Always You

J. MORALES

Dedicated

To my daughter, thank you for pushing me until the end and for being so interested in it, although you're only nine and you cannot read it. Maybe someday when you're older. Thank you to my husband and sons for your support and encouragement. I love you all.

And this is where you stop and do not read further.

Playlist

Dancing With Your Ghost—Sasha Alex Sloan
Honest—Kyndal InsKeep
Trial Run—Jenny Baker
Breakeven—The Script
Always Remember Us This Way—Lady Gaga
Nothing Compares 2 U—Chris Cornell
When We Were Young—Adele
Let Somebody Go—Coldplay-Selena Gomez
Tattoo—Jordin Sparks
Bleeding Love—Leona Lewis
I Still Love You—Night Traveler
Got You (Where I Want You)—The Fly
Drive—The Cars
Lovesong—The Cure
Here Comes My Girl—Tom Petty
This Love—Taylor Swift
Perfect—Ed Shearan

Full Playlist on Spotify
https://open.spotify.com/playlist/
6dpTO1O0ZwGIRbHitLxJ8J?si=b3107506ca60430b

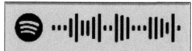

J.MORALES

Always You

Prologue

Mila

AFTER SPLASHING a moderate amount of water on my pale face, I notice hollow dark eyes and dark circles around my eyes. "Deep breaths, Mila," I tell myself as I look at my reflection in the mirror in the hospital restroom. *One, two, three, breathe.* My knuckles turn white when I grip the porcelain sink. "I can't lose him," I mumble to my reflection, composing myself, before exiting the restroom to walk numbly into Dominic's room.

I am rooted to the spot, but there's an invisible force tugging me toward him. My movements seem to happen with no conscious effort of my own. The smell of cleaning supplies and astringent hand soap makes me nauseous. The constant beeping of the IV machine near Dominic's bed tugs at my heartstrings as I watch him. His eyes are closed, and he's snoring faintly, his chest rising and falling. I can't shift my gaze away from his figure; his olive skin and chiseled features, the scar above his eyebrow, and those lips that I yearn for. How I wish to spend eternity with him. The bedsheets rustle as he exhales a gentle moan.

"Angel," he says in a broken whisper.

"Come here." He pats the side of the bed so I can sit. He shifts over. "Lay down with me." He kisses my temple. He trails kisses along my cheek, nose, and lips.

Our lips part as he kisses me softly. I'm trying to memorize the taste and the touch of his lips. I need to remember this eternally.

He pulls back when he sees my wet tears. "Baby, I love you." He wipes my tears with the pad of his thumb.

"I-I love you too. I don't want it to be our last time together. I want to be with you forever." I choke on each word.

He places my hand on my chest. "I'll be right here with you always, Angel."

I stare into those big brown eyes that remind me of whiskey. He gives me a small smile that makes his dimples pop out. Wiping my tears, he kisses my cheeks.

Rachel, Dominic's mother, transferred him to the Arizona hospital at Harold Children's Cancer Center three weeks ago. They have the finest doctors. His disease had advanced, and Rachel warned me he has only weeks to live. How unfair life can be. I lost my parents, and now the man I have fallen wholly in love with is leaving me. The day Rachel informed me, I fell to my knees. He's all I have left besides my nana. The pain in my chest tightens, making it unbearable to breathe, to live without him.

"You're so beautiful. I'm so lucky to have found you," Dominic croaks out. "Mila," he says gingerly, barely above a whisper. "I want you to live life to its fullest. I'm sorry I won't be here." He takes a slow breath. "You've been through so much. I found my soulmate, and I hope you will find a second chance at fate. I'll likely be jealous as hell." He lets out a small chuckle. "But I want you to find happiness." Tears trickle down; he swallows it all in. I wipe his tears and kiss him.

"Dom, I'll never find a love like ours." Tears streaming down my cheeks, I carefully trace the ink etched onto Dominic's chest. He wanted a line tattoo depicting a man and woman together; the man's lips resting on the woman's forehead in a tender kiss. As our relationship progressed, he'd mentioned getting a tattoo resembling us.

"Did I ever tell you why I got this tattoo and what it means to me?"

"No, you didn't," I utter between sobs.

He kisses my forehead. "A kiss on the forehead is not just any kiss; it possesses so much more meaning to it." He takes another deep breath and swallows. "A forehead kiss means protection. Even when I'm not here, I'll protect you, watching you from the heavens. It also says you're mine, although I have to leave you. I will be with you in spirit and your heart. It says I love you, even when I'm gone. Thank you, Mila, for showing me what love means." He lets out a sharp breath.

"I love you," I whisper softly.

He clears his throat. "I wanted to get this tattoo to have you imprinted on my soul eternally. I read this in a book and the statement was meaningful. It was fitting."

Understanding the significance behind his tattoo makes me even more in love with it. Just as he takes a big breath, his body trembles. Looking up through my wet eyelashes, I see Dominic crying. He holds me tight and we both cry in each other's arms for the last time.

"I-I love you; I-I love you, Dominic. I'm going to m-miss you. Everything about y-you: I'll always have you here," I say, broken up, pointing to my heart. I wipe his tears away, wanting to comfort him as well.

"I'm sorry, Angel. I'm trying to be strong for you. I hate leaving you."

I kiss him deeply, tasting our salty tears. This is the last time I'll feel and taste his lips. I end the kiss when my phone beeps. "It's my ride," I tell him with my mouth pressed against his chest.

I don't want to let go of him. I hug him tightly, a knot of emotions in my stomach. I silently wish that the darkness would take me away with him. I kiss him all over his face. Dominic cups my face and gazes into my eyes. Our faces are mirror images of pain. His eyes flutter. He exhales and inhales. My heart races as I watch how tired he is.

His brown eyes sparkle with sincerity as he cradles my face in his hands. "I'll love you endlessly, Mila," he breathes. "You've made me the happiest I've ever been," he says wholeheartedly, his voice breaking with every word.

I close my eyes and slide off the bed. Taking a long, deep breath, I make my way to the door. With one last glance, I blow a kiss to him.

"I'll love you forever. Til the end of time, my heart belongs to you, Dom, only you."

"I love you too, Angel."

As I falter in the parking lot where my driver awaits, a soft, sultry breeze picks up my hair, blowing the strands around my cheeks. I close my eyes, taking a deep breath before getting into the car.

They diagnosed him with leukemia months ago. Dominic's mom, Rachel, had flown him to a specialist in Arizona for treatment. Life took an unexpected turn. We had made so many plans after graduating high school this year. He was my future, the man I wanted to spend the rest of my life with. Once I board my flight. I unzip my bag, pull out Dominic's T-shirt, and snuggle into it, inhaling his scent, then drift off to sleep as my chest becomes hollow by emptiness.

One

MILA

Five years later

THE SUN IS SHINING MERRILY. Layering sunscreen all over my body and listening to the sound of the waves crashing on the rocks, the peacefulness reminds me of how much I've missed living in San Diego. I missed the California sun. Although it holds so many memories of Dominic and me, it's been hitting me hard. It's been five years since I've been to California. These past years have been so challenging; I've pulled through with the help of Nana and Uncle Roger. I moved to Manhattan three weeks after returning home from saying goodbye to Dominic in Arizona.

Averting my gaze from a couple of men and women playing volleyball, I lay my towel down so I can sunbathe while reading a romance novel. This is as much romance as I'm getting. It's been so long since I've been in a relationship. A part of me has guarded my heart, and the other half still mourns his loss. One would think after five years, I'd be in a relationship or even married. Moving on became unthinkable, especially after leaving Dom in the hospital room for the last time. My head snaps up when a ball smacks my book down.

"Ahh, sorry." A man around my age runs up to me. He grabs the ball.

"Don't worry about it," I say, squinting from the sun, which is blinding me.

"Mila?"

I look up, using my book as a sun visor to block the sun. *Oh, it's Brian. From the café.*

"Hey, Brian." His sandy blond hair drapes over his eye. His blue eyes sparkle with the sunlight as he takes in my profile.

"Any good?"

My eyebrows arch, confused.

"The book?" he says with a smirk.

Oh. I set the book down and smile nervously. "Yeah, it's good."

Jeez, Mila such a big talker, aren't you?

He studies me for a minute too long with a lazy grin I find boyishly cute. His gaze lands on the little man playing in the sand. He smiles at him before the guys call him back.

"See you tomorrow at the coffee shop?" he questions, raising an eyebrow.

I wave bye. "Yes, see you tomorrow."

"Mommy, look what I found, a seashell."

I hear my baby, Dante, running to me. He has the biggest smile on his face that looks like his father. I found out I was nine weeks pregnant two weeks after returning from Arizona.

"Let's put it in the bucket, baby, with the rest of them, okay? Are you hungry? I packed you a snack."

"Yes, Mommy, I hungry," Dante mumbles.

I pass him a peanut butter and jelly sandwich.

Days after returning home, I futilely tried to contact Dominic's mother Rachel, his brothers, Mark and Santiago. Rachel blocked my calls, and the calls to his brothers went unanswered. They completely ghosted me. I'm not surprised—she always despised me for who knows what reason, and from the moment Dominic and I started dating. Rachel's invariably been a bitch to me since day one. Her words to him were about how I was not good enough. Luckily, he never paid attention to what his mom had to say.

He would always say, "You're more than enough, Angel," in his husky tone.

"I'm done, Mommy. Can we go make a sandcastle now?"

"Yes, baby, let's make a big sandcastle. Then we have to go home. Okay? You have a big day. Tomorrow's the first day of preschool."

"Okay, Mommy, I'm a big boy now."

I smile at his adorableness. He has olive skin like his father, and big dimples, and black hair like mine. Dante is the spitting image of Dominic. He's my precious gift, my treasure, my light who saved me from the darkness. I can't believe he will start pre-k tomorrow.

We gather our items and walk back to my vehicle. A man with a fruit stand waves at us.

"Mommy, can I have some?"

"Sure." It's a healthy snack, so why not? I hand the man a ten-dollar bill. As we wait for the older man to prepare our fruit, my eyes narrow as I study a man who seems strangely familiar. I'm certain I've seen him before. The man leans against a wall. He's wearing aviator sunglasses. He seems to be in his late twenties or early thirties, and his eyes turn toward me. He slips his phone into his jeans.

"*Gracias, señorita.*" The older man hands me a cup of fruit.

I twist around to see if the man is still there. He's gone. I feel like I've seen him in Manhattan before, but that can't be why he would be here. I brush it off and buckle Dante in his seat, heading back home to our townhouse in the suburbs of San Diego. My best friend Sophie and I share a townhouse. My mind drifts to how I met Sophie in New York. I had just entered the University of Photography with the help of Uncle Roger, who is a photographer himself, and his connections. Sophie had taken one look at me and asked if she could rub my pregnant belly. We've been best friends ever since. I smile thinking about our move out here to California where we are now the proud owners of Glamours Photography Studio.

I look up at Dante through the rearview mirror and say, "Let's see if Auntie Sophie's home, okay?"

He takes a bite of his fruit and nods.

I STUMBLE down the stairs after groggily waking up. I brew myself a cup of coffee and grab two painkillers for my throbbing headache. The front door swings open. Sophie walks in from her morning run. She pulls out her AirPods, studies me, and shakes her head. I sigh, knowing she's going to hound me. Since we moved to California, she's been badgering me more than ever.

"How did you sleep?" my best friend asks, arching her brows as she examines my puffy eyes.

"Fine," I lie.

She huffs, opening the fridge for a water bottle. After setting it on the counter, she puts her lengthy, blonde, wavy hair in a bun.

"Dammit, Mila, do you think after all these years I don't notice you're lying through your teeth?" She narrows her eyes and crosses her arms, her mouth tightening into a thin line. Her gaze is piercing, as if she's looking right through me, making it clear that she knows I'm lying.

Screams from the night of the fire have been a constant presence in my dreams. Since my dad passed away, I have had the same dream every night.

"Sophie, I'm good. Honestly." I love my best friend like a sister. I know she means well, but fuck, I'm tired of being badgered by her.

"Mila, you can't go on like this, sleep-deprived, carrying this burden; it's bringing you down. The nightmares of the fire, losing your mom and dad, and losing Dominic. He would have wanted you to move on and be happy."

I throw a bagel in the toaster and do my best to ignore her repetitive lecture. But she continues.

"Losing Dominic and your father... You suffered a great deal of trauma because of it. Which is understandable. I think you should attempt going to therapy again." Leaning against the counter, her sparkly blue eyes bore into mine.

My bagels pop up from the toaster, and I spread a generous amount of strawberry jelly on them.

"I went to therapy in Manhattan—"

My best friend cuts me off. "Fuck, Mila, you went for two weeks. You can't live like this with the guilt of your dad dying in the fire. And not letting Dominic go, I know you didn't get closure with his family ghosting you, and not telling you shit about him or the funeral. You promised me you would try to live. To date, to fall in love, to be happy, Mila."

I groan, growing irritated.

"And I've told you I'm not going to therapy; I don't need it. Yes, I said I would give dating a try and start fresh in California. I will when I feel ready."

She gives me a worried look. And she's not done. "Mila, you have been through so much. Just think about it, please. I just want to see you happy."

I heave in annoyance. "Yes, sure, I'll think about it," I lie, and she knows it.

"Thank you, that's all I ask."

I give her a tight hug. She's always been there for Dante and me.

I went through two weeks of therapy. The first week, she suggested I write in a journal, jotting down my feelings. So, I did. I wrote to Dominic about how my life was not the same without him. I missed his voice, the way he said my name. The way he felt.

I told him about college life and how we were supposed to attend college together. The second week, the therapist suggested I try to have guy friends and date. She asked if any guys at school had caught my attention. I told her about a guy who was constantly flirting and asked me out. She suggested I take him up on the offer. So, I did, kinda.

While in line at the café, he offered to buy my lunch, so I let him. The next thing I knew, we ended up in a vacant classroom, where he kissed me savagely and bent me over the table. The next minute, he was thrusting inside me. Once, we both came off our high, I panicked. I ran out of the room crying. Guilt consumed me. I had erased Dominic's touch, his lips on mine. He had been the last man to kiss me, to touch me. I felt like I was sinking into a deep, dark abyss, full of sorrow and despair. I never returned to counseling.

I SCURRY up the stairs to wake up my sleeping baby for his first day of pre-school. "Morning, baby, time for your big day."

He rubs his sleepy eyes. "Okay, Mommy, I get dressed by myself. I am a big boy now, okay."

I hand him his uniform. I had enrolled Dante in a private school, St. Mary's Catholic School, one of the best. I'd applied for tuition assistance and was blessed with them paying half of his tuition.

My heart breaks; he's gotten so big. I can't believe five years have passed. I wish Dominic were here. He'd be so proud of him. *Dammit, Dominic, I miss you. I wish you were here to see how beautiful he is.* "Okay, baby, I'll be downstairs making you breakfast."

Thirty minutes later, I buckle Dante in his car seat, then we head off to school.

Once we arrive at St. Mary's, I pull my camera out to capture the best memories of Dante's first day.

"Smile," I tell him.

He raises his eyebrow and smirks arrogantly, just like his dad, which makes me chuckle as I walk him to his class where Mrs. Hooker is waiting.

"You must be Dante." Miss Hooker beams.

Dante gives her a shy smile. "My name is Dante Delgado, and this is my mommy, Mila Amaro."

Mrs. Hooker shakes my hand. "Mrs. Amaro, nice to meet you."

"Nice to meet you as well. Dante is ecstatic to be in your class."

She smiles warmly.

I lean in, smacking a big kiss on Dante's cheek. He wipes it off with an eye roll. What a little booger.

"Have a good day, love you."

Dante whispers, "Love you too, Mommy." As happy as he can be, Dante scurries into his class.

I blow out a scant breath, swallowing the lump in my throat and letting the tears fall. Driving to work, I tell Dominic all about Dante's first day.

———

I DRAG my ass into the studio. Sophie positions props for her clients, who are supposed to arrive in twenty minutes.

Glancing over her shoulder, she says, "Hey! How was our little man when you dropped him off?"

I let out a long, dramatic sigh. "Went well. He was more than excited, he completely forgot about little ole' me." I slump into a chair behind the desk.

"Aww, I'm so happy. I can't believe he's in pre-school. I remember when little peanut was born. So whatcha gonna do today?"

"I have a client meeting me at the pier for family photos." I smile just thinking about it. Being a photographer is something I love. Capturing beautiful memories—it's satisfying. I see love and happiness. Every picture has a beautiful story. I love being the one to capture them. My uncle is an incredible photographer. I've learned so much from him. My heart breaks when I have family sessions. It's the longing, the sadness for what I wish I could have. Maybe someday I'll find someone to grow a family with. A year ago, Dante asked me where his dad was. I told him he was in heaven with the angels. The day I found out I was pregnant, I called the hospital, but they said he was gone and wouldn't provide me with any information. For a month straight, I called Dominic's brothers, Mark and Santiago, leaving voicemails with my new number. Uncle Roger had given me a new phone with a new number because my old one had disconnected when Nana lost her financial ability to pay. They never returned my calls, so I stopped trying. God, I miss him so much that not a day goes by that I don't think of Dominic.

WHAT A LONG DAY. Time seemed to drag. Once I picked up Dante at school, I was relieved to go home.

"Mommy, I had a really good day," he says, swirling the spoon around his bowl, chowing down his mac and cheese.

"I'm so happy, little man. Make any new friends?"

"Yes, Mommy. John and Aaron. We wrestled."

"Dante, you can't be wrestling at school."

His perfectly shaped eyebrows scrunch up. "But, Mommy, I don't have anyone at home to wrestle with."

"I can wrestle with you." Grabbing a bowl, I scoop myself a helping of mac and cheese.

"No, Mommy, you're a girl." He stares at me incredulously, his mouth forming a perfect 'O' of surprise.

I can't help but smile; my boy is too adorable for words. Just then, the corners of his lips turned up in a smirk and I know he knows he's being cute. When I look at Dante, I see so much of

Dominic: his facial expressions, his smile, and his attitude. I recall the day I met Dominic.

It was at my father's diner. He had closed it for a Christmas party for his employees. Dominic's mom had worked there for six or seven months before my dad's passing. Rachel oversaw accounting/payroll for the diner.

The night Dominic strolled in the front door with his brothers, I stood frozen in place like an ice sculpture. But more like an ice sculpture being melted under Dominic's gaze. Taking a deep, steady breath, my heart raced, galloping out of my chest. He had gazed into my lust-filled eyes, taking my breath away. Ogling his six-foot-tall frame, olive skin, sharp jaw, broad shoulders, muscular, and the most beautiful brown eyes, I had whispered to myself, "Oh my God." Before I knew it, he was standing in front of me.

"Hi," he says breathlessly, as his eyes trail down my body.

My entire body heats at his appraisal. I've never been the type to want a guy's approval, and, well, I've never had a boyfriend. I stand there like a complete idiot. I can't get the damn words out of my mouth.

"Hi," I sputter out. His smile is the size of Texas, which shows his perfect white teeth and big dimples.

"So, do your parents work here?" he asks, then bites his lip.

"My dad's the owner." He leans his hard, sexy body against the counter.

"Oh yeah, Leo's your dad? He's really cool. I've met him a couple of times when I drop in."

"Yeah, he's a great dad," I murmur and smile nervously, thinking I might throw up.

He keeps his gaze on me as if he can't peel it away. He breathes out, "I'm Dominic, Rachel's son."

Dominic fits him perfectly.

"And you're?"

Oh God. *Like a complete fool, I'm still staring at him.* "Mila," *I say, feeling my cheeks grow warm.*

"Mila," he repeats softly.

Ahh, and the way he says my name has my insides burning. Dominic is so handsome, I can't seem to peel my eyes away. My cheeks go hot with scarlet when Dominic catches me gawking and drooling—sliding a hand into his soft brown hair.

"Uhmm, do you want to get out of here and go for a walk?" he asks, nervously chewing his bottom lip. He's fidgeting, eyes darting around the room, unsure of how to take the conversation forward. "We can stay here if you want. I was asking because it's getting crowded." His voice catches in his throat, and he scratches the back of his neck absently.

We wander around the pier in comfortable silence, the breeze ruffling his hair as it blows in from the ocean. I can feel his eyes on me every now and then, studying my features with shy admiration.

"You're very beautiful," he breathes, his eyes never leaving mine.

"Do you have a boyfriend?" Dominic asks, and his voice is heavy with anticipation.

I shake my head.

His shoulders slump with relief. His smile grows wider, and he moves closer to me, slipping his hand over mine. "Good, because you're mine now."

In this instant, I feel a jolt of electricity run through me. The connection between us is electric, our chemistry undeniable. I know at this moment he is the one.

A SMILE STRETCHES across my face as I recall he had kissed me then. It was our first.

"Mommy, why you smile at?" Dante scrutinizes me with a frown.

I chuckle. "Come on, little Dominic, bedtime."

He laughs. He knows he looks a lot like his father.

After a leisurely shower, I put on shorts and a tank top and pull my long black hair back into a ponytail before going to bed. I slide into bed, praying the nightmares won't come to haunt me in my sleep. Sometimes, they bring pleasant dreams of Dominic, though not as often as I'd like; no matter how much I wish it were possible, he never lets me dream of him.

Dominic and I are walking back to the house hand in hand. I see the large flames heating the night. The fire truck's sirens piercing my ears. I run to the house screaming, "Dad, my dad! He's in there. Did you get him out?" I'm screaming so loud I can't hear anything else. I'm desperately searching for him, but I can't seem to find him anywhere.

"Dad!" I scream with such intensity that I can taste the smoke. "Please, someone, my dad, he's in the house!"

As I try to run into the house, Dominic grabs me. "No, Angel, you can't go in there!" Dominic shouts, holding me in his arms.

Two firemen run out without my dad, just as the house collapses. I run to them, pleading with them, begging to get my dad. One of them whispers something to the police officer.

Dominic is holding me so tight I can't breathe. An officer comes up to me. "Sweetie, is there anyone you can call?"

I ignore his question.

"Did you find my dad?" I howl.

"Honey, I'm sorry we couldn't find him. Is there a relative you can call?" the officer says helplessly.

I drop to the floor, where Dominic cradles me—weeping in his arms.

I stir from the haunting dream, the guilt of the night I snuck out is still fresh in my mind. Every now and again, I can't help but think about how things could have turned out differently. I know my father would be relieved that I'm alive, but deep down, there's a part of me that keeps wondering what if? The longing for him is almost too much to bear. My dad was a great man. The love he had for me was unconditional. I never saw him with other women. His affection for my mom started in high school and lasted until the day he died. He had opened the restaurant when I was about ten years old; my mother had a dream of opening her own diner. My dad wanted to fulfill his dream for her. They had a love I've always wanted for myself. The day I lost Dominic, I felt I would never find love again. I tried dating. Well, I shouldn't say dating. It was more like friends with benefits. I can't commit to anyone. Having a child makes it more complicated. Men my age don't want to date a girl with a child. I've hoped to find love and a second chance at fate. I'm not sure when that will be, and I'm in no rush. If it happens, it happens.

Two

MILA

Photographing newborns always warms my heart. The smile on the parents' faces is priceless and makes my job worth it. I had three newborn shoots this morning. Two slept through the entire session. One cried the whole time and finally stopped fussing with a pacifier. Once she settled down, I swayed her to sleep, took the pacifier out, and I snagged a shot of the precious baby.

I have so many pictures of Dante. I never wanted to miss any moments. I tried to capture as much as I could to look back at as he gets older.

"Hello." Sophie waves her hand in front of my face. "I've been calling your name."

"Sorry, what were you saying?"

"Let's go to the coffee shop next door. The hot guy who works there always asks for you. Seems sweet; you should go on a date with him." Sophie winks at me with her big ocean-blue eyes.

I chuckle. "He is sweet, but I'm not going to ask him."

We walk to Joe's Coffee Shop, and Brian, the barista, greets me, his smile wide, his teeth strikingly white on his tanned face. A swath of wavy, golden hair falls casually on his forehead. His shoulders, a yard wide and molded bronze.

"Hey, Mila, how's it going? Having the usual?"

"Hi, Brian, how are you doing? Yes, the usual, you know what I like." *Jeez, that sounds like flirting. I haven't done it in a long time. I probably sound like an idiot.*

Brian gives me a wink.

"It's on me. I'll get it right to you." His blue eyes dance in the sunlight as he scans my profile.

"Oh... Thank you, that's sweet of you." Sophie and I sit next to a window.

"I'm going to wash my hands. I've got some sticky stuff on my hand," Sophie says as she walks to the restroom.

Brian emerges to our table, iced coffee in hand. The cup is decorated with a bright-colored dot, and the straw is balanced between it.

"Here you go, pretty girl. Your iced coffee." He then pulls a chair up next to me, our faces only inches apart.

He looks into my eyes with an intensity I haven't experienced in years. The warmth of his stare fills me with a strange sensation of comfort and fear, as if I'm experiencing it for the first time. My palms begin to sweat. It's been a hell of a long time since a man has looked at me this way, or maybe I just never noticed.

"How was the beach yesterday? I saw Dante building a sandcastle. I haven't seen him stop by with you."

"It was good. We had fun. Weekends are pretty lazy for us, so I rarely make it in to get coffee, we usually make some at home."

He nods. "Yeah, I get it." He clears his throat and licks his plump lips. "I would like to know more about you if you let me... Have dinner with me on Saturday?"

Oh, wow. This is so sudden. I said I would date, but this is too soon. Beads of sweat trickle down my back. It's just dinner. He's handsome and kind. *You can do this, Mila.*

"Uh... okay, I need to find a sitter first," I declare, with so little enthusiasm.

"I can babysit," Sophie blurts out as she stands behind Brian.

I'm not sure if I want to strangle her or thank her. *No, no, I can't do this*. It's not just dinner. It's a date. The last date I was on was with Dominic. I muster a smile.

"Okay, Saturday it is. I'll pick you up. Let's say seven. Does that work for you?" The corners of his mouth turn up.

I bite my lip nervously. "Sure."

He stands from his seat. "Better get back to work. See you Saturday, pretty girl."

I nod. He walks back to the counter. Sophie sits in his spot with a stupid smile on her beautiful face. "Whoa, is it gettin' hot in here? Did you see the way he was looking at you?"

"Thanks for babysitting," I grumble, rolling my eyes.

"Are you not attracted to him?"

"Yes, he's sweet and handsome..." I pause.

"No buts," Sophie murmurs with pleasure as she savors the taste of her espresso, and licks away the foam from her lips.

I sigh. "You know how I feel. I've slept with a total of three men and had one relationship. It's been two years since I've had sex. My heart can't take another heartbreak. I've lost so much in my life. More than anything, I'm scared to fall in love. Will it erase Dominic? God, Sophie, I miss him so much. I loved watching him at his baseball games. During his practices, he would sneak me under the bleachers to make out." A tear rolls down my cheek.

"Oh, babe, he will always live in your heart and through Dante. Always. He would want you to be happy."

I wipe my tears with a napkin and then take a sip of my iced coffee. I take a moment to compose myself and focus on Sophie.

"So, how are things with you and Ryder? Are you guys official?"

Sophie has been seeing a guy she met at a bar. She went out with him a couple of nights ago. Sophie is the fun, adventurous, and free type, while I'm the introvert—her complete opposite.

"I'm not sure; I don't want a serious relationship; I feel like he does, but I'm just not ready to settle down again yet."

"I know you and Eric dated for a little over three years. He did you dirty by cheating on you with one of your friends."

She guards her heart like armor. Staring out the window, I notice a man who looks just like Dominic on the phone. He's a couple of feet away—my heart races.

"What are you looking at?"

I squint, trying to get a better view. As if it even helps.

"That guy looks just like Dominic. I think it's one of Dominic's brothers, Santiago or Mark."

Sophie hisses. "Those fucking assholes. Let's confront him and ask him why they treated you like shit—ignored your calls, didn't even tell you when his service was or where he's buried. You didn't even get the chance to tell them you were pregnant." She grimaces, shaking her head.

"It's been five years, Sophie; I don't want them to know about Dante now. They had their chance. Since we've moved back, I've thought about calling funeral homes to see what information I can come up with."

The front door squeaks open as the guy who looks like Dominic walks in. God, he looks just like him. His powerful well-muscled body moves with ease. His chiseled jaw stretches across his smooth olive skin, and his short brown hair is slightly tousled. There's a light stubble on his gorgeous face—a face so familiar, it makes me gasp for air.

"Why don't you go talk to his brother?" Sophie whispers.

I can't breathe. I feel my insides caving in. My heart is pounding beneath my rib cage. I feel the color draining from my face. *No, no, it can't be Dominic.*

"Sophie," I squeak. Then I see the scar on his eyebrow. I think I'm going to pass out. All I feel now is betrayal. He lied to me. I want to run to him, hug him, kiss him. But I can't stomach it. His betrayal seethes through my soul. He doesn't see me. He orders a coffee when he gives Brian his name.

I hear him say, "Dominic," and I bolt out of my chair, running out the back door, which leads outside the coffee shop. Sophie runs after me.

"Mila, wait! What's going on?" Sophie shouts.

My legs feel wobbly; my palms hold onto the wall for support. I can't breathe. He's been alive all this time. What the *hell*... I feel like I'm going crazy—is this it? Have I actually fucking lost my marbles? I'm so confused.

"Mila, I think you're having a panic attack. Breathe, please breathe." I'm trying to talk, but the words don't come out.

"Dominic, he-he's in there, Sophie," I croak and point to the coffee shop.

"Mila, It's okay. I think you're having a panic attack. It's an illusion; you miss him. His brother resembles him."

"*No, it's him!* I saw him, the scar on his eyebrow, then he gave Brian his name. I'm not fuckin crazy." Now I'm hyperventilating, crying in an alley. *Five fucking years.*

"Dominic's been alive all this damn time while I have been mourning, going crazy over losing him." Sophie wraps me in a hug, soothing me.

"That can't be, Mila; this is so crazy. Do you want to go talk to him?"

"No, I can't, Sophie. I can't. He avoided my calls for an entire month. I tried calling him at the hospital, his mom, and his brothers. He fucking lied to me. He wanted nothing to do with me."

"Let's get you home so we can talk about this." She holds me around my waist to keep me from falling. Damn, I'm so bewildered.

I SIT CRUMBLING on the sofa, overwhelmed with sadness. My heart feels like it has been split into a million fragments. I can't comprehend why he never reached out or tried to contact me. The only logical reasoning that comes to mind is that once he went into remission, he didn't need me and told his brothers to ignore my calls. I thought he loved me. Was it all a lie? Did he and his family make it up to get rid of me? No, he couldn't have lied, right? But he did. I think back to the night after his first baseball game of the season.

I sit in the bleachers, waiting for Dominic to come out of the locker room. They just won their first game. The door swings open. I spot him with Liam, freshly showered, walking out. His whiskey eyes search for me. When he spots me, he smiles from ear to ear. I run to him, and he catches me jumping into his arms.

"Yeah, baby, you played fucking impressive out there."

He kisses my lips. "That home run was for you, Angel."

"Mila, maybe we should look him up on social media. He could be on there."

I'm terrified even to look. I've never searched because he didn't have a social media account before his cancer. What if he's married and has kids?

"Okay, let's look to see if he has an account." I watch as she presses buttons on her phone.

"So, what's his full name?"

"Dominic Dante Delgado," I rasp out. I'm shaking like a leaf —beads of sweat trickling down my back.

"Oh, I found him." I watch her facial expressions as she frowns.

I jump off the couch to sit next to her. "Let me see." My fingers scroll. My heart races. Five pictures of him and a blonde, beautiful woman, *his fiancé. No, no, it can't be.* How could he do this to me? *To us.* My heart sinks into my stomach. I crumble onto the floor. Sobbing. Angry, heartbroken, and betrayed is how I feel. Sophie holds me and lets me cry on her shoulder. I never moved on. I grieved for him, reminiscing everything about him day and night. In contrast, he moved on and is now engaged. How could he?

"Are you going to tell him about Dante?" Sophie asks.

I choke in between sobs. "I'm not sure. I can't even think straight right now."

"How about you lie down? I'll go pick up Dante from school."

I genuinely have the most amazing and caring friend. I nod. "Thank you."

I DROP into the comfy chair in the corner of the studio. All night I thought about Dominic with another woman—*his fiancée.*

Opening up social media, I glance at Domenic's picture again nervously. I've never had a social media account, never thought of making one. Now I'm creeping on him, I have to. He has a big smile on his face, the kind of smile he once gave me, but now it belongs to her. I read the caption on the bottom of the picture that says, "Just asked Samantha Williams to marry me, and she said yes."

Fuck. Then my heart breaks all over again. I can't wrap my head around Dominic being alive after all this time. I've cried for him, struggled to raise our son, and been through so much shit. And here he is, fucking engaged.

"Mrs. Amaro, I'm here for my two-thirty appointment." I jump out of my seat, startled; I didn't hear the door.

"Oh, sorry, I didn't hear you come in." I was so lost in thought looking at the asshole smiling at his bimbo... ugh, she's probably nice, and I am taking my anger and jealousy out on her too. *Damn, it.* I forgot I had a photo shoot—a husband scheduled a photo shoot for his wife in lingerie. I rarely get these types of appointments. I'm all for a woman wanting to feel sexy. Of all days, not today, all I can think of is the woman posing for Dominic and how long they have been together.

"Mrs. Ellen, please change in the dressing room, and I'll be waiting in the room when you're ready." Mustering a smile, I point to the changing rooms.

SATURDAY CAME IN A BLUR. Tonight, is my date with Brian. I'm pacing in my room, thinking about what to say to cancel. Sophie insists that if the asshole Dominic is engaged, I must move on and, at least, try to have a good time. I slip on a black off-the-shoulder, sleeveless, short dress. It hugs my curves in all the right places. I rarely dress up, although I feel sexy tonight. I'm twenty-three and feel like I'm an old maid. I hardly go out. Devoting my life to my son means so much more. Hell, what do I even talk about on a date?

"Let's do your make-up and hair," my best friend says excitedly. "Damn, you look beautiful. Brian's going to lose his mind."

Sliding my black heels on, I do feel beautiful.

"Mommy, you look pretty. Where are you going?"

I tenderly press my lips to Dante's forehead. I am overwhelmed with emotions, feeling like I might throw up. I never go anywhere without my baby other than work.

"Just out with a friend, okay? You listen to Auntie Sophie."

"Love you, Mommy. I watch Spider-Man."

"Love you more, little man." There's a knock at the door. Sophie takes Dante to the living room.

Brian stands with his hands in his pockets, dressed in jeans, and a blue button-down dress shirt. His short, sandy-blond hair looks ruffled, like he just rolled out of bed. Brian is exceptionally handsome with his boyish smile and his sparkling blue eyes.

"Wow, Mila, you look gorgeous, so stunning," Brian drawled, his blue eyes roam my profile.

"Thank you, and you look handsome, Brian."

He gives me a flirty wink. "Thanks, beautiful." We drive off in his blue Jeep Wrangler.

"I'm sorry. I forgot to ask if you're okay with Italian. I didn't think to ask if you have food allergies, or maybe you don't eat gluten; we can go somewhere else." His cheeks flush, and his words stumble, making him all the more endearing.

"Italian is perfect. I love Italian, actually."

He immediately relaxes, his shoulders deflating with ease.

"How's Dante doing? How's he liking school?" He glances at me and smiles boyishly.

"He loves it. I thought he would miss me, but nope. He has a school play, *Peter Pan*, and guess who he is?"

He chuckles. "Peter," Brian voices with a raised eyebrow.

"Nope, Hook."

We both laugh. The tension and nervousness are immediately gone. Talking to Brian is easy.

"I thought he would be more of a Peter Pan than a Hook since he's always wearing Spider-Man clothing."

I giggle. "I know, right? He's taking the Hook role seriously."

We arrive at the restaurant, Stefanos Italian Cuisine. We enter, making our way to the hostess. Brian wraps his arms around my waist to speak to the hostess. I wasn't expecting that. Feels a little too intimate.

"Reservation for Brian Prestly," he tells her.

"Yes, sir, your table is ready," the host mutters with a half-smile.

The restaurant is pleasant, not overly upscale, just perfect.

"What can I get you both to drink?" the waiter asks, his eyes pinned on my chest.

Brian clears his throat. "Can you get us some wine, Franciacorta, please?"

The waiter's eyes are back on Brian. He nods. "Sure, be right back."

"Never played you as a wine expert. You sound like you know your wines?" I ask as the server storms off.

He chuckles. "Honestly, I don't know shit about wine. I just ordered the first thing on the list. I was trying to get the server to leave. His attention was fixed on your chest. And, pretty girl, I don't like another man staring at my date." The light of desire brightens his mellow blue eyes.

I smile nervously; I'm not used to a man's attention.

The waiter takes our order. I requested lasagna, and Brian chose the trio platter with lasagna, spaghetti, and chicken parmesan. I'm enjoying our conversation. He's easy to talk to and has a good sense of humor. Brian shares his love of surfing with me.

"We can go surfing next week or when you're available." His fingertips brush mine.

"That would be great, Brian. It's been a while since I've surfed. I might be a little out of practice. My dad would take me as a kid until freshmen year in high school."

"That won't be a problem. I'm an excellent teacher. I can refresh your memory and show you my superior talents." He gives me a wink, and I blush, like a tomato.

We continue talking about how he's attending the university and majoring in marine biology. I'm impressed by his grounded and intelligent demeanor.

"Wow, Brian, you're amazing. A marine biologist sounds like a brilliant career. I'm excited for you," I say earnestly.

He lightly takes my hand and kisses my knuckles.

"Thank you; I'd like to take you and Dante whale watching sometime." His kind gesture to include Dante swoons me.

My head springs up so fast I think I just got whiplash. *Oh my God! What the fuck! What the hell? He's here.* Dominic and his fucking fiancée with her lovely, polished nails, blonde hair; she looks very well kept. Dominic looks gorgeous. He's wearing denim jeans that fit perfectly and a black button-down shirt that shows every muscle in his body bulging out.

Dominic speaks to the hostess, and he stops talking as if he can feel me, turns, and our eyes meet. He stiffens his stance, his gaze burning with such intensity I feel my soul shiver. His mouth gapes open. Then he closes it. He peers at me with longing, maybe love. In a split second, his eyes go cold. He's trailing up and down my profile. I can't seem to look away. His fiancée is talking to him, and he's not even listening to her.

Dominic notices Brian, and he turns around. The hostess seats them. A little too close for comfort. The knots in my stomach churn painfully. The taste of betrayal seethes under my skin. He kisses, her trailing kisses down her neck to her mouth, and that asshole looks at me and smirks. His eyes grow hot with hate. Averting my eyes, I turn back to my date, and I smile brightly at Brian. I'm not letting Dominic's little show bother me. What happened to *my* Dominic? He seems so different.

Bile rises in my throat, and there's a twist in the pit of my stomach. Brian leans to take my hand, peppering me with small kisses.

"Are you okay, pretty girl?"

I snort inwardly. *Am I okay? Fuck no, I'm not.* The man I love, who didn't let me know he was alive, is sitting next to me with his fiancée. Instead, I give him a flirty smile.

"I'm good, sorry, just the wine. I think I had a little too much since I hardly drink."

"If you're ready to go, we can leave."

Thank God, I need to get out of here. Fuck, why does he have to be here tonight?

He presses his lips to hers once more, his expression is malicious and scornful. *Bastard.* Brian still has his hands over mine, stroking my hand with his thumb. My eyes are still on Brian. A loud growl erupts from the table across from us. I know it was Dominic.

Before Brain turns to glare his way, I tell him, "I need to use the restroom, and then we can leave."

"Sure." Brian glances at me worriedly.

My face must show sourness.

After washing my hands and grabbing a paper towel from the dispenser, I open the door to walk out, and a hand grabs my arm and pushes me back into the restroom. Dominic pins me to the wall; his hand is up above my head. I can't breathe. My heart is palpitating so fast it's going to explode. His mouth instantly covers my neck, his hot breath soaking into my pores.

He whispers softly, "*Angel.*"

I haven't heard that name in such a long time. Goosebumps scatter all over. I can't talk, words are not spilling from my mouth. He kisses my neck, assaulting me with his mouth. Next, he sucks hard, licking my neck up and down. He groans. And goes back to sucking like it was a meal of its own. My body stays pinned to the cold tile. I'm like an ice sculpture stuck in place, frozen and paralyzed to move or talk. I'm trying so hard not to moan. Damn, it feels so good, so bad my traitorous body wants him. He sucks so hard that I hear a pop at the end.

He distances himself from me. He licks his soft pink lips. His eyes find my breasts. He inhales, then exhales. The sparkle in his eyes burst with lust, but in a second, his blood boils with hate. He clinches his jaw so tight it might snap, his breath heavy as he fists his hands into a ball.

"I fucking marked you. Your fucking date, or whatever the fuck he is to you won't want you now. I'll ruin you for any other man. You're mine, Mila," he growls possessively. With that, he storms off back to his fiancée.

Shit! I finally let out a long breath I had pent up. Immediately, my insides defrost. I step closer to the bathroom mirror, eyes widening at the sight of the new hickey marring my neck. I can still feel his soft lips and warm breath against my skin.

Thank God, I have my compact. I try to hide it. I can't let Brian see; how embarrassing that would be. *Jesus,* I can still smell him on me, musky and masculine. What the hell was I thinking? I'm so pissed off at myself. I should have pushed him away and told him to fuck off. What a piece of shit. He left a hickey on my neck, telling me I couldn't have anyone, when clearly, he left me to think he was dead. To top it off, he's engaged. My mind is still in a fog. He's been alive five damn years. He jostled me into the restroom to assault me and manipulate me.

Straightening my hair to cover the hickey, I hope Brian won't see it. I return to my seat.

"Is everything okay?"

I lean to stroke Brian's cheek pecking a kiss next to his lips and mustering a smile. "Yeah, everything's good. Are you ready?" I don't spare a glance in Dominic's direction.

Brian holds my hand as we walk out. I can feel Dominic's eyes boring holes as we walk out. Fuck him.

Brian walks me to the door of my apartment.

"Mila, you look so beautiful tonight. I had a great time. I would like to see you again if you would like to."

My mind falters back to Dominic and how he's engaged. It's time I let go of the past. Dominic certainly has.

"Sure, that would be great. I'd like that. I'll take you up on surfing sometime."

He bites his bottom lip, contemplating what to say. "Perfect."

"Have a good night, Mila. Thank you for tonight." He leans in and kisses my cheek.

"Goodnight, Brian."

Three

DOMINIC

My heartbeat races a hundred miles per hour as I walk back to my table, where Samantha waits. I lick my lips, tasting the sweetness of the woman who betrayed me. She left me five years ago. Out of pure spite and jealousy, I followed her to the restroom. The second I pinned her to the wall; the scent of cherry and coconut invaded my nose. Her scent woke every organ in me and fuck did she smell good. Hell, did it make a bulge in my jeans?

Selfishly, I needed a taste, a touch of her skin, her warmth. I savored the sensation of her delicate skin on my tongue, relishing the pleasure with every stroke. I moaned with delight. I missed everything about her. It was a shitty move to make when my fiancée was waiting for me. I lost control with Mila, letting jealousy and lust take over. Leaving an enormous mark so that blond Ken doll fucker can see it. Where in the fuck has, she been? I know she hasn't been in San Diego. The last time I saw her was the day she walked out of the hospital room. We both agreed our last moments would not be by phone.

"Baby." Samantha's smile widens as her beautiful honey eyes search mine. I lean in to kiss her lips. "What took you so long?"

"Long line, sweetheart."

Samantha's a beautiful woman, but to be honest, she's high

maintenance to the extreme. I met Samantha through my mother. She works for her dad at William's Law Firm. She's their accountant. My mother begged me to date her. She loves Samantha and her family. I took it as an advantage, a Band-Aid to cover the wound Mila left.

"I scheduled our engagement photos for next week. Make sure you put it on your calendar, and I'll find you an outfit," Samantha says in her high-pitched voice.

My kiss was tender, I'm aware I'm not the best fiancé, but I'm certain I'm far from the worst. There are measures I need to work on, like maybe cuddling with her. Every time I tried, the memory of the one girl I'd always been in love with came to mind. Samantha and I started dating about a year ago and I proposed to her a couple of weeks ago.

"Sure, sounds like a plan."

The hairs on the back of my neck stand, as they invariably have when Mila is close. Her figure is curvy and regal as she sways to her seat. Long black silky hair, big pouting lips I once kissed perpetually, her gorgeous green eyes sparkling in the light, her delicious curvy body, large breasts, and that tight black dress. *Jesus.* She bloomed into a beautiful woman.

The waitress arrives with our pasta dishes and breadsticks. Samantha moans as she bites into her carbonara. She scoops some into my mouth. "Good?"

Wiping my mouth, I nod. "Yeah, so good." My eyes turn to the woman who betrayed me.

She kisses the mother fucker on the cheek. He winks and grins. She keeps her hair wrapped around her neck, hiding my mark. Mila hiding my mark pisses the shit out of me. Her forest green eyes stay pinned on him. His hooded eyes lust over her, probably intoxicated by her beauty. The pain in my chest digs deeper. They walk out hand in hand. A small growl vibrates through my chest. Samantha chuckles, oblivious to what's going on around her. I've never spoken to her about my past relationship with Mila.

"That good, you have to growl like a dog?"

My stomach lurches. My appetite is gone. I never thought I'd run into Mila again. I called her numerous times once the doctors gave me the good news. Her phone was out of service. I presumptively thought they disconnected her phone since she was living with her grandmother and money was tight. I kept trying to call. Finally, my mother had gotten a hold of her. She announced the good news that I was in the clear and Mila hung up on her, basically saying I was a burden to her. "I think I ate too fast. I have an upset stomach now. We should go," I lie. Seeing Mila has opened a wound that's raging with pain and bitterness.

I wrap my arms around Samantha as we walk to my truck. As I'm starting the engine, she leaps onto my lap. Her dress rides up, revealing her laced thong. Her long, blonde hair flows beautifully as she straddles me, and my dick is currently not interested in her —limp. It simply has one girl in mind, and it only took five minutes of her beauty, her taste, and her touch. Samantha trails kisses all over my neck. I had thought we were developing a little chemistry between us, but after tonight, I realized it's just not there.

My feelings for Mila are consuming me, and it's all wrong. Mila is my past, Samantha is my present.

I'm overwhelmed and frustrated by guilt; it eats at me for pinning for Mila and cheating on my beautiful fiancée, who was only feet away. Samantha has been nothing but kind to me despite her neediness. I have reminisced about Mila throughout the years. The truth is no one measured up to Mila. When I started dating Samantha, I refused to think about my past. But then I put forth the effort to move on and let myself fall for Samantha. I knew it was not healthy to dwell on a Mila who had completely disregarded me. Samantha became my remedy for all the pain I had experienced. Samantha's my Band-Aid to my wounds. I proposed to her when my mom insisted it would be a great idea to settle down.

"What's your problem, baby, you seem angry."

"Nothing, I'm just tired. I had a long day, and you wanted to go out for dinner."

She maneuvers her way to the passenger's seat annoyed, and tucks her legs, folding her arms across her chest. "Stay the night, baby, at my place, or I can stay at yours?"

"I can't tonight. I have a lot of work to do tomorrow, and I have to go to the office early." My words come out harsher than I had intended. I could sense her frustration, as she rolls her eyes and tries to blow off her disappointment through a series of huffs and puffs. She tends to display childlike behavior when she doesn't get what she wants.

I WALK UP and down my small, cramped office, raking my fingers through my hair. All night I stayed up staring at my ceiling, recalling last night. I felt her the minute I walked in. Her beautiful emerald eyes were already on me. So many emotions flashed through her, one in particular, hurt. A pained look marred her face for a quick second before a stony glaze seized her.

Being the asshole that I am, I kissed Samantha, to see what Mila would do. It was a fucked-up thing to do, but fuck it, she left me. The bitter bastard in me took over. She's definitely not the same woman I fell in love with. No kind-hearted woman would abandon a man in his time of need, especially when he is ill. I showed my love effortlessly to her. I gave her my heart, my soul. I treated her like a queen. I was there for her when her father died in a tragic fire. I grieved her every day for the memories we built together. Promises for our future she disposed of.

I slam the door of my truck shut, the sound echoing through the still night air. I run up her driveway and stop on her porch, a wilted corsage in my hand. Tonight is our winter ball, and I want tonight to be special for her.

Mila's nana opens the door, her eyes widening as she takes in my nervous energy.

33

"Mila!" she calls into the house, and I wait anxiously for her to appear. When she finally steps into the foyer, my breath catches in my throat—it is almost as if time itself has stopped.

She's beautiful.

The baby blue of her dress highlights her emerald eyes. We enter the gymnasium at the school. I tightly embrace her. As the DJ changes the tune to a slow song, I look into her eyes and murmur, "Let's dance, Angel." With that, I take her hand and lead her onto the dance floor.

She chuckles. "You didn't give me time to say yes."

"It wasn't a question," I say, embracing her tightly.

She responds by coiling her arms around my neck and pressing her lips against mine. We intensify our kiss rapidly, pressing our lips together heatedly and forcefully. We sway together to the rhythm of the music. "You look beautiful. I love you so damn much, Angel."

She pants into my mouth, our hot breaths mingling. "I love you too, Dominic."

"Let's get the fuck out of here, baby." I take her hand, and we walk out back to my truck to be alone so I can show her just how much I love her.

I force myself to emerge from my daze. Mila's been fucking with my head. I resume going through paperwork and creating my list of the supplies I'll need for the restaurant. The past has been slamming right through me and taking me back down memory lane.

I TRUDGE inside my spacious yet still somehow lonesome two-story condo, hurling my keys onto the entryway table and stumbling to the kitchen. I grab a beer from the almost bare fridge, wishing it were more stocked as I walk back to the living room. As soon as I plop down on the couch in an attempt to forget about my shitty day, my phone pulls me back into reality with a shrill ring. I check the screen, it's my older brother Santiago, who is the oldest of us three. He's five years older than me. He's the womanizer in the family, has a different girl every week. I can't recall him ever having a girlfriend.

"Hey bro, how's it going? How are things at the restaurant?" He sounds chirpy. He probably just got laid. *Fucker.*

Before it all went to shit, and I got sick with cancer, I wanted to honor Mila's parents before I declared we would open a restaurant. Her face lit up like the Fourth of July. When my health improved, I chose to go to culinary school—opened up Delgado's Steak House. With an inclination to find Mila and show her what I did for her, for *us*. I kept my word, even after her betrayal.

"Doing good, bro. Just got home from work. You know, same old shit."

"How are things going at the shop?" Santiago just opened his own automotive shop a year ago.

"It's good, dude; it's picking up getting busy."

"Good to hear." Not sure how Santiago will react once I tell him I saw Mila. When Mila and I dated, he got along with her. Until shit hit the fan when she brushed me off. He fucking hated her. Clearing my throat, I'm not sure why I feel so damn nervous telling him this.

"Last night, when Samantha and I went out to dinner, Mila was there." I hear him take a deep breath and sigh.

"Dom, you're fucking engaged. She's in the past, she was your high school girlfriend, sweetheart, or whatever. You've moved on."

It's my turn to sigh as I run my fingers through my hair. "I know, bro, but I haven't seen her since she walked out of that hospital room. You know how I've always felt about her."

He's quiet for a few seconds. "Did you talk to her?"

"No, she was with someone, and we just glared at each other. She just had this look in her eyes I can't quite understand."

He hums.

Fuck I'm keeping the part where I pinned her down to myself.

35

"Dom, leave it. She moved on, and so have you."

My chest stings with pain. The pain I thought subsided years ago is back. She bites at me with her venom seeping through my flesh, eating at me. Once I was cancer-free and we moved back to California, I went feral, searching for her everywhere. As I questioned her friends, everyone shrugged; it was like she disappeared.

"You're right, I'll let it go. Fuck, I just don't get why she never called. How could she tell Mom I was a burden to her?" Bile burns the back of my throat.

"She's a cold-hearted bitch, man. She called none of us to check on you. It is not worth thinking about her." Ignoring the bite in his words. "All right, man, I gotta go shower and head to bed."

"See ya, bro," I groan once the line clicks. Throwing my head back on the couch, maybe he is right. I need to erase her—forget her. I have no idea who the guy she was with was; maybe a husband, boyfriend, or an ex now since I left a hickey on her. Mila was once everything to me—my world. And now, seeing her here, could be the closure I needed.

I strip down and jump into the steaming hot shower, reminiscing about the night I took Mila to the beach for our first date.

I lay out a blanket. We sit close to one another and gaze at the beautiful orange-red sunset. Mila is always simple; the smallest things make her happy. I cast a longing look in her direction. Her complexion is like the color of cream, and her lips are gentle and inviting. Sparkling green eyes draw my attention. She's absolutely beautiful and perfect in every way.

"Angel, is it possible to fall for someone this quick? Because I'm constantly hard when I'm around you."

She blushes ten shades red, which makes my dick press even harder into my zipper. "I feel the same way, Dom. Except for the being hard constantly." She giggles the words into my neck as she leans into me.

Cupping her cheeks, I press my lips against hers kissing her softly, our tongues collide, and I taste the sweetness of her perfect hot mouth; it has me going into overdrive. I need more. I press my lips harder into her. The sensation of her lips on mine sends a thrill through my veins. My dick pulses against my jean shorts, begging to be set free. Pleasure radiates off of me as I kiss her. I can feel my heart pounding in my chest like we're running a race, and I've never felt so alive with someone else. I've kissed plenty of girls, none have given me this much pleasure.

I groan, shaking off the memories. Dammit, just thinking of her has me aroused. I stroke myself as water droplets run down my body. My free hand is pressed against the cold, wet tile of the shower wall, stroking until I reach completion—the soap suds slide down, milking every last drop. *With her in mind. Fuck what just happened?* I need to let her go—forget her. I'm engaged now. She clearly wanted me out of her life.

Four

MILA

As I open my eyes, the aroma of freshly made pancakes greets me. I rub the sleep from my eyes and make my way to the kitchen. Sophie stands, flipping pancakes on the griddle with a goofy smile. My head spinning, I only slept a couple of hours after Brian dropped me off. The pain in my heart weighed me down. Watching him with another woman pained me. Words can't describe how I feel. How does someone move on from this? Believing he was dead. Believing he loved you.

"Coffee is ready. Sit and tell me all about your date last night." Sophie grins.

I groan, deliberating over Dominic shoving me into the bathroom and pinning me on the wall with his wet lips on my neck. Last night was one of the strangest nights of my life. My breath caught in my throat, and my heart seemed to stop beating when I saw him. It was like the pain of a thousand knives piercing through my chest and squeezing my heart until it could take no more.

"Wait, is that a hickey? Dang, girl! So, I guess things went quite spectacular last night."

A cringe-laugh drifts from my throat. I pour myself a cup of strong, steamy hot coffee that tastes like heaven. I hide the red mark on my neck with my free hand, letting my hair drape to the side.

"Not from Brian."

Her mouth gapes wide open in shock and confusion, with the spatula in hand.

"What do you mean, not from Brian? Didn't you have dinner with him?" Her pointed blue eyes drift to my hickey.

I grab a plate, sliding a warm pancake onto it before adding a generous pour of syrup. Sophie's gaze is fixed on me, waiting for my response. Why I left with one man and came back mauled by another man. I tell my best friend everything that happened and how the ghost of my past showed up with his fiancée and pinned me to the wall.

"Holy shit!" she shouts.

"So that asshole sucked on your neck, said you're his, and ran back to her?" Her eyebrows furrow into a deep crease.

I sigh in frustration. "Yup, some fucking night I had."

I feel a deep rage bubbling up in me, knowing he's been alive for the past five years. He disregarded my calls. I was always the romantic and emotional one in our relationship, while he was the dominant one and showed emotion to those in his inner circle. I've read several romance novels with similar plots after so many years, they run into each other and live happily ever after. In my case, this is no fairytale. He came back from the dead and is now engaged.

As I watch my son Dante gracefully climb the jungle gym while I call my grandmother Nana, I feel a deep longing for her and Uncle Roger. They are the only family I have left. Nana is my father's mother. She's always been like a mother to me. She took on the role when my mother died in a tragic car accident when I was a year old.

"Hello?" Nana's sweet voice lilted with happiness.

"Hola, Nana, just calling to see how you're doing. I miss you."

"Hola, *mija*, I miss you too, honey. How's my little grandson doing?

I miss him like crazy."

My nana's family originated from Mexico. My mother's family was part white and part Hispanic. I know little about her family. She was an only child, and her father and mother separated. She lived with her mother. She died of an illness. That's as much as I know about her family.

"Getting big; he started pre-k, and he loves it."

"That's wonderful. How's the studio coming along?"

I can hear Nana clinging pots and pans in the background, and a smile plasters on my face. Nana cleans like a madwoman inside and out. She would go as far as mopping the cement outside. The house smelled like Fabuloso cleaner, to the point my nose burned.

"Sophie and I have been busy, you know. California is a hot spot for tourists, so there's always business." I take a few moments to settle my nerves before informing my grandmother that Dominic has been alive this whole time. I hope she doesn't faint when I tell her the news.

"So, Nana, I have something crazy to tell you; hopefully, you're sitting." I exhale sharply. "Dominic is alive."

"Alive? How is this possible, Mila?"

"I saw Dominic twice. First at a coffee shop. I freaked out and ran out. He didn't see me then. Last night, I caught sight of him with a woman who he's engaged to." I let out a shaky breath. Nerves tingle throughout my body with what feels like the weight of an elephant on my chest.

"I'm confused, honey. I just don't get it. I'm speechless. All this time, why didn't he call you to at least say something, you know? Did you talk to him?"

It upset Nana when we thought Dominic died. She felt sympathy for me because I lost both my parents and him. Only Nana understood the anguish I was going through when she saw me break down in grief. Year after year, Nana watched me silently as I cried, her weathered hands clasped together in her lap as if to contain some of the pain that engulfed me.

"No, I didn't. I'm still shaken up by all this. You know what I've been through, and it hurts he never called. I have always loved him, not a day has passed I didn't think about him, and for him to let me think he died is low. He glared at me in shock. He had a conflicted look on his face and remained cold, as if I had never mattered to him."

A brusque hiss escapes her lips through the receiver.

"That's so strange. What the hell is his problem, *pendejo*, idiot? Do you plan on talking to him when the time is right and letting him know about Dante?"

Honestly, part of me wants to move on and let Dante think his father is dead. He's not the same man. But part of me feels monstrous lying to my son.

"Yes, when the time is right, I'll search for him. I don't know, Nana... what to think of all this."

"I'm shocked, honey. You went through so much, and all this time he was alive, you grieved and cried for this man for five years."

I swallow the lump in my throat. "Yeah, I know, Nana, but I'll let you go, we'll talk soon."

My eyes roam to Dante, my sweet boy.

WEEKS HAVE GONE BY. My headspace is overflowing with so much shit that's been going on. As I prep the studio for our next client, memories from Arizona five years ago invade my mind. I was so broken because I lost so much. I festered in a dark place, pain eating up my insides. I had already lost so much—my father, then Dominic. A storm was brewing in me, sinking me further and further into the darkness. I struggled to contain the demons inside me, having lost the will to battle them any longer. The idea of living without him was too much to bear, and it sapped away any will to live I had left. After finding out I was pregnant, my baby growing inside of me gave me the purpose to live.

I unpacked a box of recently delivered photos. We've been tremendously busy. *European Magazine* asked us to do their photo shoots. I'm pretty sure Uncle Roger had a part in this. He's worked with many magazine companies. We spent half the day photographing hot European men in swimsuits. Yup, my inside melted like a popsicle. Glancing at the photos of the hot models we took, my insides melt all over again.

"Oh, shit, I double-booked two for three o'clock," Sophie voices with a hiss.

"I'm sure if I call the school, they can wait for me for fifteen minutes more. I can stay. I'll call the school," I tell her.

"Are you sure?" She frowns. "Yes, should be quick. Engagement photos don't take long."

The door chimes as it opens, and my head jerks up to greet our clients. I'm greeted by a tall, devilishly handsome man, wearing black slacks, and a white button shirt that hugs his muscular biceps.

What the fuck! Dominic and his fiancé—with all the luck, why me? Why here? She's dressed in high-end clothing, a maroon off-the-shoulder dress, high heels that presumably cost more than my rent, and her Gucci bag. Her nose is stuck up in the air. A snob indeed. Overly dressed as if she was posing for a runway. Her curves, breasts, and long eyelashes flutter. They scream fake. I'm sure if a gust of wind breezed through, they would fly right off. She's definitely not someone I pictured Dominic dating. She looks complicated and seems uptight, while he's simple.

He stares at me with a cold, calculating gaze as we connect stares. Part of me feels it's an illusion after all these years, a dream I'm not in with him. My heart gallops like a stampede of buffaloes. Sweat trickles down the back of my neck. He harbors the same expression, shocked to see me again.

"The feeling is mutual," I mutter silently. I raise my chin and straighten my shoulders. The last thing I want is for him to see how much he affects me and how heartbroken I am—peeling my eyes from his cold stare. I muster a bright smile, rendering unaffected.

The woman struts to the counter, her polished nails tapping at the counter.

"We are here for our engagement photo shoot. We just got engaged a couple of weeks ago, right, babe?" Her voice comes out pushed and high-pitched. A wide smile spreads on her face. She leans in and kisses his cheek.

I side-eye him. Dominic nods in agreement, his lips press together tightly. His Adam's apple bobs as he swallows, his demeanor seemingly uncomfortable and tense. No greeting, just straight to the point, rubbing their engagement right in my face. Pain funnels through my pierced, bruised heart. What a snobby-ass bitch. I wonder if she knows about us. No, of course not. He doesn't give a shit about me. Why would he mention me? A forced smile paints my unblinkingly pale face.

"Congratulations," I say, grinding my teeth. The pit of my stomach twitches in knots, and the sourness erupts, causing indigestion and acid reflux. Twisting my way around them, not acknowledging Dominic's presence, I point to tell them where to stand. I exhale softly as I enter my office with trembling hands. I grab my camera, while I blink away unshed tears. I won't give him the pleasure of seeing me cry.

Thank heavens, Sophie emerges from the back room. Her eyes stretch wide as saucers when she spots the couple.

"I got this," she whispers in my ear. Then grabs the camera from my hand.

I nod, thanking her. Dominic's presence intoxicates me, the feel of his eyes burning a hole right through me. I turn to gaze into his eyes. His are burning directly into mine. The Dominic that appears in front of me is not my Dominic. He shifts between hot and cold. I won't let him belittle me. He's the one who hurt and betrayed me. I feel my eyes throwing daggers in his direction. His gaze is cold.

I built a wall to protect me from the pain I've been through. He disposed of me like a piece of trash, never giving me the chance to tell him I was pregnant.

Sophie has them posing. They pick the poses from our sample book where Dominic wraps his arms around her waist, and they press their lips together. Sophie snaps a couple of different photos. Sophie mutters words to them I can't quite hear by her facial expression she's annoyed. I notice Dominic glaring at her, then me if I'm not mistaken. My best friend is giving him a cold, hard stare.

"So, how did you two meet?" Sophie asks, making conversation. I'm sure she's asking because, one: She's a straightforward person and, two: she wants to see Dominic's expressions. Samantha beams.

"Dominic's mom works for my dad, and she introduced us about a year ago, and now we're engaged."

I roll my eyes, of course, that wicked lady fixed her son up with an uppity, snobby bitch. Apparently, I wasn't good enough for him. I'm sure that was part of the reason he dropped me like a hot cake. Her manicured fingers trace the lines of his muscular chest. My heart races. I want to tear her hands off of him. Jealousy rips through me, a burning sensation deep in my stomach. I rustle around the front counter, texting clients, their photos are ready for pickup. Muttering unkind things under my breath.

"We are so in love, right, honey? He proposed in such a romantic way." She looks at him sweetly, batting her eyelashes. He returns the smile; his eyes meet mine, smirking his lips twist as his husky voice bellows the room.

"Yes, baby, you're the love of my life, the only one I've ever been in love with. Can't wait to make you, my wife."

She gasps in shock, throws her hands over his neck, and kisses him passionately. Sophie clears her throat. He steps away, smirking.

What an asshole.

My chest burns as if acid has been poured all over my chest, eating me up. The treachery stings. The smirk on his face proves he deliberately hurt me. He fell out of love with me. Who am I kidding? He just said she's the only one he's ever loved. The betoken of his cruelty is infuriating. He's treating me as if I did something wrong. He's so confusing, one minute he's being all possessive at the restaurant, pinning me to a bathroom wall. Next, he's giving me a death stare.

He's getting married, he loves her. I have to remind myself I'm just a part of his past. My temper is rising, wanting to shout at him and ask what the fuck his problem is, does he not remember what we went through?

"We are all done. We will contact you when your photos are ready," Sophie mutters as she walks them to the front desk counter.

"Great, thank you."

I turn to walk into my office, not sparing them another glance, shutting the door behind me. The dejected feeling of a broken heart is watching the man you love walk out with another woman hand in hand. He was never mine. He found what he didn't have with me. Someone with a family, I assume. Not an orphan. Someone capable of giving him more than what I have.

"MOMMY, let's play hide and go seek," Dante shouts, jumping up and down.

"Okay, I count you hide."

"One, two, three, four, five, six, seven."

I hear giggles hiding under the table in his Spider-Man suit. Pretending I can't see him.

"I wonder where he went?"

"Mommy, right here, silly."

Crawling under the table, I tickle him. He giggles.

45

"All right, time for bed, brush those teeth. I'll be up to read you a story." He marches up the stairs, groaning as he stomps into the bathroom. I pour a good amount of wine into my glass. What a shitty day. For the past five years, I have raised my son while going to college. Taking him to the park, teaching him how to play baseball, and how to ride a bike. I longed for love every time I tried to take that step. My thoughts linger on the man I gave my soul to. I hand Sophie, a glass of wine. She takes a sip and looks up at me.

"You know that woman is an airhead," Sophie says, sneering.

"And he's a handsome asshole," I add, sighing.

"You know he kept staring at you. Just watching you." She swishes the wine in her mouth. "He doesn't look like he's really in love with her," she protests.

An airy laugh escapes my lips. "You heard what he said. Dominic loves her, and he loved no one else. He never loved me like I thought he did. I spent years talking to him, thinking he was listening from heaven, sent balloons with a message for his birthday and the anniversary of his passing." Glaring at my best friend with a grimacing smile. I shrug my shoulder.

"I just don't get what happened. He loved me. We were so in love. Well, I thought he was. It's been five years, Sophie, long enough for him to move on and fall in love."

"I think you need to be the big person and go talk to him, find out what happened, and see how it goes. Depending on how things go, you can tell him about Dante."

She's not wrong. We need to talk like adults. He's been acting juvenile. She tosses me the card his fiancé handed her. Fetching the card, a small smile creeps onto my lips. He owns a restaurant, Delgado Steak House.

"He owns a restaurant, Sophie. Before he had gotten sick when my father passed, he said, 'Let's open a restaurant together in memory of your parents.'" I scratch my head in confusion.

"Do you think he opened this up because of us? I guess that's silly. Of course not." We sip our wine in unison.

"Men are so confusing. He looked at you as if he wasn't sure if he wanted to fuck you or strangle you."

I cough up a laugh. Shaking my head definitely not fucking me.

———

I sit in my Range Rover in the parking lot of Dominic's restaurant. My nerves are spiraling, rubbing my sweaty palms on my jeans. Hell, I'm so nervous.

"Keep it together, Mila," I tell myself. Taking a deep, long breath, I get out of my car, walk through the double doors, and ask the host for Dominic Delgado.

"He's in his office toward the kitchen in the back." She looks at me up and down—sizing me up.

Okay, I don't know what this is all about.

"Can I help you with something?" A flicker of irritation and impatience shines in her eyes.

I give her a fake smile. "No, I'm a friend. I want to speak to him in his office."

She points back toward the kitchen. His restaurant is very exquisite. I pass a jukebox as I walk to the back. There's a waterfall and beautiful décor around it. Dominic's voice booms as I get closer. I hear a woman's voice, speaking to him, the high-pitched voice sounds familiar. Her sharp, high-pitched voice has me cringing; it is his fiancée.

"Baby, I picked the date for our wedding. I was thinking of a March wedding. Are you okay with that?" she questions him.

"Can't wait, baby, whatever you want."

My heart is pounding. I plant my hands on my chest, feeling my heart racing. Damnit, why did I come? I scoot a little closer without getting noticed. I peek in, hopefully, they can't see. He sits in a chair. She's on his lap, straddling him. Kissing his neck, then running her hands up and down his chest. He presses his lips on hers and devours her mouth. She moans. He retrieves from their kiss. *He will be married in five months.* What does he see in her that I don't have? Money, of course, and his mother must love her. It was supposed to be *us* getting married. I take a steady breath. Fucking hell this hurts.

"Dominic, once we get married, I want to start a family," she purrs into his neck.

He shoves her off. His jaw clenches so hard it might snap.

"Samantha, I told you I don't want to have kids right now."

I feel a sting in my chest. I can't tell him about Dante. He doesn't want kids. I turn and walk away. Once I'm in my car, I shed the tears I'd been holding.

Five

MILA

It's been a week since I stepped foot in Dominic's restaurant. I realized this was the closure, I needed to move on with my life. He made it crystal clear he had no intention of having kids. Protecting my son is my number one priority. I won't force Dante on him. At this point, it's best to keep things the way they are. I'll be dammed if I let this asshole break my son's heart.

Honestly, I am torn because it's not what I had expected from him—

five years changed him for the worse. It's time I move on and honestly, I'm ready. It's time I let Dominic go.

"Girl, don't let the douchebag get to you," Sophie scoffs.

He will always have half of my soul and my heart. He was my first love. The father of my son. He betrayed me. Not something I expected from him. We dated for a year and a half. I don't understand why he did what he did. I've been through so much. You'd think he'd have mercy on my soul.

"An asshole, douchebag, and every name in the book," I grumble as my eyes narrow on Dante sliding his bottom down the stairs. Dante's *Peter Pan* school play is tonight. My trusty Canon camera is in my hand, given to me by Uncle Roger when Dante was born. If only my parents were alive to see their grandson's first play performance.

"Mommy, are you ready? Let's go. I'm Hook. Arg!" He makes a pirate face, closing one eye.

Silly boy. I laugh.

Sophie, Dante, and I arrive at St. Mary's. Ryder stands leaning on his Harley as he walks straight to us. Ryder's Sophie's boyfriend, or should I say, 'friend with benefits,' which is what she calls him. Sophie's anti-boyfriend, afraid of commitment at this point because her past relationship ended badly. He slips a quick kiss on her red lips. Brian calls my name from a distance, waiting at the entrance. Sophie convinced me to invite him. He was more than happy to join us.

"You look beautiful." His eyes wander up and down my body. The smile in his eyes contains a sensuous flame.

"Thank you," I manage to say.

Dante shuffles next to me.

"Hey, little dude, ready for your play? You're going to be outstanding. Hook is the best," Brian says, ruffling Dante's hair.

Dante smiles at him shyly. He nods.

We all gather in the auditorium for the play's start. The proud parents and grandparents quickly produced cameras. After taking a few snapshots with my phone, I quickly send them to Nana and Uncle Roger. By the end of the show, the kids all sing "You Can Fly" and a few tears fall down my face, a testament to the immense pride I feel as a parent. My baby is getting so big. He will be five in two months, a week before Thanksgiving.

I search the crowd for what I don't know. Maybe it's families I see embracing one another. Husbands and wives. I crave the love my parents had. I want a family. I want Dante to have siblings and a father. I want a man to see me as if I were their entire universe and recognize my value. I want to experience love and happiness.

We all head back to my apartment. The guys come over for pizza, celebrating my little guy's first play. We enjoy the night with beer and wine. I pour wine into our glasses, and Sophie and I drink it down like thirsty teenagers.

"You did great, baby. You're a magnificent pirate."

He puffs his chest with pride. The pizza finally arrives, and we all gather in the living room. Brian plops down on the sofa next to me, and I can't help but sneak a glance at his toned arms and attractive physique, which are apparent even beneath the plain muscle shirt and jean shorts he is wearing. His lips turn up in a slight smile as he lounges against the couch cushions. He catches me ogling him. He winks with a smirk. My face turns scarlet red.

"Brian, you want to play cars with me?" Dante asks Brian shyly.

I'm startled by Dante's confidence in asking. He's never been around another man.

"Sure, bud, do you want to play in the living room or your bedroom?"

He tilts his head to the side... thinking. "I bring them to the living room." He runs up the stairs excitedly.

Watching Brian and Dante play—tugs the strings in my chest. Dominic should be playing with his son. I sigh.

"Don't they look adorable playing together?" Sophie squeals excitedly, grinning stupidly.

I take my glass of wine and take a long sip. I nod.

"They do. I'm happy he feels comfortable asking him to play with him, but Brian and I have been talking. We haven't stated what we are at this point. I don't want Dante to grow attached to him. I don't want different men coming in and out of his life."

She groans. "Jeez, are you done rambling? you act like you're marrying him tonight. You went on one date, and he's hanging out tonight. You see him every day when you kill for coffee."

I glance back at Dante and Brian; Dante is laughing so hard. I love that Brian's not running for the woods just yet. His heart is full of warmth and kindness. Oftentimes, he'll text me just to say hi and ask how Dante and I are doing. He knows I have a son and that he matters to me. He's good with Dante. He deserves a chance.

"You're right. I'll take it slow and see how it plays out."

She shakes her finger at me. "Girl, I'm always right. You're lucky you have me."

My eyes pass to Ryder, who's on the phone, leaning on the counter.

I ask with a mischievous expression, "So, how're things going with you two? He stayed the night last night, didn't he?"

Her blue eyes open wide like saucers as I ask. She had been keeping his overnight visit a secret from me; I wasn't sure why.

"W-what? He did not."

"You're such a liar. I heard you. Put a sock in your mouth next time." I laugh so hard that my stomach clenches. Her eyes bulge even wider, her face turning bright red, she lets out a loud laugh.

"Omg, really, I'm sorry."

Well, shit, at least she's getting some. A couple of nights ago, I fantasized about Dominic touching me in places that are begging to be touched. I groan, frustrated.

Brian says his goodbyes, as I walk him out to his Jeep.

"Thank you for inviting me. I had a blast tonight," Brian husks, his eyes linger on my lips.

"Thank you for coming."

He takes a couple of steps closer to me, his heated breath on my lips. "I want to kiss you," he whispers. "Can I?"

I nod.

His tongue traces the softness of my lips. Slowly and steadily, he slips his tongue into my mouth, intertwining with mine. The palms of his hands cup my cheeks, bringing me in deeper. His kiss is passionate and all-consuming, like a raging wildfire. My skin tingles when he touches me, and I feel a wave of desire course through me. His hands move to my waist, pulling me closer until my heart feels like it is going to burst from within my chest.

God, he tastes so good.

The perfect combination of sweet and salty, it's like a delicious reminder of all that I have been missing. He grinds into me and moans into my mouth. I take a step back, panting, our lips red and swollen. He blows out a slow breath. He looks at me with concern.

"Are you okay? Was this too soon?"

"No, it's fine. It's just... I want to take things slow, with Dante and all."

He strokes my cheek, kissing the corner of my mouth. "I understand, and we can take it slow."

I tug on his shirt, pulling him toward me, we kiss some more, exploring one another.

Six

DOMINIC

I've been in a horrendous mood, taking it out on my staff. On top of all that, Samantha wants to start a family once we get married. The thought has my stomach in knots. Damn stupid engagement photos, of all places, it had to be with Mila. She has her own studio. Proud, to say the least, she has had it hard losing both parents. She looked beautiful as always as she appeals to it effort-lessly. She was wearing tight jeans shaping her ass to perfection and a cotton V-neck shirt showing a small amount of skin.

God, her voice is like a melody, so beautiful you never want it to end. Sending bolts of electricity through my whole body. Being a dick to Mila was not my intention, but fuck it, her rejection from our past wounded me. It was a low blow, saying Samantha was the only love of my life. Mila, avoiding any eye contact, was pissing me off. Her body stiffened uncomfortably, pinching her lips together tight, to keep them from trembling. I saw the torment in her eyes as she side-eyed me, I knew, I hit where it hurt.

Good, I want her to feel the rawness, the pain searing every part of her.

I never treated Mila badly. I'm not the same person. She changed me when she left me, when I was down, when I needed her. The woman I loved sliced and ripped open my heart, molding me into being bitter and cold. Where was she when I needed her during my recovery? She left me, disposed of me like a dead carcass on the side of the road.

———

MY TRUCK PEELS out of my driveway as I make my way to my mom's for my weekly family dinner. Her rule is to have her sons meet for dinner once a week. My mom has been my superhero, taking care of me during my sickness. When Mila left me with a broken heart, Mom was there to pick up the pieces. I scrutinize the upscale neighborhood my mom lives in, I can't help but notice it's beautiful. Her home fits right in. California homes are overly expensive, but she managed to save up money to buy her dream home.

"Knock, Knock!" I shout as I walk in.

My brother Santiago and the youngest of us, Mark is sitting at the table drinking a beer. Mark is three years younger than me.

"Mmm, smells good, Mom."

She moves around from the kitchen sink to kiss my cheek.

"Hi, honey. How's the restaurant?"

"Going good, busy, like always. I had to fill in yesterday, I had some call-ins, as usual. I need to hire more people."

She nods.

"If you need help, I could help you out with payroll. I have weekends off." Her brown eyes beam with hope.

"Thanks, Mom, I'll keep that in mind."

"Good, honey, dinner's ready. Let's eat."

We all sit at the table and eat dinner. Mom prepared us spaghetti, freshly baked bread sticks, and a side salad. My favorite. Mark talks about his classes. He is attending the university for computer science. Mark's the quiet one in the family. Today he's rather talkative, maybe it's the beer he's drinking. Mark's not of age to drink, but the fucker drinks now and then. He carries a fake

ID, which Santiago gifted him. At his age, we all carried a fake ID to get into bars and clubs.

"Mark, you better be passing those classes. I'm not paying so you can flunk out." My mom glares as she chews on her breadstick.

"I know, Mom. And I'm passing," he grumbles.

She nods as she turns to look at me.

"Santiago told me Mila is back in town." Her voice grates, her nostrils flare.

I turn to my brother, giving him a what the fuck look. I turn back to my mom, frowning with worry. "Yeah, I saw her the other day."

She wrinkles her nose. "Stay away from her, Dominic. She's trouble, and she walked out on you. You were a burden to her. She said it herself. Do you not remember?" Mom stands up, placing dishes in the sink.

She's quiet for a split second.

"You're engaged, and Samantha is wonderful, beautiful, and she loves you. She's perfect for you." Her words hit me like a tidal wave.

Apparently, my heart and dick are not getting the memo. I want to roll my eyes. Samantha is a pain in my ass. Too fucking needy. Samantha's parents do everything for her. She grew up with a silver spoon. But she's right, Mila is not good for me. A woman who leaves you when you're sick, at your worst, needs to be forgotten. Samantha's been pleasantly good to me.

"Yeah, Mom, I know, and I don't plan on talking to Mila." Which is a lie; she's all I think about, more than anything, I deserve answers. I want to kiss her, feel her, hold her in my arms. It pisses me off that she gets under my skin. Thinking about her arouses me.

"She's with someone else, Mom. Could be her husband, nothing to worry about," Santiago claims, wiping his face with a smirk.

Jealousy funnels into my heart. The image of her being married kills me. I'll rip him apart.

"That's good to hear. See, Dominic, she moved on, honey, therefore Samantha is good for you. She will care for you. What if your cancer returns? Samantha will be there for you." She takes a drink of iced tea. "The day I met Mila, I knew she was not good for you. A mother knows, Dominic. Look how she left you. She's an orphan with no sense of direction."

My insides cave with pain. I was there the night she lost her father. The night I took her to the beach and made love to her.

I perch above her windowsill, my heart racing as I wait for her to appear. She finally emerges, her face aglow with excitement. I open my arms and help her to the ground, then load up a bundle of blankets. We head out to our spot, a huge rock at the beach. It's a school night. I've been dying to see her; we don't attend the same school. I lay out the blankets. The place is privately hidden from bystanders seeing us—the rock covers up anyone who would pass by. The beach is empty, just us, and the sound of the waves. It's a full moon tonight, the bright silver light spills across the water. Mila sprawls herself on the blanket, her hands behind her head. She looks up at the stars twinkling in the night sky. I've been waiting all day to see her.

"Such a beautiful night," she whispers softly, feeling content.

"Uh-huh," is all I manage to utter, because I'm staring at her like I want to rip her clothes off.

Throughout the day, I've sported a huge boner and had to read-just myself numerous times. All I could think about is if we shared the same school, what I can do to her—in the locker room, utility closet, bathroom, and even walking her to class.

She closes her eyes when a falling star shoots across the night sky.

"What did you wish for?" I ask, running my fingers along her cheek.

"Can't tell you. It won't come true if I did." Her beautiful smile stretches to her ears.

"Is it about me, at least?" I ask, sounding a little desperate. Fuck

if someone had told me I'd be falling in love at the age of seventeen, I would say they're fucking crazy. Here I am, looking like a lovesick puppy. She rolls over to her side, facing me. Her elbows are supporting her weight.

"Maybe." Her voice comes out breathless when her emerald-green gaze wanders to my engorged erection.

My dick is getting larger by the minute, stretching in my elastic basketball shorts.

"Kiss me," she demands.

So, I do.

Our mouths meld together, and I can taste the sweetness of her cherry lip gloss. A sound of pleasure escapes her lips as I deepen the kiss. Sliding my hands under her back, I unclasp her bra and tug off her shirt. She's so beautiful, and it's not a meaningless hookup like usual. She's the first girl I've ever loved and my first girlfriend.

"Mom, she lost her father in a tragic accident. Just because...."

"You're defending her? After all, she did to you," she snaps.

"No, of course not." Santiago clears his throat.

Thank God Santiago changes the subject by talking about his shop.

"I hope the shop of yours is making money, Santiago." My mom is on one tonight. Her hands are on her hips as she glares at each of us.

I'm certain it has to do with Mila moving back and stirring shit up. Well, that's my cue to leave.

I SHUFFLED past the door and into my condo, the hum of the refrigerator being the only sound. My eyes are drawn to the vast, marbled kitchen island with its steely reflectiveness. As a chef, I'd expected to be in the kitchen more often, cooking up elaborate dishes, but cooking for myself doesn't bring me any joy. I'd rather eat at the restaurant, Mom's, or Samantha's place. I sink into my huge sectional couch, thinking about what Mila is doing. "My Angel," only she's not mine, she's with someone else. And I'm engaged. I want to hate her with a passion. My heart twitches every damn time I try to. The memories of our past rush right back.

I spent the afternoon cooking a meal for Mila. I cooked the ground beef until it turned a golden-brown color. I found a box of taco shells inside the pantry and heated them in the microwave before filling them up with beef and topping them off with lettuce and tomato. I knock on her bedroom window. She smiles faintly as she slides the window open.

"Hey, Angel, I brought dinner," I say as I walk into her bedroom.

I have been concerned since Mila has eaten little since her father passed. Her grief is consuming her, preventing her from taking care of herself.

"Thank you." Her voice is soft and velvety.

Opening the container, I hand her a taco. "Baby, eat, please, for me."

She takes a bite and swallows. "Thank you, You're going to be a talented chef."

I snag a taco; I take a bite. Fuck. I spit it out and smack the taco out of her hand. The shells are fucking stale.

"Angel, it tastes like shit."

She's so sweet, she ate the damn taco. Not wanting to hurt my feelings.

"No, it's good," she proclaims.

"Baby, it tastes like ass."

She chuckles for the first time in weeks.

MY RECOLLECTIONS of how she abandoned me and never looked back are shattered with a click. I turn on the faucet for another measly cold shower for the millionth time. My dick goes back in time to when we were teens again, every time I think of her, I grow hard. A deep groan escapes my throat as I run my hands through my wet hair. *Damnit Mila, what are you doing to me? I need* to forget Mila—Mom's right, she's toxic she fucked me over. It was a high school fling. She's in the past.

I'll go stay the night with Samantha. I'll spend the entire, day with her tomorrow, take her shopping and spend the night fucking her until I fail to remember Mila. Getting her out of my system. Samantha is the one for me. I'm engaged to her.

SAMANTHA LIVES in a classy new development neighborhood. I wave at the security guard at the gate.

"Hey, Dominic, how's it going? How have you been, man?" Ron is an elderly man who retired from the Air Force.

"Good, man, same old shit." My life consists solely of work, with nothing else.

"Take the miss on a trip. Maybe it's just what you need." He waves me off with a cheerful smile.

I sigh. He could be right, maybe taking a trip is just what Samantha and I need. I pull into her driveway, hopping out of my truck, I head to her front door. I knocked twice. She opens the door, surprised to see me. Her beautiful smile glistens in the sunlight.

"What are you doing here? Shouldn't you be at the restaurant?"

I wrap my arms around her, cupping her cheeks. I swoop down to claim her lips.

"Can't I spend time with my fiancée?" I ask, raising an eyebrow at her.

She squeals, "You never show up like this. You just caught me by surprise, that's all," she moans as I kiss her. She's wearing one of my T-shirts. "You look beautiful wearing my shirt, baby." My words are strained. I run my hands under the fabric of the t-shirt.

I shake my head inwardly, repressing any thoughts of the woman with raven hair who is clawing her way inside.

"I want to take you shopping." I lift her onto the kitchen counter.

"Oh, Dominic, baby, you know I love shopping." She twirls a strand of hair, batting her eyelashes.

"I know, that's why I want to take you out and spend the entire day with my girl."

She kisses me on the lips, hungrily.

"Get dressed, baby."

———

WE'VE BEEN at the mall for three prolonged hours—why does it take so long to pick clothes? Why do women have to try it all on? I grab a hold of her bags as we walk back to my pickup.

"Do you want to go grab something to eat, sweetheart?" I ask her while opening the door of the truck. I lean in and give her a peck on the lips.

"Starving... shopping makes me hungry." She exhales a long sigh of contentment.

No one can deny Samantha is beautiful. Yet, kissing Mila always felt like a fireworks show, and with Samantha, it's... dry. *In time, it will get better,* I convince myself.

"How about Chinese?"

A warm smile clings to her lips. "That sounds good."

I pull her in for another kiss.

Lunch goes by quickly as we chat about how she's close to finishing law school. Her father's plans are for her to take over his business when he retires. Samantha's upbringing as an only child radiates off her, generations of wealth are visible. She has no knowledge of what it's like to struggle or what surviving is like. They have handed everything down to her. She is lucky to have that.

As we pull into the Target lot, I remember the restaurant

needs more paper goods and cleaning supplies. Samantha doesn't seem to mind accompanying me on my errand.

Walking down the aisle, I grab a couple of cleaning products. Samantha walks off to go fish for a phone case while I make my way to the paper products aisle. I toss a bulk pack of paper towels into the basket. My ears perk up like a damn chihuahua when I hear the sweetest voice, the voice that never leaves my memory, in the aisle next to me. My heartbeat quickens like it always does in response to her voice. She makes my body react in ways no woman can. She's kerosene, igniting every part of me. I push my basket slowly to peek into the next aisle. Mila kneels close to a small boy, but I can't see his face. I wonder if she's babysitting or if she has kids. Is she married to the Ken dude?

Oh, fuck, I feel a stab right in my chest. *Stab, stab, stab.*

"Honey, we can get you a toy in just a minute. Let me get what I need first," she coos to the small child.

"Okay, Mommy."

Oh hell, it is her son. Gasping for air, I feel as if my ribs are collapsing. She turns around to see where the noise came from. I attempt to make a run for it before she sees me, but it's too late. Her forest green eyes are on mine. Her eyes darken with anger at the sight of me. A growl escapes her lips.

The little boy stands next to Mila, his brown eyes behold mine. He tilts his head, squints his eyes as he observes me. My breathing picks up beads of sweat trickling down my forehead. He looks so familiar, with his long black eyelashes, big dimples... olive skin, and Mila's black hair.

Mila stiffens as she watches my gaze bounce back and forth from the boy to her. I'm perplexed. His features resemble mine when I was a child. It can't be, can it? I'm about to open my mouth to speak when I hear Samantha's voice.

"Hi, nice to see you again. Sorry, I forgot your name. What is it?" she asks coarsely.

"Mila," she says icily.

"Is this your son?" Samantha snickers dryly.

Mila chews on her bottom lip as she holds the little boy's hand. "Umm... yes, this is my son." Her eyes dart between us before she cuts our gaze.

My mouth drops open, and I can't speak. He looks so much like me when I was a kid. He has to be mine. How in the hell can this be? It's been five years.

Her son looks up at me, his deep dimples are visible.

"Hi, my name is—"

Mila interrupts. "His name is Dante." Her breath comes out shaky.

My eyes widen.

"Nice to see you two. We better go." She's about to sprint off when I grasp her arm, squeezing softly in desperation.

I whisper close for her only to hear, "How old is he, Mila?"

"Four," she snaps.

Shoving me away, Mila dashes off.

Dante turns around and smiles at me. He waves. The air whizzed into my lungs. A stream of fiery blood rushed through me, pulsing at my fingertips. My chest feels like it's going to burst. Why didn't she tell me? My mind is churning with so many emotions and confusion.

Our son, we have a son. Where in the hell has, she been all this time? Why did she leave me if we have a son? Mila named him after me. Dante is my middle name. Shit, I completely forgot Samantha was with me.

"Why are you staring at her like that, Dominic, and why did you whisper in her ear?" Her voice is sharp with jealousy. "Like you know her. Do you know her?"

"I don't know what you're talking about," I bark out, irritated. "Let's go. I need to get home." I'm not in the mood for her interrogation.

The drive to Samantha's is quiet, she glowers out the window. I get out of my pickup to help her out.

"Samantha," I call out.

She slams the door viciously, and I hand her the shopping

bags. She seizes them from my hold without a word and storms off. Pulling out of the driveway, I speed back to my place. I'm outraged that Mila excluded me from the role of being a father, hiding my son from me. Trailing back, she was pregnant at the hospital when I last spoke to her, wondering if she knew then. From what I remember—I was told you're not fertile when on chemo.

Shit, but he looks just like me. It's not the fucker's kid she was with he looks nothing like him. Tomorrow I'll set foot in her studio. We need to talk about Dante. So many questions, and I don't intend to be friendly about it. She owes me an explanation. Her betrayal cuts deeper than I realized.

Seven

MILA

I scroll through my mental grocery list as I wander down the aisle of Target: lasagna ingredients, and a chocolate cake for dessert. *Crap, I forgot to grab the paper towels.* I turn my cart around and head back to the household goods area.

"Mommy let's go get a toy, please." Dante looks at me, pleading and pouting with puppy eyes.

"Honey, we can get you a toy in just a minute. Let me get what I need first."

I hear a groan and someone gasping for air with a lengthy breath, and I'm startled by the sound. I turn around, and I see Dominic staring at us. His gaze is drawn more to Dante than to me. The way he's glaring at Dante has me worried. I'm not sure if he sees the resemblance. He opens his mouth, then closes it repeatedly. My momma bear's instincts kick in. We hardly know each other anymore. I don't know what he'll reveal in front of Dante. My stomach churns queasily. This is not the place for him to find out, and Dante thinks he's dead, for God's sake. Ahh, here comes Miss Snobby, I mean Samantha, with her snarky voice.

"Hi, nice to see you again. Sorry, forgot your name." Her eyebrows furrow into a sour lemon face.

The need to roll my eyes is unconscionable. She's clearly over-dressed in her 4,000-dollar outfit. Her annoying voice makes me cringe.

"Mila." My tone comes out icy. I direct my haughty stare toward Dominic. The damn bimbo keeps talking.

Dominic has yet to open his mouth to speak. His eyes stay pinned on us.

"Is this your son?"

I feel my anxiety crawling in on me. I see the wheels turning in his head. I turn my back to her sour face, mustering a smile.

"Umm... yes, this is my son."

Fuck I just need to walk away from them.

Dante stares at Dominic, his head tilted to the side. He might recognize him. I need to leave; I don't want him to say he looks like his dad. Dante has seen pictures of Dominic.

"Hi, my name is—"

I cut Dante off when he's about to say his name, not wanting him to reveal his full name. Then Dominic will know. Hell, they look alike.

"His name is Dante," I reveal with a shaky breath.

Dominic's eyes widen.

Shit.

"Nice to see you two. We better go." Fate has a way of fucking with us. As I round my cart and pass directly in front of Dominic, he grabs my arm and whispers in my ear. His hot breath prickles my skin.

"How old is he?"

I feel the need to pull away and say, *Fuck you. I don't owe you an answer.* But I do.

"Four," I snap, giving him a grimace of a stare, pulling from his hold.

My head is pounding and splitting in two—this was not how I had hoped Dominic would find out. When I overheard his outburst about not wanting kids, my plans changed. Picking up the phone, I call Sophie.

"Hello?"

"Hey, guess what just happened?" I blurt out.

"You overspent at Target like always."

I want to laugh because she's right. Just this time, I didn't get the chance.

"No, I ran into Dominic and his fiancée," I tell her everything that happened. I'm sure she can hear the worry in my tone.

"I don't think he will go looking for you. He made it clear about not wanting kids, and if he wants to talk, then lay it all on him."

Sighing, I feel a tad better.

"Thanks for letting me vent. You're the best."

She laughs. "Girl, I know I'm the best of the best."

"One of these days, your ego is going to pop," I say, popping the P. I laugh.

"I'll grab something to eat. I'll be on my way in ten." I grin as I turn off the phone. I'm fortunate to have her in my life.

I scan through the applications, searching for a front desk assistant, when I hear the bells on the door ring. I quickly jerk my head up in surprise. Dominic bursts in like a raging bull, and before I can say anything, he starts talking.

"Is he, mine, Mila?" he shouts.

I ignore his outburst, narrowing my eyes back at the applications. Having him in my space is too much. A part of me wants to say no, he's not yours. So, we can all move on from this, but that's not who I am.

"Why did you hide him from me all these years? If you didn't want to be in my life, you could at least tell me about Dante."

I spun around, my fists clenched at my sides, eyes blazing, teeth grinding. Rage bubbles up inside me like molten lava, and I stomp toward him like a bull ready to charge. A deep-seated hatred surges up inside me.

"How was I supposed to tell you when I thought you were fucking dead, you moron!"

A devilish laugh erupts from his chest. "You knew I was getting better, Mila. Quit playing the martyr. You're the one who told my mom I was a burden to you. You left me, don't fucking lie to me." His breathing is so heavy, he's so close, it's like a sauna to my face.

My lips curl in disgust. Veins pulsing, hammering throughout my spine. Taking two steps so we're eye to eye, I won't let him intimidate me.

"Your mom is a fucking liar. I called her and your brothers for a month straight. I left several voice messages, but your bitch mom blocked me. The minute I left the hospital, they ignored every phone call I made to them. I called the hospital; they refused to give me any information. So, don't give me your bullshit, Dominic." I expel a heavy breath, swallowing the dry patch in my throat.

I raise my chin, struggling to meet his towering height. My cold eyes bore into his. His confusion is palpable, and I can feel the tension radiating off of him. I step closer, pointing at him, my finger jabbing into his chest.

"Do you honestly think so poorly of me, to think I wouldn't give a shit about you? I fucking loved you so much! I couldn't function without you." I try shoving him, but his hard muscular body is too big.

His eyes soften to a whisper, and the furrows in his brow deepen. I slap his hands away as they attempt to touch my face.

"You don't understand the pain I've gone through. I wanted to give up on life and felt like I couldn't go on without you. Losing my dad was hard, but losing you made me feel even more alone."

Unbearable.

"One morning, I awoke feeling unwell and had to rush to the bathroom to vomit. Realizing that I hadn't gotten my period the previous month, I immediately drove to the store for a pregnancy test. That morning, I knew my life had a purpose again. My son was like a beacon in the darkness, a miracle to me."

He was about to open his mouth to talk, but I cut him off with my hand.

I'm not done talking, asshole.

"Nana couldn't afford to take care of me and a baby, so we all moved in with Uncle Roger in Manhattan. I wrapped up my senior year of high school there and completed my studies to graduate. Dominic, I grieved for you for five fucking, goddamn years. It was up to me to take care of our son, so I worked hard—taking two jobs and continuing my studies. I was working at a gas station and helping out at Uncle Roger's studio while you were playing dress-up with your stuck-up fiancé."

He winces. "Angel, I'm..."

I interrupt him again.

"I'm not your Angel, you're anything for that matter," I exclaim.

His brown eyes pleading.

I shake my head. "How dare you think so little of me? You, Dominic, belittled me and annihilated me. You chose to believe the lies your mother spilled from her venomous mouth. If you ever loved me, you would have known where my heart was at."

"Mila, fuck, I'm sorry—" He runs his fingers on his chin, pacing up and down the studio.

Luckily, I'm here alone today.

"Mila, I searched for you. I was a broken mess, baby. I fucking searched for you, Mila."

I laugh. "Oh yeah, you searched for me. Sticking your dick around town, parading around with your artsy, soon-to-be trophy wife. Don't play the martyr with me, Dominic. Get the fuck out of my studio, get back to your fiancée, you're so in love with,

69

right? The love of your life, you said oh, and the only woman you ever loved." My voice comes out hoarse and raspy from all the shouting.

His Adam's apple bobs, and his shoulders hunch forward. He sighs, as I walk to my office, tempted to shut the door and scream cry. He follows behind, shutting the door to my office.

"Mila, it's true I looked for you, but I was hurt and pissed. I thought you left me. And I do love you, I still do. But why would my mom lie, Mila?"

His words hurt. What does it matter now? Five years have passed, he's moved on.

"Just leave." I grit my teeth. "You chose to believe your mom over what we had. She's always loathed me. You might have looked for me at first—it wasn't because you loved me enough to believe I would never leave you. It was because you believed what your mom claimed and wanted to hurt me with your words. You made it clear."

"Are you with someone?" he blurts out as his hand shoves its way into his pockets. His body is tensed, and his jaw is clenched. He catches me off guard. His muscles twitch as his jealousy courses through him.

He has some fucking nerve to ask.

"That's rich considering you're engaged, and it's not any of your business who I date or fuck, but if you must know, he's my boyfriend."

He growls and leans into me, pushing me against the desk. "Mila, let me talk, please, I'm sorry, I want to be in your and Dante's lives."

I shake my head at him. *He thinks saying sorry will make it all better. Is he kidding me?*

"First of all, I overheard your conversation. I decided to come to the restaurant to speak to you. I heard you say you didn't want kids. Dante and I don't need you, get back to your fiancée. Leave, please. I don't want to see you again. You're five years too late." I snake around him, walking back to the front.

"Mila," he begs, trailing behind me.

I want him to leave—his presence is too much for me. His eyes scrutinize me, full of regret. That's on him. He believed what others said rather than following his own heart.

"Angel, I lo—"

I spin around to his chiseled face. My brows furrow in disappointment.

"Don't you dare say it."

His mouth crashes on mine unexpectedly. His lips intertwined with mine. The heat in his kiss feels like wax melting under the fiery flames of desire. The familiarity of his lips I missed so much. His arms wrap around my waist, lowering down to my ass, circling his palms around my ass as he squeezes. He groans and moans into my mouth. His legs wedge between mine as he deepens the kiss, making me dizzy and lightheaded. Waves of pleasure heat my core. His erection grinding on my belly.

I'm panting—angrily for allowing myself to be degraded over lust. *He's engaged, for God's sakes.*

"Go, Dominic, you're engaged, and you made it clear when you said you loved her and only her." I jerk away from him. My chest rises and falls as I rapidly take in breaths.

"Angel," he whispers softly.

"Leave, please. We're done. We have closure now. You clearly moved on. It's time I do the same. Go, I'm sure your fiancée is waiting."

Dominic's jaw tightens, his fists clench into a ball. His lips are swollen and tinged with red, his eyes reflect pain and pleading. His breathing is shallow and desperate as if panic is squeezing his throat.

I close my eyes, not wanting to bear witness to any more of his pain and turn away. The door slams shut behind me like a thunderclap, and my knees buckle beneath me as I sink into my chair and break down into sobs. My chest tightens painfully. His family did this. I know it's not entirely his fault they manipulated him, but what hurts is he belittled me. I loved him with everything I had. He once was the oxygen I needed to breathe. We lived a life without him. A part of me will always love him. It's time for me to let him go and move on with my life. I'm with Brian now. He's safe, compassionate, and cares for Dante.

Eight

DOMINIC

"Fuck, fuck, fuck," I shout as I jump into my truck, startling the old lady walking her dog. *Goddammit,* I pound my fist into the steering wheel.

My flesh and blood lied to me, kept me away from the only girl I've loved. I lick my lips, tasting her remains lingering on my lips. All this time, I thought Mila betrayed me when it was me who betrayed her. I feel like an ass flaunting Samantha around, kissing her in front of Mila, fucking with her head. The bitter asshole in me took over. Five years, five damn years, they lied to me. My own mom—why would she lie?

I pull the truck out of the driveway, speeding to Santiago's auto shop. I'm paying a visit to my lying shithead of a brother.

I stalk across the garage, my boots crunching gravel and leaves. When I reach Santiago, he is bent over an engine, grease, and sweat glistening on his face. On hearing my approach, he lifts his eyes to meet mine.

"What's up, little bro?" he says, a hint of amusement in his voice.

But I'm not laughing. All I can think of is the red haze that clouds my vision, and before I know it, my fist has connected with his jaw. He stumbles backward, smashing into the toolbox with a clang.

"Fuck what's your problem, asshole?" He rubs his jaw as his frantic eyes bore into mine.

My muscles seethe with tension. "You lied to me. Mila called you, didn't she?"

He sighs. "You punched me because of her?"

"Answer me!" I shout so loud that the guys in the shop stop what they're doing to watch.

"Fuck, what's your problem, asshole." His eyes burn into mine as he rubs his sore jaw.

I feel my muscles clenching with anger. "Yes, she called and left messages. We never listened to them, we just erased them. Mom said she talked to her, and Mila couldn't handle your illness. You were a burden. No point in answering her calls if she couldn't stick around." A shrug rolls over his shoulders.

Mother fucker.

He collects a wrench twisting a bolt off under the hood. Like it's nothing. Knowing I had been drowning in misery.

"She was pregnant."

He drops the tool, his eyes are back on me. He frowns. "She was pregnant," he repeats.

"Yes, asshole, she was pregnant. That was why she was calling. Mom lied and said she never spoke to Mila. Mom had blocked her. Mila then moved to Manhattan. When she realized she was pregnant, she moved in with her grandmother and uncle–thinking I was no longer alive after all this time without contact from anyone."

"When did you find out all this? Do you think she's lying?"

I swallow a sip of water.

"Dom, why would Mom lie?"

"No, Mila's not lying. I should have never thought less of her. The more Mom drilled it into me, the more I believed it. It pisses me off. Mom meddled with my life. You know the way Mom treated her."

"I'm sorry, bro, we should have answered her calls, but I just don't know about all this. How old is the boy?"

"Four... his... name is Dante. He looks just like us, dimples, and all." I smile at the thought of his dimples when he waved at me.

Santiago's shoulders slump. He rubs his jaw, a purple bruise already beginning to form.

"What's going to happen now with you two?" he asks.

I slid my fingers through my hair, uncertain of how to go about it. "I'm not sure. I just came from her studio, where she told me all this. My head's spinning." I sigh, inhaling a long breath. "Samantha scheduled our engagement photo session a couple of weeks ago, which happened to be at Mila's studio. Yesterday I bumped into her at Target with Samantha, where I discovered I had a son because he looked just like me. Now that I know the truth, I feel like a complete asshole. I said horrible things to piss her off and hurt her. Now she wants nothing to do with me. Also, she overheard me talking to Samantha, telling her I didn't want kids."

He whistles when he looks up at me from under the hood. He shakes his head. "Come on, man, she moves back and finds out you're alive and engaged. You really can't blame her for being mad."

I close my eyes and feel my anger rise.

"Fuck you, if you would have answered her calls," I snap.

He pushes off the car and looks up at me. "That's on you, Dom. You chose to believe our mother's story. She was your girl-friend, not mine. The only reason I believed it was because I didn't know her like you did. Do you still love her?"

I feel a pang of emotion in my chest. I can still picture the look of disgust on her face when she pulled away. But I can also still feel the longing that came over me when our lips met for the first time.

"Yeah, I never fell out of love with her."

"You'll figure it out, bro, but, fuck, you're engaged now." He taps my shoulder as he gets back to work.

I RAISE MY ARM, signaling the bartender for another beer. I slump my shoulders and tuck my chin, resting my elbows on the wooden bar top at Rocko's—the dive bar in the heart of Ocean-side. Visions of Mila's fiery eyes play on repeat in my head as her long, slender finger jabs into my chest, leaving a crimson bruise that seems to pulse in time with my racing heart. I groan. The look on her beautiful face, those emerald, green eyes filled with so much disappointment. The thought of having kids with Mila was always an option when we dated and mapped our future.

With Samantha, I'm not ready, I care for her, even love her. After she left, I figured in time, I would fall in love with Saman-tha. Perhaps I should try harder with her, maybe moving in together and taking trips. Mila wants nothing to do with me. She made it clear. Her words pierced my soul at the thought of her contemplating suicide and feeling emptiness and loneliness because of me. I could never live with myself if something happened to her. Why didn't I just talk to her the day I cornered her in the restaurant bathroom? Because I let my machismo chauvinism take over, that's why. She doesn't need me. She raised our son on her own and wants me to have no part of it. I admire her as a young, single mother. My mother struggled. I can only imagine how hard it has been for her. She was right. I should have tried harder to find her. I knew her uncle lived in Manhattan.

Liam, my best friend since elementary school, slid onto the barstool beside me. He slumps his shoulders and runs a hand through his dark, disheveled hair before ordering a beer.

"You look like shit," he says with a smug grin.

I quirk an eyebrow and take a sip from my drink. "Thanks," I snap.

Liam laughs at my irritated expression. "Shit. Who pissed in your Cheerios this morning? Did you piss off Samantha again?"

"Mila is back in town. I ran into her at a restaurant."

His eyes bulge with shock and concern. "Don't get drawn into her again, you're happily engaged now."

I scoff. *Happily?* Far from it. I reluctantly explain to him what has been going on. I can feel my teeth grinding together as I speak.

"I can't believe she was pregnant with my son, no wonder she looked so alarmed when she saw me with Samantha at the restaurant. She thought I was dead, and I stroll in with a fiancée."

Liam slams his glass on the table and orders two shots of tequila. "Fuck man, sounds like a telenovela my grandmother watches."

A weak laugh erupts from my chest.

"So, what are you going to do? How will Samantha react now, knowing you have a child?"

"I'm not sure how she will take it. I'm not sure if I should tell her or just call it quits with her. I'm still trying to wrap my head around all this."

"Do you still love Mila?"

With no hesitation, I answer Liam's question. A year ago, he stopped mentioning her name as if she never existed. In my heart, she has always been mine, no matter how hard I tried to let her go.

"Yeah, you know I do, after all this time. Not once did I not think of her."

He nods. Liam has always had a soft spot for Mila since they got along. When Mila stormed out of my life, he was just as hurt as I was.

"Wow, you're a dad now. Who knew? As my best friend, I guess it's my job to give you some advice, though I don't really know anything about love."

I quirk an eyebrow, Liam giving me women advice. I never thought I'd see the day.

"If you still have feelings for her, you should fight for what you two once had. It won't come easy, however. If you marry

Samantha and she's not the one for you, what then? You and Mila will need to stay civil when your son is around. Plus, the chemistry between you two will always be there. It's been five years! I've never seen you look at Samantha the way you looked at Mila. But look, you don't want to live in regret and spend time agonizing over 'what ifs'. You should at least think about it. Unless Mila doesn't have any feelings for you left...?"

The real question is, does she still love me?

I FIND myself at Mila's studio, contemplating what to say to her. It's been four days since our argument. She's all I think about. My head quickly jerks up when I see her step out of her shop. She's not alone, the same guy as last time is with her. She throws back her head in laughter as he gazes at her as if he's falling for her, and he whisks a few strands of hair away from her face. Her lips are pressed against his, and he wraps his arms around her waist and draws her close. My heart beats so fast, like I just ran a marathon, and my stomach lurches at the sight of him touching her.

Grinding my teeth, I feel the need to jump out of my truck to rip him off her. *Mine.* I want to shout at him to stay the fuck away from her. Acid fills my throat, eating at my insides. He walks to his car as she digs in her purse for her keys. I take this chance to leap out of my truck.

"Angel."

A smile escapes her lips when she tilts her head to meet mine. A frown creases on her forehead.

She smiles for him.

"What are you doing here, Dominic?" Her voice is flat.

"Can we go somewhere to talk?" I drawl.

She stays quiet for a second as she straightens the crease on her skirt, which hugs her curves perfectly. I picture my hands roaming over her body, slowly gripping her firm ass. I bite my lip at the thought.

"We have nothing to talk about." Her bright green eyes flicker coldly.

"Mila, I'm sorry for how I treated you these past weeks. I never intended to hurt you."

She snorts. "You did more than hurt me, Dominic, you tortured my mind, and damaged my soul, and not just these past weeks. How about five years? I realize your mom manipulated you. The pain that rips inside of me comes from knowing how crudely you thought of me. Do you not remember me crawling into your bedroom window to take care of you when you were sick in bed throwing up? Or how I was at the hospital with you here and in Arizona. How could you presume you'd be a burden to me?"

I swallow the enormous lump in my throat. I had forgotten. Occupied with searching for her and love-hating her, I neglected to remember. Dipping my head down, I kick the rocks.

"Mila, I can't change the past. I want a chance to meet my son. I'm so fucking sorry for everything." I gaze at her, maybe the coldness in her eyes softened. But the coldness remains, her eyes are piercing daggers.

"I don't trust you or your family around my son. Or your fiancée. We don't know each other anymore, Dominic. You're not the man I once knew."

Stab, stab to the chest.

"I'm the same man. I promise you, only with you."

Her eyes blaze with fire. She gives me a cold look and shakes her head. "I trusted you, but now your words mean nothing because your actions speak the truth."

I take a couple of steps toward her. "You don't trust me, but you trust the fucker you're with. How many men have you introduced our son to?" I sneer with jealousy. I know I hit too deep by the dark glare in her eyes. I've screwed up again.

"You think I whored around, asshole? I'm not you. For the past five years, I've been with only two men. I've only slept with two men, Dominic. It was just a hookup, quick fuck. Those men weren't you. I've spent five years grieving you, dedicating my time to raising my son, going to college to better myself to provide for him, so no, Dominic, I didn't whore around; my son has never met another man until now. Tell me how many women you've been with. I'm sure it's more than you can count."

Shit.

Narrowing my eyes away from her, I can't look at her. I've slept with a couple of women. They meant nothing. Then I dated Samantha. I stopped.

"That's what I thought, Dominic. I gave you my tears for five years, no more tears... because I didn't lose you, you lost me."

She opens the door to her car, and I slam it closed before she gets in. Rubbing my chest, the pain throbbing from her words, her pain, rips me to shreds.

"Who is he?" I ask, through gritted teeth. I lean into her car.

"Who?"

"The guy you're with, the guy from the coffee shop."

She blows out a hot breath. Staring at her lips as they form an 'O.'

"We just started dating, not that it's any of your business."

I know it's the boyfriend she told me at the studio, but I needed to hear it again.

"Why him?" I bellow, my voice strangled in my throat.

"Because, asshole, for the past five years, I've been fighting, struggling. I'm tired of fighting for once. I want to be fought for. If he accepts my son and wants to fight for a chance with me, then I'm willing to take it."

She starts the engine and drives off without sparing a glance, leaving me standing alone with a broken heart.

THE BUZZING of my cell phone startles me as I get into my pickup.

"Hey, baby, I miss you. I'm sorry about our fight, I overreacted. Can you come over?" Samantha's voice is gentle on the other end.

I should have felt bad for embracing Mila and betraying Samantha. After all the things Mila said, I feel like I'm being unfaithful to her by being with Samantha.

"Hey, sorry for not getting back to your message sooner. I've been busy at work. I'm on my way," I reply.

"Okay, I'll be waiting for you; Make-up sex always does the trick," she teases.

"Yeah, I'll be there in ten minutes." I slip my phone into my pocket, press my foot harder on the gas pedal, and head to Samantha's place. I'll fuck her, get Mila out of my head, and try to make it work with Samantha. When I reach Samantha's door, she opens it before I have a chance to knock. She pushes herself against me, locking her lips with mine. Her legs wrap around my waist as I close the door behind us. We kiss each other fervently, with a raw passion between us. But as our lips touch, an image of Mila pops into my head. When I kissed Mila, it felt different—like I was complete. Her lips were heavenly.

Fuck, fuck I don't want to think of Mila.

I kiss Samantha harder, frustrated with where my mind's taking me. The buttons on her silk blouse fumble under my fingers. I pick her up with ease and place her on the plush sofa. Rage consumes me, and in frustration, I rip the buttons of her blouse open with a loud tear and unclasp her lacy bra. My hands go to her breasts, kneading them firmly and I suck her nipples into my mouth, nibbling them.

Samantha throws her head back in pleasure, arching her back and moaning. The sound of Mila's name is on my lips as I once again see her beautiful face in my mind. I suck harder on Samantha's nipples as she winces with pleasure, then move my hand to tear off her thong savagely, hiking up her skirt. With two fingers, I enter her center and begin pumping harder.

Samantha moans, "Yes, Dominic."

I bite my bottom lip hard until it bleeds, tasting the metallic taste on my lips. My mind is filled with thoughts of Mila sprawled out on my bed as I plunge my finger into her center, savoring her sweetness. I shake my head inwardly.

Fuck, I don't want to think about her.

Pushing further, faster, until Samantha comes. She closes her eyes and flutters her eyelashes before leaning in to kiss me. She undoes my belt and unzips my jeans.

"Your turn." Her voice comes out high-pitched.

I grasp a fist full of blonde locks as she opens up for me, her tongue running up and down my cock. Her lips stretch around me, and her head slides up and down my shaft. I cling to her hair as I thrust deeper, wanting to take in the full sensation of her. She gags but keeps sucking despite the discomfort. I can almost feel Mila's sweet embrace, those red-cherry lips around my dick. Samantha lets out a moan that only serves to increase my agitation. I know this isn't Mila, so I push Samantha away and hastily tuck my dick back into my jeans. I throw her bra and blouse back at her.

"W-what's wrong, Dominic?" she stutters and worriedly slips her clothes back on. "This isn't working, Samantha. It hasn't for a long time," I admit.

"What do you mean, Dominic? You asked me to marry you." Her chin trembles.

Shit. I feel like an asshole.

"Yes, I did, Samantha, and I shouldn't have. I'm not the man for you. You deserve someone who can love you. It's been a year, Samantha, our relationship is not where it should be."

She stumbles toward me, her eyes pleading. She rubs her palms on my chest. "We can make it work, Dominic. I love you. I'm sorry school's been crazy, but I'll be better."

I run my fingers through my hair. "No, Samantha, it won't. I just found out I have a son."

She gasps. "What do you mean you just found out?"

"He's four years old. I haven't seen his mom in years. She moved away. She was my girlfriend. I loved her; I still do. It would never work between us because I'll always love her, and she will always have my heart," I say honestly.

Tears spill from her beautiful face. She sniffles. "You don't want kids, you told me. I-I can make you forget her. We can have our own family." She stays quiet for a second. "It's her, isn't it? The girl at the studio and the store with her son."

I nod. She doesn't need to know anything else.

"In the studio, you said all that so she could hear. I thought you loved me."

Shit. I feel like a complete dick.

"I'm sorry, Samantha, it's over. It would never work out. You deserve someone who will love you."

She wraps her arms around me. "No, Dominic."

I draw myself from her.

"I'll wait till you're ready. You're just not thinking straight," she pleads.

Shutting the door, I feel a weight lifted off me. Samantha and I are two different people. She's better off with someone who will love her and show her love, but it can't be me.

A LONG WEEK HAS PASSED, my shoulders go rigid, and the tightness in my chest unfolds ten times more in pain. The feeling it's being crushed in a vice. Liam's conversation lingers in my mind. Fight for what you can have again. Mila's beautiful voice plays in my mind: I'm tired of fighting; for once, I want to be fought for.

Baby, I'll fight for you, for us.

I might not have tried as hard as I wish I would have, but I'll fight tooth and nail this time. I'll grovel on my knees, asking for a chance, pleading for you to take me back. To prove to her, that I'm the same man. I'll be a better man for her and Dante. To be a damn good father, the father I never had. I sound like a pussy, but I'll do anything to earn her trust and love again. Even if it means begging on my knees, worshiping the ground she walks on, and making love to her day and night. A woman like Mila deserves the world. She's one in a million. I won't let that prick take her from me. She's mine.

"Hey, Andrew, my man, long time no see," I said as I embraced my buddy in a bro hug.

Andrew runs the Rock 'N' Roll Tattoo Shop. His towering frame is covered in a full set of sleeve tattoos on both arms. Andrew arranged his long black hair in a tight ponytail, and his face is etched with a permanent frown. But for all his gruff exterior, he's an amazingly skilled artist and a cool dude. Santiago and Andrew have been long-time, good friends since high school.

"It's been a while, man; do you know what you're getting?"

"My son's name on my forearm–Dante," I reply.

He raises an eyebrow in surprise. "I didn't know you had a son."

I let out a loud breath before I say, "I just found out when I ran into my ex from five years ago. It's a long story."

He nods in understanding, and forty minutes later, I leave with Dante's name etched into my arm. Pride swells in my chest at the thought of having a son.

I pass a couple of shops in the market plaza. I jerk my head back so fast it causes whiplash. Hearing the most beautiful laugh sends chills down my spine, a laugh I recognize. Observing who's making her laugh sends a pang of jealousy to my chest. At an ice cream shop, I notice asshole, pretty boy Ken sitting with my girl and boy. Clenching my fist, I feel a burning sensation in my chest. I yearn to make her laugh and see her smile. I long to say goodnight and press a kiss on her forehead. I ache to be close to her, embracing her in my arms. Fuck, I wish I could hit him hard in the face.

She's mine, my boy, my family. I'm going to fight to get them back. To win her heart.

Angel, baby! I'm coming for you; I'm taking what's mine. *I don't fucking share.*

Nine

MILA

I head toward Brian, the sound of waves crashing on the shore filling my ears. I sent him a text last night, asking if he still wanted to go surfing. Today is my birthday and I woke up at the crack of dawn, eager to catch some waves.

"Good morning, pretty girl." His perfect lopsided smile graces his face and my heart thumps unsteadily. He drinks in my profile: my shorts-shorts, lowcut sports bra, and my midsection.

"Good morning, Brian."

His lips press onto mine. "I'm guessing Dante's not a morning person?"

I love how he's always asking about Dante. This is the main reason I find myself wanting more of him.

"Nope, that little stinker is still asleep. Sophie offered to watch him and drop him off at school."

He chuckles. Hoisting his surfboard onto his shoulder, we begin trudging through the sand toward the shore. Brian pulls his shirt off over his head, revealing the sun-kissed skin of his chest and abdomen. His bright blue eyes twinkle in the light reflecting off of the rolling waves, and a few strands of golden blond hair fall messily in front of one. Leaning forward, I brush the strands of hair to the side. His eyes are on my lips as he lifts my chin so that my face is tilted up.

"From the very first day, I saw you walk into the coffee shop, I wanted to ask you out. That smile, those beautiful green eyes captured me. Every day I was eager to see you stroll through the door." He pecks my lips.

I don't know what to say. I'm so inexperienced with dating. My eyelashes flutter.

"Brian," I whisper.

He smiles.

"Let's do this before we have to head on to work."

"All right, let me remind you, I'm pretty rusty right now. It's been a long time."

"Don't worry, I've got you."

A light breeze passes through us, causing strands of hair to stick to my cheek. Removing the scrunchy from my wrist, I tie my hair into a tight ponytail. Dipping my feet into the cold water, I shiver.

"Do you mind if I'm on the board with you to help guide you? Once we get further out, I'll jump off."

"Nope, not at all." I kneel with my butt resting on the surfboard. I lay on my belly, holding my knees to my chest for support. He holds onto the board and wraps a thick white nylon strap around my ankle. The leash is just long enough to allow me a few inches of slack in case the board and I fall in a wave. He grips my torso, hoists himself onto my back, and nearly doubles over in laughter.

"Is this okay, Mila?" he asks. His body is heavy, but I can stand it.

"Yeah."

He guides us deeper into the rolling waves.

"I'm going to jump off in a bit—this is a small wave, but not too complicated. Get up to your knees first, then bring one foot up at a time," he shouts.

"All right, got it." Excitement races through my veins.

"All right, pretty girl, I'm jumping off."

After conquering the waves, I paddle back to Brian with a huge smile plastered on my face. Wow, this was amazing. My dad loved to go surfing now and then; he was no pro, but he enjoyed it. Brian envelopes me in a massive hug. Adrenaline burst through me.

"You did it, Mila, you looked hot taking those waves."

His lips are on mine, and I can taste the saltiness of the ocean water. Our kisses get heated, melting down to my center. The sensation of his erection pressing against my stomach makes me feel truly desired and desired by him. I crave the need to be loved and desired, and when I'm with him, I truly feel wanted and desired. Maybe it's the fact that Dominic moved on. The thought of Dominic engaged and belittling me all these years left a treacherous mark on my soul.

I wrap my legs around his waist, he leans me onto a massive rock, kissing me roughly. The palm of his hand feathers up and down my spine.

"I know this is too soon, pretty girl, but God, I want to feel you," he pants as his swollen red lips kiss from my cheek to the lobes of my ears.

My mind is in a fuzz. I know it's too soon, but God, I need to feel something. I haven't felt instant chemistry, but I do feel attracted to him. Do I want to have sex with him? God, I do. He's sweet and kind. But, fuck, a girl has needs. I press my lips on his.

"I want you too."

His eyes linger on my face for a split second. He slips his wet trunks off. The sun sculpted his body perfectly. A moan escapes my salty lips. My eyes stay pinned on his naked, toned body. His erection is hard and ready. I peel my wet shorts off. He sucks in a breath. Luckily, it's empty here; it's so early in the morning.

"Leave your shirt on just in case someone shows up. I don't want them to see you completely naked."

I nod. My fingers graze the ridges of his toned stomach as I pepper kisses on his neck, chest, and finally down to the impressive bulge. His body ignites with heat under my touch. He tastes like salt and sun. I work my way down to his hard, thick length, which throbs in my mouth. I take it deep and slow, and he groans.

God, this is so not me, but here I am giving a blowjob at the beach.

"Fuck, Mila, this feels so fucking good."

My tongue swirls like a pro, well, not technically. Taking him all in, I taste every part of him from the base to the tip. He grips my head bobbing, it down. He moans. Fluttering my eyelashes as I watch him.

"Come here, Mila," he rasps out.

Our lust-filled eyes meet. My lips hungrily explore every part of his mouth. My breaths quicken with excitement as we pull our bodies closer together. I watch as he takes a condom out of his wallet and then lifts me. I bite my lip as he enters me, feeling myself become swollen and wet with desire. He pushes deep inside me and holds himself there for a moment as I squirm, and a moan escapes my lips.

"Oh, Brian," I moan with pleasure.

His tongue circles my nipples, which peek over the fabric.

"Ahh, pretty girl, you feel so good." His thrust gets deeper.

Oh, God. My orgasms breakthrough. Brian keeps thrusting and kissing me. Our kisses get sloppier.

"Fuck," he grits. "Damn, you are beautiful," he grunts as his body trembles in release. Panting.

We stare at one another. He's looking for any sign of regret. There's none. I don't regret it. Slipping my shorts back on, I watch as Brian rolls the condom off and slips his shorts back on.

"Are you okay?" He frowns, concern written all over his beautiful face.

"Yeah, I'm fine." Biting the bottom of my lip, I wrap my arms around him.

"You would tell me, right, if there was something wrong?"

"Yes, of course. I don't regret it. It was great."

He captures my lips. "Good, Mila, it will be better next time. I'll have you on my bed."

Brian is truly beautiful.

"See you tonight, birthday girl."

I wave as I get into my car. "See ya later."

MY DAYS HAVE CONSISTED of interviewing multiple applicants for the front desk position these last couple of days. We finally came to terms and hired Daliah. She's a college student getting into photography, so she fits in perfectly. A soft smile flickers on my lips when Daliah walks in with her short purple hair, slender tall body, pierced nose, and eyebrows. She's sporting a short black skirt, a Tom Petty t-shirt with compact boots.

"Mila, good morning. How's my favorite boss doing?"

I shake my head, laughing.

Sophie yells from the back, "Hey, you said I was your favorite."

A shrug rolls off her shoulder. "Did I?" A lopsided smirk pinches at her pale cheeks.

She fit in, and we warmed up to her. We hired her just at the right time because Dante came down with strep throat. Once Dante recovered, Brian dropped in, offering to take us out for ice cream. His words were like honey, and his smile was like sunshine. And, he's great with Dante.

"Yo, Mila, the delivery guy dropped these off for you," Daliah yells from the front as she strolls into my office, Sophie trailing behind. Daliah's holding a beautiful bouquet of red roses.

"Damn, are they from Brian?" Sophie squeals with excitement.

I read the note attached to it: *Happy Birthday, Angel, with love, Dominic.* Conflicting emotions swirl in my head.

"Dominic," I whisper softly. He remembered my birthday. I turned twenty-four today.

Sophie lets out a gasp. "Is guilt consuming the asshole? I bet Ms. Prissy would have a fit if she knew her fiancé is sending you roses."

I bit my bottom lip. Why in the hell is he sending me flowers? *Oh, of course, it's out of guilt.* Why else? It's been three weeks since I last spoke to him in the studio's parking lot. The way he looked at me as if I was the star in his universe. It's too late for us. He made his bed now he has to lie in it. The audacity of him sleeping around and now being engaged all this time sends a bullet straight to my heart.

"Who's Dominic?" Daliah asks, a puzzled look on her face.

Sophie fills her in on all the drama I've had going on. How did my life get so complicated in the last three months?

SOPHIE HAS PLANNED a get-together for my birthday. I groan when the cranberry vodka coats the back of my throat.

"Happy Birthday, pretty girl." Brian leans to my side, embracing me as he places a soft kiss on my lips.

"Thank you. Can I get you a drink?" I ask, remembering this morning... Brian's toned body, thick thighs, and huge calf muscles.

"Sure, I'll have a beer."

Seizing a beer from the fridge, Brian's eyes stay fixed on me, burning a penetrating stare. It could be the alcohol or the after-effects of this morning's sex causing the tingling sensation between my thighs. Daliah and Ryder emerge shortly. Obviously, not simultaneously, but separately. My birthday has always been something I've tried to avoid. The memory of my father always comes to mind. He would make me a chocolate cake every year. I miss my dad dearly.

"Happy Birthday, Mommy," Dante squeals as he hands me a card.

Aww, cute stick figures and squiggles.

"Thank you, sweetheart, this is the best gift ever!" I lean down and give Dante a big fat kiss on the cheek.

Sophie then pipes up, "Who wants to play Hot Seat?" She wiggles her eyebrows with mischievous glee, and Ryder chuckles, looking at Sophie in admiration.

"Oh, come on, you guys. It's so much fun. You pick a card. Everyone writes their answer on a piece of paper. The person in the hot seat has to answer."

"I played this at a college party. Some of those questions can make you squirm," Daliah injects as she takes a sip of her mixed drink.

Brian drags a chair for me to sit close to him. Our knees touch, he slowly slides his hand on my knee.

"I'll go first," Brian says, a boyish smile spreads across his lips. *God, he has the cutest smile.*

Brian picks a card that reads: *What's the most embarrassing thing I've Googled?*

I smile widely, waiting for his answer as he rubs his chin.

He chuckles. "When I was seventeen, I Googled how to put a condom on. My mom caught a glimpse of my search history. She asked me about it, then told my dad. He said it's common sense to put one on. I should've just asked him."

Ryder shakes his head with laughter.

"Yeah, it was embarrassing being a teen having your parents all up in your business," Brain says, just as Daliah picks her card and reads it.

"What did my last text read?" She grabs her phone from her pocket. She smirks. "Meet me at my place," she reads the last text her boyfriend sent her with heart emojis.

"All right, Mila's turn." Sophie tosses me a card.

Brian's hand strokes up and down my thigh, sending shivers down my spine. *Whoa, the Vodka's warming me up.* "My card reads, what has the power to make you intensely horny?" *O.M.G.*

Brian squeezes my thigh once again, as his eyes are on my lips.

I clear my throat. Sophie rubs the palms of her hands together in anticipation.

"Come on, girl, spit it out."

Damn her. I squirm in my chair. My thoughts immediately go to Dominic. The last time I felt whole during intimacy was with Dominic. Yes, I've had two hook-ups in the last few years. It was to take the edge off. Brian gives me a subtle wink. Sex with Brian was great, but we just started our relationship. It's still new. With Dominic, I felt whole instantly.

"All right, this is awkward and embarrassing. What gets me intensely horny?... Sucking, kissing, licking on the neck that does it for me." I swirl the glass of cranberry vodka nervously.

The memory of the bathroom episode with Dominic resurfaces; I could tell he was manipulating me. I quickly dismiss this thought of Dominic. I'm with Brian now, and we just had sex this morning.

Brian's blue eyes wolfly drink me in. He's been staring since I confessed what makes me horny. The game goes on as we all take turns, laughing and drinking. I might have had a bit too much to drink. I can feel the alcohol consuming me. I chug a water bottle to sober up as I head upstairs to check on Dante. He's sound asleep. I stumble down the stairs feeling tipsy. I hardly ever drink. After tonight, I'm sure I won't touch a drink for a while. Brian leans up against the kitchen island, spreading his arms on the counter. As I stalk toward him, a ghost of a smile crosses his lips.

"Come here, birthday girl." He loops his fingers into the belt loops of my jeans, pulling me in. His thumb brushes my lips.

"I've been dying to kiss you all night, pretty girl." He's so close, I can taste the saltiness of his beer breath warming me up.

"Then kiss me," I say.

His lips brush mine, and our tongues tangle as he presses me harder onto his lean, firm body. We pull back, catching our breath. He licks his salty lips. Sophie and Ryder are on the couch, watching Netflix.

"Let's go outside for a bit," he whispers breathlessly.

I nod.

He holds my hand as we walk outside. It's nearly midnight. The night is a peaceful haven of tranquility as we step out. He leads me into his Jeep, kissing me hungrily. Brian makes it easy to fall for him. It's been so long since a man has made me feel wanted.

"I wanted us to have some privacy," he says in-between kisses. His arms envelop my waist. His lips brush the slope of my neck— a gush of wind waves through us. A moan escapes my alcohol-infused lips. Brian opens the back door of his Jeep.

"Get in, pretty girl. Let me take care of you." His blue eyes scan my body. "You're beautiful, Mila."

Brian shut his car door and crawled onto me, pressing his lips against mine. His hips move in sinuous circles against my pelvis as he slowly works my shirt up, planting light kisses across my not-so-flat stomach. He undoes my jeans slowly, sliding them and my lacy underwear off before kneeling on the edge of the seat of his compact Jeep.

My breath catches as he trails his fingers across my inner thigh and then moves between my legs. His thrusts leave me dizzy and overwhelmed as I throw my head back in ecstasy.

"I'm dying to taste you, God, Mila," he rasps lustfully, as his fingers thrust heavenly.

My throat is dry and hoarse from the liquor. A small moan vibrates in my throat. His mouth is so close, I can feel his hot breath in between my legs. Suddenly, the car door jerks open. Brian's yanked out.

Ten

MILA

"What the fuck!" Brian shouts.

Dominic's eyes darken with rage.

"Put your damn jeans on, Mila," Dominic commands in a lethal roar that vibrates from his chest, which causes the car window to tremble.

Jerking my jeans back on, and sliding my sandals on, I jump out of the Jeep.

"Who in the fuck is this, Mila?" Brian shouts.

Swallowing the large lump in my throat, I don't know why I feel like I did something wrong when he's the one with a fiancée and the one who played dead for five years. Dominic clenches his fists, and his jaw quivers with rage. I'm about to answer Brian when Dominic's husky voice sneers.

"I'm Dante's father, surfer boy." A sneer of empty laughter flickers over his curled lips. "You think you can finger fuck my girl and get her off with your spindly fingers? Only I know how to work her body, where to touch her, how to get her to cry out in pleasure. Only I know where to hit all the right spots. Don't I, baby?"

My girl.

He strides up to me, and I lick my lips nervously. Dominic's jaw is locked tight, and I can't help but admire his muscular physique outlined through the thin fabric of his t-shirt. His powerful thighs as he moves closer. He looks jealous and angry, but so attractive that it almost takes my breath away.

Snap out of it, Mila, you have a boyfriend, and he has a fiancée. My mind is in a haze. Why in the hell is he here?

"You're drunk, Angel." It's more of a statement than a question. He turns to Brian.

"Asshole, she's drunk, and you're trying to fuck her. Taking advantage of her. Get the hell out of here, Ken."

Who in the fuck is Ken?

"Dominic, what are you doing here?"

Brian steps closer to me—Dominic steps in front of him.

"I said, get the fuck out of here." His voice is lethal.

"Dominic, you need to go, and he wasn't taking advantage of me, he's, my boyfriend."

He balls his fist. "I'll leave once he leaves; you could have fooled me, Mila, you were getting finger fucked in the backseat of a car—drunk."

I straighten out the strands of hair lacing my forehead as the wind picks up. I know if I don't have Brian leave, Dominic will make an even bigger scene. It's late.

"I'll be okay, Brian, you can go." I see the hurt reflecting off of him.

"Are you sure?" His stare bores into Dominic as if they're fighting for dominance.

They might as well pee on the tire marking their territory.

"Yeah, I'm sure. Goodnight. I'll call you tomorrow."

He nods, wrapping his arms around me to place a kiss on my lips.

An animalistic growl vibrates the quiet night behind us. Brian gets into his car and drives away.

"What the fuck, Dominic? You didn't answer me. Why are you here?" I ask, narrowing my eyes at him.

He leans back against my car, the streetlight glinting off the metal surface. His broad frame blocks my view as he hands me a small box. I take it from his outstretched hand, skepticism clouding my features.

"What's this?"

"Your birthday gift," he says in a low rough voice. His eyes darken, and his nostrils widen. He's definitely pissed.

"How do you know where I live?" I ask, my brow furrow.

He shrugs. "Followed you home the other day," he admits unapologetic.

"Why did you barge into the car, Dominic? We are not together. He's my—"

Dominic takes three strides toward me. He's so close that the smell of his body wash is intoxicating, invading my nose. He cups my face gently with his warm hands.

"Because, Angel, I can't handle another man's hands touching you. You were mine first, baby. I'll fight to win your heart back, your trust back. I'll fight for you, baby–*for us.* Isn't that what you want? To be fought for?"

His eyes flicker, his breathing picks up.

"Angel, it fucking hurts seeing him touch you like that; it fucking hurts, Mila, right here." He points to his heart.

For a split second, I feel a pang of guilt for what just happened this morning. But why should I? He's the one engaged. He's the one who betrayed me all these years. I just started dating Brian, and things are going well. He has some nerve to make me feel guilty.

I throw my hands up in the air. "What the hell is this about, knowing where to touch me? When did you become a sex whisperer, huh? Oh, I know, when you slept around. So, all the other women you fucked, you know all their right spots, including your fiancée?" Jealousy spikes like a needle pins to my chest.

Dominic leans forward, placing both palms on the hood, pinning me in. Closing my eyes, I feel his hot breath scatter across my cheeks. His lips brush the top of my earlobes.

"No, beautiful, it's only you; it's always been you. All the others meant nothing. Meaningless. Why do you think after all these years, I still remember what you felt like, what you taste like, every beauty mark underneath your clothes, Angel? Because you mean everything to me." He kisses my cheek.

I open my eyes; he smiles cockily as he walks back to his truck. In a sudden surge of feeling, a million emotions course through me like a tidal wave. I'm in shock that he's said these things to me when he is so clearly committed to someone else.

"Good night, beautiful, get some rest. Happy Birthday."

"Thank you for the gift and roses," I squeak. My heartbeat speeds up. Being around Dominic is like being at a fireworks show. My body lights up around him as sparks fly in every direction. My hands tremble as I open the small box, I gasp upon seeing the silver heart locket necklace Dominic gifted me years ago. He engraved my initials on the top. My heart melts instantly at the sight of it. I had left it at his house a few days before he went to Arizona for treatment. My eyes widen... speechless when I open it I find the same picture of us on the Ferris wheel. Tears skate down my cheeks. The sentimental thought means a lot to me; he's kept it all these years.

Why Dominic? Why now? It's too late for us.

———

KNOCKING on Brian's studio apartment, my stomach churns with guilt. The door swings open. He's caught by surprise, but a lopsided smile curves his handsome boyish appearance. "Pretty girl."

"Hey, can I come in?" My voice comes above a whisper. I am embarrassed by Dominic's behavior. The fact that I sent Brian away and not Dominic has me wholeheartedly unworthy of his smile.

"Of course." He steps aside as I walk into his small living space.

"Brian, I'm sorry about last night. Honestly, I wasn't expecting him to show up."

He rakes his finger over his lips. "I wasn't expecting him, either. You had mentioned he wasn't in the picture," he says, his voice full of irritation.

He deserves to know the truth. I hadn't mentioned it because when we met, I still thought Dom was dead. Then seeing he wasn't, my head was a mess, and he was engaged, it was just too much with our relationship being so new. His hand stretches out for me to take, leading me to his sofa. I sit down and tell him about Dominic.

"I'm sorry, Mila. You've spent all these years grieving his death, only to discover he's alive. It must be extremely difficult for you."

More like a blow to the gut. Brian rubs my back in a circular motion. His comforting embrace warms my heart.

"It's me who should apologize for last night. I'm sorry I sent you home when it was him, I should have sent away."

He strokes my knuckles. "Do you still love him, Mila?" He swallows, visibly nervous. His body is rigid as he waits for my answer.

The events of the past few weeks have been like a million needles piercing my chest—Dominic's treachery, the way he mistreated me, and seeing him again. Last night, I could feel jealousy radiating off him; he clouds my thoughts.

The sentimental gift he gifted me meant so much. My body heated at his sight, the sensation of butterflies fluttering in my stomach. What right do I have to feel this way when years have passed, and he's engaged? I've told myself I need to move on. I turn my eyes to the baby blues glaring at me.

"I do love him, Brian, but several years have passed, and he's engaged now. We no longer know each other. We've both moved on, but he's my son's father, my son, so I'll always have feelings." My heart deflates with a pang in my chest.

"He clearly still harbors feelings for you," he retorts, bitterly. Shrugging.

"He's engaged," I repeat, mustering a smile.

His stare lingers on my chest. My black v-neck shirt reveals a significant amount of cleavage.

"Let's pick up where we left off, before we were rudely interrupted."

His soft lips claim mine in an unexpected embrace. His hands hike up my skirt, and his long, gentle fingers run along my skin, teasing me with each stroke. "Pretty girl, you're all I could think about last night—how you felt, how you tasted. I need to see all of you. Our first time should have been somewhere else, somewhere special. You certainly deserve that much."

The sound of my moans grows louder in our kiss as my arousal intensifies. He tears off my shirt and unclasps my bra, and his gaze settles on the tattoo inscribed on my chest under my breasts. I open my mouth to explain, but he silences me with a kiss.

"Mila, you don't need to explain," he mummer on my lips.

"Goddamn, you're sexy, baby."

That's what I love about Brian, he's easy and understanding. He hungrily pulls each nipple into his warm, inviting mouth. His strong arms lift me effortlessly, placing me on his lap.

My breath comes in short gasps as I blurt out my desire, "I want to be in your bed!"

He scoops me up, and I feel the heated press of his body against mine as he carries me to his bed. He slides my skirt off and rolls off his shorts and briefs. His sun-kissed skin glows in the dim light, and I see a flicker of desire in his eyes. I watch as he strokes himself.

Fuck, that's hot.

I'm terrified to fall for any man. I've been hurt by Dominic and left by my parents. Brian's warmth engulfs me and makes me feel safe. For right now, sex is just sex. I need to feel his touch, his need for me.

"Brian, I need you," I murmur before he groans in response.

"Pretty girl, I need you. I've never needed another woman like I need you." He claims my mouth with savage kisses. He reaches for his wallet, pulling out a condom. His fingers stroke in between my legs. "Are You wet for me, Mila?" A hum of satisfaction leaves his lips.

Brian's muscular arms hold my thighs apart as he pushes deep inside me, sending a wave of pleasure through my body with each thrust. His strong, steady breaths fill my mouth, and the tension between us grows. I open my eyes and see the look of desire in Brian's eyes, and I know he's falling for me. The thought scares me. I'm not sure I can return those feelings. I lift my hips, grinding deeper into each thrust.

"Fuck, pretty girl, are you close?" he, rasps.

"Yes," I say, as I shudder in his arms. I can feel him trembling inside of me, filling me in.

After laying together for a few minutes, I pick my clothes up from the ground, Brian fastens my bra. I smooth my skirt out over my hips. I feel something fall from my pocket, and Brian kneels to get it.

He pulls out my silver locket and peers into it at the picture of Dominic and me inside. His blue eyes harden as he takes a harsh breath. "How is this going to work, Mila, if you still have lingering feelings for your son's father? I know these are new emotions you just discovered, since you didn't know he's alive. Mila, how do I fit into all this?" Brian waves his hands in the air. Worry lines crease his forehead.

"He's engaged, Brian," I bite. Irritated.

"Pretty girl, fuck, I like you so much..."

"But?" I snap.

"Mila, I think we should put things on hold between us. Until you two sort it out. I don't want to be second. You have a son with him. He will always be in your life."

I pinch the bridge of my nose. "Brian. Yes, you're right. We do need to discuss certain things when it comes to Dante, but as for

Dominic and me, it's over." I wrap my arms around his neck. I kiss the corner of his soft lips.

"Mila, he might be engaged, but he was furious, for fuck's sake. He tore the door open and shoved me off you. Beautiful, we can't start a relationship if you have feelings for him. If he's going to be coming around ripping you away from me. I'm sorry, Mila, I don't need the drama." Brian retreats. He brushes his lips on my knuckles.

Fuming, I step away from him. "We just had sex, then you dump me? Brian, that's a dick move." Disappointment knifes through me.

"Mila, I'm sorry; I wasn't expecting all this to happen. I'm not —fuck, I didn't expect this to happen after sex. No, I'm not using you, Mila. I care about you so much, pretty girl." He sighs.

I get the hint and gather my keys and purse before walking out to my car.

"Mila!" he shouts.

I turn to peer at him.

"Honey, it's just with school, I just don't want the drama right now. Once things get settled, we can get back together. I like what we have."

"Sure, Brian, see you around," I murmur under my breath.

Well, shit, so much for him fighting for me, or rather trying. He doesn't need the drama. Seriously, I'm drama. I'm cool with it, and therefore, relationships are a pain in the ass. Jumping in my car, I put it in gear and drive off to the studio.

Eleven

MILA

The weekend couldn't come quicker. It's been a rough week between Brian calling things off with us and Dominic showing up at my house. Lately, my head has been in a cloud. Just when things between Brian and I were going good, and I was moving on, Dominic selfishly created problems.

I sigh as I put the car in drive, heading back home. Dante and I did a little shopping for his Halloween costume. I promised him a Spider-Man costume. He's an obsessed fan.

"Mommy, how do you send letters to heaven?" he asks. His brows draw in a deep frown.

My heart feels like it's going through a shredder; no, it pretty much feels like it went through a meat grinder. I blink away the tears that are falling.

"Honey, I wish that was possible."

He sighs and mumbles, "I wanted to tell Daddy about my day."

I grip the steering wheel, a wedge of anger mixed with tears fills my throat. My stomach churns. My love for Dominic has come at a high cost. I thoughtlessly offered my heart to him when we met, yet he has never returned it. My love is not free; it has to be earned. I'll talk to Dominic soon and ask if he wants to be in

Dante's life for good, or if he chooses not to. He needs to let me go.

———

"MOMMY, SOMEONE'S AT THE DOOR," Dante shouts from the living room.

Not sure who it could be, I swing the door open, I'm startled to find Dominic standing at the door. I see a rapid blink of surprise as my eyes peer into his whiskey-brown eyes. He looks handsome, wearing jeans and a black t-shirt that shapes his hard muscles. He rocks the balls of his heels back and forth. He clears his throat and swallows.

"Mila, I brought you both dinner from the restaurant," he says, in a low husky voice.

I close the door behind me, worried Dante might recognize him.

He scratches his beard. He's nervous.

My eyebrows jog up. "You brought dinner?" I question with a puzzled look. Is he serious?

"Yes, it's close to dinner. I thought I'd save you the trouble of making dinner." He sighs as his eyes search mine.

The pain in my chest sharpens as I ponder the pain he has reflected in me.

"Angel, the truth is I wanted to see you and talk to you." His shoulders slump.

"Dominic, I agree we need to talk, but now's not the time..."

"Baby, please just let me talk. You need to hear me out. I hate myself for letting my mother manipulate me, pushing you away from me, and believing in her lies. I hate myself even more for missing five years of your and my son's life. Angel, not a day went by when I didn't think of you. You always lingered in my mind. All those women meant nothing to me. All they were—was a distraction. Samantha was another one of my mom's guilt trips she laid on me. To date her, to propose to her, I went along with it because my heart was empty. It was wrong of me to lead her on when my heart and soul belong solely to you, Mila. I broke it off with her."

He steps closer and brushes a strand of hair stuck to my cheek. *He broke it off with her. What a fucking lame excuse his mom forced him.*

. "Dominic, I don't want to hear it."

He exhales, ignoring my protest. "I fucked up big time, hurting you at the restaurant and at the studio. I'm sorry, baby. I thought you left me. It hurt, so I wanted to hurt you, wanted to make you jealous. It was a dick move. What you heard about me not wanting kids? I said it to her because I didn't want kids with her. Only with you, Mila, I want to be a father to our son. I want to be in his life." His voice is hoarse and pleading.

I lean back against the brick wall of my townhouse, knitting my brows into a scowl, confused. He broke up with her. He doesn't love her. He wants Dante in his life. It's been five years. Closing my eyes, I draw in a lungful of air. He's watching me with pure adoration, melting every wall I build.

"I don't recognize you anymore, it's been five years. You've changed."

He sets the bag of food down on the porch, then steps closer. His thumb grazes my lips as I take in his spicy, masculine scent. His biceps bulge as I feel my heart quicken. His presence, powerful and commanding, clouds my mind. My pulse speeds at a carnal rate.

"Living this life without you has changed me, Angel; how could it not? I'm not the same person, but my love for you will never change. Any amount of time that has gone by can't change what I feel." He leans in, kissing my cheek down to my neck.

Startled, not expecting him to be so sudden, I jolt away from him. This makes him growl with frustration.

He says, "Is it because of him?" A hot surge of jealousy rips across his face. He's talking about Brian.

"No, Dominic, it has nothing to do with him. You can't

expect to knock on my door and inform me you left the woman you've been in a relationship with for who knows how long and expect me to throw myself on you. I've spent years thinking you were dead. My son thinks his dad is dead. How am I supposed to explain that to a four-year-old? If you want to be in Dante's life, I need to be able to trust you. I can't have you appear in his life only to disappear." My voice shakes with the violent emotions churning in me.

He runs his hands through his thick, brown hair before slipping them into the pockets of his faded jeans. He tilts his head slightly to the side, revealing a strong jawline and high cheekbones.

I can't tear my gaze away, the image of him is permanently etched into my mind after all these years. I never thought I'd see him again.

"First off, I only dated Samantha for a year."

"Only." I snort.

"Mila, I never lived with her, and she never stayed at my place. I never allowed her to. It wasn't a normal relationship. It wasn't like what we had. My heart only belongs to you, beats only for you, always you. Second, I would never disappear from Dante's life. I will never be like my father." He runs his finger down my cheek. "Give me a second chance, baby." He interwinds his fingers with mine.

I let out a sigh, letting go of his hand to massage my temples.

"Have lunch or dinner with me. Let's talk, and we can catch up; we can do this until you feel comfortable telling Dante about me. I understand you want to protect him."

I stay silent, thinking if it would be a good idea. I know Dante would love to have him in his life, of course, he would, after all, Dominic is his father.

"Mila, do you still love me?"

My brain fizzles. When I lift my head to glance at him, his eyes are on me. The glare in his eyes sparks like a fire dancing on a dark night. I want to lie so we can move on from each other. The distance between us has been too long, but I can't do that.

"Yes, I love you. I never stopped loving you. It feels like a dream to know you're alive."

He smiles beautifully.

At the same time, I want to choke him until he turns blue.

"I'm sorry, Mila, I'm, fucking sorry, baby, for being such a bastard to you. My bitterness got the best of me. Baby, I'm so goddamn fucking in love with you. I'm wholly unconditionally in love with you," he rasps, his voice full of emotion.

I choke on a lump lodged in my throat with his confession when there's a squeak at the door.

"Mommy, is it the pizza man?" The door cracks open, and Dante's small nose peeks through.

"No, baby, it's not. I'll be right there, okay."

"Mommy, can you play Spider-Man with me?"

"Sure, give me a sec."

He shuts the door.

I turn to look at Dominic. He raises his chiseled stubbly chin up. With a sly smile. He scratches the back of his neck nervously.

"Baby, you've done an amazing job of raising him. He's lucky to have you as a mother."

I swallow holding the tears in.

"So tomorrow, lunch, I want to know everything about him." He raises an eyebrow.

"Umm.... I don—"

Dominic cuts me off, "Please, Angel please." his voice turns faintly pleading. Dominic has never been the type to beg; it's unlike him.

For Dante, I say to myself.

"Okay, where?"

"Give me your number, and I'll text you the place."

I nod absently. Butterflies begin to swim in my belly. I hand him my phone, and he adds his number to my contacts, then sends himself a text with my phone.

"Got It," he says, as his phone pings. He leans in and kisses the corner of my mouth. "See you tomorrow, baby, and here's your food."

I laugh.

He winks and walks off.

Twelve

MILA

Droplets of perspiration appear on the nape of my neck. I fidget in my seat at Heidi's Deli, waiting for Dominic. I'm sure people must think my knee-bouncing is a sign of drug use. Dominic sent me a text message late last night, and it disrupted me while I was getting ready for bed.

Dominic: *Hey Angel, you awake?*
Me: *Yes.*
Dominic: *What are you doing?*
Me: *Getting ready for bed.*
The dots come and go.
Dominic: *Mmm! Bed, huh, so what are you wearing?*
I frown. He's texting like there hasn't been five years of distance between us. He used to ask me these same questions years ago to send photos.
Me: *Nothing.*
Dominic: *Whoa, Angel, I'm fantasizing about you naked.*
Oh God, this is not what I meant to text him. I slap my forehead.
Me: *I meant to text none of your business. Damn, phone.*
Dominic: *Sure, whatever you say, baby.*
He's so damn arrogant. That hasn't changed.

Dominic: *Meet me at Heidi's Deli on 12*^{*th*} *St. See you at 12.*
The dots come and go. So, I just texted back.
Me: *See you tomorrow. Good night.*
Dominic: *Good night, Angel.*

MY HEAD JARS up when I see him walk into Heidi's Deli looking devilish in jeans and a long-sleeved button shirt. *Jesus, he's so handsome.* He swags toward me, his bulky physique catching all onlookers ogling him.

"Hey, sorry, one of my chefs called in, so I had to call someone to fill in. I hope I didn't keep you waiting long?" He raises an eyebrow, staring at me as if he can see through my soul. He lifts my chin and kisses the corner of my mouth.

I freeze. He keeps doing this as if we're a couple.

"Not long, five minutes," I whisper. His presence is so intoxicating, and it makes me so damn nervous.

The waitress hands us the menu smiling at him. "Hey, good to see you," she says flirtatiously as she flutters her long-ass eyelashes. Ignoring me.

That's rude. Dominic pays no attention.

"What can I get you to drink, handsome?"

He clears his throat. "Soda for me and whatever my girl wants."

Her jaw drops. She musters a smile and takes our orders.

My girl.

Should I be swooning? Probably not. I'm not his.

"Do you come here often? It seems like the waitress knows you."

The side of his mouth twitches. "Maybe, like twice a month, Mila. Does that make you jealous?" He grins like a fool.

I roll my eyes. "No, not at all. Why would I be?" Ok, so I'm a little jealous. He does not need to know that.

"Sure, Angel, whatever you say." He looks so relaxed as he leans back in his chair.

I never thought I'd be sitting with him again. For years, I believed he had passed away. It feels like I am living a scene you would see in a movie; I just can't believe he's sitting across from me.

"You shaved your beard?" I kinda of liked him with a beard. Made him look sexy as hell.

He runs his hands over his smooth face. He must notice my disappointment. "You liked my beard?" he questions, sounding surprised.

Maybe his fiancée didn't like him with a beard. The waitress returns with our drinks. I take a sip of my iced water.

"Yeah, I actually did like it... looked good on you."

"I'll keep that in mind." His eyes darken as they flicker on my lips. His legs rub under the table with mine.

"What can I get you two?" the waitress grumbles, looking at Dominic.

"Two club sandwiches," Dominic says, handing her the menus.

"How do you know if I wanted a club sandwich?"

"Because those are your favorite," he simply says.

I wrinkle my forehead. He smiles a shit-eating grin, making me want to twirl my tongue in those dimples.

He suddenly blurts, "Are you still seeing Ken?" His shoulders tense up.

"Why does it matter who I see, Dominic? We're not together. And why do you call him Ken?"

A low growl vibrates from his chest. "It matters to me, baby. I can't with take seeing you with another man. Baby, I don't share. I'm a jealous man when it comes to you. And Ken is not your type. The fucker looks like a damn pretty boy, a Ken doll. You know those Barbies," he deadpans.

I bite my lips to stifle my laugh, and he hangs his head in defeat. His eyes flash angrily for a moment, but I can't tell if it's at me or himself.

"So, what's my type?" I ask.

He lifts his head up. "Angel, you like them rough around the edges. You want a man who will bend to his will for you."

I squirm in my chair, glaring into the pool of desire floating in those whiskey eyes of his. I take this as a way to fuck with him; after all, he put me through.

"Hmm, you're right. I'm sure I'll find him, my soulmate." My smile widens wickedly.

He sneers with jealousy. "Mila, I'm your damn soulmate. Five years ago, in that hospital room, I told you that I'd hoped you'd find a second chance at fate. I'm not dead; you get no second chance. You keep your first, and if you're so damn determined to find a second chance, I'll be it. I'll be your first, second, third, whatever it is, it's me." He pounds his chest, like a damn gorilla.

My anger rises. How dare he get all caveman on me?

"You had a fiancée. Did you bend for her? Did you not propose to her? Damnit, Dominic, why tell me this bullshit when you belittled me and had a life outside of me? Why are you trying to control me?" I blow a hot air of steam.

"She was never my queen to bend for, and I would have never bowed to her or any other woman. A king has one queen, and that's you, Mila." His gaze is so intense it is almost tangible.

My heart gallops hastily.

"No other woman stood a chance. You, baby girl, are the only woman for me. I was empty—hollow inside without you. She might have had me, but you, baby, always had my heart, and no one could have taken that from you. No other woman can replace you." Dominic laces his hands over mine.

His lopsided smile makes him look love-drunk. He was moving on, so isn't that replacing when you're getting engaged?

"Mila, what are you thinking, baby?" he murmurs as he rubs the pad of his thumb on my knuckles.

"You were engaged and in a long-term relationship. So please don't tell me no other woman could replace me." At this moment, I regret coming here.

"You're so damn beautiful, Angel. You're heart-stopping

beautiful. I was a fool for trying to, baby. In my heart, you were irreplaceable. I never looked at another woman the way I look at you." His voice is smooth as silk.

His words seem sincere, but I don't trust him yet.

He literally sucked the air out of me. I hope he's true to his words. My body floods with heat as I swallow the knot in my throat. With a shaky breath, I reach into my purse and hand him pictures of Dante.

"Oh, Mila, he's beautiful, Jesus, he's perfect," he beams with so much pride.

My boy is handsome.

"What's his full name?"

"Dante Delgado."

He sighs in relief and quietly murmurs, "Thank you, Angel, for giving him my name. He looks so much like me," he says, his voice strained.

"He does, and has your protectiveness and arrogance."

His shoulders deflate as he stares at the photo. He looks sad. "Does he know about me?" His voice comes out raspy and airy.

"Yes, I spoke about you to him and showed him pictures of you," I admit.

He clears his throat and swallows hard. He is still peering at Dante's baby photo. He looks up at me his eyes a little glossy, and whispers softly, "*Thank you.*"

"He doesn't know you're alive, he thinks you're in heaven," I say, trying to break it to him gently.

"Baby, when I earn your trust, how will we tell him about me? I know he's small, and it will be confusing to him." He takes a sip of his drink and adds, "I'll do anything, Mila, to earn your and Dante's trust."

"When the time comes, we will think of something that will help him understand and not confuse him."

Lunch with Dominic felt familiar and comfortable, but we're not eighteen anymore. He asked me when Dante's birthday is, what he likes to play, and the school he attends. He offered to pay his tuition. I refused. I need to see how things go first—time passed too quickly. Both of us had to return to work.

"I wish I could spend the day with you. I've missed you so much, Mila. God, you have no idea how good it feels to be here with you today."

I know exactly how Dominic feels because being in his presence feels like a dream. I've missed him so much. The way he drinks me in as if I'm the ocean he deeply wants to get lost in.

"I missed you too," I murmur faintly.

Dominic walks me to my car. I lean my back against the window of my car. He runs the pad of his thumb along my cheeks.

"Thank you, Angel, for meeting me today." He licks his lips. "I want to kiss you, baby, embrace you in my arms, and never let you leave. However, I intend to respect your decision to take it slow, and I want you to trust me. If I have to spend the rest of my life making it up to you, Mila, I will. You're the woman my heart desires."

My eyes flutter at the sight of his soft lips. My heart deflates. Maybe I do want him to kiss me. Hold me in his arms and never let me leave. Although he is right in front of me, there remains space between us, despite the years of yearning for his touch.

His betrayal comes to mind as I recall he chose to believe what his family insinuated about me. I shiver at the brush of his lips along my cheek. I close my eyes, savoring his touch. When I open them, he steps back.

"I'll see you soon, Mila... lunch on Friday?"

I nod. I'm flustered by his touch and terrified of giving in.

DANTE and I sit watching Spider-Man. We have watched Spider-Man a gazillion times. I chuckle as I observe Dante sitting next to me, wearing his Spider-Man suit. He's rehearsing every line; he has them all memorized.

"Mommy, did you see I want to be like Spider-Man?" One eyebrow rises as he watches me.

"You're so strong, like Spider-Man," I tell him. "I bet It's because you eat your vegetables."

He flexes his muscles, giving me a wink.

I giggle. I love my little guy. He makes every struggle I've endured worth it.

"Yup, I strong. All the girls at school like my muscles."

I bust out laughing. This kid makes my heart so full. "You're a silly boy." I tickle him, and his big dimples pop out.

The front door opens, and Sophie walks in with Ryder. Dante runs to her. She swoops him into her arms and gives him a kiss on the cheek.

"Auntie Sophie, I missed you." He frowns at her.

She had been staying at Ryder's for the past couple of days. She still denies anything is going on between them.

"I'm sorry, buddy, I missed you too. How about we hang out today? I brought you cookies." She knows how to butter him up with cookies.

He reluctantly takes the box of cookies, his anger temporarily forgotten.

"Aha, you sure know how to win his affection."

She throws her hands up, laughing.

"Hey, sweets make you forget anything." Ryder stares at Sophie, then lets out a husky laugh.

"I'll remember next time you're pissed at me." She narrows her eyes at him.

"Oh, you'll need more than sweets to make me happy."

She gives him a soft smile.

I'm glad Sophie found Ryder. He may serve as a diversion from her ex-boyfriend, but he's good for her.

"I made enchiladas if you guys are hungry." I retrieve a green enchilada casserole from the oven. Nana taught me how to make her Mexican dishes. She always makes the best food.

"Damn, these are the best enchiladas I've had," Ryder moans.

My New Yorker best friend can't handle the heat. She chugs tons of water.

"Omg, you made these so hot, Mila! Are you trying to kill me? Sheesh," she breathes out, fanning her face.

I laugh, shaking my head at her. "You're such a wuss."

"Hey, this white girl doesn't do super-hot chili," she groans in her New York accent.

Thirteen

DOMINIC

"Hey Dom, two call-in today," my head chef, Mario, comments as he walks into my office.

Lately, many of my employees have been making call-ins because of sickness, and family issues.

"Damn, who called in?"

"Melissa and Eric. We're short-staffed in the kitchen." He sighs and shakes his head. He's clearly just as stressed as I am. "I called Jimmy to see if he could come in today. He said, maybe in an hour he can make it in, but I couldn't get in touch with anyone else."

Fuck. Just what I needed today. I'm swamped with paperwork, I need to do inventory, and complete the payroll. I have so damn much to do. Fucking hell can't find reliable people.

"All right, I'll step in to help throughout the day, man."

Mario taps his fingers on the desk. "Thanks, boss. I appreciate it. I'll head back to the kitchen. Dinner is the busiest, I assume we'll be good until later." He steps out.

My body is so tense from working so hard to catch up, and to be honest—I need to distract my mind from thinking of running to Mila. Jesus, she's stunning; her entire being is. Her flowing, long, black hair, porcelain skin, emerald eyes, and luscious lips make my mouth water. A mouth to devour. Her curvaceous figure and gorgeous big breasts fit perfectly in my mouth. Goddamn, I want her. I have never wanted anyone like I want her. She wakes every inch of me. I feel alive. Fucking hell, I missed her so much. Her laugh, her smile. I need to feel her against my skin, feel every inch of her; claim her as mine.

"Dominic, I have been calling you."

Fuck. She's the last person I want to see right now. She drives into my office like she owns the place.

"Well, hello, Mother."

I know she's found out about Dante. I spent weeks trying to figure out if Mom was the one lying to me or if it was Mila. I went along with my gut instinct and heart. After seeing Dante, I realized Mila would never betray me. She has always been kind-hearted. I glance up from the mountain of papers. She's fuming. I couldn't care less what she has to say. She played me—watched me heal from my illness and a broken heart. She has been feeding me lies all this time. She watched as I suffered for five years, but she never dared to say anything. I love Mila and Dante. I'll be damned if I let her keep them from me. I could have been there for my son.

"What is it you need, Mother? Did you come to confess how you lied to me and kept Mila from me? And how my brothers ignored her calls. You wanted her to believe I was dead, and you wanted me to hate her; to think she didn't want me." I jolt out of my seat and walk toward my mother.

She curves her lips and sneers. "She's not suitable for you, Dominic. You're smart and successful. She's nothing but a weight on your shoulder. You deserve much better than that tramp."

My jaw twitches. She didn't deny it. "Don't you dare talk about Mila that way. She's more than enough for me. She's everything to me. She was pregnant with my son. Tell me, Mother, did you know? Did you know she was pregnant?" I bellow.

She scoffs. "Of course not, and how do you know it's yours?

117

Hmm, she's nothing but a slut. I'm sure she's pinning it on you, claiming it's yours."

Raging heat flushes through my body. How could she be so cruel to her? What has Mila done to her? She never treated Samantha this way.

"Mom, you have no control over my life. I have no idea what you have against Mila, but I'm positive he's, my son. Never speak little of my girl. You might be my mother, but my girl and my son come first." I stare into her hostile, cold eyes.

"You would think after her being left an orphan, without parents, you would've been more maternal toward her; she doesn't deserve your cruelty."

All I see is red, fisting my hands. It fucking hurts for my mother to lie to me and treat Mila this way. Her expression shows she doesn't give a shit about Mila, and she never has. No sympathy for the situation she was in.

I yell angrily, "Get out, Mom."

She stares at me, pointing her index finger at me. "How dare you speak to me this way. I helped you, cared for you, and was there when you were dying, Dominic. She sure wasn't."

And there she goes with the guilt trip she repeatedly takes me on.

"You know I appreciate you, but Mila would have also been there for me, but you pushed her away from me for your selfish reasons. If you could please leave. I'm done talking to you."

Her cold eyes stare into mine as she walks off, slamming the door behind her. I lean back in my chair and run my fingers through my hair. I don't know what my mom has against Mila; I won't let her come between us again.

AFTER THE LONG NIGHT, I stumble into my silent condo. Its walls echo with my heavy steps. I grab an ice-cold beer from the fridge, peel away the tab, and collapse into my worn recliner. I take a long swig of the beer, letting its carbonated bubbles wash away my exhaustion. I haven't heard from Mila since yesterday's lunch. I've been so busy I haven't had the time to text her. I'm worried she might change her mind about our lunches. I'm unsure if she still sees that guy. I'll do what I can to win her back. I know it bothers her that I was engaged and that I believed every lie my mother had declared to me. She may not believe it, but my mind always wondered where she was, and who she was with. My body only craves hers. All other women were meaningless fucks to get release. I meant everything I said to her at Heidi's. She's my queen, the only woman for me. I pull out my phone to text her. She might be in bed already. Just the thought of her in bed has me yearning to be the person lying next to her.

Me: *Hey baby, are you still up? Sorry, I haven't texted you, been so busy we had two call-ins today and I had to work the kitchen.*

I click send and wait like a desperate man for her text. I see the dots bubble so she's awake.

Mila: *Hey! No worries, I understand. I've had a lot of clients; been busy myself.*

I breathe a sigh of relief as she texts me back.

Me: *How's my boy doing? How was his day?*

I recognized myself in the photos Mila had given me. He's perfect with his goofy smile. I'm eager to see him again. I want to be the dad I never had.

Mila: *He had a great day at school. He did get in trouble today for wrestling ☺ According to him, he's Spider-Man and his friends were the villains, and he had to catch them, and they wrestled. This boy is an obsessed Spider-Man fan.*

This has me laughing so hard. I can imagine the faces of the nuns scolding him for wrestling. It reminds me of one scene in *Nacho Libre.* One of my favorite movies. My brothers and I always watch it and we crack up, every time. Maybe sometime soon we can watch it together.

Me: *That has me laughing hard, Angel. So, my boy is obsessed with Spider-Man? Don't blame him, Spider-Man's cool. Ha, I was always wrestling with my brothers as a kid, must've picked it up from me. Baby, I miss you! Can we meet tomorrow for lunch? I can't wait until Friday.*

I feel like such a lovesick puppy. When I said she only likes those who are men rough around the edges, I meant me. Damn, this woman brings me to my knees. She awakens every organ in me. I have never felt so possessive of anyone. I want her all to myself, and the thought of another man talking and looking at what's mine, makes me infuriated. On my fucking deathbed five years ago, I told her I wanted her to find happiness and a second chance at fate. My words were spiked with a hint of jealousy. God gave me another chance in life to be a father, and like hell, I will I let her, or Dante go. Four long minutes pass before she responds.

Mila: *Yes, must have picked it up from you. I can't do lunch tomorrow. Sorry, I actually have plans for lunch tomorrow. How about Thursday at one?*

What the fuck! Lunch plans for tomorrow with who? I can feel my jaw clench. I get another beer from the fridge and gulp it down. Is she going with dickhead Ken, or someone else? The thought of that makes me so...

ME: *Lunch with who?*
She answers immediately.
Mila: *A friend.*
Me: *Sophie?*
Mila: *No, not Sophie.*
Me: *Who's the friend?*
What the hell! I'm clutching my phone so tight it might crack. So, if it isn't Sophie, then who? All she says is a *friend*, like she doesn't want to say who. Like hell, she's going with another man to lunch or anywhere matter-of-factly.

Me: *Is it a man you're going with, Mila? Because it better not fucking be, Mila, You're mine! You're fucking mine!!*

Fuck, she drives me crazy. I know I have no right to go caveman.

Mila: *Dominic, what the fuck!! If it is or isn't, it's not your business. We are not together. We are friends, for Dante's sake. This was our agreement. Have a good night. If you want to meet on Thursday to talk more about Dante, let me know.*

Goddamn, this woman is going to have me bust a nut. I throw my phone on the couch. Just when I thought things were going great, I fuck it up with my jealousy. Hell, doesn't she fucking see I want her and her only? She's hurt and I don't fucking blame her. If the roles were reversed, I would be too.

Me: *Fuck I'm sorry, baby. Thursday is fine at one. Meet me at my restaurant. We can have lunch there. Good night, Angel. And you are mine always have been.*

God, I'm such a pussy. She has me wrapped around her finger, and she doesn't even know it. I wait to see if she writes back. Five minutes later.

Mila: *Sure, that's fine. See you at 1.*

She's pissed.

"Hey, Dom, how's it going?" Will greets me as I enter Rocko's Bar.

Will's great, great grandad Rocko was the founder of this pub, and we've been coming here since before we were of age—even if it meant using fake IDs.

I take a seat on the bar stool and tell him, "Doing fine, Will. Just had a long day—time to relax."

As he looks at me, he strokes his long gray beard with his fingers. "What can I get you?"

"Whiskey on the rocks and two beers man."

121

He frowns. "That bad, huh? So, word on the street is you broke your engagement off?" he asks, raising his gray brows.

I'm sure my brothers blabbed about it. Santiago comes here regularly. I blow out a breath.

"Samantha was never the one for me to begin with. We're complete opposites. I found out I have a son with the girl I've always been in love with. She was my high school sweetheart."

He whistles. "Well, hell." His eyes widen in surprise.

I've never talked to anyone about Mila. It hurt to talk about her.

"This woman you're in love with, what happened? How old is this son of yours?"

I take a sip of whiskey, feeling the warm sensation coating my insides. We talked briefly, and I told him how my mom deceived me. I'm uncertain if Mila will provide me with an opportunity. I am unsure about her feelings for the other person she is with.

"Well, that's some crazy shit, son. Sorry, but your mom's a bitch. Word of advice don't let anyone butt in on your relationships. I had a mother-in-law just like your mom. Why does she dislike Mila so much?"

A shrug rolls over my shoulder.

"I have no damn clue." Every time I've asked my mom, she's never answered the question. All she says is Mila's not good enough.

"Is she single? She's not married, is she?"

A growl erupts from my chest. Just thinking of her married pains me.

"No, she's not married, thank the fuck."

Will chuckles. "Good luck, man." He pats me on the shoulder and walks off to attend to others.

Liam walks in wearing his uniform pants and a plain white t-shirt. He must have just retired for the night from work. He's a police officer for the San Diego Police Department. He pulls out the stool next to me. Waves to Will for a beer. Liam scans my face.

"You look like shit."

I take a sip of my beer.

Will drops a beer in front of Liam.

"You keep saying I look like shit," I toss back to him, annoyed.

He chuckles. "How are things going with Mila? By the looks of it, not well, I'm guessing."

I give him the run-down of everything going on and letting out a sigh, I continue. "She looks at me with disgust and hurt. I told her how I felt. When we had lunch, I poured my soul out to her. Every time I felt she was going to give in, she pushed back."

"Dom, it's been five years. You have to be patient with her. You have a lot of catching up to do, it will take time. Don't rush her or you will push her away. Let's not forget you were just engaged."

Fuck, I want to pull my damn hair out. All I want to do is show her how much I want her. How much I need her. I want to meet my son and be a father to him. It's killing me she hasn't texted me today.

"You're right, but fuck it's hard. I know I screwed up, and now I'm paying for it. I'm having lunch with her tomorrow. She said it's strictly to meet about our son nothing else."

His husky voice rumbles with laughter. He takes a sip of his beer. "Don't get all caveman on her. You always got all possessive over her."

Fuck is, he's right. Mila makes my blood pressure rise to an extreme level. Her beauty has men glancing in her direction every time.

"Too fucking late, man, I've already gotten all caveman on her more than once."

He chuckles. "What'd you do?"

I snort. "First day I viewed her at that restaurant, I pinned her to the wall and fucking marked her neck. And the second time, I ripped the mother fucker who was on top of her off." I grumble. She knows damn well how to press my buttons.

Liam barks a laugh so loud the entire bar is staring right at us. "Shit, she has you by the balls."

He has no idea.

Making my way back to my place, I never realized the loneliness and emptiness in my apartment until now. The thought of coming home to a family—a wife and kids —is something I have always dreamed of. I never experienced a normal family where my dad would come home to us. I longed for something like—*a family*. After showering, I crawl into bed. I fall asleep with the anticipation of seeing my Angel tomorrow.

Fourteen

MILA

I sit in my office, sipping coffee and going over my schedule. I have five photo shoots and a lunch date with Dominic. Throwing my head back, I glare up at the ceiling, remembering Dominic's text from two nights ago. Jealousy and anger fumed from his text. His possessiveness had me outraged that he had some nerve to question me when the asshole was engaged weeks ago.

A curve of my lips smiles mirthfully at the thought of Dominic being jealous. Serves him right after him flaunting Samantha around, making out with her in front of me. If I had mentioned having lunch with Brian, Dominic would've hunted me down. Just like the night he busted down the door of Brian's car, tearing Brian off of me. Brian had called and asked if we could talk. I agreed to meet him at Panera.

Walking in, Brian is waiting for me by the window. His beautiful eyes bounce up.

"Hi, Mila," he says, placing his soft lips on my cheek. He pulls out a chair for me.

I've missed Brian's company. He's sweet, but the way he left us left an unpleasant taste in my mouth.

"Thank you," I say.

He sits back down, squirming in his chair nervously. "Um, what do you want to eat? I can go place the order."

I smile at him. "I'll have a Caesar salad and iced water please."

We have lunch, he apologizes for how he acted and asks for another chance to work it out. I wasn't expecting it, not by a long shot.

"Mila, I really, really like you. I would like another chance with you. But, I need to know, are you getting back together with Dante's father?"

I tell him the truth. I tell him, "Right now, Dominic and I are working on getting to know each other again for Dante's sake." I tell him that Dominic and I are only friends and I'm not sure if Dominic and I can repair things.

Brian's sweet and kind, but right now, it's best Brian and I stay friends. He doesn't need the drama like he said. I watch as Sophie sets up her props.

Thoughts of being at Panera with Brian remind me of the creepy feeling I got when I left. There was a man there, a man I'd been seeing more and more often. It started in Manhattan and now, I'm seeing him here. The man in the aviator glasses. I've seen him at the beach and again, just leaned up against a red pickup truck.

Something in me tells me it's the same man, but what are the odds?

He must be the same man I can't see his face, so, I'm uncertain if he always has glasses on. Maybe I'm just overthinking it. He bites his bottom lip, turns, gets into his pickup, and drives off. How strange.

I WALK into Dominic's restaurant. He's talking to the hostess, the same one from last time. The vulgar host. He doesn't see me walk in; I watch how she flirts with him, twirling her hair with her finger.

My stomach churns with jealousy. The way she's eyeing him as if they know each other on another level. Maybe he slept with her. She laughs at something he's saying. I'm positive he has, which makes me sick to my stomach. I turn to walk out before he sees me. My chest hurts, and stings.

I wish I could quell the awful emotions that are ripping me apart, but I simply can't. I want to be unaffected by his presence so that my heart won't be in pieces every time I see him. When I see him, I'm reminded of how little he believed in me. And how he went on with his life with other women—not to mention the fact that he was engaged.

"Angel," he shouts in his smooth husky voice.

Closing my eyes, inhaling a deep breath, I remind myself I'm doing this for *Dante.* I turn around. The pools of his whiskey-browns are on me. Relief washes over his face. His smile widens at the sight of me, along with those dimples I love. He strolls right to me, leaving the hostess talking.

I suck in a sharp breath. Dominic is beautiful, his smooth, olive skin stretched over high cheekbones. God, the way he's looking at me like I'm the only one in the room. His piercing eyes scan my whole profile with desire. A shiver runs down my spine as his lips press onto my cheek. He smirks knowing what he does to me.

Asshole.

"Angel." His hot breath scattering around my cheek.

O' God. *Keep it together Mila.*

"Dominic," I reply.

"Why were you walking out?" His confused frown deepens into one of despair.

"You seemed busy." My eyes roam to the girl—the hostess behind him.

He clears his throat. "No, work-related."

I stare intensely at him, trying to read him like a newspaper. Ahh, he has slept with her. It shouldn't bother me, but it does. She still works here. I know I'm being juvenile about his past. The stings tug when I think about how much I hurt in the past, and he moved on. Was she his girlfriend or friend with benefits?

I scoff dramatically. "Sure, maybe today, but other times not too work-related right?" I muster a smile.

"Nice to see you, beautiful." He winks. Ignoring my observation, he glares over at the hostess giving me a pitbull face. "Alicia, we'll be in the private lounge. Get us drinks," he snaps.

Alicia is still glaring at me as if I stole her man. "Sure, Dom." She grabs the menus, handing them to him.

I raise an eyebrow. He only lets those close to him call him Dom. They must be close. He must've noticed my observation. He clears his throat once again. "It's Dominic," he says in a deep tone.

As he pulls the chair out for me. I blurt out, "You slept with her?"

He frowns. "Why do you say that?"

I laugh. He must think I can't read him anymore. "Really? Dominic, it's obvious."

He groans, combing his fingers through, his silk hair. He seems nervous as he narrows his eyes above my head not looking into my eyes.

"Just once, a long time ago when I first opened."

I was fucking right. My stomach clenches painfully.

"You fuck her, and she still works here. Are you still sleeping with her?" I shout, not meaning to. *Great now I sound jealous.*

He reaches for my hand I pull away.

"Angel, no, I'm not with her and I'm not fucking her. It happened so long ago. I was in a terrible place at that time. I wasn't thinking. I wasn't in a relationship with her—"

"Wow, your fiancée was a moron to have her working here knowing you slept with her, especially when she practically throws herself on you like... she did when I walked in," I said, opening the menu, not really seeing what was on it. He pisses me off. He slept with her, but he still has her around, like—why? Is it because he plans on sleeping with her again at some point?

. . .

GOD. *Mila, calm down.* I have to keep my heart in check. My heart is in turmoil. I want to deny that he has any power over me, but even as I try to push my feelings of love to the side, they keep creeping back up. I can't allow myself to be affected by him. He has moved on as I was trying to—until he appeared. I need to remind myself we are no longer a unit, no matter how much my heart wants it to be true.

"Angel."

"It's fine. It doesn't matter. We aren't together, you don't have to explain."

His shoulders drop as mine stiffen. His expression slides into a frown. "I'll let her go. You're right; I shouldn't have kept her on staff. I don't want you to have the erroneous impression that I don't respect you. She's of no significance to me."

I stand from my chair. "I should go; this was a bad idea. I'm sorry this is not going to work, Dominic. We carry too much pain from our past. It's been too long... the years and pain has distanced us."

He jolts up and pulls me close to him. "Mila, no, don't go, please... Let's talk about it," he whispers, his voice hoarse, his gaze pleading. "I'm sorry, baby." He kisses me repeatedly on my cheek and forehead—his voice quivers with so much emotion.

I pull away from his hold and focus my gaze on his. My heart drops—the sight of his expression drawn in agony.

"Dominic, this is all just hard for me. I won't lie. It hurts to know you had a life. While I was stuck on the other side, I grieved for you every damn day. I-I cried myself to sleep holding a photo of you w-wishing you were here with me... holding me. I looked into our sons' eyes, and I would see you. I-I-I cried when Dante said Mama because I wanted him to say Dada. I cried when he took his first steps, I wished you could see him, experience it with me. *I-I fucking missed you.*" A stream of tears skates down my cheeks.

"It maims me to know while I was in pain, you l-lived a life. Fucking every woman, you could get your hands on. It goddamn hurts that you thought so little of me; enough to hate me; to treat me like shit. It p-pains me... I-I don't know you anymore like I wish I did. The w-woman you were engaged to knows you, not me. She had a ring on her finger. She had you." I hiccup, and tears keep flowing, I'm not capable of holding them in.

Then, with a flicker of my wet lashes, I direct my gaze toward Dominic. A tear runs down his cheek. He swipes it with his thumb before it drops.

"Baby, I wish I could have been there to hold you, to be a part of our son's life, Mila... Angel, we would have been married by now, I promise you. Please know... no other woman has mattered to me, Mila. It wasn't like that. I fucked up. I didn't enjoy it, I promise you. It meant nothing. Samantha never knew shit about me. She didn't know the tattoo on my chest was about the love of my life. She didn't know what my favorite color was, what toothpaste I use, my favorite song, or how I like my coffee; she knew shit about me. You baby, you know me. I'm sorry for being an asshole with you all these years and thinking wrongly of you. I thought about you every damn day. I missed you, Angel. *I missed us.*"

He cups my cheeks and kisses the tip of my nose.

"I love you, baby," he whispers.

I Inhale his masculine scent, enveloping my arms around him, in this moment. I need him to hold me, leaning my head on his chest. The thumping of his heartbeat, the familiarity of our heartbeats beating in unison. *Home.* His arms feel like home. He rubs his hands up and down my spine.

"Are you all right, baby?"

Nodding. I sniffle. I'm sure I drenched his shirt in tears and boogers.

"Fuck baby, I'm sorry. Don't cry, Mila."

Taking a shuddering breath, I lean into him again, needing his closeness.

"Are you okay?" he repeats, running his fingers along my spine.

"Yes, sorry," I whisper. I wipe my tears with the back of my hand.

"You have nothing to be sorry about, Angel. Do you want to eat still?"

"Yes, I'm starving."

He chuckles. We sit back down.

"So, what's good here?" I ask, wiping my tears with a napkin. "I really like it here; it is a great atmosphere. I love all the classic car pictures you have hanging up. Aww, and rock band posters, Willie Nelson pictures, and so many." I scan the room, taking in the homey atmosphere. Log-style chairs and tables fill the space, and a jukebox is tucked away in the corner with its glowing lights and vintage charm. I hadn't observed the restaurant until now. I smile when my eyes meet Dominic's.

He studies me with piercing scrutiny. He shifts his chair closer to mine. Dominic leans into me, his hand caressing my cheek, pulling a strand of hair behind my ear. His voice breaks in a husky whisper, "Everything is wonderful, baby; I made the menu."

A feverish chill tingles down my lady bits. He's so close, I can feel his hot breath. His lips brush my ear, trailing kisses behind my ear down to my collarbone. My breath quickens at the touch of his soft lips. I am aware I need to guard my heart and resist giving in right away. I can't get hurt. My life has been tangled with complexities.

He, though, makes my brain fuzzy. I've lost my mental clarity. My heart says yes even though my brain is telling me to back off. Moving my head to the side, giving him more access, I haven't felt this in so long. His lips all over me, it is nice, besides when he mauled me in the bathroom. He drops kisses on my cheek and on the side of my mouth. Pressing his lips to mine, we hold a stare filled with desire. His lips crash against mine, a frenzied wave of desperate hunger. His hands press firmly against my cheeks as our tongues dance in a blaze of passion. The kiss feels like molten metals brought together, our desire bubbling over, melding us together in one explosive moment. His lips sear against me as I suck on his bottom lip, the heat all-consuming until we have to part to catch our breath. Our lips are glossy, swollen, and red. I lick my lips, tasting him, he does the same.

"Angel, no woman has ever made me feel like you do."

I take a slow, steady breath to calm my racing heart. I don't know what to say. My mind is in a confused fog. He sees it in my confused glare.

"I'm going to the kitchen to give them our orders."

A couple of minutes later, he returns with our order. Two delicious burgers with cheese and bacon, slathered with a secret sauce.

"Mmm, this is so good, so juicy."

He looks at me with those gorgeous brown eyes.

I ask, "What made you want to be a chef? I know you liked to cook, but I remember you saying you wanted to open your auto shop."

"You," he says softly.

He stays quiet for a second too long.

"I loved cooking for you, seeing that smile on your face when I did. I wanted to open this place in memory of Leo. Do you remember we talked about this?"

My heart breaks thinking of my father. His kind gesture melts my heart. I swallow the knot in my throat as memories begin to resurface of Dominic making me meals when I would go over to his house, or he would drop by with something to eat at my house. I lean in to kiss his cheek.

"Thank you. I do remember, of course. It means a lot to me, Dominic," I say, earnestly.

"Don't thank me, Mila. Leo was a good man. He always treated me with kindness. I told you I would open a restaurant in his memory and your mother's."

My heart squeezes again. His smile is drop-dead sexy; he stands up and walks to the Jukebox, drops a coin in, and *Love*

Song by the Cure plays. He brushes his thumb on my lips and sings to me. His voice is smooth as silk and rough all at the same time. His eyes stare into mine. I melt to his touch, to his voice. I close my eyes taking, it all in. The song ends.

"Mila," he whispers.

Opening my eyes, his long, thick eyelashes flicker.

"Baby, I know I can't make up for lost time. You were right when you said I didn't try hard enough. I should have. I belittled you and thought low of you. I spent all these years angry with you. I wanted to find you to confront you for leaving me. I guess after so long it was better to believe I was a burden to you. I'm sorry about how I treated you. I will repeat it as many times as you need to hear it," he says, swallowing hard as he continues. "As for living life, how could I possibly live life without my queen by my side? Mila, you hold the power to my soul, the key to my heart. I promise not to let my mom or anyone else come between us ever again. Will you give us a chance? I want us to be a family. I'm sorry for everything that's happened, and the pain I've caused you. For the last five years, baby, I was a broken man without you. I need you, Angel, like my lungs, need air. I'm here; let me love you, embrace you, be a father and the man I need to be for you. I'm not going anywhere. I'll be with you until my last breath." His voice is rich with promise.

The light in his eyes twinkles, showing how sincere his words are. I need him, we need him. I love him. Trembling in anticipation, I fight the urge to embrace him. I'm not sure I can handle any more pain in my heart.

Fifteen
DOMINIC

She's so beautiful, the most exquisite woman I've ever seen. I linger over those plump lips wanting to taste them all over again. My thoughts are racing as I wait for her reply. I asked her to allow us to become a family and to let me be a father to Dante. My love for her is so strong. I ache to see her again and to finally meet my son. Memories of my father abandoning us when we were young rush back to me as I recall him packing his belongings in his vehicle.

My mom rocked back and forth in a brown rocking chair, cradling Mark. He opened the door to the yellow Volkswagen. He glanced at Santiago and me before he slammed the door and drove off. That was the last time I saw him. My mom did not shed a tear. She kept rocking back and forth with a haughty stare in her eyes.

I promised myself never to be that man. Beads of cold sweat form on my forehead, waiting for an answer. She glances up at me with those big green eyes. She smiles.

"I want to give us a chance. I've spent five years yearning for you, living without you. I need you; we need you, Dominic."

The tips of her nails brush along my cheeks. Her touch ignites a blazing fire; she's my kerosene. A simple touch sets me in flames.

"I want you to be a father to Dante. I want you to see how

incredible and sweet he is. How special he is." The light in her eyes sparkles as she describes our son. She smiles sweetly when she speaks of him.

I'm relieved she wants to give us a chance. I take her hand, placing soft kisses on her knuckles.

"Don't let me regret this, Dominic," she softly whispers.

I see the pain behind her eyes. She's afraid to let her guard down.

"Thank you, baby, and I promise I'll never hurt you intentionally. I promise to be the best father. You mean everything to me."

She squeezes my thigh, sending a twitch straight toward my cock. I want to touch her, hold her. As I sit her on my lap, she lets out a squeal.

"What are you doing? Dominic, there are people here!"

"Baby, we're in a private room. It's just you and me. I want to hold my woman and kiss the shit out of her."

She giggles in my ear.

I skim my lips along the sweep of her cheek, teasing her, kissing her softly along her neck, inhaling her scent of coconut and cherry. She smells so good. I suck hard, leaving little bites on her. I know how to get her off. That always ignited a fire in her.

"Mmm, you smell so good."

She lets out a soft moan.

I'm about to explode in my pants, with just the sound of her voice. "Stop teasing me," I tell her as she moans again.

I grab onto her waist, digging my fingers into her soft, delicate skin. Her low-cropped shirt rises, and the tip of my fingers featherily brush along the soft pale skin. She wiggles continuously on my lap and I know she can feel my hardness for her. A growl erupts from my chest.

"Stop wiggling around, baby." I slam my lips on hers, begging for entrance. Immediately, she opens, our tongues tangle with one another. My tongue thrusts unmercifully, I want her to feel how much I want her; how much I need her—kissing her desperately, assaulting her mouth—the feel of her fingers sliding into my hair. I groan in her mouth. She tastes so damn good I can't get enough of her.

How could I be such an idiot to go five years without her? *Mine. She's mine.* We part needing air. We lean our foreheads together.

"Fuck, Mila, you're so beautiful. I can't get enough of you."

She pecks a small kiss on my lips. "I feel the same," she murmurs.

The smell of cheap perfume stings my nostrils. I glare up at the woman foaming with jealousy, Alicia is standing there.

Fuck.

"What do you need, Alicia?" I bark out. I'd told her and the staff not to come in. I wanted to be alone with my girl. My fingers grip Mila's waist, holding on to her tightly, the last thing I need is her running off because of Alicia. I know Alicia does shit on purpose. I should have terminated her long ago. She agreed when I explained to her at the time that she had no meaning to me.

"W-wanted to see if you needed anything," she stutters.

"No, I fucking don't. I told you, along with everyone else, not to come in here." I grimace. I'm going to fire her once Mila leaves.

"S-sorry," she says, running out.

Mila rubs my shoulder. "I see you're still very much hot-tempered, huh?"

The smile she wears is alluring. This woman is my weakness, the definition of beauty. I capture her lips with soft kisses. I laugh, she knows me so well. Although she thinks she doesn't.

"With others, yeah, but never with you, baby."

She snorts. "That's because you know I'd let you have it. And you have gotten hot-tempered with me." She makes a fist. Proving she would let me have it. I burst into laughter, making my chest rumble—her tiny fist. *God, I love her.* It's been so long since I've felt happiness.

"Ah, I see still a firecracker," I tease, mimicking words she's used before.

She replies, "Of course." Her smile stretches. She glances at her watch and sighs. "I need to head out. I have a client in about thirty minutes. Thank you for lunch and the other stuff."

I raise an eyebrow at her, giving her an overconfident smirk. "Other stuff? Are you talking about our erotic, deep tongue kiss?" I tease, knowing she will blush. I loved making her blush.

She looks at me through her long eyelashes, cheeks turning a splash of pink. She huffs with a twitch of a smile. "Yes." She waves her hands in the air. "Anyway, I will talk to Dante tonight about you."

Immediately, worry sets in. What if my son doesn't want to meet me? What if I'm not good enough for him? She must see right through me. She cradles my cheeks, kissing me softly. The taste of her sweet, sugary lips diminishes me. I wrap my arms around her waist, holding her tight.

"Everything will be fine, he will be confused, but you're his father, he loves you. He will be happy. He always looks at photos of you. You know, the day you first ran into Dante and me, I'm surprised he didn't recognize you. But you were young in those photos."

Letting out a breath of relief, I say, "Do you need me there?"

"No, I need to do this alone with him. I'll call you tonight." With that, she jumps off my lap.

Immediately, I miss the heat of her body. I want her back in my arms.

I LEFT work early and informed Mario to take over right after Mila left. Before leaving work, I asked Mario for advice on what I should do when I meet Dante. His advice was effortless, just purchase him some toys, and the rest will take care of itself. Yeah, well I hope so. I've always dreamt of being a dad.

I blame my mom for the shit she pulled. She's always controlled our lives. She manipulated me. My mother manages

Santiago's shop. She's always used my disease to get what she's wanted to guilt trip me.

"Dominic, I'm your mother. I took care of you, took you to the best doctors. You're alive because of me."

I'm grateful for her love and affection. She never left us like my father. But I'm not letting her fuck with my life. If I have to cut her off until she accepts Mila, and Dante, I will. I pull into Target to pick up toys for my little guy. I've never shopped for kids before. I load up my cart with everything Spider-Man, grabbing some web shooters, a Venom costume; *holy shit, army guys,* haven't seen those in a long time. My brothers and I always played with army guys and He-man... *oh shit,* and Ninja Turtles. I was always Raphael, *damn, this is fun shopping for toys.* I feel like a kid again. Smiling foolishly, I make my way to the sports aisle, throwing baseball gloves into the cart. I'll teach him how to play. I was team captain in high school. I was the shit back then.

When I heard the news that I had cancer, it felt like I'd been thrown into the depths of a raging ocean. But even as the waves dragged me down, Mila's beautiful smile and bubbly laughter kept me from giving into the shadows. She gave me the strength to fight for my life. She remained my beacon of light, in the darkness even after she was gone.

Heading to the check-out, I spot Ken glowering straight at me with his tiny shorts and a muscle shirt with no damn muscle to his body. What a joke.

"What's going on, Ken?" I cringe at his short shorts and scrunch my nose in disgust. I'm surprised his dick isn't hanging out; probably a tiny dick, I snort.

"It's Brian," the dickhead snips. He glances at my basket. "Is this for Dante?"

I want to pound him right in the face. The fact that he's met my son and I haven't pisses me off, and the asshole knows it. I'm not letting it show he irks me. The image of him sleeping with Mila ignites me. Fuck I'm not sure if she's been intimate with him, but the way he had her in the backseat of his car says otherwise. I could hear her moaning. The sound of her moans are engraved in my mind.

"You know it, Ken, heading to see my son and my woman later tonight." I flash him a cocky grin.

His eyes widened with rage. He barks a laugh. "Until you screw it up, then she'll come running to me. I'll be the one warming her bed and tucking your son into bed. She savored my dick in her mouth. The way she moaned my name. Yeah, she'll be doing it again. When she comes back to me."

Mother fucker. With my jaw clenching, I drift toward him without making a scene.

"No matter what, this is where you are mistaken. I'll stay in Dante's life forever, and he'll always be my son. Even if she is not with me, my woman is still *mine*. When any other man is fucking her, she will think about me because no one can fulfill her the way I can. I damaged her for all other men, and no one comes close to me. As a result, Ken, if you believe you can warm her bed, well just know it won't be you she'll be thinking about it. Do you really believe you can endure living in another man's shadow? And just to be clear, I won't ever let her leave."

Jealousy pours over me like acid.

"Her soul is and will always be *mine*. Selfishly, I'll never return it. You know shit about mine and Mila's history. Stay away from my family. If you even breathe in her space, I'll rearrange your face."

If looks could kill, dickhead would be six feet under. Grimacing, I give him one last look before I head to check out.

———

I ROUND the corner of my condo. Fuck. The two women I'm not in the damn mood to see. They don't know how to back the fuck off. I park my truck in the garage. Samantha runs in her Louboutin heels, throwing her arms at me.

"Baby, I've missed you so much. How about I order us

dinner, and we can cuddle and watch a movie?" She strokes me with the palm of her hand.

I rip her hands off my chest. My mom stands milliliters from Samantha.

"What are you both doing here?" I bellow.

"Dominic! Is this any way to speak to your mother and fiancée?" She gapes, shoving her hands in her pockets. "I came to see you. And drop Samantha off with you. We went dress shopping, and she found a beautiful wedding dress. Can't wait for my future daughter to walk down the aisle." She beams.

What in the fuck. Goddamn.

"She is not my fiancée. I've made it very clear. It's fucking over between us. You both can go. I'm with Mila like it should have been."

Samantha breaks into tears.

Shit.

My mom sneers at me. "Fix this, Dominic. I have somewhere I need to be." She rounds herself, her heels clinking on the pavement, then she gets into her Audi and speeds off.

I'm left with Samantha whimpering. I sigh. "Samantha, we are over. I'm not in love with you nor will I ever be. I'm sorry for hurting you. We should never have become a thing. My heart was never mine to give away. It has always belonged to another woman —my first and only love. I'm sorry but you need to leave. We were not meant for one another. You know this."

"Dominic p-p-please," she says, pleading.

My heart aches and guilt eats at me for giving her false hope. A superficial relationship.

"Samantha..."

Fuck.

She throws herself on me, her lips crashing onto mine.

I shove her off of me, enraged. "What the fuck Samantha?" I grimace.

"You're going to pay for this, Dominic," she shouts. Her eyes bore into slits. Her heels crush the pavement as she stomps away.

Sixteen

MILA

As I fold laundry, I keep pondering how to address the situation of telling Dante his father is alive. When there's a knock at the door, the shock of finding the one person I despise—Rachel—fucking Rachel—I'm surprised the sourness in her face hasn't aged her. She has a tall, slender figure, light brown hair, and olive-tan skin like her sons. She stands gloating over me. She glances over my shoulder as Dante plays with his toys. I shut the door. I don't want this evil, crazy woman to see my son.

"What can I help you with, Rachel?"

Her mouth twists. The audacity of this woman showing up at my doorstep.

"I see you're back in town. Pursuing my son all over again. You just had to come back; he was engaged to beautiful Samantha. You're like a roach we can't get rid of. A nuisance. It won't take long before he leaves you. You're nothing," she seethes, grinding her teeth.

Bitch. I'm not a teenager anymore. I've grown thick skin. I keep my head held high, refusing to back down from the manipulator. Her sons always cowered behind her. I'm not them. She's notorious for using mind games to control those around her, but

I will not succumb to her tactics: I have no intention of giving her satisfaction.

"Listen here, Rachel. This is where you're wrong, your son pursued me back into his life. If your son wants out, that's fine by me. I don't need a man to take care of me and my son. You're just pissed he chose us. Never step foot on my doorstep again. You're not welcome. If you have a problem, take it up with your son. We have nothing to talk about." My breath, heaves. I slam the door in her damn face.

Fuck, Fuck. Why does this woman loath me so much?

"Mommy, who was that?"

Sigh... My poor baby.

"No one, honey, wrong house." My hands shake. How did she find out where I live?

My phone beeps in my pocket. It's Nana. I texted her for advice on how to explain to my son that his father is alive and kicking. He's four going on five soon, so how do you explain such a critical situation to a child?

Nana: *Tell him Dominic was in the hospital the whole time, and he got better.*

I could tell him something similar. Yanking on my hair, I groan with frustration. I won't let Rachel get under my skin. My insecurity hits me with a warning label. If what Rachel claims is accurate, will he leave? When the fire inside of us extinguishes, will he get his final taste before he leaves me? It's been much too long; these may all be old sparks and wounds needing to be closed. The walls I built are crashing down a little at a time. I'm terrified of letting them all crumble. Once I do, I might regret it. The last thing I want is my son with a broken heart. That's something I can't live with. I can muster living with a broken heart I've done it before.

"What's wrong, Mommy? Bad day?"

His beautiful face lights up my world, I kiss him on the cheek. Jesus, he looks just like his father.

"I had a good day just a little tired."

He sighs "Me too, Mommy. I played all day, so tired." What it is to be a kid.

"Baby boy, come sit here with me. I need to tell you something."

He frowns. "What is it, Mommy?"

I sit him on my lap. I take a deep breath. "You remember how I told you how your daddy was in heaven?"

He nods.

"You see, your daddy was in hospital when you were in my tummy. I moved away with Nana and Uncle Roger. Doctors told me he went to heaven, but he really didn't. When we moved here to California, I found out the doctors gave me the wrong information, and your daddy didn't know how to find me to tell me he was better. I saw your daddy. He actually lives here. I told him about you, and he's so happy and wants to meet you." My blood pressure is sky-high; my pulse is speeding rapidly.

With wide eyes, he grins. My shoulders deflate, the tension dissipating.

"My daddy's not in heaven?" His nose scrunches up. His beautiful brown eyes twinkle.

"No, baby, he's not. I just saw him today."

With a squeak, he jumps off my lap and screams. "My daddy's alive. Mommy, can we go see him please?"

Awe, I can feel my heart melting. When Dominic asked for another chance, I realized sometimes we lose people in our lives to find them again. We've been through a lot these past years. As much as the engagement and the other women irked me and the fact, he belittled me, I know I need to move on and start fresh, not dwell on the past. We need Dominic back in our lives. I won't lie. I'm terrified of letting him in my heart. It's easier to tell myself I'm doing this for my son. I'm not sure what our outcome will be.

"How about I call him to see if he can come over for dinner?"

"Okay, Mommy, call him, get your phone." He nods and runs

upstairs and returns with a photo I had hanging up of Dominic and me. He would consistently glance at it.

Dialing Dominic's number, I'm hoping he will pick up, but I am not sure what his work schedule is like.

"Hello, beautiful."

The sound of his husky voice sends goosebumps down to my core. How I missed the familiarity of his voice.

"Is everything okay?" He questions with worry in his tone.

I'm not sure If I should tell him about his mom dropping by unwelcomed. That could wait.

"More than okay. I talked to Dante and explained to him in a way he could understand."

"Is he okay? How did he take it, Angel, is he confused? I've been thinking about this all day."

I smile so wide it makes my cheeks hurt. "He wants you to come over," I say, wiping a tear sliding down. I hear Dominic swallow. I clear my throat. "Can you come over for dinner? If you can. I understand if your bus—a"

He cuts me off. "Baby, of course, I want to come over to meet my son. God, I've been waiting for this moment, Mila. I can grab dinner, whatever you guys want."

I'll admit I'm a little shaken up with mixed emotions. I just hope it all works out. "Sounds good. How about The Taco Shop?"

He chuckles knowing tacos are my favorite. "I know my girl is a huge taco fan. I'll grab a little of everything. What should I get, Dante?"

Dante runs to me. "Mommy is that, Daddy?" he whispers softly.

"Yes, baby, it is."

A boyish smile pops his dimples out. Dominic's laugh rumbles on the other end of the line.

"He's not picky. You can get him some beans and rice."

Dante frowns and whispers, "I want a burger and fries, Mommy."

This boy.

"Sorry, he would like a burger and fries, if you can; if not, don't worry about it, he can eat whatever you get."

"No, I'll get him what he wants, baby." A shakiness in his voice bounces off the receiver. He's nervous.

"I'll be right over, give me like twenty minutes, Angel," he says with a low husky voice.

"Ok see you soon."

A knock at the door twenty minutes later, has me giddy and so excited to see this father and son reunion. The photographer in me grabs a camera. As soon as I turn the doorknob, Dominic's silhouette appears from behind it. His white t-shirt seems to hug his biceps perfectly, and I can see the outlines of his firm muscles through the fabric. His biceps bulge against the sleeves as his olive-tanned skin gleams in the light. A chiseled jawline and thick eyebrows enhance his rugged good looks even further. It's evident that he puts a lot of time and hard work into keeping himself in good shape.

Man, I'm jealous of those long black eyelashes. *Lord have mercy.* He's like a daydream. His shirt is so tight I spot the tattoo on his chest. Jesus, the perfect lines of his eight-pack. I see another tattoo on his forearm, but can't make out what it says. I snap myself out of the trance. I realize he's staring at me the same way, seeking me out.

"Angel," he breathes out. His eyes scan every part of my flesh.

"Here, let me help you." I reach out to grab the food. I hear little footsteps coming down the stairs. The door swings open.

"Daddy!"

Dominic places the drinks and food on the doorstep. When Dante runs to him, Dominic catches him in his arms. There's a startled look in Dominic's eyes. Dante wraps his tiny hands around his dad's neck and cries on his shoulder. Dominic is clearly choked with emotion holding his son so tight, afraid he might disappear from his arms.

"My boy, my Dante," Dominic whispers. He wipes his and

Dante's tears, he kisses him on each cheek and his forehead. They stare at one another. Dominic's eyes pained with guilt.

"I missed you, Daddy."

I wasn't expecting Dante to run to him, but I'm sure he feels the connection.

Dominic swallows the rock in his throat he replies, "Me too, son."

God, I'm ugly crying as I watch my son and Dominic together. Dominic reaches for my hand, then wipes my tears.

He whispers, "Thank you."

I nod. He leans in to kiss the top of my head. I wrap Dante and Dominic in a bear hug. My two loves. With a rumble in Dante's stomach, he giggles.

"I'm hungry, Daddy carry me inside, and don't put me down."

He kisses him. "Never, my little man, never."

AFTER DINNER, the two stuck together like partners in crime. Watching them interact warms my heart. They are too much alike; the similarities are crazy. A smile reaches my eyes as I take them both in. Dante sits on Dominic's lap as he tells him about preschool and what he likes to do. Dante scrunches his nose and frowns.

"Daddy, you, okay? You're not sick no more?"

Dominic turns his gaze toward me, a deflated emotion criss-crossing his face.

I nodded, assuring him it was okay.

"No, Dante, I'm good."

Dante smiles gracefully. "Come on, Daddy, let's wrestle, or do you want to play Spider-Man?"

Dominic chuckles. "I have a surprise for you in my truck. Let me get it, okay?"

"I come with you, Daddy?"

"Get your shoes on," I tell him, "And you can go with Daddy to the truck and get it."

He runs upstairs to get his shoes. This has gone better than I thought. I knew Dante would love to see his father, but I didn't expect him to warm up to him this quickly. I'm cleaning up the kitchen when I feel tree trunk arms wrap around my waist—peppering kisses along my collarbone. I tense at his touch. This is all too new to me.

"I missed you," he murmurs, his hot breath on my neck—liquid heat courses through my veins.

My body heats with his soft touch, my heart beating at a carnal speed. His hands roam to my ass; he grabs and squeezes. Genuinely, I feel like I'm in some dream. They led me to believe he was dead. But here he is, standing before me... kissing me. The pain of his betrayal has me gripping the counter. *Give it a chance, Mila. You won't know unless you try,* I say to myself. *For Dante,* I add silently.

"Been wanting to do this since I walked in."

I look up, resting my head on his chest to get a good glance at him. He winks with a cocky grin. Dante runs down the stairs breathing heavily.

"Ok, Daddy found my shoes."

"All right, little man, let's go to the truck." Dante's eyes widen, he looks at Dominic up and down.

"Daddy, you're so strong; you have lots of muscles. I want to be like you, strong and have lots of muscles."

Dominic barks a laugh. A light in my heart lights up.

"Oh yeah? Well, you've got to eat your vegetables and exercise."

Dante scrunches his nose. "Okay, I'll try, but I don't like vegetables." He sighs.

Oh, Lord, they walk back in with bags of toys from Target, like eight, maybe ten bags full.

"Wow! That sure is a lot of toys," I say.

Dominic's smile falters, but he shrugs his shoulder and leans into a whisper, "I haven't been around for him. I want to make up for the lost time. I know I'll never get lost time back. So, I want to start now by giving him everything I can, Mila."

I smile in awe.

"O. M. G.!" Dante screams. "Look, Mommy, Spider-Man." His face lights up like a Christmas tree.

"Give your dad a hug and tell him thank you."

He runs into Dominic's arms, hugging him. "Thank you, Daddy, you're the best dad ever."

Dominic swallows and replies with a choked emotion, "You're welcome, my little man, anything for you. I love you so much, Dante."

"Love you too, Daddy, like this much." He extends his little arms, showing him how much.

Man, I'm a crying mess again. God, and the tattoo on Dominic's forearm is the icing on the cake. It's beautiful. He said he had gotten it a couple of days ago.

The evening passes pretty quickly, and today I feel complete. It eats away at you when you're engulfed in grief for a long time. The pain of losing my father was unimaginable. He was my best friend and my rock. When you lose the love of your life, your soulmate, the pain renders you terminally ill and lifeless. My insides shattered. Dante was my purpose to keep going. Without him, I wouldn't have survived.

Dominic's thumb skims along my cheek. The warmth of his callous touch vibrates a hum throughout my body. We sit on the couch watching Venom with Dante. He was in shock when Dominic confessed to him that he'd never watched Venom before. He gasped with his little mouth. The facial expression had me laughing.

Throughout the night, Dominic's eyes hold mine, hostage, and I can't seem to look away. I'm afraid to look away. What if this is all a dream?

He must feel the same. He traces his thumb along my lips. He softly whispers, "So beautiful."

His touch sends a bolt of electricity, waking me up in a way I'm not sure how to resist this beautiful man. I've missed his touch, the tingling feeling you get in your stomach. When butterflies are ready to erupt. Only Dominic has the power to make me feel this way. Only *him*.

The soft sound of little snores makes me giggle and a relaxed smile tugs on my lips. Dante is sitting between us, sound asleep.

"So much excitement, he didn't even make it through the movie. You really know how to party," I tease with a big grin.

He replies, "He's amazing, Mila. He's perfect. I hate that I missed so much. I'll make it up to you both for the rest of my life. You've done a fantastic job raising him, Angel. I'm so fucking proud of you. I didn't expect him to warm up to me so soon. It feels incredible, Mila, like we didn't just meet today." His hoarse voice cracks with emotion.

He's correct. Dante felt at ease right away, perhaps because of my conversation with him about his father. No matter what, their bond is strong. I sensed it the moment he took him into his arms. I stare into his beautiful whiskey eyes that keep me hostage.

"He loves you, Dominic, he feels safe with you. You showed him love, immediately, without hesitation. Your aura is so strong and positive he felt it. This is how a father should make their child feel, and you did just that. You made him feel loved and special."

He's quiet, then sighs with a breath of relief. His whiskey eyes gaze up at the ceiling for a few silent moments. "Baby, I haven't been this happy in so long. I'm afraid I'll blink, and you will both disappear from my life."

I see the desperation on his face.

"I'll be here as long as you want me, and Dante will always be in your life. You're his father. Let's put our son in his bed. Can you carry him?" I want to take back my words immediately. *You idiot Mila, why would you say you can have me as long as you want me?* I'm not a toy he can play with and then toss.

149

He pulls me to him as I lift off the sofa. "Mila, I want you forever. If it's not you, it's not anyone."

I frown because he had someone else.

He sighs. "Let's put *our* son to bed. Then we can talk."

Seventeen

MILA

Dominic chuckles. "Damn, I'm jealous; this is a kid's dream room."

Dante's room is awesome. I spent a lot of time decorating it. Red comic Spider-Man curtains, a blue car bed, I had printed out Spider-Man pictures on photo paper and hung them up in his room. Spider-Man wallpaper as border trim. Let's not forget the bins of toys he has. Dominic lays him on his bed and tucks him in under the sheets. Dominic smiles with so much love for him, and he kisses him on the forehead.

"Good night, buddy." He glances at the nightstand where Dante has the picture of Dominic and me. Picking it up, he smiles.

"I remember this day like it was yesterday. I won you the teddy bear at the fair. After losing your father, I wanted to make you smile again." His chin dips in remembrance of the day.

When I lost my father, I sank into depression. He never left my sight. He made sure I ate. Helped me shower. I was a zombie, barely living. An orphan. He brought me to life day-by-day. I'll always be grateful. Nana tried to help me the best she could, but she was battling her grief for the loss of her son.

"It was an amazing night. I hadn't left the house for two months. You made me smile again."

Dominic sets the picture back, then grabs my hand. "Come on, let's go downstairs."

He sits on the couch, pulls me onto his lap, and gently tucks a strand of my hair behind my ear. His lips brush tenderly against mine, sending a wave of warmth through me.

"Mila, you're so damn beautiful. You're mine, baby. You've always been mine." His soft lips press against my own, sending sparks through my body as he kisses me passionately. His fingers tangle in my hair, and I grab a fistful of his brown locks in response. The intensity of his desire is palpable, and I feel a wave of heat course through me.

"Goddammit, Mila, I can't get enough of you."

His voice is a seductive drawl to me. He strokes his thumb on my lips. His hooded gaze stays pinned on my lips.

"I can kiss these all day, baby," he murmurs in a husky voice laced with lust. He tugs me tighter onto his chest. So, close I can feel the vibration of his heartbeat. His bulge presses against my thigh.

"Dominic," I reply softly.

"Angel, I need you, and I want you to know. The only reason I dated and proposed to Samantha was because my mom was pressuring and guilting me. She was a Band-Aid. I thought I could forget you. I never had another girlfriend, only you, even after all these years. Dating Samantha never felt real. I never gave her all of me, baby, never." He shakes his head. "I want you to know I've never loved another woman, nor will I ever. I've missed you so much, Mila, you are the love of my life."

He kisses my nose, then my cheek.

"Listen to me," he says, emphasizing each word. "You, Mila," Dominic growls. "It's *always* been fucking *you, baby*."

A tear escapes.

He catches it with the tip of his finger. I have no words. *Nada.*

Running my hands through his hair, his head tilts back, I crash my lips with his. This is all I needed to hear to reassure myself, it was always me. He lifts me off the couch. I wrap my legs around his waist, kissing him, not wanting to part from his lips. We shuffle our way up the stairs.

"Where's your room?" he breathes into my mouth.

I point to it. Shutting the door quietly, he locks it.

"I need you, baby, so damn bad; I want to respect you and take it slow for you."

Fuck slow. I've been without *him* for too long. My body aches for him, with so much damn longing. I shake my head and wrap my arms around his neck.

"I need you to, Dominic, I need to feel this is real... you're here. It's been so long. I've dreamt of this for years."

He blows soft kisses on my collarbone.

"It's real, baby, from the very first day I saw you in the restaurant, you awoke every part of me. I haven't had sex with anyone since you came back into my life, not even Samantha, I couldn't. I knew you were back, and you're all I wanted, all I needed... Have you?"

I'm so heated I can't think straight. I know he's asking if I've slept with Brian. Guilt sours in my belly. *He hasn't slept with anyone*. I had sex with Brian. But fuck, I shouldn't feel guilty he hurt me. He was engaged.

"Dominic, I have. I-It was just umm. We used protection," I fumble with my words and swallow the lump.

Dominic closes his eyes, and hot breath fans my face. He swallows. I know jealousy is brewing inside him when his eyes darken. He lays me on the bed without a word. He crawls into bed next to me and slides his hand along my jawline. I close my eyes and breathe a sigh of relief.

His touch is soft and delicate, almost a promise of things to come. Dominic kisses me softly, but I can taste the urgency just below the surface. His tongue grazes mine, tiny flicks leave me quivering. He tugs my tank top off, tossing it to the floor. His fingertips glide over my skin. He sucks in a sharp breath and locks eyes with me.

"Angel," he gasps. His fingers trace the tattoo just below my breasts. His Adam's apple bobbing.

"When did you get it?" he says, slowly releasing his breath.

Thinking back to the day I walked into the tattoo shop, with shaking hands numbly, I walked in. The wretchedness of my shattered heart needed to feel the blazing of the gun on my skin, the desperation to feel alive. A year and a half after I thought he passed away. I asked Mike to tattoo a single red rose and in place of the stem, Dominic's name. In memory of Dominic, symbolizing my love for him.

I watch as he traces it—kissing the ink on my skin. Closing my eyes, I moan at the touch of his hot lips.

"Mila, when did you get it?" he repeats.

"A couple of months after I had Dante," I reply, biting my lip at the electric shock of his fingertips skimming my skin.

"It's beautiful—fuck, Mila, my name on your beautiful body. I'm honored." He lowers his lips to my stomach, the heat of his soft lips kissing me. He removes my bra and slides my shorts and panties off. His eyes burn into mine with a passionate intensity. He groans.

"Mila, let me worship you tonight; this body needs to be christened by me all over again, every inch, every crease. This beautiful body belongs to me and needs to be reclaimed by me, I need to obliterate the touch of another man touching what's always been mine. Let me show you how much I love you and how much I need you. Let me show you it's always been you."

Oh, God, yes. The sound of his lustful, husky voice sends shivers down my spine. Igniting my core in flames, I know by reclaiming, he means Brian. He wants to fuck him out of me. I know Dominic.

He sucks on one nipple. Then the other.

"I want you to reclaim me as much as I want to reclaim you," I whisper seductively, sucking on his earlobe.

"I'm very possessive over this body," I say, honestly trailing my fingers down his abs and then placing kisses on his neck. Teasing him. I let my fingertips stray up his biceps, then down his chest, before clasping onto either side of his shirt. With a gentle tug, I draw it up, exposing his olive skin to the air and feeling the warmth radiating from him. Trembling, I ease my hands down to the waistband of his jeans and slowly undo each button, one by one, until they slip away.

"I want to feel you are mine. Show me it's mine, Dominic."

He groans. "Baby, I'm all yours. My body is yours; do with it what you want. I want to feel you tonight, baby, bare, no condom. I haven't been without one since you. Is that okay?"

I nod. "I'm on the pill."

God, he's beautiful—so perfect. He hikes on top of me, kissing my neck, his tongue exploring my neck down to my breasts. He slowly kisses down to my thighs, his tongue making its way in between my thighs. He inserts a finger, then another. "I want to taste you. I've never gone down on another woman. I couldn't," he proclaims.

That thought alone sends me into overdrive. *Holy shit.*

I feel pleasure coursing through me as he licks my wet folds. My back arches involuntarily, and I grasp a handful of his hair. I've never let another man do this to me; it was always him. His tongue thrusts deeper, punctuated by the occasional insertion of his finger that intensifies the sensations. I moan and move my legs over his shoulder, urging him closer to me; I want more.

The waves of my orgasm are building up. His mouth is on mine, kissing with urgency, I moan, tasting myself on him. He slides his finger inside, and thrusts in and out, the bulging muscles in his arm straining with the motion. He gently takes my hand as I reach for his boxers, pressing a soft kiss against my knuckles.

"No, baby, it's all about you tonight. Let me take care of you. Angel, I've missed you, your body, your heart, your touch, the way you taste."

With that, I come undone, muffling, my screams as I come on

his fingers. He peels his boxers off as I scan his whole toned body admiring every inch; he's certainly not a teen anymore, he's all man now. Damn, he's perfect. Dominic grabs both of my legs, spreading them, making room as he slides into me.

"Fuck, Mila, you feel so good." His relentless thrusts ram into me repeatedly. "I missed being inside you."

I dig my nails into his back, and bite on his neck as he groans. "Oh God," I moan in pleasure.

I let him worship me, make love to me. With every thrust, every kiss, every appraising whisper in my ear telling me how beautiful I am and how much I mean to him. Reminding me, I'm his, as he is mine ruining me all over.

"Mine," he whispers in my ear. "Mine all mine, baby."

I've missed the weight of him. The only man who makes me feel whole. Capable of making me orgasm until I go boneless in his arms. The man who ruined me from the very beginning, who took my soul and never returned it, is back in my life.

SNUGGLING INTO THE SHEETS, I haven't slept so good in so long I moan it to my pillow. After years of nightmares, tonight was the first night I woke up without one. When I first started getting nightmares, Dominic would sneak in through the window of Nana's house. He would lie in bed with me and sneak back out early in the morning. Up until, they had diagnosed him with cancer, and as it progressed, I would sneak into his window.

My body aches like a damn lawnmower ran me over—a very sexy lawnmower. I shift my body toward a hard muscular body, sprawled wrapped in a silk sheet. He's sound asleep. I take the time to ogle him. God, he's sexy as hell. His long eyelashes flutter in his sleep. Running my fingers up and down his hard-as-stone abs, tracing the tattoo on his chest, he groans as I press kisses on his chest. I yelp as muscular arms wrap around me, lifting me to his chest.

"Good morning, Angel."

His alluring, raspy morning voice sends a rush of heat through my naked body, which is pressed against his very naked body. "Good morning," I say breathlessly.

"Mmm, I could wake up to this every morning," he says, in a sexy raspy voice. He presses his lips on mine, we kiss wantonly. His breath mingles with mine. "Should I go before Dante wakes up?" His searing gaze cascades into mine.

"As much as I want you to stay, it's too soon for him to see you wake up here."

He licks his lips as he pecks kisses all over my face. "How about I go home, change, I'll grab some coffee and doughnuts, and come back. We can go do something, anything you two want."

A beaming smile shines across my face. "That sounds perfect."

He stands his naked ass up to get dressed.

"Oh, there's something I need to tell you."

"What is it, baby?"

"Your mom dropped by."

He growls. "When?" He slips his shirt on and frowns.

"A couple of hours before you came over."

Shit, he's pissed.

"What the fuck did she say? She didn't mess with you. Did she?"

"She was pissed and wants me to stay away from you. Said I'm a nuisance."

His jaw twitches. "Baby, you are everything to me. You're my world. Don't let her push you away." He slips his pants on. He raises an eyebrow scrutinizing me. "Baby, don't listen to her. I'll take care of it."

I nod, blowing out a stream of air.

"I'll be back, baby. I'll tell her not to come here again." He kisses my cheek and heads out while I lay in bed memorizing last night. The way he worshiped my body—hours of lovemaking.

"Mommy," Dante calls out.

Oh, shit, I'm still naked.

"Hold on, baby, be right there." I throw on some shorts and a shirt. I open the door to find my little guy standing there with his hair ruffled up and groggy.

"Where's Daddy? Did he leave?"

"He went to his house, but he will be back in a bit, okay?"

He sighs dramatically. "Okay, I want him to live with us like Josh's parents they live together. Are you going to get married?"

Oh jeez. I wasn't expecting that question to pop up this soon. I scratch my head thinking how to answer him.

"Baby no, not right now. Daddy has his house, and he can come to visit anytime, okay? We can visit him as well. As for marriage, that's not happening right now. Maybe later, okay? Let's not worry about it. How about you brush your teeth, let's get you ready for the day?"

"Okay, Mommy."

Eighteen
DOMINIC

A cool draft of air brushes past me causing a chill in the air. October has always been my favorite month; leaves falling and pumpkin spice. I've been a sucker for anything pumpkin spice since Mila introduced me to it six years ago. Mainly because it always reminded me of her. I've never been the sentimental type, but Mila brought me to my knees. From the first day I glanced at her, I was a goner. Her beautiful emerald eyes can cast a spell on you. Last night was fucking amazing, I bite my lip, just thinking about it. Savoring her taste, reclaiming her. Her beautiful body is spread out for me to glorify. The way her body responded to mine, molded herself onto mine, the longing in her eyes.

She's everything I dreamt of and more. The tattoo rose with my name was enough to have me come right on her breasts. These past years, the only thing that gives me consolation is my name was imprinted on her body. My name on her skin is like a staked claim to ward off any of those men in her past– touching what was mine. When they viewed and tasted what is etched on her beautiful cream skin. Especially that fucking shithead Brian. I fucked her so hard she whimpered in pleasure.

"Get out of the way, asshole."

Aww, fuck. I hadn't realized I'm blocking the entrance to Lee's Bakery.

"Fuck you, shithead," I yell at the dude on the bike. I walk in.

Mrs. Lee greets me, "Nice to see you, Mr. Delgado, on this fine Saturday morning. What can I get you?"

"Hello, Mrs. Lee. I'll have a dozen doughnuts, two pumpkin spices, and a chocolate milk."

She nods. "I will prepare the order."

I wait patiently as she busies herself behind the counter.

"Here you go, Dominic, have a good day."

"You too, Mrs. Lee."

Just as I walk out, I spot my mom a couple of blocks down the street. She's talking to someone in a red pickup truck. The person hands her an envelope. Not sure if it's a man or a woman I can't see as they're sitting in the driver's seat. They drive off. She shoves the envelope into her purse. It aggravates me she went to Mila's. Why in the hell does she have to make it her business?

"Mom," I shout.

She whips her head up. "Dominic, what are you doing?" She traipses toward me.

"Came to get doughnuts and drinks. What are you doing? Who was that you were talking to?"

"Just a client. They asked if I could take these papers into the office for them." She smiles. Reaching for a coffee.

"This is for Mila. I can buy you one if you'd like, and by the way, what business do you have, Mom, stepping foot at my girl's place."

She huffs, crossing her arms. "Dominic, when in the hell are you going to wake up from this? She's not good enough for you."

I interject. I'm tired of this shit. She always talks down about Mila. To arm's length, she's kept me away from her. "Mom, I will not tell you again. Mila is more than enough for me. I don't want to hear you talk down about her. I'm the one who is not good enough."

"You're a fool. That boy is not yours," she hisses.

My heart aches for how she treats them, and only if she would give in.

"He's my son, Mom!" I shout. Some onlookers peer at us.

"What about Samantha? How dare you leave her. Her father is disappointed."

I roll my eyes. You can never win an argument with her. Sometimes I wonder if she drove my dad away.

"I gotta go." I don't spare a glance at her. I know she's pissed. It's all about control with her.

I'M A BALL OF NERVES, standing in front of Mila's door like a teen knocking on his date's door for the first time. She drives me mad, only she has the power to make me feel. Five, long, mislaid years without her.

"Hey, so are you planning on coming in, or are you just going to stand there because I would love a doughnut, and oh, is this pumpkin spice I smell? Mmm."

Fucking hell, she stands there staring at me, leaning on the door, wearing short shorts and a low-cut shirt showing her belly button. I drink her in, scanning her body with pure adoration. My eyes trailed up and down, biting my lip. All I can think about is slamming her against the wall and having my way with her. I let out a loud groan that sounds like a damn bear wanting to mate. She gives me a bright smile. That little devil knows what she's doing to me.

"Later tonight, grizzly bear," she whispers. "Now get your ass inside."

A smile tugs at the corner of my mouth. God, I love her so damn much. "Is Dante still asleep?"

"No, he's in his room playing with the spider shooter thing you got him." She takes a sip of her coffee. "He was looking for you this morning."

She grabs the box of doughnuts from my hand. The idea of

my son asking for me makes me want to burst. I *want* this. I *want* a family. I *want* to come home to her and Dante every night. Fuck. *I want to marry her.* Why waste any more time? I know it's too soon. She barely trusts me.

"What did you tell him?" I ask.

"I told him you went home and would be back later." She shrugs. "He asks if we are going to live together."

She pauses for a second, and I wait for her to tell me how she responded.

"I told him not right now, not anytime soon. And we don't know how things will end up with us yet."

I feel a stab in the chest. She has major trust issues; I get it. She lost her mom and dad at a young age. Everyone she's loved has disappeared from her life, including her friends. I hurt her painfully. Her fear is of me walking out on her. Her feelings are relentless. I'll do anything to reassure her that I'm not leaving her. I know I screwed up these past months with her, taunting her, adding gasoline to the fire. My betrayal, belittling her all these years. I walk up to her, keeping my gaze on her, cupping her cheek. I brush my lips against hers, and our breath mingles.

"Listen to me, baby, you are my forever. I need you like I need air. There will *never be no* us. You got it? You're my world. The woman I'm madly in love with. I will do anything you need me to for you to trust me, but all I ask is don't push me away. I want it all with you, a future, marriage, more kids, a shit load of them. I will repeat it as much as you need to hear it until it sticks in your stubborn head." I kiss the tears from her beautiful face.

"Dominic," she croaks.

My heart is breaking with each tear she sheds. "Hmm," I say while kissing her neck.

"I love you too."

"I know," I say in between kisses.

"Ugh, you're such a cocky bastard."

I gently squeeze her plump ass, which I admire. Then chuckling, I slap her ass and head upstairs with Dante.

Standing in the doorway, I watch Dante with amazement as he lines up his army guys. Being a father is the most precious gift. I will be nothing like my own father. Part of me will never understand how he walked away from his kids. I've always wondered why he left. Mom never mentioned to us his reasons.

The one thing that terrifies me is cancer, cancer-consuming me once again. However, I get checked yearly and have been in the clear. With Dante and Mila back in my life, I ask God to grant me more time; years if possible. I sneak behind him, squatting next to him. He feels my presence and turns to look at me. He greets me with a perfect, boyish smile, his dimples visible. My heart radiates with love. He cocks his head to the side. Hell, how did I get so lucky?

"Daddy!" He leaps into my arms, causing us to both fall to the ground.

I tickle him all over, he lets out a squeal, panting.

"Daddy, no stop." He laughs so hard that his stomach shakes.

We both roared with laughter. I peer into my boy's eyes, which resemble so much of me. My little mini-me. I gently kiss him on the forehead. Jesus, he's perfect.

"I got doughnuts and chocolate milk for you."

He licks his lips, then shoves a hot wheel's car in his pocket. I laugh.

"Yum, come on, Daddy, let's go down the stairs." Dante reaches for my hand.

I take his small hand in mine and swallow the clogged knot forming with emotion. We make our way downstairs.

"Daddy, I think Mom's happy now. She cried for you."

Damn, my chest hurts—the pain I have caused them. "I'll make her happy, Dante, I promise."

He smiles all dopey and nods.

Mila stands leaning against the kitchen counter, talking to Sophie, who must have just walked in. I suck in a breath and take a moment to admire her. She's strong, confident, intelligent, and beautiful. The way she holds herself up, has me beaming with pride. The world has not been fair to her. I will do everything in my power to give her happiness and show her the world.

She turns when she hears us, her emerald eyes are locked with mine. With a raised eyebrow, she looks over at her friend. By her glowered stare, she can't stand me. The last time I met her, I was getting engagement photos and making shitty remarks to Mila.

"Sophie, you remember Dominic?" Mila bores her green eyes into her friend. As if they can telepath with each other. Without looking away.

"Of course, I remember him. Last time was at the studio when he was getting his glamour shots done with his ho," she bellows and narrows her glare at me. She slowly turns to look at me with a look that could set me on fire, and I know she'd spit on my ashes. I don't know much about Mila's life in the last five years. Sophie seems protective of her, and I'm glad. Mila needs someone in her corner.

I open the box of doughnuts, handing one to Dante. I look to Sophie. "I apologize for how I acted and how I treated Mila. It was uncalled for. I let my anger get the best of me. I should have been man enough to confront her respectably, to get the answers we both needed. My mother manipulated me into believing Mila was the bad guy in our story."

Sophie's lips form a straight line.

"I'm to blame for believing what my mom accused her of or rather lied. I should have known better. I love Mila and Dante."

She studies me, then looks over to Dante, still holding my hand, munching on his doughnut. He's in a doughnut coma, not paying us any attention. Sophie's royal blue eyes pierce right back to me.

"I met Mila at the university we attended; she was three months pregnant. My heart sank; she looked heartbroken, lost, with dark circles around her eyes. She didn't have the pregnancy glow."

I swallow the bile from regurgitating. I let go of Dante's hand

and shove my hands in my pockets, trying to keep myself in one piece.

Sophie continues, "She went through hell these past five years trying to move on, letting the ghost of her past go, and when she just started to move on, you pop up. You should've been fucking man enough to defend her from your mother. I love her and Dante. God help me, if you screw up, I will hunt you down and stab you in the eye." She whispers the last part. Her palms press on the counter—giving me the stink eye.

"Sophie, I won't, you have my word. You're an amazing friend from what I can see. I'm grateful you have been there for them."

With a nod, she takes a sip of her smoothie.

Mila laughs nervously with a mouth full of a Boston cream doughnut. She mumbles sarcastically, "You guys are going to be great friends."

I glance at Mila, she's worried the two people she cares about and loves are going to be at each other's throats. Sophie has the don't fuck with me vibe. I'm positive the New Yorker would stab me in the eye. Mila's my everything. I will prove it to her and Sophie. I shift myself to look Sophie in the eye, letting her know I'm game.

"I'm guessing, I won't be your favorite person for a while, Sophie. I'm willing to prove to you they mean the world to me. I'm grateful they have had you in their life."

With a sip of her drink, she gives me the stink eye again. I get it. Don't fuck with her.

"I hope you prove it to me. I need to see my best friend happy. She's the closest I have to a sister." She turns to Dante, kissing him and makes her way upstairs.

I cup Mila's face, leaning in to lick the cream from her lips. I can't get enough of her.

"Don't look at me like that," she softly whispers.

"Like how?"

"Like you want to eat me alive."

"I do." I trace her lips with my tongue. "There's a lot I want to do with you, baby," I say, earnestly.

"I'm sorry about Sophie, she's overprotective of us she's always been there for me. She means well. She doesn't hate you."

My lips brush her soft lips. "Don't be sorry, I'd rather her care than not."

Dante sneaks up next to us. "Mommy, can we go to the zoo today?"

She tilts her head. "What are you doing today?"

"Anything you two want to do."

Nineteen

MILA

After a couple of hours at the San Diego Zoo, a downpour of rain erupted from the dark clouds. We packed up and left; we had forgotten our umbrellas. On our way back, we stopped at the market to pick up some ingredients to make Caldo de Pollo, *chicken soup*. Nana always said soup warms the soul on a cold rainy day, which is why she always made soup on rainy days. I try to keep some of her traditions alive. I know my dad would love for me to learn all of Nana's recipes. We had a fantastic time. It's the happiest I've been in so long. It feels too good to be true.

"Mom, can I have a baby brother?"

I nearly chop my finger off while prepping the vegetables. Where in the hell did that come from? Setting the knife down, I stoop down to his level and cup his cheeks. Glancing at Dominic, a smile jots across his lips with amusement.

"Baby, that can't happen right now, but how about we get a pet for now?"

He huffs dramatically. "Okay, Mommy, can I get a spider monkey like me, and he can swing on trees and buildings like Spider-Man." He beams with so much excitement.

Dominic snorts a laugh. Dante stares and turns to glance at Dominic with a bright smile that can make you melt. Dominic blinks a couple of times, ready to run for the hills, unsure how to answer his question.

"Can we get a monkey, Daddy?"

Dominic chews on his bottom lip and looks up at me, smiling. "I need to use the restroom... be right back."

What a chicken shit. Dante has been on cloud nine since Dominic drifted back into our lives. He's been attached to him at the hip. It makes every nightmare, heartbreak, and tear I've shed worth it to have my son smiling and happy to have his father back in his life. If I had to do it all over to get this outcome, I'd do it for Dante.

"Dante, a monkey would be too much work to take care of. How about we start with something simple? Humm... How about a kitten?" I suggest.

He wrinkles his nose, thinking. "I'll think about it." With that he heads to the living room to play with his toys.

Dominic walks back from the bathroom. I've been noticing he keeps checking his phone. I wonder who's texting him—is it another woman, maybe Samantha? The heaviness in my chest sinks in. His hot breath fans my neck, wrapping his solid bulky arms around my waist.

"Is it almost done?" he breathes out.

I can smell the mint on his breath. Sending goosebumps from head to toe. I turn to meet his eyes. "Twenty minutes," I say, with a bite to it.

He frowns, putting his palms on the counter. "What's wrong, Angel?"

I blurt out, not meaning to show any signs of jealousy or insecurity, "Why do you keep checking your phone? You have been doing it all day. I don't want you to feel forced to be here." I avert my eyes to my toes, not wanting him to see how bothered I am.

He lifts my chin, my gaze cuts to his. His lips brush over mine. "Sweetheart, there's nowhere else I'd rather be than with you two." He kisses my mouth, then my cheek, he sighs. "It's my mom, she keeps texting and calling. It's unimportant; she's just pissed. I'm not going over for dinner."

"Oh, it's okay, you can go."

He kisses my mouth to silence me. "I don't want to go. Also, I made it clear to her that I couldn't be around her if she didn't accept you and Dante. After what she did to our relationship, I'm pissed at her." He shrugs. "Remember I told you I wouldn't let her come between us? I won't, Angel, it's you and me forever."

Forever.

Hearing his words reassures me, but I'm still uncertain. After all, this is all new, it's been five years of separation. His mom's words linger in my mind.

He'll leave you. She will always try to come between us. What kind of life and future will we have with those dynamics in our lives?

"Stop thinking," he says as he presses his lips on mine.

We kiss until someone clears their throat.

"Do you guys mind? I'm hungry. The smell of food woke me up."

I glance at my New Yorker, who is staring at us disgustedly. "Uh-huh." My eyes go back to Dominic, and I grab a fist full of his hair, get on my tippy toes, and kiss him hard. I turn to the cabinet to get bowls without sparing him a glance.

"Fuck, that was hot," he breathes out.

"OMG, you guys get a room."

We both exchanged a chuckle.

Since Dominic returned to our lives a week ago, everything has been just wonderful. Twice this week, he left before Dante usually wakes up at the crack of dawn. I believed it would be preferable to go slowly with Dante throughout the period. We have been making up for lost time. We discussed what had occurred after his recovery and remission. I inquired whether he has been receiving checkups. I can't lose him, and I'm scared to death that the cancer will come back. He said once a year.

"I'm good, baby, I'm in the clear. I eat healthy and exercise, I do have cheat meals." He gave the most adorable smile.

The door to the studio chimes open. My eyes dart to a tall, handsome, muscular man in a police uniform. I haven't seen Liam in so long, not since high school. He was always sweet and made all the girls swoon and stare after him with desire. He's never been the relationship type of guy, from what Dominic has told me.

"Liam, it's been so long."

A smile ruffles his lips. "Hey, beautiful, Dominic told me where to find you. I wanted to stop by to see you. You look amazing, hot, and beautiful, just like Dominic described you."

I chuckle and blush. "Whoa, I feel like I need to fan myself, Liam."

He wraps his arms around me for a tight hug. I love Liam. He's a fantastic friend. We always joked around. Being one of Dominic's best friends, he always treated me like a best friend too.

"You have a son; it's amazing, Mila; I'm so fucking sorry for all you went through these past years. I wish... you would have called me." He sighs. There's a deflation on his shoulder with sadness. "I missed you so much, Mila, when you left. I won't lie. I was angry. I thought you left him." I see the sorrow in his eyes.

"I did go looking for you, Liam. I asked around since we didn't go to the same school; it was hard getting a hold of you. I bumped into Skylar the day I was leaving for Manhattan. I asked her for your number; she said she didn't have it. I also informed her I was moving to Manhattan. I never told her why—"

He cuts me off. His eyes bulge out the size of a golf ball. "Wait a minute, she knew where you were this whole time?" he asks. Okay, he's acting strange about this.

"Yes, she would call me and ask how I was doing."

His expression is confused and angry. He rubs the stubble on his chin. I'm about to ask him what he means by this and why it makes him disoriented and angry when Sophie walks in.

"Hey, Chica, I'm going to grab food from one of the food trucks out there; want something?" she says, walking toward me. She does a double take on Liam.

I know my best friend, and she's drooling at him with hungry eyes. I've never seen her look at Ryder this way or any man. She takes a long breath as if she was holding it too long. She glances at me clearing her throat.

"You want something?" she repeats.

I look over at Liam; he's taking a long brush over her body, staring with a cocky grin. That asshole knows he's hot, especially with his uniform on. "Liam, my best friend Sophie," I introduce the two, who keep eye fucking each other. "Sophie, this is Liam, Dominic's best friend."

"Hey," she squeals.

This is strange she has never acted this way with a guy. She's never shy, always upfront. The way he's ogling her, you'd think he'd never seen a woman like Sophie before. She is one of a kind and absolutely beautiful.

"I'll have some teriyaki chicken," I answer, as her blue eyes brush his profile.

"Ugh, okay, nice to meet you, Liam." She walks out, glancing back to take another quick look at him.

Liam is in a drunken daze. This was interesting. Maybe I should play matchmaker. I glance back at Liam. "So, what was it you were saying?"

He shakes off the haze he was in. "Oh yeah..." Just then, a call comes in through his radio. "Shit, I have to go. It was nice seeing you again. Glade to have back." He envelops me in a hug, just before he walks out saying something on his radio.

THE PLACE IS BUZZING with people. The music is blasting, and people are laughing. I drum my fingers on the table nervously.

"Baby, relax," Dominic whispers in my ear.

We are at his restaurant tonight having dinner, waiting for his brothers to get here. They asked if they could meet Dante. My headache throbs as if a hostile squatter occupies it. A tightness in my chest burns with the thought of seeing Dominic's brothers. I was wounded by how easily they ignored me when I tried to reach out to them five years ago. If they had only listened to me then, things could've been different. I know I shouldn't dwell on it.

"Hey, brother."

I look to see Santiago and Mark—a beautiful blond, slender girl attached to Mark's arm. Dominic stands up to hug his brothers. I stand next to Dominic to greet his brothers. Dominic rubs my back, comforting me. Santiago scans me up and down. It only makes me more nervous.

"Hot. Damn, Mila, you turned into a bombshell."

Dominic grinds his teeth. "Watch it, brother."

Santiago grins.

Yup, he still knows how to irk his brother.

"Still so possessive over her." Santiago was always a womanizer. He never did relationships. I wonder if he's still the same.

"Hey, Santiago."

He envelops me a hug, so does Mark. He introduces me to his girlfriend, April. Mark was always sweet and quiet, the complete opposite of his brothers. He was in his early teens when I met him. He's grown into a beautiful man.

Dante is beyond ecstatic to meet his uncles. Dominic swells with pride as he reaches for Dante lifting him into his arms.

"I want you to meet my brothers, your uncles."

Dante frowns. "You have brothers?"

"Yeah, this is Santiago, and Mark."

Dante has a huge grin. It warms my heart to see Dante so happy with family. This is all I've ever wanted for my son. To have a family.

"He looks just like you." Mark smiles at Dante.

Both brothers gaze at me with remorse.

Santiago is the first to speak. "I'm so sorry, Mila. I just... I didn't know. I should've answered you. You called many times; we should have picked up." He exhales with regret. "We see it now. If you hadn't cared, you wouldn't have called us continuously. It's just our mom... I-I don't know what her problem is with you. We should have heard you out first. Fuck, Mila, we should've told Dominic about you calling." He looks at Dante, then at me. He puffs out a breath. "We all missed out on his life."

My heart is beating so fast; their words mean so much to me. I feel the immediate love they have for Dante. Nodding, I let a tear slide down my cheek. Dominic wipes it with a kiss. Thankfully, the food arrives at our table. Unfortunately, I'm too choked up.

Twenty

MILA

We made our way back to my home. Now Dominic is tucking Dante into bed and reading him a bedtime story. As I walk to my dresser to collect my pjs, Dominic's phone keeps buzzing. The nosy and curious side of me wants to know who it is. It's buzzed like five times, maybe more. Would it be wrong if I snooped? *No, right?* Since we are a couple. Chewing on my nails, I cast a gaze at his phone sitting on the nightstand. *Fuck it.* I pick up the phone to find messages from Samantha. My heart is drumming against my ribs. I hold my breath, reading through them.

Samantha: *Hey baby, call me. I miss you. We can work this out.*

Samantha: *I love you, Dominic, so much, I know you still love me.*

Samantha: *Dominic, I know you feel something for me. Remember the other night? You undressed me, ripping my clothes off, baby. You were fingering me until I came undone. You kissed me with so much eagerness. I know you love me. I felt it in our kiss.*

Does he still love her? Did he tell her? They were together for a year. What the fuck? He ripped her clothes off. This must have been recent. Fucking asshole, he goes all alpha, pulling Brian off of me when he's out doing shit with his fiancée. Those two are old

174

messages he never responded to. The new messages have me wondering.

Samantha: *Baby, I miss you so much. Come back to me. I know this is some old fling you have going on. She was just a high school girl. You might think you have it for her. It will fade. You need closure. You proposed to me because you love me.*

Samantha: *We can still get married. I haven't canceled our arrangements. I know you will come back to me. She has nothing to offer you.*

Samantha: *I'm not giving up on us. You'll realize I'm the one for you. I'm it for you, baby.*

My stomach churns; according to the texts, he was just with her. He had sex with her. He lied. Is this what this is a fling, an itch he needs to scratch? I repeatedly blink at the text.

"He's sound as sleep, Angel."

I hadn't noticed Dominic walking in.

He frowns "What's wrong?" I hand him his phone. He slides his fingers through his soft silky hair, he reads the messages.

"Oh, baby, this woman is full of shit. She knows nothing about us or me. I'm sorry, I will delete her number and block her." He sits next to me on the bed and lifts me onto his lap.

I'm struggling to get out of his hold, he holds on to me tightly.

"Baby, please stop," he murmurs.

"Let me go, Dominic," I growl. I'm so fired up.

He possessively holds me in place.

"What the fuck was the text, Dominic? You ripped her clothes off just weeks ago and fucked her," I shout.

"I didn't fuck her, Mila, and it wasn't what you think. And it happened before we got together."

The electricity between us thunders a storm brewing.

"Oh no, then what is it? Didn't you slip your finger in her? What else did you have her do? Suck you off?"

He winces as his gaze darts to the ground. Oh, so he did, then he came asking me for a chance. I might have slept with Brian, but

175

Dominic was engaged for a year and betrayed me. I was starting a new life, trying to move on because he betrayed us.

"Mila, please listen to me. The day at your studio, you had told me you wanted to be with that guy Ken."

"Brian," I mumble.

He sighs. "Samantha called. I went over it in my head. I thought if I tried with her, maybe I could feel something for her since you said we were over. The whole time I was kissing her, I kept thinking of you. Yes, I slipped my finger into her, but it felt wrong, Mila. When she tried to suck me off, I pushed her away; she wasn't you, Mila. That's when I told her I couldn't be with her. I wanted to fight for you, for *us*, Mila; I promise it meant nothing." His hooded eyes gaze into mine. He presses a kiss softly on my lips.

I don't open for him. I turn my head.

"Don't even think about it. I can see it in your face, Angel, only you, baby, always been you. I fucked up listening to my mom. I'm sorry, baby; I'm so fucking sorry, but fuck, Mila, you fucked that shithead. How do you think it makes me feel, huh?"

Oh, hell no. He didn't just say what I think he said. His chest deflates as his shoulders slump. The rapid palpitation of his heart vibrates through me.

"Mila," he whispers softly, but I shake my head, trying to maneuver myself from his hold.

"You keep blaming it on your mom, Dominic. Yes, she manipulated you, but how far are these excuses going to go? You're a grown man; you dated her and proposed to her. Your reason is, oh, I just didn't care because I was dead inside. Seriously, Dominic, was it so you could have someone to fuck when needed? Because I was dead inside, I didn't search for a man just because I needed a side piece. I'd rather be alone than with a man I'm not in love with, much-less propose to or be married to. What would've happened if I'd come back and you were married to her, huh?"

I lick my dry lips, anger burning deep inside me. I expel a puff of steam full of air. He stands, and a deep furrow lines his forehead. His gaze trails a visual sweep across my face. He takes a step closer to me, but I shake my head at him.

"How dare you point the finger at me for being with Brian. You were engaged. You made it clear you moved on when you kissed her in front of me, so yeah, I did fuck him. He was my boyfriend. You pulled him out of his car when he was on me, when you were doing the same with her. I was with Brian, trying to move on from the truth you spilled from your venomous lips. I had sex with him when I found out you were with another woman... *engaged*." I'm breathing so heavily my chest tightens. Without thinking, I take a step back. Maybe it's the jealousy, hurt, his betrayal, and lack of belief in our love swimming in my scabbed soul. His brows perched low. A fire fizzles in his eyes.

"You're right, baby. I'm a coward. I allowed my mom to manipulate me; I should have stood up for you, for us. I regret dating her and proposing to her, Angel, I never loved her—"

I interject. I feel my walls coming back up. "I don't know if I can do this anymore, Dominic. You should go back to her. Our past, the years apart, has destroyed us, Dominic. What kind of life can we have if your mom will always rip us apart?" Sobs escape. "She despises her grandson. I-I can't give my son this life. You chose your mom's lies over our love. H-h-how do I know you won't do this again?" Tears skate down my cheeks.

He takes a step forward I take a step back.

"It's best if you leave, Dominic. You loved her. I saw how you looked at her. It's best you marry her. It will be better this way. Your mom will approve. I can't let you choose me over your mom again. She will always come between us. At some point, you will choose her. Our past is too painful. I'll move back to Manhattan."

He fists his hands at his side. His whiskey browns pained with fear. I look away. "Baby, don't you fucking push away, goddamn it. I just got you back. Look at me, baby!" he shouts, pleading.

I can't look at him. The pain is blistering inside me. He needs to leave, this hurts too much.

J. MORALES

"Angel, please," he says in a raspy voice, searching my face with his whiskey brown eyes. He gently takes my face in his hands. "I fucking love you. What you saw at the restaurant was me acting the whole time. I never cuddled on the couch with her, I never held her in my arms. I never made love to her. I never looked at her like I look at you, Angel. I never told any other woman I loved them, only you," he croaks, his Adam's apple bobs. "Guilt eats at me for treating Samantha poorly. I despised her because she wasn't you. The fucking rock on her hand wasn't your hand. What I hate the most is myself for allowing all this. For not..." he exhales a long breath. "For not believing in our love and belittling you for betraying you. Damnit, Mila, not once did I stop loving you." He kisses the salty tears rolling down my face.

"Dominic, we won't work," I say, my voice strangled in my throat.

"S-stop, baby. We fucking will, I made a promise to you. I will not let my mom come between us. You and Dante come first. I will never allow her to degrade you or Dante. Never, do you hear me? Fucking never. *You're my world.*" He seizes me by the neck, gently slamming his mouth on mine. His tongue battles for entrance. His erection presses against my belly.

"Fucking kiss, me, goddamn it," he growls.

I stare into his hooded profile for mere seconds. Replaying every word, he spoke. His lips and tongue keep brushing my lips, fighting for entrance.

"I'm yours *now*, and forever, even in our next life, Mila. Don't fucking push me away, baby. I-I can't live without you." His voice is so raspy. He closes his eyes, shielding the vulnerability in his gaze. His hands still wrapped around my neck—the pain in his eyes sears.

My walls are halfway up, contemplating if we will work. How a future with him will hold with his toxic mother. This is not the life I want for my son or myself involved in. But, I love him; I love him more than anything.

His mouth slams back onto mine, fighting for entrance. His

178

engorged erection presses on my core. He bites my lip when I gasp. He takes advantage of that, slipping his tongue in. He thrust his tongue fucking my mouth. Giving in, I bite his lip. He runs his finger along the soft fabric of my jeans and lacy underwear, softly caressing my inner thighs, sending shockwaves throughout my body with each gentle stroke. His lips are so full and delicious, it feels like he is stealing my soul with each kiss. His touch grows bolder and more urgent as his finger begins to thrust in and out of me, leaving me breathless. I let out a moan of pleasure before retreating from his hot mouth, both of us now panting heavily. He licks his lips.

"Now let me show my queen how much she's made for me." His forehead presses on mine. "Are you made for me, baby?"

All I can manage is a nod, yes. I'm hypnotized by his eyes, the lust swimming in them. His soft lips caress my neck with sloppy kisses.

"Words, baby, are you made for me, Mila?"

"Yes," I breathe out lustfully.

"I love you so fucking much, Mila. I'm sorry, baby. I'll spend the rest of our lives making it up to you," he pleads, which makes my heart crack.

"I love you too." I kiss the tip of his nose. "I'm sorry."

"No, baby, don't apologize. It's me that has to apologize. I hurt you. I deserve it. Let me show you." A soft breath leaves his lips.

He peels my shirt off, unclasps my bra, and runs his index finger over my nipples.

"Mmm, all mine, so perfect for me." He lifts me with so much force I squeal. "Wrap your legs around my waist, baby."

I do as he says. He sucks on my breast I throw my head back, griping a fist full of his hair, holding on. Dominic walks us to the shower, still latching on to my breast as he walks. I moan his name. He unbuttons my jeans sliding them down along with my panties, his gaze ignites me and I burst into flames as he scrutinizes me fully naked.

"You're so beautiful, Mila, you turned into such a gorgeous woman. You've always been beautiful."

My heart swells. "Thank you," I say breathlessly. My hands brush along the ridges of his firm chest as the shirt slips off of him. With a shaky hand, I unzip his jeans as he slides them off. Dominic's beautiful body is sculpted to perfection. He turns the faucet on, droplets of lukewarm water trail down my body. Dominic's heat and his large erection pressing on me, submerge me in a wave of euphoria. He reaches for the bar of soap, washing my back and shoulders. He squeezes a generous amount of lavender shampoo onto his palm, he gently massages the locks of my raven-black hair, moving up as his fingertips stroke my scalp deliciously. I moan.

"Baby, stop it. I want to take care of you. It's all about you, Angel. I want to pamper you and show you what you mean to me. I don't want to lose control. Fuck. I'm trying so hard to keep it together. You drive me crazy."

I smirk with a twist on my wet lips. Turning to face him, I crash my lips on his. It's exhilarating how Dominic wants to take it slow, showing his love for me without sex. I love it. Right now, I don't need slow. I need him, to feel the rhythm of his heartbeat the melody his body sings to me as he makes love to me. I need to feel him inside me. The way our bodies mold into one another. The way his eyes stare into mine as he fucks me raw and ends the night making love to me.

"I don't want gently tonight, baby. I want to lose myself with you, I need rough. Fuck me, Dom. Take my breath away, love me recklessly. Show me who you belong to."

"Fucking hell, Angel, thank the fuck, yes. I fucking belong to you, baby. You belong to me." He lifts me, pushing me against the wall. "Legs on my shoulders," he orders.

I do as he says. His hands squeeze my ass hard, kissing his way up my thighs down to the center, swirling his tongue. *Holy Hotness.*

"You taste like heaven," he mouths in between my legs as his tongue laps over my folds.

I have to hold on to his wet silk hair, as he sucks so hard, my body trembles. *Feels so good.* I cover my mouth to suppress my cries. His gaze is hungry as he continues thrusting his tongue violently. His long dark eyelashes flutter droplets of water and flicker as he licks the juices from his lip.

"Baby, keep quiet; you're going to wake our son." He continues feasting, lapping up water droplets with his tongue.

No man can ever compare to him. The liquid heat of his love courses through my veins. I bite my lip hard, tasting blood as I orgasm. His grip holds me down, steadying me as my legs wobble.

"Baby, turn around," his husky voice rumbles.

I place my palms on the wet tiles. He takes me from behind slowly as he picks up speed.

"Shit, baby, you feel so good."

The heat from his body mixes with my own as the passion between us reaches its peak. His deep, primal groan echoes in my ears as his hips thrust against mine. His strong hands grab my breasts and massage them with a mix of gentle and vigorous intensity. My entire body trembles as I feel his hard cock throbbing inside me.

"Oh, God, Dominic."

He grunts as he thrusts deeper, harder. "That's it, baby."

I'm coming so hard. My body shakes. He hands me a towel, after shutting off the faucet, while keeping his beautiful eyes glued to me and gazing into my soul with his magnificent eyes.

"We're not close to being done, Angel. You wanted rough and hard, and that's what we're doing all night." He lets out a possessive growl. With a fist full of my hair wrapped around his hand, he kisses me, devouring my mouth and sucking the air out of me.

It's a little after midnight. There's no way I can manage sex all night, after round two, I tap out.

"Can't handle the beast, huh? I'm a machine, baby," he scoffs with arrogance.

"When I said rough and hard, I didn't say break me in half and maul me like an animal," I tease.

A frown cuts across his handsome face, he shifts his body, facing me. "Did I hurt you? Was it not good?"

He's so cute. He always wants to please me. I rub my hands on the stubble of his cheeks, loving the sensation. I tilt to drop soft kisses on his lips.

"It was perfect, amazing. Always is. I didn't just see stars, baby, you gave me the universe. That's how good it was."

He raises an eyebrow showing his signature cocky smirk. "Damn, that's good huh, just call me your sex machine."

I snort a laugh.

Dominic flips me on top of him, kissing me slowly with a steady rhythm, grinding my hips. He moans. "God, baby, I can never get enough of you." He lifts me slightly and inserts himself inside me.

I guess we're going for round three. As he arches his back, I rock my hips. We ride the waves of pleasure.

"You're my universe," I whisper in his ear, right as we both doze off.

Twenty-One
DOMINIC

Four weeks have passed; it's been perfect, except for our argument. About fucking Samantha's texts. Guilt eats at me for stringing Samantha along. I was attracted to her beauty, yet she was always a distraction. I was never in love with her. Mila is the most beautiful woman; no one compares to her. The pain in Mila's eyes fucking hurt; it shattered me. She's fucking terrified of me breaking her, betraying her.

The fact she doesn't trust me, fucking wounds me. I chose my mother over her once. I'd never make this mistake again. I meant what I said. She will always be number one. Her words from that night hurt. *"It's best if you leave, Dominic, we won't work."* Fucking hell. Felt like knives slicing through my heart. I fucking love her. If only she would let me show her. I'd rip the heart from my chest just for her.

The last time I was this happy was the day I met Mila. We were inseparable. It didn't help that we went to different high schools. After practice, I would rush to her house, or she would drive to my school to watch me practice. I knew then she was meant for me. I couldn't keep my hands off her and definitely not my mouth. The night I peered through the restaurant window at the Christmas party, she glistened, angelically beautiful just like an

Angel, with her sparkly green eyes, which captivated me with her illicit smile, and took my breath away, knocking me to my knees. I'd never experienced love until that moment. She was for me to love, cherish, and worship.

"Your mom is here." Mario peeks his head through my office door.

Fuck. I haven't answered her phone calls in weeks. Being controlling is her nature; the fact she can't control me any longer has her fuming. She waltzes in like she owns the place, shooting daggers and sharp cheekbones that can shave ice.

"Nice to see you, Dominic. Did you forget you had a mother? You have not joined us for dinner or returned my texts and phone calls. Is it because of her?" She stands with her hands on her hips.

I scoot my chair back and rub the back of my neck. "Yes, it's because of Mila. I love her. We have a son together. It's always been her, and it will always be her. I've loved her since I was seventeen. You know I wonder, shouldn't a mother want to see her son happy? *She* makes me happy. She is everything I want in a woman and more."

I lift myself from the chair, shuffling beside her, I shake my head at her.

"I can't comprehend what you have against Mila that prevents you from wanting to meet your grandson. You have not once mentioned him. The hate you carry for Mila is sickening. You want to be part of our life, Mom?" I roll my shoulders back, wishfully praying she will accept our relationship like a normal mother would and love her grandson.

Her lips flatten into a curl flaring her nostrils. "Of course, I want to be in your life, Dominic."

"No, Mom. Our life. As in mine with Mila and Dante. If you can't accept them, then I can't be part of your life. This is where I put my foot down. I will do anything to protect Mila and Dante from anyone, especially your mother. You're missing out on meeting Dante. It's your loss. She will always come first." My jaw twitches with the coldness and selfishness she abhorrence.

"What about Samantha, she loves you, and you're still marrying her. I will cancel nothing, Dominic; you're so delusional over this woman all she is your high school past, an itch to scratch," she bellows. Anger rising, she breathes heavily.

I stop her from saying more, I don't want to hear shit about Samantha. "Listen to me, Mom, there will be no wedding with Samantha. One day, there will be a wedding with Mila. I left Samantha, I was never in love with her. She was never the one. You're the one who set me up with her. You insisted on the relationship, Mom. I've had enough of this shit, you deal with Samantha and her father." I rake my finger on my lips as I survey her as she bursts into flames.

"And you were happy with her, Dominic. This woman comes back, and you forget all about Samantha," she hisses.

"Mom, we are done here. You need to leave."

She stiffens. "Dominic, Samantha has been calling me crying. You better fix this; she loves you."

I roll my eyes. I doubt she loves me. It's not something I felt from her. She slams the door on her way out.

AFTER WORK, I head to Rocoo's for a drink and to meet Liam, Santiago, and Mark.

"I went to see Mila did she tell you? At her work a few weeks ago." Liam raises an eyebrow grinning as he scratches his lottery ticket.

"Yeah, she was happy to see you, and she also told me you drooled over her friend."

He snorts a laugh, focused on his ticket. "She was hot, that's all."

"Really, bro? You're not interested in hooking up with her or asking if she's single?"

He tosses the ticket and turns to look at me. "So, is she single?"

I snort. "No, she has a boyfriend."

He barks a laugh. "Then why in the hell tell me?"

I shrug. "Mila said you eye fucked her, or rather eye fucked each other."

Liam smirks. My best friend has never had a girlfriend, and I don't think he plans on it. He says he doesn't need women's drama.

"Fuck, she's hot dude, like damn, and those eyes. How good of friends are they?"

"They're best friends. She's like a sister to her—roommates."

"Who's hot?" Santiago asks as he takes a seat next to Liam with Mark trailing behind.

"Liam is drooling over Mila's roommate," I answer him.

"Hey, has she told you that she kept in touch with Skylar?" Liam questions.

My jaw tenses. Hearing that is a stab to my heart. When I got back to San Diego from Arizona, I'd asked her if she'd heard from Mila, begged her to tell me where Mila had gone, but she'd denied knowing anything.

"What?" I ask with a bite to my tone.

"Yeah, she's known this whole fucking time where Mila was. Had her number and everything."

"That fucking bitch." I'm steaming. She has spent the last five years trying to get into my pants, but she used to sleep around, and I have had no desire to be another of her conquests.

"Come on, let's go play pool," Liam suggests.

We make our way to the pool tables.

"Damn, dude, we're spanking your ass again," Mark gloats at Liam. They bicker like a married couple when they play pool.

"Are you going to Mila's after?" Mark asks.

"Told Dante I would stop by to tuck him in bed."

Mark grins. "I'm happy for you man. Dante's an amazing kid. I fell in love with him instantly. Damn, it's surreal to have a nephew."

Aiming the cue, fuck I miss. "Thanks, bro, I'm so fucking

happy with Mila and Dante. God, Mark, I've always dreamed of being a dad someday with the right girl. Now I have my girl back and a son; it's a dream come true. I'm so fucking scared of failing him."

Mark lifts his hand up, shaking his head. "I'm going to stop you there, bro, you will be an amazing dad, and you already are one. I saw you with him the other night, the love in your eyes. We never had a father in our life, Dominic, and at that moment, I saw you with him, and all I thought was I want to be a father someday like you, and be a great dad just like you. The love you and Mila have for each other is special. You look at her like she's your world and she looks at you the same way. I want what you have, Dominic. When two people love each other as you and Mila do. You will be an outstanding father. That's what love does to you, Dominic; it makes you a better person."

I suck in a sharp breath. Mark's words mean so much to me. Mark has always been the soft-hearted type. He's always been good with words and the romantic type. I've only shown that side of me to Mila. Mark's the complete opposite of all of us. I pat him on the shoulder with appreciation.

"Thanks, bro, it means a lot," I say earnestly, my chest tightening with emotions.

I lean in to make a shot when arms wrap around my waist. I jolt back to see who it is. Fuck, it's Skylar, and the anger I've been working on shedding since Liam shared what he'd discovered comes rolling back over me. I shove her off me.

She has no fucking clue Mila is back. I turn to face her ripping her hands off me.

"What the fuck do you want, Skylar?" My voice rages with venom.

She bats her long fake eyelashes at me her blonde hair up in a ponytail. "You." She smirks her red lips. "I want you, Dominic. Don't you think it's time to give us a chance? Mila is long gone. I know that's why you've been holding back and you're no longer engaged," she says in a seductive tone that sounds clogged.

I push her gently against the wall; she moans and rolls her eyes back, as if I'm about to fuck her against the wall.

"Skylar, you're nothing but a desperate conniving woman.

I want nothing to do with you. I never have. I'm not into desperate. Especially the ones who betray their friends." I'm not the type of man who hits women as much as I wish to strangle her. It's agonizing how everyone is out to hurt Mila. Fuck it pisses me off. Jealousy and envy are all they have over her.

"Have you talked to Mila? Do you know where she's at?" I ask. Baiting her. Fucking backstabber. All this damn time she knew, I had been searching for my girl. She lied to us just so she could get to me. My jaw twitches with rage and my blood boils.

She presses her palms on my chest.

I swat them away. I pound the wall with my fist. "Answer me!"

"I-I don't know. I told you I don't know! It's been so long. Don't you think it's time to move on? I can treat you good. I've always been in love with you. Mila never cared about you. She never deserved your love. She left you," she pleads, hopeful.

I bark out a laugh.

Liam shakes his head at her in disagreement. "I contemplate it's you that needs to move on from Dominic, Skylar. He doesn't want you. Dominic never will, you know why he's with Mila. Dominic and Mila, have a son together. And you're a lying, cold-hearted bitch. You knew where Mila was and you knew she thought he passed away. You fucking knew she was hurting inside." Liam gets in her face, his nostrils flare. "She went through hell. She thought she lost Dominic, and you kept quiet. It's fucked up, Skylar. How could you stoop so low?"

Her eyes grow as big as saucers. "W-w-what do you mean she has a son with you, Dominic?" she stutters with a pout as if I betrayed her.

"None of your damn business, stay the hell away from me and my girl you hear me?"

She cringes. "Yeah, ok got it." She gathers her belongings and makes her way to a table with her friends.

Thank the fuck.

I take one last sip of my beer before slapping a $20 on the counter. "Thanks, Will," I shout as I walk to my truck, heading back to my girl, *my family*. What a shit of a day first, my mom comes in with her bullshit. Then, Skylar, the twit, is delusional. The world seems to think they can keep us apart. So many lied to us; my family, Skylar.

What they don't know is how strong our love is, how the fire in us can literally start a fire, it burns so strong it seeps down to our souls. Every soul has a partner, and no matter how far apart they are from one another or what elements they are in, they will always find one another. This is our destiny, and love is what makes it so. As they say, if it's meant to be, it will be, and fate has a way of finding its way back to you. Mila found her way back to me. God, Mila turned me into a sappy fool.

Twenty-Two

MILA

"Dante, get your pajamas on, it's getting close to bedtime."

OMG, boys! He comes out of his room sweaty and sporting his Spider-Man costume, I pinch the bridge of my nose.

"You just took a shower and now you're all sweaty."

"Sorry, Mommy, Mary Jane needed help. Venom was after her."

"*Huh.*"

He cleans his forehead, wiping off sweat from trickling down. He gazes at me with those big brown eyes with a smile that lights up my world showing those beautiful dimples.

"I saved her, she's fine now." He lets out a relieved breath.

There's a knock at the door, my handsome man is wearing jeans, and a tight button shirt, showing every inch of bulging muscle. He stands holding a single red rose just like the one he gifted me the day we met.

"Hey, Mila."

I do a double sweep of his profile, biting my glossed lips needing a taste. "Hey back."

"For you, Angel. I missed you all damn day." He gives me a beautiful red rose.

I step back, letting him in. "Thank you."

He pulls the strings on my pajama pants, yanking me close to him, and he kisses me sweetly.

"Daddy, you here?" Dante runs into his dad's arms.

"Of course, buddy. Why are you so sweaty?"

He throws his hands in the air dramatically. "Mary Jane needed help from Venom I had to fight him, Daddy."

"Did you save her?"

Dante has his hands on his hips. "Yes, she's good now."

Dominic chuckles, ruffling his hair.

"Good, a man's got to do what a man's got to do to save his woman."

Dante cocks his head and nods.

I chuckle at their conversation, and my heart melts every time. We head upstairs to get Dante ready for bed. I kiss his cheek, tucking him in before heading back downstairs to clean up while Dominic reads Dante a story.

I scrub the counters, and pop my air pods, on, and *Shake It Off* by Taylor Swift plays. I sway my hips from side to side, scrubbing the counter and dancing to the beat. I bump my hips into a pillar of muscle. His brown eyes sparkle with amusement as he watches me. His lips curve in a twist.

"By all means, baby, keep swaying those hips and that ass. I like what I see."

Color flames my cheeks. "Stop spying on me, jeez how long have you been watching?"

He grins. "Long enough to give me a major hard-on."

I groan at his stupid, sexy, beautiful, lopsided smile. He flusters me. I throw a dish towel at his face. He catches it with a deep rumble laugh, sending a shiver up my spine.

"Come here." Stretching for me, he pulls me in close and kisses me wantonly with his heated lips on mine. He intensifies the kiss and moans tasting the saltiness of the beer.

"Fuck, Angel, you're all I think about. I crave you. I missed you, how was your day?" he says, sincerely as he snuggles into the nap of my neck.

"I missed you too, and I had a good day." I press a kiss on his soft lips.

He kisses me like there's no tomorrow, lifting me on top of the kitchen island. His tongue thrusts in cadence, he sucks the air out of me. I am dizzy and flustered. I squeeze my thighs around him. We pull away, hearing Sophie clear her throat.

"Just getting a glass of water, guys, and a snack." She stops and stares at us. "Jeez, you guys look like horny teens."

I'm breathing so hard trying to catch my breath. Dominic's hot breath fans my neck. I compress my moan, by pressing my lips together.

He whispers, "Going to the bathroom, be right back." Dominic closes the door.

Sophie glares at me. Watching me. "I've never seen you like this, Mila, so happy and Dante, God, he's so happy with his dad. It's as if he was never gone. The bond they have is so unreal so soon, you know?"

I nod in agreement. They warmed up to each other, instantly. Dominic has been excellent with Dante, showing him so much love. Children feel the love a parent has for them.

"I'm happy, Sophie, so happy. I never in a million years would have thought I would be with him again."

"And your dreams, are you still having them?"

"Yes, the days Dominic stays over, they subside. But some nights it's not about my dad, Sophie. Some are of Dominic walking out on me." I haven't uttered a word to anyone about this. Not even Dominic.

My best friend wraps me up in a hug. "I love you, Mila. I'm so damn happy to see you smile so beautifully. Your face lights up when he's around. You deserve it. Honey, have you talked to him about these dreams you're having?"

"No, I can't tell him. I love him. All this with his mom is too much. What if I let my guard down all the way, Sophie? And his mom interferes. What if he goes back to Samantha? I just can't

192

handle any more heartbreaks. I had a shattered soul for five years." I rest my head on her shoulder.

"Take it day by day. Give yourself breathing space. If you need to take it slow, then do so. Don't let his mom ruin shit. Talk to him, Mila. I see he loves you. At first, I was unsure, but I see it. I love you, my best friend. I'm always here for you."

"Thank you, I love you too." I notice her eyes water and her shoulders fall. "Hey, are you okay?"

She sniffles. "Yeah, I'm good. It's just, Ryder called it off. He wanted more of a title to what we have, and I can't, Mila."

"Do you love him?"

She closes her eyes. "No, I'm not in love with him. When I saw how you and Dominic act together, I realized I was missing something. Mila, your face lights up. The way he looks at you. It wasn't us. I'm hurt a little, but maybe because I got dumped." She laughs weakly. "I'm good, Mila, goodnight. Get back to what you were doing." She wags her eyebrows.

"Goodnight."

Dominic steps out of the restroom, I notice his knuckles scraped.

"What happened to your knuckles?" I reach for his arm. As I grip his hand, I place kisses on his knuckle.

He blows a hot breath. "Let's sit."

My nerves are pulling in every direction; the pit of my stomach sinks in. He leans in to kiss my cheek.

"I love you so much, Mila."

Oh, God. Is he breaking up with me or going back with his ex? His face is grim.

"Just get with it, what do you need to tell me? I can tell by the expression on your face."

He sighs. "Baby, you still talk to your friend Skylar?"

Oh hell, did he sleep with her? Is this what this is about?

"I haven't talked to her in like three years, why?" I swallow the ball of nerves. "I bumped into her a day before I left for Manhattan.

I asked her for Liam's number, and she said she didn't have it. I told her where I was going, and we exchanged numbers. I *never* told her I was pregnant. She called once in a while, and we would talk at times. When we talked, I'd cry, telling her how much I missed you. Her calls were always short. She would tell me it was best to stay where I'm at. Too many memories of you in San Diego."

His hand's fist, his jaw locks.

"Why, Dominic? Did you sleep with her?" My pulse quickens.

He cups my cheeks. "Fuck no, baby, I would never touch her, especially a friend of yours."

I relax my stiff shoulders.

"That bitch played you, us, baby. All this time she knew I was fine. She has been interested in me for the past five years. She was trying to get with me. I had asked her so many times if she knew where you were. Every time she said, to forget you and be with her."

Blood boils within me, clenching my jaw. That fucking bitch. All this time she knew. It makes sense she would call to make sure I wasn't coming back. She made a fool out of me.

"She was at the bar tonight. When the guys and I were playing pool, she wrapped her arms around my waist. I pushed her away. Liam had mentioned you spoke to Skylar a handful of times, and she knew all along, so when I saw her tonight, I let her have it; so did Liam. I punched the wall baby. Fuck, it pisses me off how they all tried to keep us apart. My mom, and Skylar, and my brothers."

OUR GAZES MELT into one another. He strokes the pad of his rough thumb along my lips. He kisses me on my lips, on my cheeks, and down to my neck. His touch dissolves all my anger, replacing it with love and lust.

"My beautiful Angel, so sweet, so perfect. I'll never let a soul tear us apart. Baby our love has been written in the stars, destined to be together. We will always come back to each other even in another life, it will always be us. Let me take you to bed, beautiful, to show you how much you mean to me. The love I have for you is beyond words, Mila, let me show you."

His voice is so husky and rough. His words leave me breathless. He makes it hard to keep my walls up when he speaks this way to me, like I'm in a romance novel.

I love how he constantly expresses his love for me, begging me to trust him. I hate how restrained I'm being and how agitated it makes me to give him all of me. Although it's fitting, he proves himself and earns his way back into my heart. I spent years loving him, missing him. My love for him was sacred. He shows me his love not just by making love. He tells me continuously how much he loves me. Dominic often drops off breakfast or lunch at the studio cooked by him. He'll leave little love notes written on the takeout box.

I whisper softly, "Show me, show me the universe."

We shred our clothes off until we're skin to skin. Dominic hikes up my body as I lay sprawled on the bed. Kisses skimming down my neck.

"What do you need, Angel?" His voice drips in lust.

"You, Dominic, inside me."

A moan mutters from my lust-induced lips as he positions himself in me. He stretches me with his thick cock. His thrust is deep, searing into me waves of ecstasy as he slams into me. He pressed harder, deeper, as he hits full speed, filling me in.

WHEN I UNLOCK the door to the studio, my heart sinks. Someone broke in, it's destroyed. Sophie walks in behind and she gasps. The studio's back door hangs open, and all our props are scattered everywhere.

"Don't touch anything, Mila, let me call the police."

My gaze goes to the register. It's not broken or messed with.

We don't leave money in the register. We lock all cash in the safe. I walk into my office and all my cameras are in place. This is not a robbery. Doesn't seem that way. I'm no detective, but I've watched plenty of shows. Tears trickle down my cheek. I've worked so damn hard to have my studio, to build a life for Dante and me. Sophie stands next to me with tears in her eyes. Her head lies on my shoulder.

"Police are on their way, chica." She sniffles.

"They didn't take anything."

"I know, I noticed."

Twenty minutes later, the police show up and one officer was Liam. They took all our information and checked for fingerprints and nothing, not one. Someone had tampered with our surveillance cameras, so it didn't pick up the intruder. Liam took pictures of the demolished props.

What the fuck.

They broke into no other shops but mine.

"How are you doing, Mila?" Liam walks toward me.

"A little shaken up, but I'll be okay," I say, earnestly, chewing on my bottom lip.

"I called Dominic. He should be here soon. He said he would be here in like thirty minutes."

"Thank you, Liam."

He nods and leans by the door. "You're welcome call me if you need anything."

Sophie's been calling all our clients, canceling until we clean this mess up and call the insurance.

The mail carrier walks in, handing me a large envelope. I open it to find pictures of Dominic and Samantha together. Having sex. One with her in red lace lingerie as he sits on the bed watching her.

Oh God, I want to hurl, are these recent? In the other photos, she's on top of him. Her blonde hair brushed against Dominic's thighs, as she arches her back. Another picture shows him on top of her.

Both fucking and naked. The temperature in the room shifts my flesh goes ghost white.

Dominic happens to walk in, startled by the mess. "Baby, are you okay?"

My chest feels so tight. The way he's looking at her in those pictures. The same way he looks at me. He loves her.

"Besides the break in, Dominic. These were delivered to me," I say harshly, slapping the photos on his chest and blinking to stop the tears from streaming.

Dominic's gaze cuts into mine, his eyes widen.

"Angel," he whispers. He swallows, then walks to the trashcan and dumps them. "Angel," he repeats.

I turn my gaze from him, I can't look at him.

"I don't know who took those, but this was way before you came back, baby. I'm sorry you had to see them," he drawls through gritted teeth. "Baby, please look at me. I don't remember any of it."

I'm so fucking disgusted. I run my hands through my hair. "The way you looked at her, Dominic, it was the same way you look at me. You love her. You fucking lied to me. You just told me you didn't love her, and you never made love to her?" Tears drop, I'm unable to hold them in.

"Baby no, I never loved her, Mila. In those pictures, I was most likely drunk, Mila, at times I would imagine it was you. I'm being honest with you."

He takes a step toward me. He wipes my tears.

"I love you, Mila. I didn't lie to you. I never made love to her. Do you believe me?" he murmurs, cradling my face. "Don't cry, baby, it hurts me to see you cry; it pains me." His eyes are shaded. His shoulders deflate. "Do you believe me, baby?" he repeats.

"I-I want to... why did you take photos of you two having sex if it was nothing to you?"

"Baby, I never took photos, honestly. I have no clue who would do it, and I never saw her with a camera."

A hiccup escapes as more tears are shed.

"We will figure out who sent you those photos. I'll let Liam know and we'll get your studio back together." Dominic kisses my temple, he wraps me in a hug.

Who would send me those photos? Samantha? His mom? Did they do this to mess with me? I don't think they would break into my place.

"Do you think it was your mom who sent me those photos? or Samantha?"

"I don't know, baby. I can't see my mom taking pictures of us doing stuff, you know."

He's right, I don't think his mom would take photos of them having sex... that would be odd. Maybe, Samantha, had a camera hidden.

"Do you think it was Samantha? Because it's clear she would. The photos are of you two. It was to hurt me."

His eyes dart to mine. As he rubs his jaw. "Angel, it could be her. Trying to cause problems by breaking us up. I know she's pissed over the breakup." He sighs.

"Whoever sent them wanted to get a rise out of you baby, from now on, I want you to be careful." He lifts my chin and kisses my lips. "I love you, Mila. You got that, baby? I'm so fucking sorry, baby. Fuck."

Sophie walks out of her office. "I just called the insurance to make a claim they will get back to me."

Exhaling. What a fucking day.

"Thank you for calling."

Dominic grabs my purse leading me out the door. Sophie walks out the door heading home.

"Let's go, baby. I'll take you for ice cream," he drawls.

I kiss his cheek. The pit of my stomach sours. The images of those photos, my studio. What the hell!

"I can't get those images out of my head," I admit.

His eye flair with anger. "Angel, you're letting whoever did this win."

I nod in agreement.

Twenty-Three

MILA

The insurance has compensated us for the damage. It took us a couple of days to get it all cleaned up. The police are still investigating the break-in. Unfortunately, the security cameras from the neighboring stores didn't pick up the perpetrator's identity. Uneasiness settles as I see those images of Dominic and her in my head. Daliah notices my pinned eyes on the trash can. Wordlessly, she takes the dumpster outside and burns it.

I'm starting to wonder if Dominic and I are meant to be star-crossed lovers. The universe seems to be conspiring against us. My heart and mind are not in the same agreement. My mind says guard yourself, build a wall. My heart says let him in. I lean back in my chair, massaging my temples.

"What are you doing for Halloween tomorrow?" Daliah asks as she goes over the client's appointment book.

At the same time, I set up props for my next appointment.

"Dante has a Halloween party in his class. I'm taking cupcakes and goodie bags for the class. Dominic and I are doing the trick-or-treating around here with Dante. And you?"

She shrugs as she taps her pen on her chin. Today she has her hair pink. It looks good on her. "After passing out candy here. I'm going with my boyfriend to his friend's Halloween party."

"Sounds like fun," I say as I set out artificial pumpkins for photo shoots.

Sophie traipses out of her office smiling.

"What are you grinning at?" I raise an eyebrow at her.

"I joined this dating app. I thought I'd give it a shot, and I have a date or hookup, I guess you can say, since I don't do relationships."

I frown. I hate that she's anti-relationships all because of one guy, but who am I to talk?

THE FALL BREEZE shimmers in the air and the crispiness of the leaves, as you walk, has me grinning ear to ear on this gorgeous Halloween morning. Fall is my favorite season. Pumpkin spice, cozy sweaters, cool weather, ah, and Halloween are some of my top favorite holidays. I take the bags from my car which contain the cupcakes I baked the previous night and the treat bags for Dante's first Halloween party. Also, really good. I dressed Dante as the well-known Spider-Man, and I'm Wonder Woman. Fits perfectly with my long, wavy, black hair. I picked up a Superman costume for Dominic. He has no clue, yet the thought of him wearing tight spandex has my mind racing into naughty places.

Mila, get a hold of yourself. I see Father David standing in front of the school at St. Mary's Catholic School, greeting the kids. Oh, forgive me, Father, I refrain myself from my filthy thoughts. Entering Dante's class, I realize all the parents are gaping at me. Yeah, maybe I shouldn't have worn this to school. A Catholic school, may I add.

Dante's first Halloween was a success. Costume parade, games, and treats. Now time for trick-or-treating at the outdoor shops. It is part of the festival they have every year on the pier. At the studio, Sophie and Daliah will be passing out candy. It's been years since I've been to the festival. Dominic sits on a stool swirling his tongue, licking off the frosting of his cupcake.

My mouth waters at the sight of his pink tongue. A tongue that works magic. His eyes darken as he catches me looking. His lip lifts with a smirk and he winks. Rolling my eyes, I pass by him, swaying my hips as his head spins. He hooks me in his arms.

"Damn, you're sexy, baby. You look incredible in that Wonder Woman costume, especially your breasts." He nuzzles in the crook of my neck, inhaling my scent, as the length of his velvet tongue sweeps up and down my collarbone.

"Dominic," I rasp out; goosebumps, prickling my skin.

"Hmm," he hums as his tongue works its magic.

"I got you something for tonight."

His head lifts, missing the warmth of his hot tongue. A bright smile lifts as he takes the bag with his costume. His eyebrows raise questionably as he inspects it. Biting my lip, I try not to laugh as he struggles for words. His mouth opens and closes.

"Mila, baby, are you out of your mind? You expect me to wear these tights?" He dangles the Superman costume in the air with a raised eyebrow.

I'm trying my best to stifle my laugh. "Men in tights are sexy."

He possessively growls. "What do you mean men in tights are sexy? Do you look at other men?" he says with a bite. Then he tilts his head in a solemn manner.

I giggle at his ridiculousness. Ahh, and there's my old Dominic, the jealous and possessive one. He's never been the type to be overly-possessive, but just enough to know he cares. Since the death of my father, I had realized how much I desire love. In other words, I want a man to look at me as if I'm their world. A man that makes me feel desired, worshiped, and loved. Someone to tell me I look beautiful on a crappy day. To keep all my secrets, close to his heart. To stop every tear. Speak of me the way my father spoke of my mother.

My eyes flicker to Dominic. He makes me feel loved. I know he's been trying extra hard, but I can't help but keep my guard up. You can't blame me, right?

"Jealous much?"

He scoffs. "Very."

"Come on, just put it on so we can go."

"Do you want women to stare at my huge, bulging package I've got going on here? Hmm." He points to his bulge.

The mention of his dick has me licking my lips, and heat seeps into my skin. "If any women stare at my man's big package, I will poke their eyes out of their eye sockets. If it bothers you this much, just tape it down."

He repeatedly blinks as if I just said the most ridiculous thing. I shrug.

"For fuck's sake, woman, did you just say to tape my dick down?"

A tickle of laughter has me clenching my stomach with laughter. He throws his hands in the air, bug-eyed.

God, this is hilarious.

"It's not a bad idea. Men do that, ice skaters, principal dancers."

Dominic pinches the bridge of his nose. "Did you just make this shit up?" He crosses his arms, surveying me.

"Kinda, well, maybe they do or is it a dance belt they use? Something like that, but it's not a bad idea, you know. Better than it bulging out."

He sighs in defeat. "I'll go get ready without my dick taped. Thank you very much," he mutters as he stomps to the bathroom like a child.

"YOU LOOK SO hot in your Wonder Woman costume, I can't take my eyes off you. I want to go home and tear it off," he whispers in my ear, sucking on my earlobe.

"The feeling is mutual."

His tight muscles strain against the tight material of the costume. Damn, and those rock-hard abs, I can see his eight-pack peeking through the material. I want to run my hands through it.

Those thick muscular thighs, I envision wrapped around me. I let my eyes wander to his ass, *Jesus* his round, tight rock-hard ass I want to squeeze while he's underneath me. Ugh, and his bulge is practically on display. My eyes rest upon his perfectly sculpted, godly body. He makes Henry Cavill look unsubstantial. I blush, thinking about where my mind is taking me. *God, Mila, you're so stupid; why did I have him wear that?* Bad fucking idea. *Stupid, stupid, Mila.*

Women chant, "Ride me up into the sky, Superman! Can I feel those muscles, hot stuff? Yum, I want a taste of that."

I grind my teeth; by the end of the night, they will turn to dust. He grins like a kid in a candy store. *Asshole.* A laugh breaks from his chest. His broad laugh reaches his eyes, spreading small lines outward. His lips brush the corner of my mouth.

"What's wrong, sweetheart? Jealous? I warned you, Angel."

What a cocky shit. My eyes narrow into slits. Squaring my shoulders and crossing my arms. "Nope, not at all," I lie.

He chuckles some more. "Someone's lying."

"Someone's going to get suffocated by a pillow tonight."

"I'd rather get suffocated by your breasts tonight, seems like a great way to go." He grins.

I erupt in laughter. Next time, he will be Bozo the Clown. I grab Dante's hand leading him to different booths and shops so he can collect his candy.

"Look, Mommy, it's Brian."

Oh shit, no, no, no. Brian's handing out candy next to the coffee shop. Dante runs up to him.

Dominic's smile fades, he sneers with jealousy, his jaw twitches, and straightens himself, dropping daggers at Brian. Brian ruffles Dante's hair.

"Hey there, Spider-Man." Brian gazes at me, his baby blues wandering up and down my body, chewing on his bottom lip. "Hi, gorgeous."

Before I can respond, Dominic wraps my hair around his hands, kissing me possessively in front of Brian. Like a predator stalking his claim. He breaks the kiss and his eyes bore into mine. His look indicates so many words without speaking. *You're mine, I'm yours, my everything, my universe.* His brown-whiskey eyes soften into mine. I nod, reassuring him *I'm yours, you're mine.* A relieved look washes over his face. He turns to look at Brian and smirks at him.

"Ken."

"Satan," Brian replies.

I snort. Brian has a backbone now. Where did it come from? I smile at Brian.

"Hi, how have you been?"

"Good," he mummers.

Guilt washes over me. He's a good guy, a sweet, caring, and beautiful man. I know there might have been something there if Dominic and I hadn't happened. He was easy, maybe too easy. I don't regret him or sleeping with him. I do know he would have never had all of me. My heart and soul belonged to one man.

"Happy Halloween, Brian. Have a good night."

He nods.

"Bye, Brian." Dante waves.

We walk a couple of blocks down to the carnival. Dante asks to ride a couple of rides. We hand our tickets to a tall man who escorts us to our seats securing us on the Ferris wheel. Dante sits between us. A flood of memories washes over me. Teenage Mila sat in this spot, making out the whole time with Dominic. I smile at the memory. Dominic gently tucks a lock of hair behind my ear. His whiskey-brown eyes blaze into mine.

"I remember it all, baby," he whispers softly.

"Remember what, Daddy?" Dante asks. His forehead creases as he glances up at Dominic.

"Before you were born, your mom and I used to come here and get on the Ferris wheel."

Dante shrugs, uninterested.

Dominic and I exchange a laugh. We begin to move, and Dante's eyes widen.

"Dad, I'm scared." Dante sniffles.

"It's okay, buddy, I got you. We're superheroes, remember?"

Dante scoots into Dominic's side. His arms wrap around Dante's tiny frame. My heart squeezes. I fish for my phone in my purse to take a picture of Dante and Dominic.

"Okay, Dad. You're Superman and you're strong and fly?" he whimpers, nestling into Dominic.

"You'll be okay," Dominic assures him.

The ride must have put him to sleep a couple of seconds later. He's passed out, leaning on Dominic. The pad of Dominic's thumb feathers along my cheekbone. He lifts my chin and kisses me. His sweet sugary lips sink perfectly with mine. The taste of his lips has always been my favorite flavor.

"Let's go home, Angel, it seems like he's done for the night."

Home.

"I WANT to show you my place, nothing special; I want to cook dinner for you two." A smile lifts from his beautiful profile.

As we step inside, he flickers the lights on. As we walk into his beautiful condo, I take in the polished marble countertops and the vast kitchen which seems not to be used much. A huge leather sectional sofa, a big screen tv hanging on the wall. A couple of paintings hanging. A bachelor pad is what it looks like. It appears lonely, with no splash of color. I wonder if he brought women here. If he brought other women into his bed. These thoughts make me frown.

"I don't cook here much, I usually eat at the restaurant." His whiskey eyes scrutinize me as I rake his beautiful home.

"It's a beautiful kitchen you should cook more often."

He flashes a huge grin. "I will now, beautiful, I have you two to cook for."

Jesus, he's so hot. I kiss the corner of his mouth. Dominic is a beautiful man.

"Daddy, I like your house, but-but you have no toys I checked all the rooms."

A deep rumbling laugh breaks from Dominic's chest. "Ahh, I'm sorry, little man. I'll have to buy you some next time I run to the store so you can keep it here. Do you want to watch a movie while I cook dinner?"

Dante pokes his nose and nods. "Do you have Netflix, Daddy?"

"I do. How about we watch *Nacho Libre*, have you seen it?" Dominic has been dying to have Dante watch *Nacho Libre*.

"No."

"Ahh, well you're going to love it."

Dante lies on the sofa watching the movie.

"Come on, let me show you around. I need to get out of this costume, my balls are suffocating." Shaking his head. He scoffs.

"We can't let that happen can we."

He stretches his hand out and I intertwine mine with his. He leads us upstairs to his room.

Twenty-Four
DOMINIC

She's so beautiful. My eyes wander up and down her body, from her creamy toned legs, thick thighs, and round ass, all of which are begging to be squeezed. She's changed from her sexy Wonder Woman costume to a t-shirt of mine and gym shorts. Damn, she's sexy in my shirt in my house. The whole time in my bedroom, she scrutinized it. Her beautiful, bright eyes kept staring at my bed. I know she's wondering if I've taken another woman to bed here. I change into some sweats.

I tear off the t-shirt and gym shorts, leaving her in her laced bra and underwear. I lay her on my bed. She squirms, uncomfortable. Dipping my pelvis into her perfect belly, I grind my swollen erection into her. I brush my thumb along her stretch marks which she always hides from me. I love them. I didn't get to see her pregnant, but I get to see the marks left by our son.

"You're beautiful, Mila, I've never had a woman in my bed," I assure her. I'm in love with her.

Fifteen minutes later, we make our way back down. She's washing the dishes as I cook the pasta. Dante wants spaghetti, so spaghetti it is.

"Angel, I got this, go relax on the stool. Just keep me company."

She pouts. "Are you sure? I don't want to be useless just watching."

I lift her, carrying her to the stool, sucking on the soft skin of her neck, sweet as honey. I suck and nibble on her neck. My mouth trails along her collarbone to the hollow of her throat. She molds into my arms. My perfect sin I can't live without.

"Jesus, Mila, you're perfect. I want you so bad that I can't breathe without you. I want you in my bed tonight."

She moans in my ear as I kiss her delicate, soft neck. I slip my hand under her shirt, grabbing her perfect breasts, and pinching her pebbled nipples. My lips find hers, and I taste her moans as I voraciously kiss and lick her. I thrust my tongue like a man desperate for more, never satisfied with just one taste of her, exploring her hungrily and never wanting to stop.

"Shush, baby, we don't want him to hear," I say as I slip my hand into her panties, inserting a finger to feel her wetness.

She slides her fingers into my hair, holding on while I pump inside her. Mila bites down on my shoulder. *Fuck,* that sends an electric shock to my cock. My dick twitches, begging to spring out. She's so close I can feel it when she clamps on my finger.

"That's it, baby, come for me," I whisper in her ear.

Right when she moans, I suck the air from her mouth, kissing her possessively. She comes on my finger, and I come in my sweatpants without her touching me like a damn teenager. Just watching her unfold does it for me. I lick the juices from my finger, tasting her. A taste I love, a taste I can never get enough of. She watches with a raised eyebrow. I shrug.

"Just sampling my dessert, baby." I wink at her.

She blushes ten shades of red. "I'm going to wash up," she says, as she makes her way to the restroom.

"All right, Angel, I'll finish up here once I run upstairs to change."

She stares at my wet, come-filled sweats. She smiles as she walks off to the restroom.

FOR TWO GODDAMN HOURS, I've been waiting for the delivery truck to arrive with my furniture. It's fuckin' finally here.

"Where would you like us to set your furniture up?" the delivery guy asks.

"In the spare bedroom," I say, my voice steeped in annoyance.

Three weeks have passed since I had Mila and Dante over to cook for my little family dinner. My home never felt like home until that night. My poor little guy slept in the spare bedroom on an air mattress. His words, "Daddy, this room is empty and scary. I need a night light."

I ran to Dollar Days to get him a nightlight. My beautiful Angel stretched out on my king-size bed as I ate her, feasting on my sweet dessert, fucking her deep and rough, ending the night by making love to her. I've never had a woman stay the night or fucked them in my bed, including Samantha. It never felt right. With her, everything tumbles into place.

For a man, waking up with their soulmate wrapped in their arms is the most incredible feeling. Now that she's back in my life, I loathe waking up alone. I hate missing her, studying her like a book, kissing her gently. A feeling I've never experienced until now. Mila and I didn't get the chance to explore each other in this way, we had our time cut short. Two teens in love, fighting to live. The tragic loss of her father destroyed my Angel and fought cancer with me. I know she still fights the demons in her nightmares when I'm not next to her. I will do everything in my power to demolish those demons in her nightmares.

The spare bedroom has a complete makeover. I turned it into a new bedroom for Dante. I make sure to hang up superhero posters, making the room welcoming and not scary like the last time Dante was here. I hope he likes it. I'm not sure if Mila's ready for us to move in together yet. I haven't pushed the idea on her, I know she's still working on letting me into my heart, and I am still trying to regain her trust.

I'll keep working every damn day until I have her heart and trust. And fuck, those photo's that were delivered to Mila. It pisses the hell out of me. I honestly don't remember the night of those photos. I know I was drunk because that's the only time I could sleep with any woman. As fucked up as it was, it took me two years to have sex with another woman after Mila disappeared from my life. I'm pretty sure Samantha sent those photos.

There's a knock at my door, and I hope it's my girl surprising me; I'm not expecting anyone.

"Hey Liam, what's happening? You don't look too good."

He's dressed in a full police uniform. His skin is pale, and he has a ghost of a grimace on his face. He rubs his forehead nervously.

"Come in, man, what is it? Did something happen?"

He walks in bewildered; his mouth opens and closes no words form. He shakes his head.

"Dom, I have some news. I'm fucking shocked, confused, shit I don't know what to think."

He pulls out a chair to sit on. Fuck, he's scaring the shit out of me. In all the years I've known him, I've never seen him this way.

"Spit it out."

He groans as beads of sweat trickle from his forehead.

"We discovered who started the fire. Who killed Mila's father."

Seven years later, I'm frozen in place. Finally, justice for Mila and Leo. Thinking back to that night, when I helped her climb out the window to sneak out was a school night. I had a late practice, and I was dying to see her, to hold her, to make love to her at our secret spot on the beach. If she hadn't sneaked out Mila wouldn't be here right now. She carries guilt for not rescuing her father that night. I know Leo, he loved his daughter more than anything, I'm positive he's happy she snuck out that night to have a life, a family, and love.

"Who is it? How did they find the person?" I turn to cast a glance at Liam.

He chews on his lip nervously. "Mila's former neighbor just came into the precinct a few hours ago. She glimpsed from her porch that night a car parked outside. She retreated into her home not thinking anything like this would happen, then minutes later the house caught on fire and the woman in the car split. She also has footage on her security cameras that she kept. She was terrified to tell." He pauses for a second, rubbing the stubble on his chin.

I'm trying to regroup from his statement that it was intentional. Someone did this. Who would want to harm them?

"This is the shitty part, man; I-I don't know how to tell you, but here's the copy of the report. I haven't turned it in yet. I can sit on it for a little while, but there are others involved and I can't wait too long. I wanted to talk to you about it first."

Nausea stirs in the pit of my stomach.

"Fuck, dude, the person who started the fire was your mom."

My legs are shaky as I support myself on the table. My chest is caving in, I can't breathe. *My mom, my mom, my mom,* are the only two words that keep playing in my head.

This can't be real. Why would she do this? *No, no, no.* It can't be. With shaky hands, I open the report, Mrs. Gibson witnessed my mother light candles around the house with a gallon of gasoline and a rag. I blink repeatedly, praying I misread it.

"Are you sure it was my mom?" I choke out, a sudden dark shadow hovering over me, sucking all the light out of me.

"Yes, I watched the surveillance video more than twenty times. It was no accident, it was intentional," Liam says in a soft, shaky voice. His head hangs low, and his shoulders slump. Liam has grown up in our home. My mom loves Liam, she treats him like a son.

"I haven't submitted the report yet. What do you want me to do? It's your mom, she will go to prison for murder. We will need to turn her in. Mila needs closure as well; she went through years of trauma and therapy. If she wouldn't have snuck out that night, Dominic, w-we could have lost her." His eyes hood as he directs his gaze to mine.

"I can't comprehend the reason your mom had. Why did she do something so ruthless." He stands and walks to grab a bottle of water. Twisting the cap off, he stares up at me.

Paralyzed by this new information, never in a million years would I have imagined my own mother to be this cruel and heartless.

"I think you should be the one to speak to Mila first, before word gets out, or she finds out from someone else."

I nod. Numbly.

I keep replaying the conversation I had with Liam, and it has me frazzled. He left two hours ago. Mila just texted me to come over. As much as I want to see her, and hold her, I can't today. I lied, informing her I was over-submerged in work. How could I face her knowing my mother is the reason she's an orphan? My mother attempted to kill her, the love of my life. I don't have an answer to why my mom did it. If I call her, she might flee. Liam asked me to keep quiet, and not to mention it to my mom or brothers yet.

How do I tell Mila? What if she leaves me? Or despises me for what my mom did? What if I remind her of what Rachel Delgado did to her and her father? She will look at me with animosity. Rightfully so, I am the son of a killer, a murderer, after all. I can't lose her. I love her more than life itself. I love my mom and loathe her at the same time. What she did is unforgivable.

All these years, she showed no sign of remorse or regret. Unsympathetic, she portrayed no sign of remorse all these years. She killed Leo, and burned him to death. She is a cruel fucking woman. She betrayed us. Our mother. *Fuck, fuck.* My shoulders slump as I throw my head back on the sofa. I grip my fingers through my hair with frustration.

Mila's going to leave me. I can feel it. I should have protected her from my own mother. Losing her all over again is going to destroy me, losing my son in the mix will leave me lifeless. Terminally ill.

I'm so sorry, Angel, I love you. My eyes fall heavy, and I drift off letting sleep take over.

Twenty-Five
MILA

A couple of weeks have passed since Halloween. I've been super busy at work, and it will only get busier with the holidays coming in full swing. Today's Dante's birthday and we're throwing him a party at Chuckie's Adventure. My head has been in a haze lately. Dominic has been acting strange these past few weeks. He has been distant. Distracted.

I asked him if everything was okay. He replies work has been hectic, and he's been behind on paperwork. I'm hoping that's the case. His eyes are as soft as a whisper when I catch him staring at me, and he then turns away. He frowns and drops his head. I refrain from being intrusive and stop asking repeatedly.

"Happy birthday, baby, the big five today." I squeeze my baby boy tightly.

"Mom, you're squashing me." He frowns, his gaze roaming around to make sure no one is looking at him. We just arrived at Chuckie's Adventure.

Dominic is on his way with Dante's Spider-Man cake.

"Mom, is Daddy almost here?" he whines.

"Yes, he should be getting here any minute. Oh, look Auntie Sophie just got here."

He sprints into Sophie's arms, and she lays a wet kiss on his cheek, which he quickly wipes. "Hi, Auntie Sophie."

"Hey, birthday boy, wow you're so big now you look taller, and omg, did you get muscles."

He flexes his arms, checking his muscles. "I eat vegetables now."

Dominic has been getting him to eat his vegetables; surprisingly, he does.

Dominic, Santiago, Mark, and Liam all stroll in together, making heads turn. Hell, they look sinfully attractive, resembling sexy firemen in one of those calendars. My man, of course, is the hottest of the group. His beautiful brown eyes meet mine as he walks toward me. The corners of his mouth curl downwards. Lust-filled eyes. Scrutinizing as I rake him, drinking him in. Dominic's wearing snug denim jeans that hug his muscular thighs and a V-neck shirt that grips his biceps. He skims a kiss on my cheek, God, he smells so good. So, masculine.

"Hi, beautiful, how's my girl doing?"

A flutter of arousal rockets to my core. I glide my palms up and down his tight abs. *God, Mila, not now it's a kid's party.*

"I'm excellent, baby. I've missed you," I pout.

"I've missed you too, Angel. I'm sorry work has been insane." His smile is distraught.

My thumb brushes along the edge of his jaw, his stubble prickling my thumb. He's so handsome. The palm of his hand sweeps my back.

"Where did the Birthday boy go?"

"He's in the jungle gym with a couple of friends from school." He wraps his finger in my hair.

"Be back, Angel, let me go find my boy." He swaggers off, looking sexy.

I notice other women gazing at him. He pays no attention.

I envelop Santiago, Mark, and Liam in a tight hug. I introduce Santiago and Mark to Sophie. Not shocked when Santiago attempts to flirt, his characteristic move. He has a charming grin plastered on his handsome face.

"Nice to meet you, Sophie." He drops a kiss on her cheek. Startling me. Whoa wasn't expecting him to go that far. Liam bumps Santiago out of the way, seething a death glare toward Santiago. Santiago breaks into a roaring laugh. Aha, so Santiago must know Liam has a spark of interest in Sophie.

"Hi gorgeous, nice to see you again."

Rolling my eyes, I maneuver away from them, looking for my two favorite guys. I find them playing arcade games. Dante's plastered in a racing car seat, gripping a hold onto a stirring wheel. Dominic stands next to him, watching him play. I sneak up behind him, wrapping my arms around his waist, and inhaling the smell of his cologne. He tips his head back, and winks. He runs his thumb along my fingers.

"Our boy is going to be a natural badass street racer." He laughs, staring pridefully at Dante with a sparkle in his eyes.

Dante holds a tight grip on the steering wheel he seems to be in a daze. He has not blinked once, he's so engaged in the game.

Getting on my tiptoes, I place a kiss on the nape of his neck. "I want him to be just like you." It's true I want him to like Dominic. He's a good man and a good father.

He turns to face me. "Mila, I want him to be just like you. You're the most amazing person I know."

I gather the kids around the table for cake. I snap pictures of Dominic and Dante. Times like this feels unreal to have Dominic. I cried when Dante had his first birthday. I wanted Dominic to be with us. "I'll take the pictures. Go stand next to them," Sophie says. "Thank You."

We sing "Happy Birthday" while gathered around the table. My favorite people are all here together, and I'm in awe of it. Dominic's brothers excitedly celebrate the birthday of their nephew. I long for the presence of my parents, whom I miss. With Dante, they would have been in love.

"HOLA, MIJA," Nana screams and waves from the pickup lane at the airport.

Uncle Roger's smile widens.

I jump out of the car hugging them both, my biggest supporters. Nana rushes to the car, kissing Dante to death.

"Mi niño, I missed you," she coos at him.

He groans. "Nana, I'm not a baby."

She chuckles and blesses him. It's a cloudy rainy Thanksgiving morning. The house smells like heaven. Last night, Sophie and I stayed up late making apple, pumpkin, and cherry pies, and let's not forget dinner rolls. Nana has been running around all morning, cleaning, and prepping at the crack of dawn. She's in her mid-seventies and she has the energy of a thirty-year-old. She swears by her nightly cinnamon tea routine. She exclaims that it's the trick to healthy, glowing, juvenile skin and is great for your health. Nana is also very superstitious.

"Mila, did you chop up the celery and onions for the stuffing? Our guest will be here at two," she screams over the sound of the vacuum going.

Arrg! The only guest we have is Dominic, for God's sake. I don't bother answering her, she pops her headphones on and sings *No Tengo Dinero* by Juan Gabriel dancing as she vacuums.

I crack a smile. I missed her. I glance at Sophie and Uncle Roger, staring at Nana with the same expression of admiring her.

Tears stream down my cheeks as I finish cutting up the onions. When the smell of Fabuloso invades my nose. Of course, Nana is mopping while I am cooking.

"Nana, seriously, can you wait until I'm done?"

She huffs with her hands on her hips, staring at me like I've sinned. "Mila, the house needs to be extra clean for our guests it's Thanksgiving. Needs to be extra."

"Nana, it's only Dominic who's coming."

She puts her hands on her hips. "Yes, and it still needs to be super clean."

"I know, Nana, it's just that I don't want you to overwork yourself."

She wags her finger at me. "I might not be no spring chick, but these old bones can handle it."

Sophie sighs. "I missed your Nana, she's a little crazy but the good kind of crazy."

Uncle Roger barks a laugh that roars through the small apartment. "I would say a lot crazy, but we love her."

That's for sure, she brightened our life. We all get back to our cooking duties.

I looked over my shoulder at Sophie peeling potatoes.

"I've been meaning to ask you, is there something going on between you and Liam? I see some chemistry, connection with you too. I didn't see it with you and Ryder."

A frown creases her forehead. "I feel something, Mila, I've never felt this way before and I'm not even dating him. We've only met twice. God, that day at the studio in his uniform, it hypnotized me. He's hot as hell, with his tanned skin, sharp cheekbones, gun-metal eyes, thick eyebrows, and let's not forget muscle on top of muscle."

Her navy blues sparkle as she daydreams about him.

"Then when he spoke a heat wave hit me. It terrifies me. He asked me out for a drink. He asked at the party. I denied him, told him I'm busy." She Bites her lip. She watches me through batting eyelashes.

"Wow, you got it bad. Give it a shot, Liam is sweet and a good person. He's not Eric."

She's about to answer when there's a knock.

As I open the door, I see Dominic with droplets of rain drizzling down his hair and face. *Jesus,* he always takes my breath away.

"Baby, you can ogle me some more inside, it's cold and raining out here."

Fuck, I got caught blushing. I take the wine, he's holding.

"Your Nana's not going to smack me with the broom, is she?" As he sweeps his wet shoes on the rug, with a twist of a smile, he leans in to kiss my lips.

"Hmm, not sure. She might stick a needle in your eye," I joke.

"I'll take the pain for you, Angel. Happy Thanksgiving, beautiful."

I stare into those dark, whiskey eyes that hold so much love. A spark of desperation mirrors his beautiful, handsome face that bloomed these last couple of weeks.

"I love you," I say, as I kiss the stubble on his cheeks.

His breath steams into my pores, whispering in my ear, "I love you more, Angel, so much more."

"Daddy, Daddy!" Dante screams.

Dominic kneels to hug him. "Happy Thanksgiving, buddy."

Uncle Roger shakes Dominic's hand. The last time they met was at dad's funeral.

"Nice to see you again, Dominic. How have you been doing? Mila tells me you're the owner of a restaurant."

"Yes, I opened up Delgado Steakhouse a couple of years ago." I beam with pride.

"That's impressive for someone so young, congratulations." Uncle Roger beams and ushers Dominic into the kitchen.

"Ahh, is that Dominic?" Nana shouts from the bathroom she's cleaning.

"Yes, Nana he's here," I shout.

She sprints to him, hugging the life out of him. She pinches his cheeks just like she does Dante's.

"Que guapo *how handsome,* Dominic, you've grown into a fine young man. I would scoop you up too if I was your age."

I groan, jeez Nana. Dominic shakes with laughter. Nana rests her hand on his shoulder.

"I'm happy to hear things are good between you two and you found your way to Mila. Dante needed his father."

Dominic sucks in a sharp breath, his eyes dropping to his toes. I can detect a dark cloud washing over him.

"Thank you," he whispers.

A sick feeling of nerves floods the pit of my stomach. He's hiding something. Worrying, maybe his sick cancer could've returned.

As Dominic, Dante, and Uncle Roger are watching football, I go upstairs to get dressed before dinner. I stand in my walk-in closet wearing just my lacy underwear and matching bra. Suddenly, strong, masculine, warm arms wrap around my waist. He shuffles my hair to the side and kisses begin to be planted on the curve of my neck. I moan at his touch. Tilting my neck to the side, I welcome more of his soft kisses on my skin.

"I need you, Angel." His dark husky voice vibrates like a melody on my skin. His erection rubs against my ass.

I twirl around to face him, interwinding my fingers around his neck and kissing him like a savage. It's been weeks since we've had sex. He says he's too busy with work and he leaves once Dante goes to bed. Somehow, I feel he's avoiding me. I'm distraught by how much distance he's placed between us. I've missed him.

"I need you too."

Dominic unclasped my bra, freeing my breasts. "I love your big tits, baby. You're beautiful." He bites his bottom lip. His brown eyes flame with lust as he pinches each nipple.

My nipples grow hard as pebbles, pressing against the fabric of his dress shirt.

"These are mine." He sucks so hard on my breasts, and I hiss with pleasure.

God, I've missed his touch, his mouth. His kisses trail down to my stomach, and he kneels to peel my laced underwear off.

"Fuck, Mila, you're so perfect and this pussy is mine." He places soft kisses between my legs.

"We don't have much time. Someone could walk in at any minute," I pant, sinking my teeth into my bottom lip.

"I'll be quick, Angel, let me just get you ready for me."

Dominic brushes the tips of his fingers in between my legs and center inserts two fingers. His touch is reminiscent of a flame burning hot searing in me as a touch of a flame to a candle.

"Spread your legs, Mila, I want to see your cum drip down your legs, baby."

Oh heavens. A man on his knees for his woman, pleasuring her isn't weakness. It is the most beautiful thing in a man, a reverence so powerful and so fucking hot. As if he could read my mind, he looks at me through his long, thick, black eyelashes.

"Only for you, Angel, no other woman holds a candle to you, baby."

My walls come crashing down. I'm so wet it drizzles down my leg, Dominic catches it with his tongue. He licks up to my center, twirling his tongue, sucking so hard my knees wobble. I hold onto the wall for support.

"God, Dominic, don't stop," I moan. "That tongue of yours works magic."

He laughs in between my legs. He slaps my ass. "Lay down, baby. Let me fuck you."

I unbutton his shirt, and my hand roams his olive-tanned sculpted, chest. He has a perfect V line. The feel of his body makes my mouth water.

I trace the forehead tattoo and then kiss it. His body is so perfect, with so much muscle. The tempo of his heart accelerates as I slip my hands around his waist and undo the button on his jeans. His cock stands hard against my abdomen, and he draws in a ragged breath.

"Mila, I need to be inside you." Precum spills from his cock. I stroke up and down with his hooded eyes watching me. He moans.

"Lay down, Dominic," I command, his lips twitching into a smirk. Kneeling down, I eagerly take him in my mouth tasting him. My tongue traces the thick veins, gliding in rasping strokes. Deep throating, I take him deeper. He grunts and moans. He dips two fingers in my center as I take him in my mouth. I moan into his cock.

I straddle him, swaying my hips as I bounce up and down, feeling his every thrust from within. His arms cinch tight around my waist, pulling me closer as I increase the pace. Our mouths crash together, our tongues tangling in a passionate embrace. With each movement, our bodies melt into one another, creating an intoxicating rhythm.

"Fuck, baby, you feel so good. I need you so bad, Angel."

Breathlessly, I say, "You have me."

God, he feels so good. He flips us over. Once I'm underneath him, I wrap my legs around his waist. I lift my bottom for him to piston in deeper. More. His perfectly sculpted body moves in perfect rhythm.

"More. Harder," I cry out.

Our mouths press, kissing hungrily swallowing each other's moans. I dig my nails into his back. We come hard and fast.

Dominic rolls off panting. "Let's clean up, baby, and get ready to eat before Nana finds us naked."

We gather around the table, Nana utters grace. I glance around the table, grateful I'm surrounded by the people I love. Surreal soul-stirring warmth drapes over me. Never would've thought, I would have Dominic at our dinner table. God is good. He holds my hand under the table rubbing my thumb. I know he feels the same way. We both study Dante stuffing his face with mashed potatoes.

"This is so good, Mommy."

I clear my throat swallowing the mouth full of turkey. "Your auntie made the mashed potatoes."

"So good, Auntie." He gives her a thumbs up.

We all chatter around the table. Dominic's gaze falls to the ground, unable to meet anyone else's eyes. My heart squeezes. What's going on with him?

"Are you feeling, okay?" I whisper faintly.

"I'm good, baby."

"I've missed you."

His smile curls. "Me too, Angel." He wipes his mouth dabbing the napkin on his chin, then bites into his dinner roll. "You did good, Mila, best Thanksgiving ever."

"Many more to come," I say, hopeful as I wipe a smear of mashed potatoes on the corner of his mouth.

He swallows hard, turning his gaze to Dante.

My stomach churns, what's going on with him? Mustering a smile, I try to ignore his reaction. Enjoying the night stuffing ourselves with delicious food.

Twenty-Six
MILA

A chilling breeze, which makes my skin shiver, kisses my skin. I reach inside my purse and take out my red scarf, wrapping it around myself to stay warm. I savor the aroma of the sea breeze and the crash of the early-morning waves. I gather my equipment, preparing for a family photo shoot. I take a breath of the morning's salty air.

Nana and Uncle Roger left for Manhattan yesterday. I miss them already. Moving back to San Diego was the best decision I could have made, not expecting to see Dominic. Our destiny was written for us in the stars, perhaps love drew us back to one another. I sound like my smutty books. I'm the happiest I've been in a long time. Every day, I fall deeper in love with him. The thought scares me while I'm falling, and he's drawing back. My walls are crumbling down and his are going up.

Could it be work? Or am I just a phase like the bitch stated in her text? It leads me to believe there's more to it, maybe it has to do with his mom meddling with our relationship.

"Hey, girls! Let's go have lunch I'm starved." Sophie rubs her belly, staring at Daliah and me. She must be hungry because her stare could kill. I chuckle; she turns into Godzilla when she's hungry or hangry.

"Sure, let's get food in you before you turn into Godzilla."

She flips me off. Daliah and I share a wry chuckle.

I love her.

We traipse our way into Jerry's Pub, the smell of food has my stomach grumbling. I didn't even realize I was this hungry. We're seated in a corner booth. We all idly eye the menu while considering what to get. Anger wells up inside of me like a lump of burning coal when I hear a familiar voice tinged with betrayal.

"Can I take your order?"

I look up at the conniving bitch. She gasps when she recognizes it's me.

"How are you doing, Skylar? I assume well, right? I heard you had been throwing yourself on Dominic these past five years like a frantic slut obsessing over my man. You've been lying to me all this time, so you can pursue him. Hearing me sob as I grieve his passing when you were aware he was still alive. You heartless shit! We have a kid, Skylar, and we had been talking for three years."

"This is her?" Sophie injects with a clipped tone.

"Yup, that's her."

Skylar's bewildered eyes bulge out of their sockets. Her color drains ghost white. "I-I-I'm sorry, Mila," she bats her fake lashes, stuttering.

Skylar's always been a manipulative bitch. I should have known better. Who would scheme such evilness?

"Fuck you, Skylar, don't fucking give me your fake apology. You knew what you were doing. You're not sorry. My son lost four years from his dad."

"I- I didn't know you were pregnant." Darkness seeps through her bones. She's so damn fake.

A malicious laugh rolls off my tongue. "You wouldn't give a shit if I was pregnant or not. You've always been a selfish tramp. You always had a crush over him. He never wanted you. He told me what transpired at the bar, you're pitiful, Skylar. You've been like this since high school."

She looks at me through her fake eyelashes and smirks.

That fucking bitch.

"You have it all wrong, Mila. He's only with you now because you have a son, and it's all fresh. Otherwise, he would've stayed with Samantha, or maybe they will get back together after he gets bored with you. You're just a phase." She shrugs her shoulder. She flips her golden blonde hair.

Fuck her.

Adrenaline spikes subconsciously as I stand up and slap her hard across the face. A thunderclap vibrates throughout the room.

She gasps, massaging her cheek. She jolts off to the restroom.

Oh God, I've never hit anyone before, this is not me. Shock heats up at me, noticing the people around me watching. I sit back down Sophie and Daliah's mouths gape wide open.

"Damn, this was amazing. Fuck that slut, don't feel bad, Mila, she deserved it." A grin jots across Daliah's face.

"Let's get the fuck out of here before we get kicked out; we can just hit the food trucks."

I nod to Sophie, still in shock, I slapped her. Honestly, it felt good. I'm not the violent type. Damnit, she pissed me off. Is Dominic with me because of Dante? He has been distant. Why are they all saying I'm just a phase? *Don't let her get to you, Mila.*

"Come on, Jackie Chan, let's get out of here." Daliah swings her arm around my shoulder.

I giggle.

WE HAVE A FULL DAY PLANNED. Dominic is taking us to pick out a Christmas tree, lights, decorations, and all the good stuff. Grayson Farms has the best Christmas trees, and an apple farm. One of my favorite recollections is picking apples and a tree with dad.

He would say, *"Pick a Christmas tree that's special to you, one that catches your eye."* My smile brightens at the thought of him.

"I can't believe you slapped her, babe. Damn, I wish I could have been there." He smiles with a face-splitting grin.

"I can't believe it either. She pissed me off, I just can't get over the fact she was lying to us the whole time and trying to get in your pants the whole time. Fake bitch." My nose swells with anger, blowing a puff of steam.

Dominic reaches for my hand, kissing my knuckles. "Don't let that bitch get to you, Angel, she's not worth it. She's not worth thinking about."

I nod in agreement.

"Mommy, Daddy, are we almost there?" Dante jumps in his seat excitedly.

"Almost there, buddy."

Twenty minutes later, we arrive. "We're here, Dante."

He squeals. The smell of fresh pine invades our noses. I jump out of the truck and stretch my legs from the hour-long drive.

"It's been a long time since I've been here. The last time was with my dad. So many significant memories," I say to Dominic.

He stiffens, and his jaw tightens. I kiss his cheek, and he immediately relaxes. He cups my cheek and presses kisses on my lips.

"I'm sorry, Angel. Allow me to make this day memorable for you both. I'm sorry you don't have your dad here to continue your tradition, baby." His mouth sinks into a sad smile. My arms lock around his neck, pressing another kiss on his lips. He wraps his arms around my waist, pulling me in more. Kissing me deeper.

"It already is... memorable," I say, inhaling a stuttering breath, still catching my breath from his hot lips.

He kisses me one last time before releasing me.

"Come on, guys," Dante shouts. "Look, Mommy, animals. Can we go see them?"

Dominic intertwines his fingers with mine. With my free hand, I intertwine my fingers with Dante's.

"Of course, baby." I adore watching Dante so animated.

He'll become fixated on remembering all the times that he's

come with his parents because I enjoy carrying on our traditions. An opportunity for him to cherish his father-son relationship the way I have.

We make our way to the petting zoo. Dante's flabbergasted, petting the goats, ponies, and chicks. When he's done, we head over to rows upon rows of trees. Dante stands tall staring at a six-foot-tall, tree. His eyes glisten alluringly. Tilting his head at an angle.

"I want that one, Daddy."

"Are you sure that's the one you like?"

"Yes, Mommy." His pink cheeks flush with the chilly breeze.

"Good job, little man. You picked a special one," Dominic praises him.

I'm in awe staring at them both, his little mini-me. Equally, hands in their pockets they stare up, grinning showing their white teeth. His wandering eyes peer into mine. Dominic's long thick lashes flutter as he winks flirtatiously.

"Are you good, Angel, having fun?" he asks, seeming very pleased with himself. He purses his lips for a kiss.

"Never been this happy I'm with my two favorite guys."

"Me too, baby."

I sigh as I breathe in the piney aroma. The smell reminds me of those scented holiday candles. "I long for us to carry on this tradition every year," I say with a grin.

He swallows hard. He shifts uncomfortably, his cinnamon-whiskey eyes pinned to the wet dirt.

"Umm, we should get someone to help us with, umm... the tree." He turns away from me and waves down one of the workers to carry our tree to the front.

I shrug it off, putting it off for now, not wanting to ruin the moment.

"Baby, let me sit you on my shoulder, so you can reach the apples on top." Luckily, we found a couple of trees left,
    as it was the last pick of the year.
    "Don't you dare drop me, Dominic."
    He flexes his biceps and bounces his pecs.
    Holy shit.
    He grins stupidly.
    "Daddy, that's so cool! You're so strong."
    Dante tries to bounce his pecs, shaking his body, he tries so hard. Instead, he puts his hands on his chest, lifting his pecs up and down.
    "See, Daddy, I can do it too!"
    Dominic's shoulders shake in laughter. I do the same. Kids are so funny.
    "Mila, I would not dare to drop you; I need my girl in one piece. Besides, these muscles you love to hold on to when I make love to you can hold you perfectly. Let's not forget you've been on my shoulder before, just facing the opposite way in the shower, my face buried between your legs," his husky voice whispers in my ear.
    A flame of heat sears my core, warming up my body from the frigid chill. My face flushes ten shades of red. His eye lasering right at my center biting his eager lips.
    "I'll reply that later," he mutters. Dominic grips my bottom as he gently lifts me over his shoulder.
    We filled a bucket of apples with enough to make an apple pie and some apple crisp, Dominic's favorite. Luckily, I didn't fall on my ass off Dominic's shoulder. His hard, broad, powerful muscles held me up effortlessly. Driving back to my place, Dante falls asleep. We stop at a drive-thru to grab burgers for dinner.
    "How's work going? You've seemed off lately, you've seemed different. I don't mean to pry, I'm just worried we don't see much of you."
    He sighs, gripping the steering wheel tight. He reaches for my

hand, bringing it to his mouth, pressing a soft kiss on my knuckles.

"I'm sorry, baby, work has been crazy. I'm hiring two new people this week. I have orientation and training." He smiles weakly.

An uneasy feeling cuts into the pit of my stomach. My shoulders stiffen. Furrowing my brows. He brushes a strand of hair tucking it behind my ear.

"Come here, baby."

I slid my way toward the center next to him. He pivots to face me. The tip of his tongue traces my lips. I inhale mint mingling in his breath. Invading my softness with his mouth, he glides over mine. His thick tongue writhes around in mine as it explores. Dominic uses the simplest of gestures to show me how much he cares about me in place of using words. He cups my cheeks in the palms of his hands.

He intensifies the kiss. His passionate kiss deepens, and my worries, and uncertainty are forgotten. Dominic's lips hungrily drink up mine, and I can hardly catch my breath. The sensation of his calloused thumb gently tracing my lips keeps me rooted in the moment. I stay in the embrace, savoring our swollen lips.

"You know, there's one thing we haven't done. I would like to take you out on a date next Saturday."

I am completely mesmerized by Dominic's striking olive skin, whiskey-brown eyes, prominent brow, and long eyelashes. Dominic has the most attractive appearance of any man I've ever seen; his full, plump lips and sculpted jaw make me fall in love. On a date? I haven't been on a date with him in so long, like a little more than five years. I arch my left eyebrow quizzically.

"A date?"

He brushes his thumb on my cheek with a chuckle. "Yes, my Angel, a date. I already asked Sophie to watch Dante, and she said yes."

"Okay, then I guess it's a yes."

"Baby, you didn't have an option."

We move to the next window as a teenage girl hands us our food.

Twenty-Seven

DOMINIC

It's been four weeks since I found out what my mother has done. Liam has been pressing me to tell Mila he can't sit on it for too much longer. I get it he can lose his job. It's been four fucking weeks of seeing less of Mila. She questions my absence, and I lie, blaming it on work. I plan on telling her everything, the day after our date.

Yes, I'm a selfish asshole. Before she ends it, I want to give her the best night. A night we will both remember. My routine consists of picking Dante up from preschool, taking him to my place or the park, and then finally dropping him off at home once Mila gets off work. She comes home with her damn tight pencil skirts, tight jeans, or short dresses showing her beautiful, toned legs. Being around Mila is like a magnet. She pulls me toward her without even knowing it. I want to touch her all over. She's embedded in my soul and my flesh.

Last night, I stayed until Dante went to bed. I was about to walk out the door when she came out of her room in short shorts and a cropped shirt. I bit my fist out of frustration so hard it bled, tasting the metallic on my lips. Her beautiful, long black eyelashes flutter, calling my name. I kissed her goodnight and left like a fucking dick.

I want to make it somewhat easy for us. Who am I kidding? It will never be easy, she will move on. *Fuck that.* The idea of her with another man, sends blazing heat seething through my body. I pound my fist on my firm mattress. Tomorrow night I'm going to fuck her so good she will see stars, galaxy, and even the fucking universe. I will ruin her for another man. Reminding her soul to whom she will forever belong. When another man fucks her, she will think of me. My dick thrusting in her, my tongue lavishing between her legs, my lips all over her body. All she will think is it's me when another man touches her. She will crave me; I'll make sure of it. No other can satisfy her as I can.

I KNOCK on Mila's door. My son opens the door. "Hi, Daddy." He's all smiles, just like his mom.

"Hi, son, what did you do today?" I bend down to kiss his cheek.

He smells of sweat and dirt. I watch as Dante walks into the living room, chest puffed, chin up, confident and arrogant. I chuckle. He's so much like me as a kid.

"Auntie Sophie took me to get movies at Redbox, and then we got pizza and poppop-corn. For our movie night. Are you and Mommy going out?" He raises his eyebrow at me. His cuteness makes me want to laugh. He is so serious.

I keep myself collected. "Yup, I'm taking your mom out for dinner."

He nods. "You take care of her, Daddy?"

The pleading in his eyes knocks the air out of me, he is a true king. A pang in my chest hits me like a bulldozer. My son protecting his mother, I'm the one who turned her life upside down. My mom was behind the scenes this whole time, and I couldn't even protect her; she lost her father because of me. My words come out hoarse.

"Of course, son." With a dry mouth, I ask, "Where's your mom?"

"Getting dressed." He glances back at the TV.

Sophie comes out of the bathroom, looking at me with a smile. "You look nice," she says, her lips forming into a straight line.

"Fuck." I gasp like a fish needing water. Mila sways her hips down the stairs in a low, tight, forest-green dress that hugs every curve of her sculpted body. Her ass, so plump and round, ripe as a peach. My mouth waters at the sight of her luscious, beautiful, well-formed breasts spilling out. God, those creamy-toned legs I want them wrapped around my body. Her long, thick, natural eyelashes flutter.

Beautiful.

Her lips parted—plumped perfectly shaped to fit on my mouth. Fuck dinner, I'd rather eat her. Raking my gaze up and down, I lush over my gorgeous girl taking her all in. A bolt of firing heat goes straight to my dick, and it twitches. My breath hitches, my eyes fixed on her, unable to move. When I finally take a step, my legs wobble like a newborn calf. I topple over Mila catches me, before crashing to the ground.

"Hmm, you're falling head over heels for me, big guy." Her voice comes out raspy and sexy. She smiles at me, showing her bright white teeth.

"You look so beautiful, baby, like so fucking beautiful." I bite my lip, gazing at her.

"Thank you, and you look handsome as always." She winks. Even her wink is hot.

I fan myself with my hand. She giggles.

I rented a private house on the beach, so we could be alone. A place where we always felt at peace. In our teenage years of dating, we would sit with blankets wrapped around us, kissing, so much kissing, and making love to her. I knew renting this beach house would be perfect.

"O.M.G., this is beautiful, Dom. I love it ah, and the view is gorgeous." She gapes.

Dom. I love it when she calls me Dom it's not often, but when she does, it turns me on.

"You're gorgeous," I drawl, keeping my lustful eyes on her.

She smiles sweetly. I hand her a glass of wine. She presses her flawless, exquisite lips to the wine glass and takes a sip. I'm so damn jealous of a wine glass. I bite my fist so hard it pierces the skin out of frustration. All I can think of is getting her out of her dress, her lips pressed on my dick. I'm throbbing, aching. Itching to touch her, make love to her. I want this night to be special and memorable. The last thing I want to do is ruin it by fucking her first. Maybe she won't mind.

Get your shit together, Dominic.

Turning the red brick fireplace on, I head into the kitchen. I plan to cook us a nice romantic dinner—something I've never done before. Shit, I don't know if I'm doing it right. A pleasant dinner and a good fuck sound like a good plan, right?

"Mmm, it smells so good, you look so sexy, my hot sexy chef. I love watching you cook. It turns me on." The smell of her perfume lingers in the air.

"Well, fuck. I'll cook for you all the time if it turns you on this much."

A twitch of a smile on her lips. "I'd like that, I'll reward you every night."

Hell yeah.

Her arms wrap around my waist. Her cheek and breasts press on my back her soft hands rake under my shirt—fingers trailing up and down my rough hard chest. I moan, I'm so damn horny.

"Baby, goddammit, you're fucking killing me. My dick has been as high as a stallion for you, dying to be set free, throbbing, aching for you. The minute your fine ass swayed all sexy and shit coming down those stairs. All I could think about was stripping you down. Now, if you continue teasing me, I'm going to have you suck me off while I cook these damn steaks." I huff with an air of sexual frustration.

She giggles. Even her giggle sends a rush to my dick. My dick is about to spring out, pressing on the zipper. She tippy toes to kiss my cheek.

"All right then, sexy chef, what can I help you with?" She wags her eyebrows.

"Chop the vegetables, I have the potatoes baking in the oven, and don't look all sexy chopping it, or we will not make it for dinner," I mutter, as I season the steaks.

"All right, Chef," she says, with a cheeky grin.

"THIS IS SO WONDERFUL, dinner is amazing. Thank you for this, I needed it." She chews on her steak, dabbing the napkin on the corner of her mouth.

Oh, baby, I needed this too. One last time with you.

"You're welcome, Angel, anything for you." I place the dishes into the dishwasher, making my way to the sofa. She sighs softly and snuggles into my arms. Unlocking my phone, I begin going through the playlist I created for us. *Butterflies* by Max & Ali Gatie plays.

"Dance with me, Angel."

We sway to the music, her hands brushing over my head and settling on the back of my neck. Her head rests on my chest. My hands roam her exposed back, skimming my fingers on her creamy, soft silk-like skin. I let them rest on her peachy ass as I squeeze it. God, she's intoxicating.

"Did I ever tell you why I call you Angel?" I brush my thumb on her cheek. Inhaling her sweet smell.

"No, you've never told me."

I smile, reminiscing about that night. "The night we met; I noticed you before I walked in. Santiago was smoking a cigarette. I fixated my gaze on you, smiling, laughing. The most beautiful smile I've ever seen, lit up my world, those sparkling emerald eyes shined so brightly. Your head tilted back when you laughed."

I kiss her shoulder.

"I kept my eyes compulsively fixed on you for ten minutes. My heart pounded beneath my rib cage; my pulse quickened with anticipation. You appeared like an Angel sent just for me at that moment, I knew you were meant to be mine. If you didn't acknowledge me and see we're meant to be, I was going to pursue you until you fell for me."

I smirk, placing another kiss on her collarbone.

"There was no way I would give you up, baby. The minute I walked in, our eyes locked deep in my soul, yours whispered in mine. The connection is raw and organic; our souls yearn for one another. Angel, I gazed into your eyes that night. I know you saw us the same way. You left me breathless."

She sniffles on my chest.

"Baby, I'm sorry, did I say something wrong, or maybe I'm wrong, you don't..." I'm being such a sap only because I don't have much time left with her.

"That was beautiful, I love you so much, no, you're not wrong, I felt the connection. The most powerful, incredible feeling the stars aligned that night."

I press kisses on each rolling tear. "Baby, I'm made for you, and you for me. I love you. Now I need you fucking naked already."

My lips brush against hers as I hungrily kiss her; I need to feel her softness and taste her sweet flavor. I couldn't possibly survive without touching her and tasting her. My hands ache from the desire to explore her sculpted body's curves and delicate, soft milky skin, the mounds that fit perfectly in the palms of my big hands.

"Angel," I mouth into hers. "Hmm." I pull from her lips.

Both of us panting, gasping for air. I focus on her swollen red lips, drunk with lust.

"I'm going to get some blankets to lay next to the fireplace."

237

My voice comes out raspy and strained. I suck on my bottom lip, tasting the lingering flavor of Mila's lips.

She nods.

I pick up some blankets from the linen closet. I spread them out on the fluffy brown carpet. "Baby, I need to feel you underneath my skin, savor every part of your body. I'm going to take you hard, Angel. Possess your soul, baby, then I'm going to make love to you sweet and gentle until you rock the heavens with your screams."

Her breath hitches. I'm a little surprised myself but Mila brings out the romantic in me.

Our eyes swimming with lust for each other, staring at one another for a long, hot minute. As I stand behind her, I unzip her forest green off-the-shoulder dress that clings to her hips. With a shaking breath, I peel her dress down. She's so extraordinary, no other woman holds a candle to her. Unclasping her bra, I begin to massage her breasts. She throws her head back onto my shoulders, my lips feather along her collarbone lightly. She shivers in pleasure as my finger hooks onto her panties, peeling them off.

"Lay down, Angel, I'm going to ruin you, baby. Tell me you're mine, I'm the only man who gets to see you this way."

She moans as I spread her legs; such a beautiful view. She's so wet for me.

"Baby, tell me you're mine," I repeat. My tongue lashes inside her, working her open. Moisture beads and drips down her leg. I lick every drop savoring it as if it's my last taste.

She whimpers.

"Mila, answer me." Fuck, I need to hear it.

"Yours," she pants. "Yours, Dominic, don't stop."

"That a girl, you taste so good," I praise. I slowly unbuttoned my shirt, my eyes never leaving Mila's face as I expose more and more of my chest. Her beautiful green eyes never waver as I move down to my jeans; I hook my thumbs into the belt line and pull them off with a single tug exposing my very engorged dick that's been dying to break free. She's so fucking wet for me. I cup the heavy underside of her sweet mounds taking each one into my mouth. Her already hard nipples tighten further with each suck and lick. My hands slide down to her silken belly, and she moans at my touch. She spreads her legs and arches her back when I tease and work her folds. Mila is the definition of beauty.

"Dom," she whimpers.

Fuck. Mila chanting my name takes me over the edge. With my free hand, I stroke my dick as I watch her watch me with hungry eyes. I ease myself into her tight pussy, savoring the sensation of her moist warmth and gentle contraction around me. I move my hips slowly and gently, gradually building momentum. Fuck, she feels so damn good.

She whimpers and arches her back, her breathing intensifying with each thrust as I drive deeper into her depths as soon as I know she's ready to take me all in. With one final push, I feel a wave of pleasure ripple through both our bodies.

"Oh, baby, you feel so good." With one final push, she shudders. I feel another wave of pleasure flows through both our bodies.

Our eyes lock. With one deep dive in right before, she lets out a scream.

"Ahh, Dominic," she cries in pleasure.

The crisp of the burning fire mingles with our moans, grunts, and screams. I take her again, right after thrusting inside her fast and slow, filling her in one after another. I hold her hips possessively as if a tidal wave will rip her from my hold. Kissing her passionately, I swallow every moan, every scream. Our hearts beat so fast. I watch her as she comes undone, singing my name. I follow right after her, panting, a sheen of sweat trickling down as we kiss continuously.

Our hearts beat as one, dancing as one. I get lost staring into her gorgeous, bright eyes, mine darken with pain. If this is our last night together, I want her to feel my need for her. I hope she will forgive me for my mother's cruelty, ruthlessness, and vicious crime.

Even if she forgave me, she would only see me as a product of my mother's crime. A crime that robbed her of her childhood, left her parentless, and alone in this world. As much as it will pain me, I understand. I'll always love her. She's the first woman I've ever loved, and she will be the last.

I'm a selfish asshole. I took half her soul that night we met, and I'll never give it back. She belongs to me. She always will, even if she's not with me. Kissing the tip of her nose, I hold her in my arms for the last time. I brush a strand of hair pressed against her cheek. I watch as she drifts off to sleep. I tighten her in my arms. I fall asleep right after dreaming of the woman I can't live without.

Twenty-Eight

MILA

The sun shines brightly through the long-draped windows. I struggle to open my eyes and reach for my phone, which sits on the nightstand beside me. Zero missed calls, so Dante must not miss me all that much, what a little booger.

"Baby, what are you doing?" His morning voice comes out hoarse.

Setting my phone down, I turn to him. My eyes scan his beautiful naked body, half on the sheet sliding off. If only I weren't so sore, I'd go for another round. His sexy, bed hair doesn't help much. He reaches for me, pulling me into his arms. Our naked bodies press against each other.

"If you keep looking at me like this, Angel, I'll pin you down for what is round four, five, six?"

I brush my lips along his neck. "Something like that but, I don't think I'll make it another round."

"Ahh, too big, huh?"

I lift my head up and smack his chest playfully. A deep rumble of his laugh sends a kaleidoscope of butterflies swirling in me. My heart cracks at his beautiful smile. He lifts my chin and pecks my lips. His free hand creases my back gliding down to my ass.

Dominic's erection grows, the warmth of it presses on my belly. My eyelashes flutter. His lips twitch in a smirk—smug bastard.

"I'll draw you a bath, baby. I got you some of those bath bombs; what's the scent you like? That relaxes you, baby?"

My smile grows. He tilts his head in thought. Jesus, I love him so damn much.

"Lavender."

"Yeah, that. I'll drop one in for you. I'll cook you some breakfast in the meantime."

My gaze lingers over him. I'm falling in love with him more each day, drowning in the depths of him. "You're too good to me." I kiss his soft lips.

"You deserve the world, Angel; anything for you." He stands up, walking his naked ass to the bathroom.

After relaxing in the vast oval bathtub, I slip on leggings and a sweater. I make my way downstairs to the smell of fresh coffee, eggs, and diced potatoes. Dominic stands in front of the stove in sweats, a t-shirt, and a backward baseball cap looking, sexy as hell. *Jesus.*

"Smells good," I say, making my way toward him. Standing on my tippy toes, I kiss his stubbled cheek.

"Here you go, beautiful, scrambled eggs, bacon, and potatoes. If I had more groceries, I would've made you your favorite French toast."

God, he's so cute.

"This is perfect. It was all perfect; the best date ever."

He sets our plates on the breakfast bar. "Would you consider this a date you'll always remember?" He raises an eyebrow.

"Of course."

He sighs, as he sits next to me.

"Is everything okay? You look lost in thought," I murmur.

He smiles faintly. There it is again. The unsettling feeling bubbles in my gut. His eyes are telling me something's going on.

"I'm good baby." His phone buzzes in the pocket of his sweats. "Hello, Mario."

I devour my breakfast as Dominic talks on the phone.

"Fuck," he shouts, slamming the phone on the counter.

I jump, startled. "What happened?"

"It was Mario, we have plumbing problems. A leak... it flooded the kitchen." He rakes his hands in his hair. "Fucking hell, I'm going to have to close down for the next couple of days. Shit, this is going to suck."

IT'S BEEN three days since I've seen Dominic, he's been busy at the restaurant. He sends text messages, asking how I'm doing or about Dante. He's been more remote, barely talking. He seems to only communicate by texting, but even then, his messages are infrequent. I realize he has plumbing problems going on, but the penetrating tug in my chest says otherwise.

Our date was amazing; I dressed in the sexiest dress Sophie helped pick out. I watched him watch me the entire night, damn, it was hot.

"Hello, earth to Mila Amaro." Daliah snaps her fingers at me.

I swat them away.

"Are you fantasizing about your hot man?"

"Kinda."

She wiggles her eyebrows.

"Your ten o'clock is here. Baby photo shoots are the most adorable, especially when it is with twins."

I prop the newborn twins in a basket, a little blue blanket propping them up. The thought of us growing our family has me smiling as I snap photos of the sweet babies. Dominic and I should discuss moving in together. I love waking up in his arms. His strong arms wrapped around me, spooning me as he grinds into me. I admit I let him crash my walls down. That last night of sex, the way he worked every part of my body.

"All right, we are all done," I tell the proud parents as they pick up their bundles of joy. "We will have them ready for pick up next week or we could mail them out to you."

"Pick up is fine." She smiles as she coos at the babies.

"Great, see you then."

As I sit in my reclining chair to eat lunch in my office, my phone buzzes. I look at my text message from Dominic.

Dominic: *Baby, can you meet me at my place in like 30 minutes?*

Me: *Sure, is everything okay?*

Dominic: *Yes, baby.*

Me: *Okay, I'll be there in 30.*

Dominic: *Okay.*

I fix my hair, smoothing out my skirt as I knock on Dominic's door. The door swings open. I swallow the knot forming in my throat. A grimace of shocked disbelief burns through me. I am peeved at seeing Samantha holding the door in one of Dominic's T-shirts and messy hair, as if they just had sex. Her ass hanging out, obviously without underwear. She smirks at my reaction.

"What are you doing here?" A feral sneer curls at my lips.

She laughs mirthfully.

"Oh, Dominic didn't tell you, we are back together. The engagement is on." She flashes her ring at me, flipping her blonde hair.

"Mmm, we had a wild night last night. He fucked me like he missed me. You just missed him. As you can see, you were just a fling, Mila. A high school crush, but he got it all out of his system. All you were, was just a phase. He told me himself. He begged me for another chance he loves me."

The memory of those photos of them having sex knocks the air out of me. He's back with her.

I hold back the tears. I won't let her see me shed a tear for them. She stumbles back, reaching for a paper.

"Oh, here, I found this. I'm assuming he didn't tell you this either, as you're not important to him."

She hands me a paper, from the San Diego Police Department. Opening the paper, I find Rachel's name, the paper claims the neighbor next door witnessed Rachel as a suspect in the house fire on Marul Lane.

My house.

What the fuck! I'm frozen in place staring at the paper. The bitch speaks.

"Dominic used you, Mila, you're nothing. His mom and family will come first and, of course, me. By the way, he screamed my name said, I'm the best fuck he's ever had." She slams the door in my face.

I felt in my gut these past few weeks something was up; he had been acting differently and withdrawing from us. The need to run, to scream, overcomes me. But my body becomes petrified stone. I don't know how I made it to my townhouse.

I texted Sophie, asking if she could pick Dante up from school. Crawling into bed, I sob, letting the tears flow. He's back with Samantha, his mom's responsible for my father's death, and she tried to kill me.

He lied to me and manipulated me. I welcomed him in only for him to push me away again. I had put a wall around my heart for a reason, not wanting it to be used as something to be stepped upon. I've been so naïve; everything was a fabrication as a part of a plan to save his mother.

So, I wouldn't file a complaint. He betrayed me once again. The thorns pricking at my heart cause me to feel as if I am bleeding, I am bewildered. The hands of that monster murdered my poor father. She took him from me.

Deep down, I know his family will come first, his mother and the woman he's going to marry. He broke my heart. I'm the fool who handed it to him and he selfishly took it. I pick up the phone and dial Dominic's number.

"Hello, Angel, I was just about to call you."

"Fuck you, w-why didn't you tell me about Rachel b-b-blowing up my house, Dominic?"

Fuck I hate he's hearing the weakness in my voice.

"How long have you known? Was it all a lie to use me so I wouldn't turn your mom in? To give you my heart so I would get over what your mother has done. You motherfucker!" I inhale slowly, my chest feeling tight and constricted. My phone trembles in my hand as I press it against my head.

"Baby, no I found out a month ago, I just didn't know how to tell you."

"Don't call me, baby, I'm not your baby. I don't want to have anything to do with you. You broke me, Dominic. Do you care about Dante, or was that a lie too?"

"Fuck no, I love Dante. Mila, he's, my son."

"I'll allow you to see him. You can pick him up on Wednesdays and Thursdays from school and bring him home for dinner and we will only talk about Dante. I have nothing else to talk to you about. I don't want my son around anyone else in your family or Samantha." I wipe my tears.

"Okay, yeah of course. I'll get him on Wednesdays and Thursdays, Angel, please let's talk about this. I haven't—"

I cut him off, "I fucking hate you, Dominic. You used me, lied to me, broke me again. You led me to believe what we had was real. You manipulated me into falling in love with you all over again. It was always her." I hang up the phone.

I splash water on my face, then, I ball myself on the bathroom floor, hyperventilating. I feel an icy chill settle over me, as if I'm not worthy of his mercy. He left me shattered to pieces. Why would Rachel kill my father? I'm positive it was intended to be me; she wanted me dead. She hated me this much. She would kill my father and me... both.

I can't believe he's with Samantha; maybe I was his sidepiece all along. Did he mean it when he told me he loved me? Was I not enough for him? The date: Was it real or a trap... A lie? Did he plan on getting back with her all this time? So many questions and no answers. I'm too shattered to find the truth. Not yet, but I will.

"Babe, what happened?" Sophie walks into the bathroom.

"W-Where's Dante?" I'm weeping, uncontrollably.

"He's in his room," she softly whispers. "Mila, you're scaring me what happened?"

I lean on her shoulder holding onto her, crying my heart out to her.

"I-I went to his place. He sent me a text. When I got there S-Samantha was there in his T-shirt, and she said they're back together, and the worst part was she handed me this." I hand her the police report.

She gasps.

"What in the hell is this? His mom, Rachel Delgado?"

Nodding, I say, "His mom started the fire. Crazy bitch killed my dad and I'm assuming she's not behind bars." I weep in her hold.

"Have you talked to Dominic?" Her forehead creases.

"I called him and asked him why he lied to me. I just couldn't talk to him. I'm fucking broken, Sophie. I feel used. I gave him my heart the second time around," I say, my heart cracking with each beat.

Sophie soothes my back.

"We will get through this, Mila. You're not alone. You have me always, sisters for life."

Sniffling, I wipe my tears with my shirt. "Why, Sophie, why? I've been through so much. I lost my dad because of her then I thought I lost Dominic. I spent five years mourning his loss. To find him engaged. He asked for another chance. For another chance at *us*. But for what? So, he can shatter me, leave me? To mess with my heart? He lied to me. God, Sophie I'm so confused. My head's spinning." My shoulders deflate as I rest my head against the bathroom wall.

"Maybe you shouldn't let him see Dante until things get sorted. His mom is dangerous. I don't presume Dominic would let anyone hurt Dante, but I don't trust his mom. We don't know what she's capable of. She's a conniving bitch."

Shit, she's right. My head is spinning; I didn't think of it.

"You're right. I told him he could pick him up on Wednesdays and Thursdays. I'll just let him know I changed my mind."

"Come on, let's go downstairs. I'll make us some grilled cheese and a glass of wine. Dante will be looking for us."

I nod, wiping the snot dripping down.

"Mommy, look, I made Santa a letter."

My heart breaks when I see, Dante standing in front of me with his beautiful big brown eyes. My innocent baby. We tangled him in this mess, and all he wanted was his father and a family. Sophie is correct, I don't know what dynamics Dominic has played in this, or what his mother is capable of. She's dangerous, after all; it's my fault I should have guarded my heart, keeping my walls up.

As a mother, keeping my son safe is my priority. I let love and lust cloud my thoughts as they say, love is blind. My heart bleeds. He's in love with another woman. It was never me; it was a lie, all of it I'm the fool, the one who got played.

"Oh, that's sweet, honey, Santa will love it."

He frowns when his eyes meet mine. "Mommy, are you okay?"

I caress his cheek.

"Yes, baby, I'm fine, just tired, and I think I'm getting a cold," I lie.

"You should lay down, Mommy. Me and Auntie Sophie will make yummy grilled cheese," he says, his smile reaching his brown eyes.

"Little man is right, lie down on the sofa, Mila, we will get dinner started, as requested by my Dante."

The gratitude I have for Sophie is beyond words. She has been my rock from the very beginning. My New Yorker is a fierce warrior, generous and devoted, the kind of friend you keep safe and never let go. She's like a sister to me.

While I massage my throbbing temple, my phone buzzes with twenty missed calls and ten messages for Dominic. I erase the messages; I don't bother reading; instead, I turn off my phone. I sigh, why me? What did I do to deserve all this? Why did my dad have to pay for all this? It was all my fault. I should have never dated Dominic. My dad might still be alive. Howling sobs escape me. I bring a pillow to my face to cover my sobs.

"Here you go, milady, a strong glass of wine. Oh, honey, I'm going to strangle that son of a bitch and his fucking psycho mother. And the dumb ass bimbo he has."

"Thank you for always having my back."

She grabs a tissue, wipes away my tears, and brushes off the boogers. I feel like a child. "Always, Mila, you, and Dante are my family."

I sip a tall glass of wine, letting the alcohol cloud my brain. I need something more substantial. *I need to feel numb*, but this will do for tonight.

Twenty-Nine

DOMINIC

My phone is grasped so tightly in my hands that it might break. I take a few breaths in an effort to compose my racing thoughts. I've lost track of how many times I've called Mila, yet she never answers. The words she left me with replay in my head: 'I hate you.' I had somehow known this would be her response. I don't blame her; my mom took her father away from her and plotted on her being there as well. I don't know how she found out, but I phoned Liam and asked if he had told her.

He said no and said I told you to tell her before she heard from someone else. I pound my fist on my desk; I need to get the fuck out of here. I've lashed out at everyone in sight. I'm so close to knocking Mila's door down. I know I can't do that; I'll scare Dante, which is the last thing I want to do. I prepared myself for this for an entire month. The truth is nothing can prepare me for losing her all over again. With my keys, I walk to my car and drive to the nearest liquor store. I grab a twelve-pack of beer and a bottle of whiskey from the cooler. Tonight, my only solace is to drink until my pain is numb.

I chugged the last lukewarm beer of the twelve-pack, leaving a foamy mustache on my upper lip. Staggering, I make my way across the room to a bottle of cheap whiskey. The surround sound system blares *Don't Let Me Go* by Cigarettes After Sex, as I pour a shot of whiskey and slump onto the sofa. The burning sensation trickles down my throat warmed my chest. I close my eyes and think of Mila as the song plays, just then there is a knock at the door.

"Mila," I say, stumbling to the door. No, it's not Mila. It's ... Samantha.

"Hey baby, I missed you," she coos, barging in. "Let me take care of you."

I let her in and close the door behind her. She throws her expensive handbag on the table.

"What are you doing here?" I slur.

Her lust-filled eyes take me in like fine wine. "I came to take care of my man; I have just what you need."

She's wearing a long, brown high priced fur coat that reaches her knees. She slowly unties the knot, and it slides down her body like a snake shedding its skin. Standing in the room, she is completely and utterly naked. My eyes roam her slim figure and land on her hard nipples. I notice she has more curves than before. Her big brown eyes are full of lust, desire, and want. Her polished fingers dance across my bare chest. I brush her fingers off.

"You need to leave," I slur.

She rolls her eyes. She licks her bright red lips. "Oh, come on, I know you want me." Her delight rings warm in her voice. She kisses my cheek. "I can make you forget; I can make you feel good." A smile flickers on her lips; Her breath comes out, panting.

I let my eyes roam her naked body. I'm not interested in her whatsoever. All she has on is her Christian Louboutin high heels. I turn to pour myself another glass of whiskey, I will require it for what I'm going to do next.

THE FOLLOWING DAY, I knew what I need to do. I begin typing, sending a group text to my brothers, informing them to meet me at my house in an hour. It's time they knew the truth.

"What's going on, Dom?" Santiago grunts. Not pleased, I woke him up.

"And why do you look like shit?"

I grab a bottle of Tylenol for my pounding headache and hangover. With two tablets in hand, I swallow it down with a glass of water. Taking a lungful deep breath, I say, "A witness came forward after all these years they found out who started the fire and killed Mila's dad."

"That's great," Mark replies.

My shoulders slump, this all feels like a big nightmare, a horror movie.

"Fortunately, Liam took the report; he's holding onto it. Detective Johnson sent the neighbor in to give Liam the report and he's been after him to turn it in. They had a surveillance camera, and the person who started it... was Mom."

Marks's glass of water slips from his grip and spatters on the floor.

"What the fuck? This can't be right, Dom, Mom would never do something like this. She wouldn't even hurt a fly," Mark shouts.

I scratch my stubbled chin. "That's what I said. I needed proof. Liam showed me the footage. It is Mom. I haven't confronted Mom yet, but I told Liam I needed to talk to Mila first. I-I- didn't know how to tell her, it's been a month," I say, stumbling over my words.

Closing my eyes, I take another deep breath.

"She found out from someone else, not sure who. She won't talk to me. She wants nothing to do with me. She's hurt and thinks I had something to do with it. I lied to her for a month. Honestly, I'm so damn confused as to why Mom would do this."

Santiago is quiet as he walks into the living room, sinking into the sofa. His eyes cast up to the ceiling.

"Why haven't they arrested her yet?" Santiago stares at me, pale as a ghost.

"Liam was waiting for me to tell Mila before word got out. Mom doesn't know anything."

He nods.

We all sit on the sofa quietly, lost in our thoughts, so many questions and no answers. Our minds whirl in confusion as we gape in disbelief.

Mark sighs. His elbows rest on his knees. Head dipped down.

"Why does Mom hate Mila so much? Why would she want to try and kill her? Jesus, Dominic, good thing you went to her house that night. You know, I remember that night. Mom said she was going to the grocery store. She came back with nothing," Mark says, in a gruff voice.

Santiago and Mark's eyes are glassy over the news. I've had days, weeks to absorb the ruckus in our lives. This is all fresh to them. Santiago stands up, taking a glass from the cabinet. He pours us all whiskey.

"Mom made Mila the villain when it was her the whole time. She lied. For five years, she kept you away from Mila, and she's forcing you to marry Samantha. I can't believe this, bro, why the hell would Mom do this? I can't grasp all this," Santiago says, as he takes the glass of whiskey to his mouth.

"Only Mom has the answers," I tell them.

Santiago slams his fist on the sofa.

"How can she betray us like this? If she had signs of remorse, we would've seen it." Mark sobs as I him toward me to comfort him.

"You can come stay with me, bro," Santiago says to Mark.

He nods.

"We can't let Mom know," I tell them.

SINCE MY BROTHERS LEFT, I have been sitting in the dark, in my living room, nursing a bottle of whiskey. Thinking of Mila and Dante. Why did my mom have to fuck it all up for my brothers and me? Why couldn't she see me happy? Isn't it what mothers want for their kids, to see them happy and in love? She never reached out to Dante or showed any type of guilt or remorse. Unfortunately, the story of my life doesn't come easy. I miss Mila so damn much. The phone rings. It's probably my brother.

"Hello."

"Dominic, I called to let you know it's not a good idea for you to see Dante right now. I don't trust your mother. She plotted to kill me, she's a murderer. I won't let her hurt or come after my son. You lied to me. You betrayed me all over again. I don't know what's true or not. If you had given a shit, you would have put her behind bars to protect your son. It's only obvious you defend her actions," she bellows with rage.

My heart deflates.

"Fuck no, I'm not defending her actions. I would never let anything happen to him, baby—you know that."

"Like I said, I don't know what's true or not coming out of your mouth. It's best we hold off until things get sorted out, and she's locked up." Her beautiful voice cracks.

"Baby, please..." I beg when she interjects.

"I'm not your baby."

My heart deflates with her rejection.

I need her.

"Mila, you can supervise our visit I just need to see him," I slur.

Fuck.

"I'll think about it, but for right now It's better to wait."

"Please, Angel, I..."

"Are you drunk?"

"Mila, I just had a little to drink."

She sniffles.

"Angel?"

The phone line clicks off. She hung up on me.

Shit, shit, tossing my phone across the room, dragging my fingers through my hair. Fuck, I want to pull my hair out. Goddammit, I don't blame her for not letting me see Dante, I don't trust my mother, but fuck, I would never let my mother hurt her or him. I respect her wish for now. If only she would let me explain things to her. Technically, I don't know my mother's malicious reasons as to why she would stoop this low to do something like this. Leo was a great man and a noble father. Thank God I picked up Mila that night; I could've lost her.

I lost her anyway. She's not mine anymore, maybe she never really was. I lost my son in the mix. Back to being shit lonely. My heart sinks with memories of our date. I knew then it would be the last night I held her in my arms. The last time she'd smile at me, kiss me, and make love with me. She'll always be the one woman I can't have. I'll have to watch from the sidelines as another man does all the things, I couldn't do for her. My black-haired raven clawed her way into my soul, leaving an imprint. I'll gladly take each claw mark in remembrance of her once being mine.

What Rachel has done is unforgivable.

IT'S BEEN four miserable days since I last heard from Mila. The only reminders I have of her are our memories, and the tattoos imprinted in my flesh. Has she forgotten about me? Was I easy to forget? It would come as no surprise, Mila is drop-dead gorgeous, smart, kind, strong-minded, and a hell of an exceptional mother. Jealousy clouds my thoughts, what if she went to Ken, or Brian, or whatever his name is for comfort. The fucker was right, I would fuck up. I'm sure he's running to her rescue. She will move on eventually. I shoot her a text.

Dominic: *How's Dante doing?*

Ten minutes later she answers.

Mila: *He's doing good.*

Dominic: *Tell him I miss him and love him.*

Mila: *Will do.*

Her words are short and cold.

"You reek of alcohol and look like shit," Santiago strolls into my office.

"You don't look too good yourself," I say, scrutinizing him.

He has dark circles around his eyes, his stubble has grown into a beard, and he smells of weeks-old clothes. He sighs and pulls a chair in front of my desk. He's been quiet for a good ten minutes solid; we both are. His hands drape onto his lap.

"I can't wrap my head around this. Feels so unreal. Why the fuck would she pull this shit, why dude, she left her parentless. A poor teenage girl and an innocent girl. I know Mom can be excruciating, but to commit murder," Santiago says, enraged as he slams his fist on the desk, his nostrils flaring.

The palms of my hands run up and down my cheeks with aggravation. I gulp through the dry patch of my throat; it feels like I just swallowed a handful of sand.

"I can't sleep, I can't eat. I think back to the past years to see if I've missed anything. Some kind of sign or something." My voice comes out throaty.

"What if she would have died that night?" Santiago's eyes widen at the thought.

For years it's all I thought about. Now more than ever.

"She doesn't trust me with Dante now. She's afraid Mom might hurt him. Since she thinks I had something to do with it, she won't talk to me," I say, looking up at the white ceiling closing my eyes.

"She's right, Dom. We can't trust Mom with Dante. We don't know what's going on in her head; I've always thought Mom had some kind of mental illness. It's time... You need to tell Liam to take her in. We need answers, and Mr. Amaro needs justice. We need closure. We need to keep Dante and Mila safe. I let Mila down. I'm the oldest; I should have noticed something. Now all I can do is keep my nephew safe and Mila," he says, disoriented, his voice strangled. Santiago stands from his seated position; he taps my desk and exhales a harsh breath.

"Give her time, Dominic, I'm sure this is all too much for her. She just found out our mother is the reason she lost her father." He pats my shoulder and walks off without another word.

I pick up the phone making the most complex phone call I've ever had to make.

Thirty

MILA

The stars are bright tonight, and the moonlight glistens off the blue water. I sit wrapped in a blanket staring at the calmness of the ocean. Two weeks have passed since I bluntly received the news or instead got a two-for-one special—Samantha's half-nakedness at Dominic's and shoving the report in my face. My stomach churns at the thought of him with her. I huff with anger. Never in a million years would I have thought Rachel would do this. I thought maybe it was an accident. I never thought someone would want to kill us, especially not her.

"I'm sorry Dad, I'll make sure that bitch pays for this." I look up at the sky as the stars twinkle. "I love you, Dad." My heart squeezes with pain for my dad and the love of my life, who made me a pawn in his game. They say grieving the living is worse than the dead. When I thought Dominic had died, my anger would rise when I heard those words. Now I understand it's the most complex and most crucial grief. When you see the person smiling, it is meant for someone else; when you see them laughing, it will be someone else making him laugh. Their hearts would belong to someone else entirely, no longer mine to call. I will witness him moving on. Dante has us tied together; what will hurt the most is

—I will have to watch it happen—missing someone who doesn't miss you.

"Hey, you."

I jump up, startled, not expecting anyone to sneak behind me.

"Shit, sorry, Mila. I didn't mean to scare you." Brian smiles boyishly like he always does.

I give him a return smile. "Hey, you back. And don't worry about it."

"Can I sit?" His beautiful blue eyes sparkle in the night sky.

"Sure."

"What are you doing out here so late?" he questions me as he glances at my profile. He frowns.

I must look like shit because I feel it. "Just needed a breather. How about you?" I ask.

"Going out for a jog."

I scan his profile. He's wearing sweats and a hoodie. Brian's incredibly handsome. "You jog here every night?"

"I'll jog in the mornings or nights depending on my schedule; you know."

"So, tell me what has you so down, honey, I see it in your eyes."

It's been more than a month since I've talked to him—since the night of Halloween. Brian's a great guy. What a shame that feelings never flourished for him. I fell in love with the wrong man.

I sigh with relief staring into the ocean waves. Brian has always been easy to talk to. I guess you can say I viewed him more as a friend than a lover. I had cut our relationship short; sex was great, that's all it was. We didn't get to explore what could have been.

"So much has happened; I'm still trying to wrap my head around it all. You remember when I told you my dad died in a fire?"

He nods.

"A witness came forward after all these years." Taking a breath, I continue. "Turns out Dominic's mom started the fire."

"Wait, what? By accident or on purpose. Jeez, Mila, I'm sorry."

I lick my chapped lips due to the cold winter breeze.

"I'm not sure, but I'm pretty sure it was on purpose. I just don't know why." My voice breaks.

He leans to hold my hand... stroking my knuckles.

"What does Dominic say about all this?"

The mention of Dominic's name has me withering like a garden of dry, wilted flowers. I dip my head down, poking at the sand—tears spill.

"I-I haven't spoken to him. I never want to speak to him. I found his ex at his place. She said they were back together. He lied to me; I'm just so confused," I say in between sobs.

I'm embarrassed to be crying in front of Brian, my ex, for another man who broke me as if what we had been nothing. Maybe it was to him. Brian wraps his warm arms around me.

I embrace his warmth, feeling secure in his arms. His lips brush on the top of my head dropping a kiss. He gently strokes my back soothingly. "I'm so sorry, Mila. If there's a way to take all this pain away, I would do it in a heartbeat."

"You're sweet, and I know you would." The truth is I believe he would, and I just can't offer him anything more than friendship for now or maybe ever. My heart will always belong to one man. I bestowed my heart, my soul, to him at the age of sixteen, and he never returned it. Dominic left me hollow inside, and I let him in knowing he could destroy me. Brian brushes my tears with his thumb.

"How about a cup of coffee at my place? I would say the coffee shop, but it's closed." His blue eyes twinkle with the moonlight.

"Coffee sounds good right now."

He stretches his hand out for me to take, helping me up. His apartment is close by, within walking distance. Once we get to his place, he pops the pod into the coffee maker. Brian talks about school and how he will be graduating this year. I'm proud he worked hard to earn his biology degree.

"How's Dante doing? Has he seen his dad?"

My heart cracks lying to my son, but I'm doing it to protect him.

"He's doing good. He asked for his dad. Lying to him has been so hard. I told him Dominic had to work out of town for a couple of weeks. I feel so bad, Brian, I need to protect him from Dominic's mother. I don't know what she's capable of. Once she's locked up and we sort things out, I will allow him to see Dante."

Brian pulls a chair out and takes a sip of his coffee. "Don't feel bad, Mila; you're a wonderful mother; protecting your son will always come first. Stay strong, pretty girl."

I don't feel like an excellent mother. Brian hands me a cup of scorching coffee. I moan into my cup as it warms me up.

"He asked if he could see him at my place supervised. I feel bad. I'm just not ready to see or talk to him yet."

"Mila, self-care is important. Take time for yourself. Your wounds are fresh; you need your time, and he has to understand that. He cheated on you, Mila. You just found out what his mother has done. This is big; take the time you need to heal."

He's right; I need time.

I stare at my cup of coffee. Brian lifts my chin.

"Things will get better, Mila."

I glance into those baby blues. His lips are so close to mine. I blink.

"Brian," I murmur as I pull away.

"Shit, Mila, I'm sorry; I wasn't trying to take advantage of the situation. I just got lost in those eyes of yours," he says bashfully.

"Don't worry about it. I know you're not like that."

"I wish things could have worked out between us. You're easy to fall for, Mila, this might not be the time to say this. But I feel if I don't, I'll never be able to tell you. I'm in love with you. I've been in love with you since the day you walked out. I regret my words," he says, with a painful expression.

I rest the palms of my hands on his. He's in love with me. If only I could love him.

"I know, Brian, I wish I'd fallen for you. But my soul belongs to another. It wouldn't be fair to you to offer you half of me. You're an amazing man, you deserve more than I can offer," I say earnestly.

His finger sweeps my lips. "I can help you forget, pretty girl, just tonight. Let me show you how much you mean to me. Give us a chance, Mila." His eyes are filled with hope—tears stream down my cheek.

I wish I could forget. Not a night goes by when I am not assaulted by these memories. I'll just end up hurting him. I can't get his hopes up. I kiss his cheek and stare into those beautiful eyes. I trace my thumb along his perfect lips. I kiss the corner of his lips. I love Brian, but I'm not in love with him. I thanked him for the coffee and walk into the night's blue sky.

THE NIGHTS GROW LONG. I stare up at the ceiling of my dark bedroom. I feel the empty space next to my bed, feeling for the spot where he slept. Is she in his bed? What part of us was true? All of it, or part of it? When did he get back with her? Was it after our date? Did he plan to end it then? Is this why he did all that on our last night together? Why would he do this to me? That night, he made love to me, I felt it in every thrust as his eyes peered into mine, locked. At that moment, I didn't see it. I was so lost in the lustful moment, falling deeper in love with him, when he was saying goodbye. I ask myself these questions repeatedly.

My dreams of the fire have increased, and I am replaying the night and the echoes of my screams. They shift to Dominic with Samantha. The photos of them together. I exhale a painful breath as sleep takes me a second time.

DEPRESSION HITS HARD, and all I want to do is cry in bed. I cry for loving a man who didn't love me as I thought, a man who lied and cheated on me. I cry for my amazing father, who I miss profoundly; he was such a great man. He did not deserve to die. It's been a long time since I've visited his grave. Sitting cross-legged, I trace the inscription of his grave, which I have memorized with my fingers. *Leonardo Amaro, beloved father.* A man who loved his wife fiercely.

He once told me, when I asked if he would ever marry again, he said mom was the only woman for him. He would say, *"Pumpkin, the greatest gift of life is finding the love of your life. Some will never find it. Others believe they will find love again if they're lucky. For me, I only have and will ever have one love. She gave me love enough to last a lifetime; she showed me how to love unconditionally. She loved with so much conviction, and so much heart. She loved me through my weakest moments and my strongest ones. She's my soulmate, destined for me. Someday, pumpkin, you'll find the soulmate destined for you; you will know it by how you feel because you won't feel that way with anyone but him. You'll just know. She was my sunshine, and her smile lit up a room just like yours. Her green eyes sparkled just like yours, honey. Her laugh was contagious; she could make a bad day good. I see her in you; that's all I need to survive, pumpkin. I'm good, honey."*

Oh, Dad, I miss you, but I know you're with mom now. I-I n-need you, Dad, so much right now. Dad guide me—tell me what to do. I'm lost without you. How do I love again? How do I trust again? I cry into the palms of my hands. I want a love like theirs. Hearing my dad talk so fondly of her always had me crave a love like their's. *I wish I could have saved you that night. I'm sorry, Dad.*

"MILA BABE, we need to get you out of bed," Sophie demands.

I haven't slept in days, weeks. I've been wearing my heart on my sleeve.

"I can't do it, Sophie," I choke out between sobs. "I'm dead inside."

"No, you're not," she murmurs comfortingly, sitting beside me on the bed. "You're just hurting. You have a beautiful boy down there who needs you."

She looks exhausted, her eyes flickering with worry. I feel a surge of guilt—while I've been wallowing in my grief, she's been taking care of the studio and looking after Dante.

"You're right." I nod finally. "I have to be strong and get my shit together. I have an amazing little boy who needs me."

"That's my girl. I love you, I'm so worried about you, Mila."

I sigh loudly, relieving the knots in my chest.

"I'll admit I'm hurting like a mother fucker. Dante is my light in my darkness I'll get through it day by day. I'm so tired of crying I think I might be completely out of tears. My nightmares have been more intense. I keep replaying the night of the fire. And Dominic's betrayal."

She nods with a slit frown.

"Let's take it day-by-day. If you still want the therapist, I can go with you."

"Thank you," I say earnestly, rubbing my chest soothing the pain burning within.

"Have you talked to Nana?"

"No, not yet. I don't even know how to tell her that my son's grandmother did it." I rub my pulsing headache. "I was waiting to tell her when Rachel gets arrested. I might just call Liam and ask him why they haven't taken her in. I'm going to file a lawsuit suit for not arresting her the minute he found out." I watch as Sophie starts the shower for me and lays out my clothes.

"You should definitely call Liam and ask him what the fuck he's waiting for."

I don't miss the grimace in her profile when she says his name.

"Have you talked to him?" I ask.

"He's tried calling me I haven't answered him." She shrugs. "He's Dominic's best friend. I'm sure he wants info."

The beads of water roll down my pale skin. I stare at my reflection in the shower. I've lost weight. *Get your shit together Mila, Dante needs you.* I give myself an internal pep talk to get me through as I have in the past. Stumbling out of the shower, I throw on jeans and an over-sized sweater, scurrying my way down the stairs.

"Good morning, baby. How did you sleep?"

"Good, Mommy. I sleep like a big boy, not a like a baby," he says with a mouth full of Lucky Charms.

A soft laugh comes from of my lips. Only my boy can make me laugh; he's the medicine for my soul. I pour myself a piping hot cup of coffee. Dante eyes me with a sad frown.

"What's wrong?" I ask.

"Mom, I miss Daddy. Can I call him?"

The look on his handsome face pains me. It's not his fault. I need to harbor my pain setting it aside for him. Picking up my cell phone, I dial Dominic's number and hand it to Dante.

"Hi, Daddy!" He smiles from ear to ear. "Guess what, Daddy, I'm going to be in the Christmas play. I'm going to be one of the twee wise men." He nods and nods pacing up and down with his hand on his hips.

I snort at his cuteness. I can't hear what Dominic is saying on the other line.

"Are you coming to my play? It is next weekend."

I listen to Dante and take a sip of my coffee.

"Ok, Daddy, I love you too. She's right here. You want to talk to her?"

Shit.

Dante passes me the phone. I press the phone in my ear hearing his husky breath on the receiver.

"Mila," he softly whispers.

No Angel or baby just Mila. Once again, I swallow the painful lump. He's not mine, I remind myself.

"Yes," I say, my voice sounding throaty.

"Can we meet somewhere to talk?"

I think of what Brian said to give my self-time when I'm ready.

"I'm not ready to talk to you or see you, Dominic."

He's quiet for a couple of minutes. "Can I pick up Dante tomorrow for ice cream I'll drop him off right after, I promise."

I take a minute to think about it. I shake my head. "No, it's not a good idea."

"Please," he pleads.

"I don't trust your mom. She loathes us. I will not put my son in danger, Dominic."

"Mila, please, can I just stop by his school to say hi or at your place just five minutes? Please."

I exhale releasing the knot jammed in my throat. "Okay, umm, you can stop by and see him here."

"Thank you," he says, his voice gruff.

Damnit, I'll have to ask Sophie to stay while I hide. I'm not ready to see him.

Not yet.

"Yeah, sure."

"Have a good day." He hangs up right after.

I grimace in disbelief seriously, have a good day after finding out his mom killed my dad, and he has bimbo all over him, Ms. High-end bitch. Yeah, I'll have a swell day, asshole. Not realizing I'm shoving a bagel down my throat eating angrily. Sophie's face looks horrified.

Thirty-One
DOMINIC

The past couple of weeks have been some of the worst days of my life. My brothers and I all gather at Rocko's, nervously waiting for news from Liam. Today is the day they arrest my mom at work. My head is spinning like a carousel. I can't get my head around it all. Thoughts and questions race through my mind like a tornado. This has been such an awful experience; one I wish to wake up from.

We hoped that maybe it wasn't my mom, or she was forced to commit this atrocity. The footage had already proven mom had been lying about Mila for years and had kept her away from me for five of them. It was hard to imagine she would take things to such an extreme, with such a cruel act. Therefore, I'm compelled to let Mila go. My family is too toxic, she will never look at me the same. Nothing could ever erase what has happened.

How could she—I'm the son of the woman who killed her father cruelly and attempted to harm her. I will always love Mila; she will always hold a special place in my heart. She's the only one I've ever loved, and devotionally, she will always be. I hate that I've hurt her. I hate that I broke her heart. If I hadn't asked for another chance and stayed with Samantha, this wouldn't have happened. All I did was break her heart all over again. The memory of our last night together plays on repeat in my head. It's better this way. I'm not good enough for her.

Mark's leg shakes uncontrollably under the table. Will approaches us with a round of beers.

"Beers on me tonight, boys, drink up no kid should go through shit like this." He scratches his long gray beard we tip our beer in appreciation.

"Thank you, Will, we appreciate it."

"Let me know if you boys need anything. I'm always here for y'all."

"Thank you," Santiago says with gratitude.

My phone buzzes. Mila's name and beautiful picture flash on the screen.

"Hello?"

"Hi, Daddy!"

I smile so big my cheeks hurt. My boy can make a bad day good. "Hi, little man, how's my boy doing?"

"Good," he breathes out.

"I think about you, every day, all day long, seriously, you're my favorite person. I miss you. How's school?"

He huffs a breath. "Guess what, Daddy? I'm going to be in the Christmas play. I'm going to be one of the twee wise men." His breath is heavy; I'm sure he's pacing up and down as he talks.

"That's cool. I'm so proud of you. You're going to be the best out there. The fucking best."

He giggles when I curse. Mila always scolded me with a look. Whenever I'd cuss, her green eyes would twinkle with reprimand, but then I would give her my signature charming smile that melted her heart. God, I miss her.

"Are you coming to my play next weekend?"

"Of course, I'll be there." If your mother lets me. "I love you. Is your mom there?"

"Love you too. She's right here."

"Pass the phone to her." My heart beats out of my chest, and my breath hitches heavily. I can hear her soft breaths that once belonged to me. When her hot air fanned my neck, tickling my ear as I fucked her hard on the bed, floor, and against the wall.

"Mila," I mumble.

"Yes." The sound of her voice is cold. I swallow hard.

"Can we meet somewhere to talk?"

She takes a moment to answer. "No, Dominic, I'm not ready to talk to you, much less look at you."

Fuck, that hurt like a jab to the chest.

My heart races, and I feel my chest tighten painfully. The pressure is overwhelming, as if a thousand-pound elephant is pounding its feet on my chest. What the fuck am I to say to that? I'll give her time.

"Can I pick up Dante tomorrow just for ice cream? I'll drop him off... right after, I promise." Praying, she says yes.

"No, that's not a good idea."

Fuck, I hate she can't trust me. I understand she's worried my mom would do something to Dante. I don't blame her. She's doing what a parent is supposed to do: protecting her son with her life.

"Please," I beg, my voice strangled.

"I don't trust your mom. She loathes us. I will not put my son in danger."

"Mila, please, can I just stop by at his school to say 'hi' or at your place for five minutes? Please," I say desperately.

She takes a deep breath. "Okay, um, you can stop by and see him here."

"Thank you," I say, above a whisper. Her alluring voice makes me weak.

"Yeah, sure," she replies, perhaps hesitantly.

"Have a good day," I say, hanging up before she changes her mind.

Santiago and Mark cock their heads, frowning.

"Have a good day; really, what kind of shit is this? Yeah, Dom, she's really going to have a good day with all this going on. What the fuck? Have some sympathy. Shit, even I know it, and I've never had a fucking girlfriend." Santiago waves his hand in the air with a gruff look.

My jaw tightens. I pinch the bridge of my nose. Fuck, I feel like a complete heartless asshole. Class A asshole.

Liam walks in quietly and takes a seat next to us. He rests his hands on the side of his face, elbows pressed on the table.

"The FBI and a couple of officers went to her work and home. Your mom was not at either place. Have you guys spoken to her?"

Fuck, his face is pale. I look at my brothers, maybe they told her something. They look just as surprised as I do.

Santiago speaks first. "No, bro, I haven't spoken to Mom or gone over. I can't even look at her. I've been making excuses. Have you, Mark?"

Mark shakes his head. "No, I moved to your place; maybe she's assuming something's up. I told her I wanted to move out, not making it suspicious." He blows a hot breath.

The guys look up at me. "I haven't spoken to her. I know she's pissed at me because I was with Mila. It's nothing new for her," I say as I turn to look at Liam.

"Where do you think she's at, man? Shit, we need to find her before I get fired for sitting on this too long. Dammit." He pounds his fist on the table. "Hopefully, she's at the store or something. The last thing we need is for her to know and be on the run," he adds.

Fuck, I should have just told Mila sooner. What if my mom's on the run? I hope, just like Liam said, she's just running errands.

I look up at Liam. "Did you go in the house?" I ask since he has a key to the house. He's like family. My mother gave him a key.

He runs his hands along his cheeks. "I went in... Her clothes are all there, nothing's been touched."

I'm relieved. Maybe she just ran errands. How in the hell will I be able to explain this all to Mila if she runs? I'll never get to see Dante.

Leaning against the wall, I wait for Dante to get out of school. Mila texted me and asked if I could pick up Dante, she had a client that was taking longer than needed. It surprised me, to say the least. She begged me to keep him safe. I assured her I would pick him up and take him for ice cream, then bring him home. I stopped at a comic store on my way to get Dante. Some stuff was not appropriate for his age, but I found a Spider-Man stuffed toy, hopefully he doesn't think it's babyish.

At times he goes from being a five-year-old to a fifteen-year-old. It's been three and a half weeks, maybe four, since I've seen Dante.

"Daddy." He leaps into my arms wrapping his arms around me.

I kiss his cheek, inhaling the smell of boy's sweat mixed with Mila's cherry coconut scent. Mrs. Hooker approaches me.

"Mrs. Amaro said you're picking up Dante, is this correct?" She bats her eyelashes at me.

"Yes, that's correct."

"Great, have a good rest of your day." She walks off as other parents approach her.

"Hey, buddy, I missed you so much. Man, you got taller," I tease.

He grins. "I did, Daddy. I want to be just like you."

That makes my heart swell. "Have you been listening to your mom and eating your vegetables?"

"Dad, I hate vegetables."

I chuckle, trying to be serious, but failing miserably with his facial expressions. He crinkles his forehead, and his eyebrows knead together. Kissing the tip of his nose.

"Daddy," he groans. "Put me down."

"All right then, so how was school?"

"Good, I played and made a gingerbread house, then we had church." He walks with his hands in his pockets.

"Sounds like a good day,"

"Daddy, Mommy's been sad. How come you don't talk to her?"

Shit, my chest squeezes, and my throat feels like I swallowed a mouthful of thorns. "Your mom's strong; she'll be okay." I fist my hand, damnit.

The nuns greet us as we exit, waving us goodbye.

"Ready for some ice cream?" I ask, trying to avoid the topic of Mila.

"Yup," he squeals.

Standing in front of Mila's townhouse door, I kept my promise by dropping him off immediately. Appreciation fills my heart for the time we shared. I'm sweating profusely as we wait. The door swings open. I was expecting Mila to answer, but much to my surprise, Sophie stands at the door. I'm not sure if I should be disappointed or relieved when I don't see Mila. I clear my throat.

"I came to drop off Dante."

Her eyes dropped to Dante. "Hey, honey, say bye to your dad." Her eyes darken with disgust and hatred.

Bending at the knees, I lower myself for a hug from Dante. I kiss his cheek. "Bye, buddy; I'll see you soon. I love you." Shit, I hate this, my heart breaks.

"Bye, Daddy, love you too." He runs inside leaving me standing with Sophie.

My eyes skim the townhouse searching for Mila.

"She's not here." Her hard-as-hate eyes bore into mine.

I admit, she's scary as shit. Where in the hell could she be? I know she's not at work; it's after five.

"Tell her thank you." I stagger back to my truck. Jealousy hits me like a ton of bricks. What if she moved on to seeing someone or... shithead Brian. He must have taken advantage; the fucker was waiting for me to fuck up to take his chance. I grip the steering wheel while driving back home.

Thirty-Two

DOMINIC

I brush through the crowd getting into the auditorium of St. Mary's, I find a place to sit. I glance to see if I spot Mila—not that she would acknowledge me; she might get outraged seeing me here. We haven't spoken since the day she agreed to let me see Dante.

As if my body senses her presence, the hairs on my neck prickle as Mila gets closer. She maneuvers through the crowd; the sound of her soft voice sends pleasant shivers through my whole body and causes my cock to twitch against my zipper. Mila whispers into Sophie's ear as they sit a couple of rows across from me. She hasn't seen me, yet I get a perfect view.

Her tight checkered skirt hugs all her natural curves, she has a tight black shirt on, emphasizing her perfectly rounded breasts. Her long black hair falls perfectly without her trying. I gaped at her beauty. God, she's beautiful. It's been close to a month since I've seen her. She's lost some weight. She looks tired. The beauty in her radiates through her whole body. You wouldn't notice unless you knew every curve, mark, scar, and mole. I know her body like the back of my hand.

The music begins to play. Mrs. Martinez, the music teacher, stands in front of the stage.

"Good evening, everyone. Thank you all for coming out to support our students. They have worked so hard."

Everyone claps. The kids sing "Silent Night." Once the three wise men come out, I pull out my phone to record Dante. I watch Mila do the same. Dante steps out with a golden robe and a pretend camel as a prop. He is carrying the oil. One of the gifts the three wise men carry. He hands it to the little girl playing Mary. They sing a couple of songs and dismiss the kids. I watch as Dante steps down and runs to Mila. He hugs her. She smiles at him proudly. He turns and notices me standing there, watching.

"Daddy!" He shouts and runs toward me.

Mila shoots me a surprised look, a haughty stare that may cut through glass. In this moment, I realize she will never forgive me, more than anything she will never see me the same. A feeling of overall heaviness akin to a molt of lava seeps through my body, extinguishing any possible hope I've had. I direct my eyes to Dante, hugging him tightly.

"I'm so proud of you. You looked awesome out there, fist bump, dude."

He giggles and fist-bumps me. "Daddy, are you coming to the house?"

I muster a smile. "No, buddy, not tonight. I'm going to your Uncle Santiago's house, and I'll show him the video I took. He will be so proud of you."

He puffs out his chest, beaming with pride. He sure is a Delgado. Arrogance at its finest.

"Did you see, Daddy? I carried the oil to Mary and Joseph."

"Yup, sure did. Your mom and Sophie are waiting for you." I run my hands along the stubble on my chin. "Take care of your momma... okay... can you do that for me?" I ask, barely able to keep my emotions at bay.

"Yes, Daddy," he says, nodding his head.

"Good little man, I love you, okay, to the moon and back."

"I love you, Daddy, this much," he says, spreading his hands as far as they can go.

I give his hair a light ruffle, he runs back to Mila, who is talking to a parent. Roaming her body one last time before she catches me, I make my way out the door with a lump in my throat. My heart is heavy.

I grip the steering wheel in my truck, thinking she'll never forgive me. Sighing, I reminisce about the way her body felt on mine, the way it responded to mine, and her soft lips brushing against mine. The way she smiled and laughed sent me to an unknown world where it was just us. She's the star shining in my darkness. I've always been the moon. She once shined her way into my soul. Only now she shines in the opposite direction while I sink back into the darkness.

Thirty-Three

MILA

I've spent the last couple of days Christmas shopping, forcing myself to get out of the house. Four days until Christmas. I breathe. Dante is my strength to keep going. Christmas is one of my favorite holidays. It's so hard to maneuver through it. Sophie and I decided to head on out of the house and get into the holiday spirit. I really wanted to show them the Holiday Market at Petco Park. I know Dante will love it. It's beautifully decorated for the holidays—magical lighting displays, Santa, holiday characters, and so many food vendors. The last time I had been there was with Dominic before Dad passed away.

Damn you, Dominic; I don't want to think about you now.

Day by day, I'm healing. I'll never be completely one hundred percent healed. I'll always have a piece of him. Sophie and Dante went to do a little Christmas shopping. They should be here in about thirty minutes. Then will head to the Holiday Market. A knock at the door startles me. It must be Sophie.

I'm surprised to see the bitch standing on my doorstep. She stands tall, her dark glare searing me with hate. Rachel pushes her way through the door.

"What the fuck do you think you're doing?" I yell. Shoving

her. My heart thumps against my ribcage as I watch her reach into her purse.

She pulls out a cold, metal nine-millimeter handgun, and I freeze in fear. Dante's adorable face flashes in my mind, and I wonder if this is how it will end. She wants me dead. She came for me. Why in the hell isn't she locked up?

"What do you want, Rachel?" My voice above a whisper, as I move myself against the wall.

She slams the door shut. She clicks her tongue on her teeth. "You want to know what I want? I want you dead. You took everything from me."

Dominic, she's talking about me taking him from her.

She's fucking crazy.

"Rachel, you took my father from me because, I was with your son. How could you be so cruel?"

She laughs viciously. She picks up a photo of Dante. She sneers at the photo. I creep up behind her, my heart pounding in my chest. She twirls around and backhands me with the gun, faster than I can move. I feel a sharp pain in my temple as I fall to the ground, and when I touch the spot, my fingers are stained with blood.

My head spins with the vibration of metal.

"Your father was a coward, just like my son. He obsessed over a worthless girl like your father with your mother. It was a great satisfaction to know you suffered as an orphan. It's a shame you didn't die with your father," she says with bitterness dripping from her venomous tongue. She cocks the gun aiming it at me.

I drag myself toward the end tables. My baby boy, I can't leave him. He needs me.

"Rachel, Dominic, and I are not together. I'll move and stay away from him." I try to compromise.

She chuckles. "I heard. Samantha told me. You should have stayed away from here. My son was happy with Samantha. Now that you're here, I'll do him a favor and get rid of you. It will be for the best for all of us." Rachel's hand shoots up to the ceiling, the gunshot reverberating off the walls.

I leap up off the floor, my heart pounding in my chest. Suddenly, movement catches my eye, and I see a figure standing in the window. Rachel notices too and starts to turn toward it. Acting on instinct, I grab a table lamp and swing it with all my might, connecting with Rachel's head and sending her reeling back. I hit the floor, scrambling for the gun that has fallen from her grasp. My arms shaking, I hold the gun unsteadily in my hands and point it directly at her.

Anger rises in me. I could end her life by taking my father from me. I could end her life right fucking now. She maneuvers, laying sideways as she rubs her head where I hit her. She looks up at me. Evil and hate seep through every part of her.

"End me, Mila. It will work out even better, you'll be locked up. My son will hate you. Your son will live with his father and new mother, Samantha."

Blood drains from my face. The thought of my son being raised by his bitch. Anger racks over me like hot coals.

"I'm not going to kill you, Rachel. I'm going to make sure you rot in jail. I'm going to make you pay for what you've done."

The front door swings open. My glare stays pinned on Rachel. When I hear Liam's voice. My chin trembles.

"Mila, sweetheart, it's me, Liam. You're okay, You're safe. I'm here. I need you to hand me the gun. I'm going to reach for it. Okay, sweetheart."

I nod. I didn't intend to cry, but tears stream down. I could have died. I would have missed my baby boy growing up. He takes the gun from my hold. Officers swarm in. Liam hands the gun to an officer. I watch as the officer handcuffs Rachel.

Liam cups my trembling chin. "You're safe," he whispers.

I throw my arms around him and sob. He kisses my temple. Soothing me.

"You're safe," he repeats.

I nod. My head resting on his shoulder. I hear Dominic's

voice speaking to an officer. I pull away from Liam's hold. His eyes water.

"It scared me, Mila. I haven't felt this scared in a fucking long time. I thought she was going to kill you." He wipes a renegade tear from my cheek. "Sit, Mila. I'll grab you some water." Fear vibrates through his body, I can feel it.

I sit and glare out the window. I spot Sophie's car and relief washes over me as I spot Dante seated in the car.

"Angel." Dominic's voice is shocked and full of uncontrollable urgency.

I don't turn to look at him. My eyes stay pinned on the window.

"Are you okay?"

I can feel his hot breath so close. "Yes," I murmur.

"I'm sorry, Mila." His voice is no more than a whisper.

I swallow. He reaches over and wipes the blood trickling down. My heart races; it's the only organ in me that seems to be working; the rest of me feels numb. I watch as the paramedics arrive.

"Mila," he says, his voice strained.

I can't look at him, not when he lied to me. Not when he left to be with another woman. When he knew his mom killed my father and had not had her arrested. I could have been killed; this wouldn't have happened if they had detained her the day they found out.

"I'm going outside to check on Dante. The paramedics are here to check on you."

I nod once again.

He sighs. The sound of his voice echoes in the broken chamber of my heart.

IT'S CHRISTMAS EVE, and I'm baking chocolate chip, peanut butter, and sugar cookies for Santa. Yesterday, I spent the day making tamales, not that I had the energy to do it. I forced myself to keep the family tradition alive. Nana insists I keep it going. Every year, Nana makes tamales. It's a family tradition passed down.

It's been four days since Rachel showed up on my doorstep, attempting to kill me for the second time. I've kept myself busy with cooking and cleaning. I haven't spoken to Dominic. I know he tried. I overheard Liam telling him now wasn't the time. Whatever that means.

The day of the incident, Sophie and Dante slept in my bed. I needed Dante close to me. Sophie was scared out of her mind. She had overheard shouting and called Liam when she peeked through the window.

I sigh as I unfold a tamal and savor it. I think back to the night of Dante's school play. I didn't expect him to show up. It shocked me to see him; it had been a while since I'd seen him. That was the night of our date. Damn, he looked good. I was expecting to see his blonde, snobby bimbo next to him. The minute my eyes met his, all I could see was his betrayal, his lies, and her all over him. My phone pings, startling me and bringing me back from my thoughts. A text from Dominic.

Dominic: *Merry Christmas, Mila. I left gifts at the door for Dante. Tell him I love him.*

I didn't envision Christmas this way, not this year. I imagined we would be together as a family. Opening the door, I find five gifts wrapped up in beautiful wrapping. Picking up each one, I place them under the tree. I find one that says to Mila from Dominic. Wow, I wasn't expecting it. I bought him a gift from Dante, so maybe he's doing the same.

Mila: *Merry Christmas, okay thank you, I'll let him know.*

I text him back, shoving the phone in my jean pocket. I miss him, but the betrayal stings, and the pain he's caused me festers in me like cancer reminding me of what he's done.

"Mom, can I have a cookie?" Dante peeks his head out of the living room into the kitchen. We are having our annual

Christmas Eve movie night. We count the hours until Santa comes while we watch all our favorite movies while cuddling under the blankets.

"Yes, of course, baby, you want some milk too? Oh, and your daddy dropped some gifts off for you." I pour a glass of milk for us both, and we dunk our cookies in our milk.

Dante licks his lips, then wipes the milk mustache off with the back of his hand. His eyes trail to the gifts under the tree. He cocks his head to the side and frowns. "Why didn't he come inside?"

"Baby, he left them on the doorstep. I think he thought no one was home."

He huffs. "Are you not talking to him? Are you mad at him or is he mad at you?"

My chest tightens. Smart kid. One minute Dominic's here constantly and now he's not. It's my fault for letting him in too soon.

"Everything is fine it's just adult stuff. Nothing you need to worry about. Let's go watch the Grinch." I take a stack of cookies with me, we all sit on the couch enjoying the night.

I SIT at my wooden desk, its deep mahogany grain almost the same color as the leather camera strap in my hands. It's hand-made, and its smooth texture is embroidered with my name in a subtle script font. I'm bewildered—I wasn't expecting something so personalized or a gift at all —and I can't help but question what this could mean. Maybe I'm just overanalyzing it, he gave it to me because I'm the mother of his son. *Right?* Ugh Mila, get over it! He's engaged. My fingers work in a circular motion, massaging my temple, when the door chimes.

I watch as a tall, handsome, well-built man walks in. Bright sea blue-green eyes and a sharp jaw suggest a late twenties age.

"Hello, good evening. Looking for a Ms. Amaro." Mr. Handsome's husky voice booms with authority, and it snaps me out of my daydreaming.

I realize I've been staring into those blue-green eyes. He smirks. I clear my throat.

"Yes, I'm Mila Amaro. What can I help you with? Do you have an appointment?"

"No, Ms. Amaro, I'm Detective Mike Johnson with the San Diego Police Department."

My heartbeat palpitates uncontrollably. My hands shake.

"What can I help you with?" My voice falters.

"Have a seat, Ms. Amaro." He gestures to the sofa. "I wanted to check up on you and make sure you're doing okay. Also, I wanted to let you know my father retired and handed me all his cold case files. Most times, we backtrack when asking around as to this matter. Many are too afraid to speak, but as time goes by, they come forward. We are very fortunate your neighbor came forward when I questioned her myself. She then called the station for an officer to obtain her statement."

Biting my lip nervously, I soak his words in. "I'm doing okay, thank you for checking in," I say, earnestly, as Mr. Handsome shoves his hands in his pocket.

"My father never gave up, Mila. I thought it was worth mentioning. We now have concrete evidence that she was the one who started the fire, but Rachel has been less than cooperative with us when it comes to finding out why she committed the crime. She's asked for her son Dominic before she will provide a statement in the interrogation room, so we are just waiting for him."

I felt my breath catch in my throat, a mix of shock and relief washing over me. I feel like I can breathe easier with a weight lifted off my shoulders. I was still in disbelief that she had been planning to kill me, and the thought of losing my father in such a violent way sent chills through me. What could have driven her to this?

She was employed by my father. It can't be solely because

Dominic and I dated. But it could be because she warned me to keep my distance from her son. Something's not right.

Ugh. My head throbs thinking about this. She's a lunatic.

"Oh, God. I'm so relieved after all these years we can finally have closure. Thank you for coming here and letting me know. This is great news. Thank you for reopening the case."

Detective Johnson hands me his card as he pulls it out of his dress shirt pocket. "If you need anything, day or night, give me a call, even just to talk. I'm a good listener." He smirks.

What a flirt.

"Thank you, I appreciate your help."

I haven't yet spoken to Nana or Uncle Roger about Rachel killing my father. Or about her attempting to kill me. Nana would freak out. This is not a matter to be discussed over the phone. This felt like something I had to do in person, so I booked a flight. My father was the youngest, and Uncle Roger, the oldest. Dante and I are waiting for our flight to New York.

Sophie decided to stay behind and run the studio while I'm gone. We hand our boarding passes to the lady at the gate as we make our way to our seats. Staring out the window, I reminisce about the day I had packed up in Manhattan to move back to San Diego seven months ago.

Never would I have thought my life would turn into an enormous mess. From finding Dominic to finding the person responsible for my father's death. In the end, Dante reunited with his father. That's what matters, right? We buckle our seat belts for the five-hour flight.

Thirty-Four

DOMINIC

Beads of sweat trickle down behind my neck, my emotions are all over the place: anger, betrayal, sadness. My hand grips the handle to the double doors, we walk into what awaits us at the detention facility where my mother is being kept until they move her to Donovan Correctional Facility. Mark and Santiago sit in the waiting area while I check in at the front desk. A petite older woman greets me with a warm smile.

"Hello, how can I help you?"

"Hello, I'm here to see Rachel Delgado; Officer Liam Rodriguez knows I'm coming."

"Okay, I just need to see your ID."

I hand my ID over with a shaky hand.

"Okay, sweetheart, take a seat. I'll let the officer know you're here so he can take you back."

"Thank you, ma'am."

Scooting a chair next to my brothers, we wait until Liam collects me and takes me to speak to my mother. She specifically asked to talk to me before she spoke to anyone else. I'm so fucking nervous to see her. Mainly, I'm angry at her, disgusted with her. I still can't believe she went to Mila's and attempted to kill her. I couldn't even look at her when they took her away when Liam called me. I could hear the sirens from his cop car. All I heard was your mom's at Mila's with a gun. The air was knocked out of me. My lungs collapsed, taking my breath away. I jumped in my truck speeding to get to her, praying she was alive. I've never experienced fear like I did that day. It was all my fault for not getting it all taken care of the day Liam told me. I'd let out a sigh of relief when I noticed she was unscathed. It killed me she wouldn't look at me. As long as she was safe, *alive is what mattered.*

Liam sits me in a small room that could be the interrogation room. A small table with two chairs.

"Take a deep breath, Dom, I'll be outside waiting if you need anything. Just tap on the door."

I nod, wordlessly. My mouth is dry as the as desert.

The door swings open, an officer shuffles in, my mother walks with chains wrapped around her waist and her ankles. He unlocks the chain and handcuffs on her wrist. My mom's round brown eyes meet mine pleadingly. Her shoulders hunch forward. My mother has always been a beautiful woman with short brown hair, and big brown eyes. My eyes downcast, fisting my hands until my knuckles turn white, my jaw-clenching with fury.

"Dominic, honey, thank you for coming. I'm so sorry, Dominic."

Infuriated, I hold my hand out to stop her. I don't want to hear her bullshit. She acts like I'm doing her a damn favor for coming.

"What the fuck have you done, Mom? Tell me WHY did you intend to kill the *one woman I've loved?* Not once but twice. She's the love of my life. She was then and still is." My voice booms echoing through the cement walls.

"You hated us dating from the get-go so much you'd take it to such great lengths, murdering her dad and trying to hurt her? It's cruel, barbaric, and callous. You're heartless. I don't fucking get it, so explain it to me."

Her chin trembles with tears in her eyes.

I roll my eyes.

"I will tell you everything. You must listen to me from beginning to end."

I nod in agreement.

"Let's sit, Dominic."

The chairs scrape the cold cement floor as I slump in the chair. She sighs with a heavy breath, wiping the tears leaking on her cheek.

"When Santiago was five years old, and you were a year and a half old, I decided to go to college. I met a woman in college; we became friends, studied together, and hung out. She had a child, a baby girl. She was also a year and a half old. We had play dates. You were so attached to this little girl. You would talk to her in baby talk. She would giggle as babies do. You would blow baby kisses on her cheek. We had many play dates. We would meet at her place to study together while you kids played. It all started when I met her husband. He was a tall and handsome man; I couldn't help it. I fell for him."

My mind is racing, trying to grasp what she's saying.

"He treated her like a queen. The love he had for her was something I wanted. Your father never looked at me with love in his eyes. I wanted what she had. My jealousy grew for a man who only considered me as his wife's friend. One day in our algebra class she confessed to me she was pregnant. She planned to go home to surprise him. I was raging with anger and jealousy. I was in love with her husband, who had no clue, his eyes were only for her. My envy consumed me in a moment of impulsiveness. I followed her home and deliberately caused an accident. Her vehicle crashed into a tree and came to a halt at the spot she died on the scene."

My eyes grow wide with shock. What the fuck.

"The friend was Mikaela Amaro, her husband, Leo."

Holy shit.

Standing up, I pace the small room. I run my fingers through my hair grinding my teeth. I slam my fist on the table, it vibrates.

Rachel jumps. "Dominic, baby."

"No, Mom, just don't... y-you killed Mila's mother, a baby who needed her mother and her father. You left her with no parents, you selfish bitch. All because you were fucking jealous."

She gasps.

I almost feel guilty for calling her a bitch, but I don't. Her actions were selfish and heartless, filled with hatred. I can't believe this woman is my mother.

"Continue," I seethe and foam like a rabid dog.

She swallows.

"When Mikaela passed away, I distanced myself, afraid of anyone finding out, never saw Leo again. Until fifteen years later, I walked into his restaurant for lunch with a friend. My heart sped up at the sight of him. My feelings for him were still there. I asked him for a job. I wanted to get close to him. I figured maybe he could develop feelings for me. So, I worked as his accountant for the restaurant, doing his payroll. Over time, I felt a connection growing between us. Leo retreated so we could take things slow, although he never looked at me like he looked at his wife. Leo had indicated if things between us escalated, they would not go further. He would never remarry, and his heart belonged to her. He could never love me like his wife or love any woman. At that moment, I said I would take whatever he gave me." She sniffles.

I roll my eyes. I have no sympathy for her, my heart races she wanted to kill Mila over her lust for a man.

"Then you and Mila met and started dating. Leo broke whatever we had between us off, which was nothing, really. He said you two were dating and in love. He had told me it wouldn't be right for us to date and it's not like things could go any further for us. His daughter's happiness was more important to him. I was furious you two were so in love. It was no surprise. You were attached to her as a baby. You would cry every time we would leave from your playdate. Even as just a baby, you were like a magnet to her." She wipes her tears. Surveying me through her eyelashes.

"It ruined my chance with Leo. I was in love with him. Mila looked so much like her mother. It made me angry that she came first. She ruined my chance with her father. I wanted her out of the picture, along with Leo. If I couldn't have him, no one could. That night I started the fire." Her shoulders shake as she sobs into her hands.

Clenching my hands on the edge of the table, I control the boiling rage of muscles, and veins straining against the skin.

"I'm sorry, Dominic."

"Don't, Rachel."

She gasps. "I'm your mother. Don't you dare call me by my first name. Who's the one who took care of you all these years? Who gave you everything? Who took care of you when you were sick, Dominic? Me." She breathes heavily as her eyes narrow on me.

"You lost the privilege of me calling you mom you're just the woman who gave birth to me. You should've just let me fucking... die. I'm already dead inside. You would have done me a favor."

"I'm sorry, Dominic."

"You should apologize to Mila; even then, it would not be enough. You robbed her of her parents. An innocent girl, Rachel. You took everything from her. You even took me from her."

"I know. I'm sorry, Dominic," she said, her voice unruffled. Rachel is the queen of manipulation and mind games.

"You're not fucking sorry. You went back for vengeance to finish what you started. I will never forgive you for wanting to take her from me," I shout.

She wipes her fake tears. "There's more, Dominic."

Fuck.

She sniffles as she wipes her tears. "When you became ill, we had you moved to the clinic in Arizona. I lied to you all. You were never dying, Dominic. I wanted Mila far away from you. When I heard she was moving, it all worked out. She thought you were no longer alive, so I saw my opportunity. I couldn't bear to watch her with you. She was the product of Leo and Mikaela and when she moved to Manhattan, I had someone watching her all the time. I kept a close eye on her to make sure you two never crossed paths again."

Oh, fuck, fuck goddamn her! My fingers curl into tight fists, and my jaw clenches as dark anger floods through my veins. Heat rises up my neck, and my face burns as bright as crimson.

"All this time, you knew where she was? You knew I had a son, didn't you?" My voice bellows with hatred for the woman who gave birth to me.

She nods. "Yes."

I punch the wall, my knuckles scrape with the force of the cement brick wall. "Did you plan on hurting Mila and my son? Did you really plan on killing her?"

Her cold eyes give no sign of remorse. She really is a sick person.

"No, didn't plan on it. If you would have stayed with Samantha, none of this would have happened."

I let out a sarcastic laugh. "I don't believe you didn't plan on hurting them. You wanted her dead, Rachel. You're fucking insane. If I'd gotten there before Liam, I would have shot you myself. As for Samantha, I never loved her. My heart always belonged to Mila, and you were well aware of it. You were determined to get what you wanted at the cost of my broken heart. You used me. You saw me weep for a girl I thought deceived me. You fed me so much bullshit," I croak, my anger rising.

My own mother *used* me as a pawn in her wicked game of destruction. It cost me the woman I love.

"You lied to me, telling me Mila had said I was a burden to her. I let myself believe it, hating her like a fucking fool. I should have known better, she wouldn't have ever done this to me, because she fucking loved me then, unlike you, never putting me first. What else is there, Rachel? Once I leave from here, it will be

289

the last time you see me, so spill it all out. It's your last chance," I seethe, trying to keep my temper in check.

"Before I started the fire, I had been embezzling money from the restaurant. I've been doing it at all my jobs. For years."

No surprise there her lies unfolding now, piecing it all together like a jigsaw puzzle. She lives in an expensive house, of course, now I see it, she paid for Mark's school, and helped put money into Santiago's shop. And she paid off some of the loans I had gotten when I purchased the restaurant. I pondered how she could afford it.

My eyes stay pinned on the woman next to me, glaring at her with coldness and disgust. The woman who raised us with blood on her hands, no guilt, no remorse for the past twenty-four years. Taking two innocent lives, attempting to take the only girl I've loved for her own selfish pleasure. The chair scratches on the cement floor as I stand up. I dip my head down to her level. Her eyes plead, begging for forgiveness.

"I hate you, Rachel. You're dead to me, you ruined Mila's life, you ruined my life. And my brothers' lives. You did it all for yourself. It was always about you. You never cared or loved us enough to put us first. *Me,* you never put me first. It was all about Rachel. If she can't have what she wants, you destroy it. Isn't that right, you disposed of them? You're disgusting. You deserve to rot in hell. I'll make sure you never get out of here."

Resting my palms on the table, I lean in. My hand throbs from hitting the brick wall.

"You got what you wanted. Mila wants nothing to do with me now, she knows what you did. Once she finds out you killed her mom, she will never let me see my son. I'm the result of a murder. She will always look at me as the son of a cold-hearted bitch. The son of a woman who killed her parents. Congratulations, Rachel, you got what you always wanted."

She reaches for me.

"Don't fucking touch me. You have blood all over them.

Rachel, rot in hell." I tap the door, and soon enough, Liam appears.

He stands with his mouth gaped open. I'm positive they heard it all. Making my way to the waiting room where my brothers wait. I signal them to the door. I don't want to spend one more minute of my life in this place.

We sit in my pickup truck, I take a huge, deep breath. They patiently wait until I'm ready to talk. Resting my head on the steering wheel, I sob for the woman I've always loved, the hard life she's endured. All because of the woman who birthed my brothers and me. The one woman who was supposed to love us, protect us, destroyed another's life. My poor Angel was parentless at such a young age. My mother, who knew I had a son all along, looked me in the eye every day, lying to me and betraying us.

My baby, Dante, spent his first years without me. If Mila hadn't moved back, I would never have known. I would have married Samantha with no knowledge of having a son. She would have never told me. I ponder about what my mother said—or Rachel, I should say.

Mila and I had a connection with each other from the very beginning. It all makes perfect sense—she's my soulmate, two souls destined to be together. Our love, our hearts, bring us back together every time. The night at the restaurant seven years ago, I felt it—it was no mistake. Our souls connected as one, as if they were home.

She's, my home.

Wiping my tears, I look at my brothers and tell them word for word what Rachel said.

———

AFTER DROPPING off my brothers at their house, I drive to Mila's townhouse. Her car is parked, so I assume she is here. I knock, no answer. No answer on her cell phone. Fuck, I need to see her. I need to tell her everything. She needs to know. She deserves to know as much as it will hurt her. I'll fight for us. We are destined to be together. She's my person, my other half. Sophie opens the door. She frowns, lips thinned she sneers when she sees it's me.

"What are you doing here?"

"I need to see Mila," I snap, frustrated.

"She's not here; she left."

"I'll wait until she gets back, I need to talk to her."

"Then you'll be waiting for... days, maybe weeks or months."

Fuck, my heart races.

"Where is she?" I bark.

"Calm down, boy, don't raise your voice at me. Why in the fuck do you care where she's at?"

"Because I love her."

She laughs. "You love her, but you cheated on her, and you left her for your snobby high-class bimbo of a fiancée, Samantha. You fucking lied to her. You betrayed her yet again. You knew what your mother did, and you lied to her."

"What the hell are you talking about?" I ask, running my fingers through my wet hair, the rain drizzling on me as I stand in the doorway.

"Are you playing stupid or is this the act all men make playing dumb?" She studies me and rolls her blue eyes.

"Come in; you're getting all wet, and it's getting in my house," Sophie growls, annoyed, fisting her hands on her hips.

"It's fine, just, tell me where she is. I need to talk to her. What's this all about, Samantha?"

She sighs. "Mila received a text from your number saying to meet her at your house. She went, and Samantha was there in one of your t-shirts with her ass hanging out. Samantha said you fucked her. She told Mila you two were back together and getting married, and Mila was just a fling. She handed the police report to Mila, saying, you basically used her in all this to protect your mom."

"What a fucking bitch." My jaw tightens. No wonder Mila's

been disregarding me. It's not just what Rachel did, she thinks I used her. Those were her words. She thinks I left her for Samantha. I blow out a breath, recalling how Samantha took my phone to spin her web of lies. It hits me she had come to my work. She wanted to talk. I left her alone in my office. She must've gotten my phone when I left the room to text her and erased it. When I went back, she was gone. I have no clue how she got into my house, but I'll be changing the locks.

Sophie stands at the door, hands on her hip with a murderess look.

"Fuck, I didn't even know all this happened. I never slept with Samantha, and I didn't text Mila that day you're talking about coming over to my house. So where is she?"

Her mouth twists. "She left for Manhattan. Yesterday," she says, dryly.

My heart pulls painfully, shivering under the icy rain droplets. She left; Mila's gone. She has no reason to stay here, too many horrible memories. I lost her again.

I pull into Samantha's place, pissed as fuck for her audacity to break into my house and stir up lies. Mila already had enough on her plate; she didn't need to deal with Samantha's stupid, juvenile nonsense; like she did the other day at my house. The door is slightly open, so I make my way in. I hear moaning and groaning. My eyebrows rise up. I spot Samantha and some older guy, probably in his early thirties fucking on her sofa. She's on him. They can't see me. There's a wall blocking it.

My eyes turn to the kitchen table—photos scattered all over the table. I glance at each photo of Mila and Dante. *What the fuck!* Mila is pushing a stroller, and several pictures show her holding Dante as an infant. One picture shows Mila sitting on a park bench. She looks broken. My heart cracks. A couple of her here in San Diego at the beach with Dante. Some of us at the zoo. There's one that catches my eye.

Mila on her knees, Brian fucking her mouth.

The blood drains from my body, it's like I slit a vein and blood is oozing out. I swallow the rock jammed in my throat. I guess this is what it feels like to get a taste of your own medicine. It's dated months ago. Now I know it was Samantha who sent those photos to Mila. I know what Mila felt. A stab to the chest. The only difference was that Mila wasn't fucking drunk. I can't be pissed at her. I hurt her. I was a man looking for revenge then... now I'm a man groveling at her feet. Why in the fuck does Samantha have all these? Recalling Rachel's words about keeping tabs on Mila. She had Samantha keep tabs on her? *Fuck.* Breaking their fuckfest.

"What the fuck is this, Samantha?" I bellow with fury, holding the photos up.

She jerks herself off him. "Baby, I-I..."

"Cut the shit, Samantha, why do you have pictures of Mila and my son?" My eyes glance at the naked dude. "Put some fucking clothes on. I don't want to see your fucking pint-size dick."

"Answer me," I shout.

Samantha smirks slipping her dress on. "Jealous?"

A malicious laugh erupts from my chest. "Fuck no. I don't give a shit who you screw. Have you been spying on my girl?"

She laughs spitefully. "I see, Mommy Dearest hadn't told you. Now she's locked up, our deal is off."

"What kind of deal are you talking about?"

She scoffs and lights a cigarette, something I'd never seen her do before.

"Angelo, here is the man your mom hired to keep tabs on Mila all these years." She points to the dude getting dressed. "You see, Dominic, I've always known about Mila and Dante. Way before you did. Your mom told me." She takes a hit of her cigarette.

My anger boils.

"In order to take over his inheritance, my father had a stipulation that I had to be married. It was when I was leaving the law firm, I caught your mom stealing from my father's firm. We made a deal. She would set me up with her poor, broken son. I would keep quiet about telling my father, and I would be married to gain my inheritance. It was a win-win. Until the lousy bitch got in our way. Why do you think I set up the engagement photo shoots at her shop? The look on her face." She hummed with a smirk.

"How did she like those photos of us fucking, Dominic? Angelo here took them. He loved to watch us. He's into voyeurism." Her laugh radiates through the apartment.

"This was all a fucking game to you, Samantha. You were just as much of a joke to me. I used you too. Do you think your pussy was so good? Fuck no, I had to get drunk to fuck you. I give zero fucks about you."

Jesus, I should have seen it. I was a pawn in their game.

She wraps herself around the guy next to her. And fucking laughs harder. The idiot next to her watches smirking.

"Oh, Dominic, it was easy, you were the poor broken bastard who followed along like a puppy dog. Angelo came into the office to report to your mother, and that is when we began seeing each other. Daddy would never approve of us; the age gap would be too much for him. It had to be you. Once I got the inheritance, I planned on leaving you."

It's my turn to laugh. God, what a fucking idiot. I felt bad for treating Samantha, the bitch, like shit. It turns out I was the one getting played.

"You knew about the fire. And did you break into Mila's place?"

She takes a drag. Her lips form into a line.

"No, I found out the day I snuck into your house, by the way, the look on Mila's face was priceless." She snorts. "And... no, the break-in wasn't me."

Fuck I've had enough of this shit. I gather all the photos; I wince at the throbbing in my hand. It feels fucking broken.

"If I ever see you two anywhere near my family, you'll have to deal with me." I look into the fucking douchebag's eyes with a grimaced glance. I shove him against the wall. "And you," I point to Samantha, "If you ever mess with my girl again, I'll make sure to call your father and let him know about the man you've been fucking you know about six maybe seven-years age gap. No inheritance for you, bitch."

She sneers. I slam the door behind me. Fuck. Samantha's a selfish bitch just like Rachel. No wonder they got along. Both evil and heartless only looking out for themselves. Thank the fuck, I never married her. What the fuck was I thinking?

Thirty-Five

MILA

God damn, it's cold. Good thing I left my big jackets here, mainly all my heavy winter clothing. It's beautiful here. The bitterness of the crisp wind brushes along my arms, prickling my skin. As I walk down the street to one of the best bakeries in town, I reflect on the previous night.

We arrived late last night. Uncle Roger picked us up from the airport. Nana stayed home, waiting for us to arrive. The winter is cold here, which adds to the discomfort of her joints. I keep telling her to move back to California; she has refused to. She's made good friends, and Uncle Roger takes good care of her.

Uncle Roger kept gazing at me out of the corner of his eye as we drove back close to midnight. Uncle Roger is the master at figuring out your facial expression. He's always been good at reading people.

"All right, so are you going to tell me what's going on? I know you didn't fly back here to just say 'hi' out of the blue."

I sigh in, desperation, as my heart tugs at what I need to tell them.

"You're right. A lot has happened in the last couple of weeks. I needed to fly back to tell you and Nana..." I blow out a hot breath. "Rachel, Dominic's mother, caused dad's death. She started the fire."

Uncle Roger is silent for a couple of minutes. "Are you sure?"

"Yes, a witness came forward along with surveillance tapes. Our neighbor had cameras, and it picked it all up."

He pounds on the steering wheel.

"Shit, all these years I wondered how it all happened. I wasn't expecting it to be her, or really anyone. I thought it was a freak accident. Leo didn't have enemies. He always lit candles. Why would this woman do this to him? Do you think it's because of you and Dominic? Why would she do all this because she dislikes you?" He shakes his head in disbelief.

"I was just as shocked. I was the target. Rachel despised me for being with her son. Also, please don't tell Nana, I don't think she can take this."

He grips the steering wheel and nods.

"She came into my home with a gun. She wanted to kill me. I've never been so scared in my life. All I thought about was Dante. Her action could have left him without a mother. At that moment, I regretted knowing Dominic. But I wouldn't have Dante." A tear ran down my cheek.

"What does Dominic say about this?"

"I haven't spoken to him about all this. He's back with his fiancée. My heart's too mangled to discuss all this right now with him."

He gasps. "Wow, I'm sorry, sweetheart. His loss, beautiful, jeez, Mila, maybe you should move back. You're too far from us. I'm scared shitless. If something would have happened to you..." He shook his head and swallowed.

A shiver runs up my spine standing in line at Degee's Pastry Shop, they have the best pastries like to die for so good, buttery and melt-in-your-mouth good. A line forms pretty early before he opens.

"Mila, my girl, how are you? Moved back already? I knew you couldn't live without me."

I chuckle at Oscar. The owner's son, he is the biggest flirt. I'm pretty sure this is how he gets business. Women melt at his big cheesy smile and when he winks at you, it nearly makes your panties wet, yeah, he's a good-looking guy.

"Nice to see you. It's been a long time, had to come to visit you. I need my morning dose of Oscar to keep me going," I tease.

"Ahh, it's the smile, right?"

"Sure." I snort.

"I knew it." He smiles, showing all his white teeth. He walks around, wrapping me in a massive hug with his tree trunk arms. "Good to see your pretty face. How long will you be here?"

"Not sure yet. Maybe a couple of days."

He nods. "Good." He scratches his chin as he drinks me in. "So, you want your usual?" He maneuvers his way back to the counter.

"Yes, please, you know what I like."

His eyes widen, and he smiles.

I shake my head. I know what he's thinking about, something sexual. His laugh booms throughout the shop. This was a pleasant distraction. It's been a while since I've laughed.

Nana pours us all a cup of coffee as Uncle Robert and I sit in the kitchen munching on the incredible pastries I missed so much. "All right, mija, what going on? I see it in your face. You can't fool this old woman."

Clasping my hands together fiddling with my fingers. "Nana, I have something to tell you. A witness came forward. They found out who started the fire and killed Dad. It was intentional."

She gasps, her hand goes right to her chest. "Who would want to hurt my Leo? Ay, Dios Mio," Nana says.

"Nana, it was Dominic's mom."

Her eyes widened. "What? That can't be. Are you sure?"

I nod.

"She's evil. I-I-I just don't understand all this just because you dated her son. No, no, there has to be something else."

She's not wrong. It's a little extreme, but Rachel is crazy, and

I've watched plenty of forensic files, killer women on Netflix's, people like that snap. She was determined to get rid of me. She could be one of those obsessed with their sons—controlling them.

"What does Dominic say? Is he shocked? It was his mother. I'm sure he must be."

I exhale and look up at Nana.

"I haven't spoken to him about all this Nana. I went to his house and found, Samantha, the one he was engaged to. She said, they're back together, and she's the one who handed the report to me. I don't want to talk to him. He's been trying to call me. I told him we can only talk about Dante right now."

Her hand rests on my shoulder with a soft squeeze. "I'm sorry, honey."

Tears strain my eyes and Nana envelops me in a hug.

"I'm shocked it was Rachel who killed my son. But I want to ask, did he tell you he was back with this woman?"

"No, he didn't. He had been acting strange since before Thanksgiving. He kept saying it was because of work. So, I left it as that. Then, when all this happened, it made sense. He's back with her and he knew about all this but didn't tell me." I sigh as I rest my head on Nana.

She rubs the palms of her hands on my back motherly. Nana is the only mother I know. I love her so much. She's my rock, the woman who helped raise me.

"I find it hard to believe he's with her. On Thanksgiving, he looked at you like you were his world, just like your grandfather looked at me. I despise his mother. She was evil always with you and now we know she killed my baby boy. We have justice for my Leo. Mila, I really think you need to talk to Dominic. He is the father of your son. Hear him out, and if you feel like he had a part or don't feel it, then it's your decision. And if he chooses to be with this woman, it's his loss."

I sigh, relieving a knot, pouring a second cup of coffee.

"I know, Nana. I think I'm just scared of what I'm going to hear. I love him. I've always had. I don't want to face the fact he's with her or he knew what his mother had done all along. I'm just confused."

She kisses my cheek. "I'm sure you'll figure it out, you're strong and smart. Honestly, I don't see him having any part of this, honey. I strongly believe it."

WITH A CLUNK OF THE SKATES, we unsteadily make our way onto the ice, Dante holding onto my arm. He is natural at ice skating, gliding across the rink, while I do my best to stay upright without falling on my butt. As we spin around in circles, a flurry of soft snowflakes begins to fall from the sky, like delicate jewels glistening in the sun. Dante sticks out his tongue and laughs as each snowflake melts on his skin. As it gets colder, we know our time is short, and the snow would make it harder to drive home, so we skate a few more laps before reluctantly leaving the rink.

It's New Year's Eve today, and the streets are getting busy, snow or not. Everyone's out in Times Square, celebrating. Nana is heading to her friend's tonight, and Uncle Roger is out with his girlfriend, ringing in the New Year. I'll stay home with Dante while he sleeps. And watch the countdown with a glass of wine— my phone buzzes. Our Uber is here to take us back to Uncle Roger's house.

I notice a couple of missed calls from Dominic and a voicemail. I haven't listened to them. Since I arrived in Manhattan, I've turned my cell off. I'm drained, not ready to face him yet.

"That was fun, Mom, I love skating."

"Me too, baby."

"I wish Daddy was here. He would love it. I could teach him how to skate."

I rub a hand on my heart, sadness invades my broken heart.

"Me too, baby, me too."

Three hours until the ball drops, and I'm on my third glass of wine, but who's counting? Dante passed out in bed. It's an overly large house with five bedrooms, so we all had our own rooms, a beautiful brick house with a basement. I'm not feeling it tonight. Turning the T.V. off, I turn on the radio, *Fingers Crossed* by Laura Spencer plays.

Ugh, great, of course, they play break-up songs on New Year's Eve, damn them. Just how I want to bring in the New Year. I take a swig of wine straight from the bottle, fuck it. I'm sure the asshole is bringing in the New Year with her. Fuck, I hate you... no, I love you... No, no, no.

Ugh, I sing the verse to the song in annoyance. Fuck you, Dominic, and your stupid snobby bitch, you—lying douchebag.

The doorbell rings. Opening the door, I am surprised to see Dominic standing there, looking as handsome as ever. My chest tightens and butterflies flutter in my stomach. It's almost as if I imagined him into existence, I said his name and he appear at my doorstep.

Okay, Mila, you've had way too much wine, you're hallucinating.

My eyes flicker at his appearance: he's wearing a hoodie, not something you wear in this harsh weather, dark circles around his eyes. A backpack swung on his back; his hand wrapped in bandages. His eyelashes flutter as the snowflakes stick to them. I frown. What is he doing here? I finally manage to get a word out.

"What are you doing here?"

He shivers in the cold. "Baby," he softly whispers.

"What are you doing here, Dominic?" I repeat. My chest tightens, and a ball of nerves erupts in my stomach.

"I came to see you, baby. Damnit, woman, we need to talk. Can I come in? It's fucking cold here."

I moved to the side to let him in.

His eyes roam my body, stopping at my breasts. I forgot I'm not wearing a bra. My nipples peek out through the thin material. I wrapped my arms around my chest. Drinking him in, I missed him so much. He's not, mine, and he still has not answered me as to why in the hell he came all this way.

"Dominic, why are you here in Manhattan?"

His voice is hoarse when he speaks. "Angel, I-I needed to see you, to talk to you. I tried to give you space, but we need to talk. You have ignored me every chance you get. You don't answer my calls or texts."

I rest my hand on my hips. Space, what the fuck space? Is he serious?

"You could've waited until I got back," I snap. "Go back to your fucking fiancée. I don't need you here."

Thirty-Six

DOMINIC

My face and hands are numb. Damn it, it is so cold here. All I brought was a hoodie and a backpack with two changes of clothes. Yeah, I didn't think much about the freezing cold. Mila stands, hands wrapped around herself, probably to keep me from staring at her perfect nipples peeking through the thin material of her shirt. She glares at me coldly.

"You could've waited until I got back," she snaps. "Go back to your fucking fiancée. I don't need you here." Her voice is laced with venom.

I walk to the red brick fireplace, warming my hands. Her lips form a tight line pressed together. Her guard is up. I look for the cut on her temple. It's covered with her raven hair.

"Angel, if you would have talked to me from the beginning, we could have talked things out—you're a damn stubborn woman."

She laughs sarcastically. "Oh, when should we have talked? When you text to go over to find Samantha right after you fucked her?"

Her pained-filled eyes break my heart.

"Baby, stop right there and just let me talk for once. I have so much to say. First, I know. Sophie told me about the text. I did not know about any of this. Samantha came to my work; she said she wanted to talk. She got my phone when I left. Remember I had the plumbing problem?"

She nods. "Yes."

"Well, I told her I was busy, I didn't have time to talk, and we had nothing to talk about. So, I left the office to talk to the plumber. She must've gotten my phone then."

She frowns, her shoulders slumping as she sits on the couch. She keeps her distance from me as expected. It tugs at my chest.

"So, how did she get in your place? Hmm, because of the way she looked as if you two were sleeping buddies," she says through gritted teeth.

"Can I finish, woman?"

"Fine, continue."

"Honestly, I don't know how she got my key, but I'll change the locks. She planned it for you to go and staged it to make it seem like we're together."

Her head tilts. Her green eyes sparkle with relief. "You're not back with her?" she asks. Unsure if she can believe me.

"No, baby, I would never cheat on you, or leave you for anyone. But, Mila, I didn't use you, nor would ever use you. Especially after Liam showed up at my house with the news of what my mom had done. I was wordlessly shocked. Fuck, I couldn't wrap my head around it. I still can't."

I sit next to her on the couch. I reach for her hands. Luckily, she lets me hold the soft warmth of her hands. An exhale blows out of her cheeks. She glowers at our hands clasped together when she turns her eyes back to mine.

"Why didn't you tell me when you found out? Why did you wait, like it wasn't important? Were you protecting your mom? She wanted to kill me, Dominic. I've never been so scared in all my life. The thought of leaving Dante terrified me. I-I couldn't stomach you raising Dante with Samantha." Her hooded eyes glare into the crackling fire.

My chest burns: the thought of losing Mila would leave me

terminal. I brush a strand of hair behind her ear, sighing with so much desperation, she will give us a chance to fight this together —my beautiful Angel.

"I would never defend Rachel for what she did. She deserves to pay for what she did. Mila, baby, I didn't know how to tell you. I was terrified of losing you. What first came to mind was that when you'd look at me, you would see what she did, baby. Fuck, baby, I've never been so scared in my life, Mila. The thought of my mom hurting you. I can't live without you, Mila. I wouldn't know how to, I would never raise our son with another woman, Mila. Never. Like I said, if it's not you, it's no one."

She pulls away from our intertwined fingers, I dip my head down. "Look at me, Dominic," she says in a demanding voice. She rubs her thumb on my cold cheek.

Diverting my eyes to meet her beautiful forest green ones. The crease on her forehead softens and I immediately relax.

"If you say you genuinely never suspected, and you had to find out from Liam, then I can't fault you. You're just as much a victim in this, Dominic. You're a fool, Dominic. I would never look at you and see your mother."

"Rachel," I correct her.

"Rachel, I don't see Rachel in you, Dominic, for her doing. I see a victim in all this. You should have been honest with me, no matter what you thought. Finding out from Samantha was a low blow, especially finding her like that," she says, with a sensuous twist of her plump, pouty lips.

I have the urge to kiss her.

"You belittled me again, Dominic." Her tone is soft.

Guilt rattles me. I did it, again, belittling her. "I'm sorry, so sorry I fucked up. Baby. God, Mila, I didn't think Rachel would want to hurt you. Fucking hell. To think I could have lost you, Mila... Fuck, it—scared the shit out of me. It would have been my fault for not having Liam take Rachel immediately into custody. Life without you is unimaginable to me. It was my responsibility to protect you." My hands shake. Exhaling.

"Dominic, I'll admit I was furious you didn't have her arrested sooner. But this is all over, and it wasn't your fault. You couldn't have known."

"I went to the detention facility to talk to her. She asked to speak to me before she confessed to anything."

She straightens herself up.

"Angel, first, I want to tell you I love you so much. These past weeks, I couldn't function without you. Loving you is the happiest I've ever been. Without you, I'm empty inside."

She stands from her seat next to me. She chews on her nails nervously. "Dominic, I love you too, so much. But you're scaring the shit out of me. What did Rachel tell you?"

Fuck.

I'm rubbing the back of my neck, preparing myself for the blow; I'm about to tell her how fucked up it is. Instead, I watch her pace the living room in her fuzzy brown slippers. I glance around the house. It's a beautiful, pretty, big house. It warms my heart that this is where Dante grew up during his first years. Rachel took it from me. She took so much from me and from Mila.

"Is this where you lived with Dante?" I ask.

"Yes, it's a big house, lots of space."

I nod. I'm glad they were taken care of.

"Baby, come sit here so I can tell you everything. There is so much to tell you. It's not good."

She bites her lip nervously. She watches me closely. "Ok, let me get wine. I feel I need something."

"You have whiskey?" I ask.

"Yes, do you want ice with it?"

"No, it's fine."

She hands me my drink, her hand shaking, setting it on the coffee table. "What happened to your hand? It looks swollen?" Her beautiful eyes are filled with worry.

After all the shit I've done and put her through. She still worries. Still loves me.

"Punched a wall."

She frowns. "Well, that's smart." She walks into the kitchen and returns with a bag of peas placing it on my hand. She sits next to me.

I need her close to me when I tell her everything.

She sniffles on my shoulder as I tell her word-for-word what Rachel said, wiping her tears with my thumb.

"I'm s-sorry baby, I'm sorry I couldn't protect you and your dad. I didn't know—if only I would've picked up on something," I croak feeling helpless.

She stops me, pressing her lips on mine—a quick brush. "Don't you dare apologize. Don't you dare blame yourself. This was all her. She took them away from me, you did not. Rachel was envious of my parents for the love they had for each other, just like she was of ours, Dominic." Her eyes search mine as she holds onto my hand tightly. A small slit smile plays on her beautiful face.

"So, you cried to be next to me when you were a wee baby."

I can't help but laugh. It feels good. "Ahh, I see you picked up on us knowing each other as toddlers."

Mila wraps her soft, warm hand around my neck as I pull her onto my lap. She leans in for a peck on the lips. Feels so good to have her in my arms. I'll take anything she'll give me. I love her profoundly. I bury myself in the crook of her neck... inhaling her scent.

"I can't believe we met as babies, and when we first saw each other at my dad's restaurant, it was like we instantly fell into each other like—"

"Like home, reunited, our hearts became one," I finish for her, kissing her cheek to her forehead.

"Yes," she breathes out slowly. Mila kisses me on the lips, a small brush on the lips.

I'm dying for more. I missed her.

"You know, it's strange I didn't plan on moving back to California. The memories of us were too much for me. Still, something was pulling me to move back, to open a studio in California. I see it clearly now makes more sense. Our hearts, our souls called to one another. We will always find our way back to each other." She looks up at me. "Sounds cheesy, but it's true."

"Yeah, baby, you're mine forever. I can't live without you, Mila. It's you and me against the world. I need you like I need air."

I love how she molds into me. I keep kissing her all over her face, I can't seem to stop. It feels like years of not having her near me. My arms wrap around her waist tightly. She tilts her head to the side.

"What are you thinking about?" she asks.

"I can't help but apologize for what she took from you, two loving parents, baby. You're so strong, my warrior."

"I don't want you to apologize. Rachel thought she loved my dad, but it wasn't love; it was a sick obsession. I'm just glad I know the entire story. I feel more at peace now, you know?"

I nod. I'm happy she has this. She removes herself off my lap, sitting next to me. She reaches for her wine taking a sip.

"I wish I would've met my mom, and none of this would've happened, but I can't live bitter with rage. They both died tragically. I miss them dearly, but they're together now, watching over us. I need to see it in a different light. I have closure now. I have you, Dante, Nana, Uncle Roger, and Sophie. You're my home, Dominic, you and Dante."

Fuck she's amazing here, I envisaged her looking at me with hate, a son of a murderer. But no, her eyes bore into mine with so much love. I can't help but lift her and sit her on my lap, smacking my lips on hers. Our tongues tangle with each other.

The moment her lips press against mine, an electric shock of pleasure jolts through my body. I pull her closer to me and run my tongue across her soft lips. They part and I deepen the kiss, savoring the taste of her as our tongues intertwine in a passionate embrace. The intensity of the moment pulses through us, and all I want is more.

I moan in delight at the intimacy of our kiss. My dick twitches against my zipper. The love I have for her is above and beyond. *She wants to see stars. I can't help it; I'll give her more. I'll give her the universe.* She deserves it all. Tearing away from the kiss, I desperately don't want to end, but fuck, there's something else I need to tell her about Samantha. We pant and breathe in each other's space. I wince.

"Baby, there is one more thing I need to tell you."

She frowns. "What now?"

I lick my lips, savoring her taste on my lips.

"Umm, well, one night I was drinking on the sofa, really depressed, kinda drunk. Samantha showed up."

Her forehead creases with worry. I rub my thumb on the top of her hand. I take a sip of whiskey and continue.

"She was wearing a long coat, then she dropped it to the floor... she was naked." She tries to jump off my lap. I hold her in place.

"What the hell, Dominic? You said you didn't do anything with her."

"Mila, listen to me, please. She tried to get me to seduce her. At the time, I didn't know she was the one who gave you the report to break us up and told you we slept together."

"Spit it out, Dominic. Did you fuck her?" she bites with rage.

"No, baby, I didn't. I grabbed her arm and shoved her out the door along with her bear coat. She's not you. No woman holds a candle to you. I kicked her ass out of the house."

"Did you get turned on?"

I snort. "Hell, no baby, she never turned me on. She disgusted me."

"Good." She huffs, I want to laugh at how cute she looks jealous.

"And another thing, I need to tell you, after I had spoken to Sophie, I went to confront Samantha." A chuckle of disbelief escapes me at the fucked-up shit Samantha and Rachel have done screwing with our life.

"Caught Samantha with her lover balls deep, which happened to be the man Rachel hired to stalk you all these years. Samantha and Rachel set the whole engagement up. Samantha would get her inheritance if she married; I was the pawn in their game." Explaining it all to her, I leave out the part where I saw a photo of her and Ken.

The image throws me over the edge. The need to toss her on the floor and bury myself in her and get her on her knees to deep throat my cock in her mouth until I spill every drop. Claim her until the image is out of my head like a wild animal. She stands up, throwing her hands in the air.

"I knew it. When I moved back, I noticed a man I had seen in Manhattan. I thought I was going crazy. He looked oddly familiar. I thought it was a coincidence, of him being here, or someone just looking like him." She shivers.

My jaw twitches at the thought of the asshole following her around.

"Mila, why didn't you tell me this?" I'm pissed she failed to mention it.

"I just kept brushing it off. I only saw him three or four times since I moved back."

Fireworks begin to pop. I look up at the clock on the mantel, it's midnight.

"Happy New Year, baby, to a better year to come. I'll protect you with my life, Mila, you, and Dante always. I'll do better." Then I kiss and kiss her like a man who can't get enough. Raw, organic, and full of need.

"So, where's Nana? And your uncle?"

"Nana went to her friend's party. She's spending the night there and Uncle Roger is with his girlfriend. I don't think he's coming home."

We walk up the stairs hand in hand. She leads me into Dante's room, where he's sleeping. My little man is curled up in a blanket hugging a Spider-Man stuffy; I lean in to kiss his cheek. Soft little breaths escape his lips. He's perfect.

"I love you," I softly whisper as I pull the blanket up.

His eyes open. "Daddy?" His voice is groggy.

"Yeah, it's me. Go back to bed. I'll see you in the morning, love you."

"Love you too, Dad." His eyes close, he's back into a deep sleep.

Mila chuckles as she watches from the door. "Come on, let's go to my room."

We lay in bed. I hold her in my arms, as we drift off to sleep. It's been weeks since I've slept. A sense of relief washes over me. From the beginning, I should have told her everything. I only tortured myself and her. I should've known better. I could have lost her—my queen. Mila would never see me in a different light because the love she has for me runs deep, as does the love I have for her. Our love is more profound than the ocean's depths.

MILA

A month later

THESE PAST COUPLE of weeks have been wonderful, taking it day-by-day, we've spent the last couple of days moving all our stuff into Dominic's house. After weeks of being apart, we decided to move in together, no point in waiting.

Although there's still a shadow over us, mainly on Dominic and his brothers, I might have gotten closure and justice. I can't imagine what the guys are going through. The woman they loved and who raised them, lived a lie. She killed two innocent people, with no remorse. Let's not forget she wanted me dead. Chills run up my spine just thinking about how crazy she was.

"Baby, I can cook. You know I'm a chef." Dominic leans to kiss my cheek.

"I know, but I want to cook for you and your brothers tonight. Just relax. You've been moving all our stuff in, and we need a family dinner tonight."

His hands roam my whole body as he stands behind me.

"Dominic," I whisper; his brothers are in the living room playing with Dante.

He kisses the side of my neck. He whispers in my ear, his hot breath feathering the hairs on my neck, "You look so sexy cooking in our kitchen. So beautiful." He keeps kissing my neck.

I bite my lip to keep myself from moaning; I don't need his brothers hearing me.

"Let's go to our room really quick."

I glance at him over my shoulder. "No, I'm in the middle of making dinner, and your brothers are here," I whisper with scant breath.

"They won't know, and I need dessert before dinner tonight, Angel."

His husky voice sends a rush of heat between my legs. "You always want dessert."

He shrugs. "It's true."

Practically dragging me up the stairs, Dominic strips his shirt off. I'm wearing a jean skirt which works for easy access.

"Get on the bed now," he demands desperately.

His hungry eyes captivatingly have me obeying instantly. He hikes up my skirt, placing his face in between my legs. I gasp as a shockwave pulse in my clit. His tongue works magically. Licking up and down. Sucking. His tongue overlaps my folds, thrusting rhythmically, he doesn't stop until I'm satisfied.

Oh, God, feels so good.

He pistons into me. The vibration of him inside has me gasping, lifting my legs over his shoulder. I can feel the stretch as he goes deeper. The force of his thrusts sends shockwaves of pleasure through me. I cling to his shoulders, my nails digging into his skin.

"I love waking up to you. I love holding you in my arms at night until we both fall asleep." His voice vibrates with pleasure. "Get on your knees, baby." He grabs my hips firmly, his voice full of authority.

His free hand smacks roughly against my butt as he pushes himself deep inside me with a groan, his hardness pulsing against my slickness. His body moves in a controlled rhythm, the circular movements increasing in intensity as we both moan in pleasure. With his other hand, he grabs my hair and tugs it back, sending a wave of pleasure through my body. His ragged breathing intensifies as he increases his pace and I feel myself on the brink of an explosive climax.

"Fuck, baby, you feel so good," he moans.

Slapping my ass, a wave of pleasure pulses through us. The slapping of flesh against my ass sends an electric shock through my whole body. We ride the wave of pleasure together. My spine goes rigid, squeezing my thighs. He wildly thrusts harder... deeper. He hits every spot so raw and perfect I can't help but scream his name, praying no one can hear.

"That's it, baby, scream my name. Look at me, Angel."

I do. Over my shoulder, I see his brown whiskey eyes; beautiful, full of lust and so much love. His thrusts pick up speed grinding harder.

"I love coming home to you, baby. I fucking love you. You're mine, Angel. Scream my name, baby, let everyone know who you belong to, no one fucks with my girl," he bellows.

I scream his name as a soul-shattering orgasm robs me of my senses. His grunts are deep and raspy. Shit, I'm sure every neighbor heard, fuck, and his brothers. Dominic spills inside me. We're both breathing heavily, panting as I flip over. He rests his head on my chest.

"I love you," I say in between breaths.

"Mom, are you okay?" Dante asks worriedly.

Dominic and I walk down the stairs. Ugh, my face turns red like a tomato.

"She's fine, little man. Why?" Dominic answers.

Dante frowns, a crease on his forehead. "She was screaming."

"Oh, yeah, well a spider jumped on her, so she was screaming for help."

Santiago and Mark burst out laughing.

Well, that's not embarrassing. I hide myself behind Dominic.

315

"Come on, baby, let's finish dinner together since I interrupted you, I'll help you."

I groan as I shuffle my way to the kitchen. "Jeez, Dominic, how embarrassing," I say, smacking Dominic on the chest.

He smiles, showing all his white teeth. I melt all over again for this beast of a man. "Don't be. My brothers are horn dogs. Well, Santiago is," he says as he waves his hand like it's no big deal his brothers heard me scream bloody murder.

An hour later, two casseroles of green and red enchiladas, rice, and beans are ready. Liam and Sophie show up. She proclaims they're not seeing each other. She says they're just friends, I find it hard to believe. I know they are both attracted to each other. But then again, they are both anti-relationships. So, who knows?

I thought my best friend would be heartbroken that I moved out of our place. However, I think she is happy to have her privacy with Liam or whoever, since she still sees guys on dating apps.

WE SIT at the table like a big, happy family, holding onto one another for support. It's been rough on the guys. Dominic and his brothers occasionally appear to be in a fog. I hate they are going through this. I hate that it was his mother who killed my parents. I would never have thought she killed my parents; my father never mentioned my mom knew Rachel.

I find it hard to believe my father had a thing for Rachel; perhaps it was all an illusion in Rachel's head. My father would never commit to a relationship with someone who knew my mom. He adored my mother.

I'm still trying to wrap it all together. Dominic and I, as babies, who would have thought? It's so bizarre how obsessed she was with my father.

"Damn, these are so good," Mark mumbles.

"How's your girlfriend?" I ask Mark, making conversation.

"She's good. She's in Oregon visiting her sister." Mark, being the youngest, I can tell he's having a hard time with this. His beautiful boyish face has bags around his eyes.

Rachel's hearing will be next week. I haven't decided if I want to go. Dominic said he would go with me, but I feel it would be difficult for them. Dominic believes we all need to be there to move on. Maybe he's right.

"Mom, do you have chips and hot salsa?" Dante inquires, his eyebrows knitting together.

"What is the need for hot salsa?" I ask.

He huffs dramatically. "Mom, Uncle Liam said hot salsa will give me a little hair on my chest."

The entire table erupts in laughter. Dominic's shoulders shake with laughter and tears. Dante always has a way of putting a smile on your face.

Santiago reaches for the tortilla chips, handing them to Dante. "Here you go, my favorite nephew, chips, and salsa."

I smile as I watch Santiago interact with his nephew, scooping some rice into my mouth. I reach for Dominic's hand under the table, intertwining our fingers. The conversation continues. We talk about what there is to do in Manhattan, and what Dante was like as a baby, the brothers mainly ask. They smile and laugh at the stories I tell. I see a pang of guilt in their eyes. I hate it. It's not their fault. We all mask the pain we harbor. The night went smoothly with just us three left.

My weight carries me to the sofa, where I lay down, feeling a little fatigued.

"Are you all right, Angel?"

"Yeah, I'm just tired. I've been feeling exhausted lately." I yawn.

His thick, long, dark eyelashes flutter as his brown eyes darken with worry. His lips twist. "Maybe you're getting sick, or just all this going on, baby, it's wearing you out. I know it is wearing me out. Everything will get better, baby, I promise."

I sigh tiredly. He kneels next to me on the sofa. He brushes his hand over my head. "I'm okay, just tired. Don't worry."

"I'll always worry about you, baby. Take Dante to bed. I'll clean up the kitchen and be up to take care of you. A warm shower or bath will help. Deal?"

My stomach flutters with the rumble of his voice. I gaze into his brown eyes, sharp jaw, and olive tan skin, his hair perfectly slicked, silk hair falls flawlessly to the side with a strand hanging down. His complete form is muscle. Dominic is utterly sexy as hell and a heart of gold just for me. *Mine.*

"Deal."

I lean my head back in the big, oval bathtub. Dominic filled it with lavender bath bombs, and it smells so good. I moan as he massages his masculine hands into my scalp.

"This feels good."

He groans. "I can tell. You keep moaning. And now I have a major hard-on, my dick is hanging heavy, baby." he says, sarcastically.

"Get in with me."

"That can't happen, Mila, I'm already losing it with your nipples peeking out from the foam, your leg draped over the tub. It's like a sex fantasy."

"Mila?" I snap, giving him a questionable look.

"My bad which one, do you prefer? baby, Angel, sweetheart, sexy, beautiful, hot mamma, big titties?"

I laugh. "All the above works." I bat my eyelashes at him tilting my head up to look at him. "Get in. My turn to take care of you."

He raises his perfectly shaped eyebrow. "You're tired. I'm supposed to relax you."

"I'm relaxed. We don't have to have sex to pleasure you. I have other ways."

He bites his bottom lip. "Is that so, big titties?"

"Dominic," I groan with a smile.

"Hey, you said all the above." His hands go up in defense.

My mouth twists with a grin. "Fine, just get in already."

He laughs, and I can't help but smile at his beautiful laugh. "All right, bossy."

He peels his shirt off, revealing his perfectly toned abs and unbuckles his jeans. His boxers slip off; he sits on the opposite side of me. I crawl to him, kissing him like a needy schoolgirl. I grab a hold of his hard thick shaft. He groans.

"Fuck, Angel, your hands work magic."

"Umm... I say the same thing about your tongue."

"Is that so." He wiggles his eyebrows.

I blush. He tilts his head back, he grunts and groans as I stroke fast and slow, getting him worked up.

"That's it, baby, keep going don't stop. Oh, baby, just like that," he moans until he comes.

"Relaxed?" I ask.

"Very. Thanks, Angel. I love you." He kisses me with his hot lips.

I mouth into his lips, "Love you too."

"Let's get you out and get you to bed." He helps me up... drying me off, then dries himself off.

I slip on some shorts and a tank top. He carries me to our big Cali king size bed. Snuggling into his arms, I drift off to sleep. Ever since Dominic's mother confessed the truth, the nightmares I've battled for years have decreased to a bare minimum, almost nonexistent. I'm positive with Dominic by my side they will fade away. As for my dreams of Dominic, they no longer exist as my heart is at peace now.

Thirty-Eight

DOMINIC

I hold Mila close in my arms as we sit on the bench at the courthouse. My brothers sit next to me. Sophie sits next to Mila for moral support. Roger and Nana flew down to be here for the trial and conviction of Rachel.

I rub the sweat off the palms of my hand onto my jeans. We scrutinize Rachel walking in, handcuffed with an officer walking her to her seat. Pain shoots through my whole body, my gut twists uncomfortably. I know Santiago and Mark have the same expression of pain seared in their hearts. I clench my jaw, color drains from their faces; they appear ghostly; hurt, betrayal, anger are what we manifest as we watch Rachel sit insouciant, chin up with no sense of remorse.

She whispers into her attorney's ear. She pauses as she turns to look at us. My brothers stiffen. Her eyes soften when she looks at us. Rachel's irises darken as her glare travels to my girl with pure hate.

I squeeze Mila's shoulder, bringing her close to me, possessively, protecting her from the woman I've grown to hate. Anger boils in me, pinning my eyes right at her, fire blazing, I let out a growl, letting her know not to fucking look at her.

Mila stiffens in my arms. Turning my head to look at Mila,

her eyes fixed on Rachel, no hate in my girl's eyes, just anger. Mila stands tall, like a true warrior. The look in her eyes tells Rachel, *Don't fuck with my family.*

Rachel turns back to her attorney.

I rub Mila's back. Leaning into her I whisper, "Are you ok, baby?"

She nods yes. "Are you?"

"I'll be okay, baby, in time. All I care about is that you and Dante are safe. You two are my world." I kiss her on the temple as the judge walks in.

Halfway through the trial, Rachel sits in the witness seat, and she confesses about Leo and Mikaela's deaths. Nana sobs in Robert's arms as he comforts his mom. Mila runs out of the courtroom as I follow behind.

"Baby, wait up," I whisper softly.

I follow her into the lady's restroom, where I find her throwing up—shutting the door to the stall, I rub her back.

"Baby, this is too much for you. We can leave."

She wipes her mouth with her hand flushing the toilet. "I just felt nauseous. I'll be good." She opens the door.

I grab a paper towel, wet it, and hand it to her. She wipes her mouth, then rinses her mouth at the sink. I hiss at the look of her.

"Angel, you're pale. We're going to wait outside. You need fresh air. Come on, I can't stand another minute in there myself." I drop some coins into the soda machine and get Mila water and soda for myself. Then, holding her hand, I lead her outside.

Later, we all sit at our restaurant, as in *ours,* I mean mine and Mila's. I built this restaurant with her in mind. It's always been ours, I just hadn't realized it. After court, we all came here to regroup.

They sentenced Rachel to life in prison. I'm relieved because the malicious depth in her eyes, the way she fixates on Mila, revealed how much hatred Rachel carries. She would do anything to get rid of her, no remorse, no sorry, nada. Life in prison is what Rachel deserves.

My heart hurts for the mother I once loved. However, with how selfishly she thought of only herself, I no longer do. I'm more than relieved Rachel will be nowhere near Mila ever again.

"To closure and a new beginning," my brother Santiago says as he lifts his drink, masking his emotions.

We all bury our emotions, the pain crippling us. We all raise our glass and drink.

Two weeks later

Opening the front door to our condo, I'm greeted by Dante running into my arms.

"Daddy, you're home." He envelopes his hands around my neck like a monkey.

Coming home to this is the best thing ever, no more coming home to an empty place. Mila's in the kitchen cooking dinner. Her beautiful face glows brightly.

"Yup, I got out a little early. I needed to get home to my two favorite people in the world. How was school?" I place a kiss on Dante's cheek.

"Daddy," he groans, wiping the kiss-off.

Putting him down, I walk over to Mila.

"Good, Daddy, I won an award today."

"Really! I'm proud of you."

Dante smiles widely, showing his deep dimples as he walks into the living room. I lift Mila's chin so I can kiss the shit out of her.

"I missed you," I tell her before I press my lips on her hot, wet mouth. Then wrapping my arms around her, I place them right on her plump round ass. I squeeze roughly. "How was your day, Angel?"

She presses her mouth right back on mine. We kiss some more. "Great," she finally answers after our long make-out session.

"I thought about you all day," I murmur as she presses her lips on mine again, kissing me like she hasn't seen me in years. I'm not complaining. I like it.

She looks at me with her sparkly green eyes like I'm a meal she's dying for, starved for. I'm not sure if I should rejoice or be terrified. Her gorgeous eyes scan my body with a lick of her swollen red lips. By the look in her eyes, she might pounce on me like a predator catching its next meal, or she might rip my clothes savagely. My cock twitches. I clear my dry throat, which has suddenly become parched and dry, which desperately needs water. Reaching for the nearest water bottle on the table, I take a long sip.

After dinner, I help Mila rinse dishes by placing them in the dishwasher. Every chance she gets, she smacks her gorgeous hot lips on mine. Horny and I mean Extremely Horny Mila is scary, but I am fucking love it. I've never seen Extremely Horny Mila. It's making me Extremely Horny Dominic.

"I love you," I tell her as I suck on her bottom lip. "It's 9:30; it's late. Go put our son to bed. I can't handle your fuck me eyes any longer and I need you naked on our bed."

She giggles. "Fuck me eyes?" she asks, innocently.

"Yes, fuck me eyes, you look at me like I'm your last meal."

She smiles with satisfaction. "Oh, you have no idea," she says seductively.

That has my dick twitching swelling in my jeans. She sways to the living room to collect Dante, then she turns her eyes hot on mine.

"Oh, and I have a gift for you." She winks.

Holy shit, my heart's about to roll out of my chest. Super-hot, sexy, horny Mila is pure heaven. I press start on the dishwasher and run the fuck up the stairs.

I am patiently waiting while Mila gets out of the shower; she even locked the door. Seriously, I think she is trying to sabotage me, torture me. For fuck's sake, she finally comes out ten minutes later. Ten. Long. Minutes. Her long, black, silky hair damply wrapped in her soft pink robe. She carries a small box wrapped in a bow. She sways to the bed next to me.

"Here." She hands me the white box with a red bow. Her smile lights up her face with a tad bit of nervousness as she bites her lip.

"Is everything ok?" I have to ask.

She nods. "Open it."

I do. My heart beats so damn fast that my heart wants to explode. I am filled with so many emotions: joy, happiness, love. Staring inside the box, I look up at the love of my life.

"Y-you're pregnant?" My voice comes out raspy with so many emotions.

"Yes." She breathes with a smile that lights up my life.

My eyes go back to the ultrasound picture, and my smile widens at the tiny baby who's represented by the tiny heartbeat. Lifting Mila gently on my lap, I kiss her with everything I've got.

"Mila, baby, you make me so damn happy. We're having another baby?"

She giggles adorably. "Yes, I'm due in November. You know, I am pretty sure this is the same time we conceived Dante. He or she might be born on his birthday."

I can't keep my eyes off the woman who's giving me everything I've ever dreamed of... love and a family. A joyful tear spills.

"I can't wait until your belly swells and the baby kicks. I get to be part of it this time and you won't be alone."

She smiles weakly. I missed out on Dante's first years. I can't get those back. All I can do now is move forward. She runs her hand down my hair lovingly.

"Yes, you do, baby." She presses her lips on mine.

Mila slips off my lap and unties her robe, it drops to the ground. She has me gasping for air like a fish out of water. My hot, sexy woman is standing in front of me, naked. My eyes travel up and down every luscious curve. I groan at her swollen breasts, which I'm sure is because of her being pregnant.

Fuck me.

"Fuck, Mila, you're so beautiful. How did an asshole like me get so lucky? I want you, baby." I reach for her.

"Nope, strip down, Dominic. Now," she demands with a hiss, and Horny Mila is back, full force this time.

Fuck is this hot.

I strip my shirt off and unzip my jeans like I'm in some kind of race.

A race to get inside of her.

"On the bed, Dominic. And take your damn boxers off, for fuck's sake."

Well, hot damn.

A woman has never dominated me, and the only woman I'll let is Mila—sprawling my naked ass on the bed for my demanding, bossy girl.

"You know, pregnancy makes me horny. I've been waiting all day for this." She cat-walks on the bed, her breasts bouncing as she makes her way to me.

This is sexy as hell, a fantasy, my fantasy.

"If pregnancy gets you like this, then you'll be pregnant with a football field of kids," I choke out.

She wraps her hand around my massive hard-on and begins to stroke. Her seductive green eyes meet mine as she watches me, eager for a taste and to take me in her mouth. Her tongue glides over my shaft in rasping strokes. She takes me in with devout desire as her tongue slurps on the tip. Her mouth is like a drug I crave. I moan and groan in satisfaction.

"Fuck baby, oh God, that feels good. Shit, Angel, just like that. You take it so well."

I don't want to come in her mouth, I need to come inside her.

Instead, I say, "Ride me, baby."

She rides me mercilessly like I'm a goddamn bucking stallion. I cup her breasts in my large hands, take a nipple in my mouth, sucking the sweetness, giving each one its undivided attention. Mila purrs with pleasure, throwing her head back as she rides me. Her hair sways to each side. I have the perfect view. I watch her as she chants my name over and over, her lip's part. My heart pounds like I raced a dozen stairs. Taking her mouth in mine, her heated mouth savors mine.

"Baby, you look so beautiful riding me. Mmm and those swollen breasts, baby." I pinch.

"Yes, that feels good," she moans with pleasure.

"I want those breasts in my mouth."

Popping each one, I twirl my tongue over them then I flip us over. Thrusting inside her, I feel her muscles tighten around my dick.

"You want me to show you stars, baby, or want the universe tonight?"

She hums with pleasure. "Universe," she purrs.

"Then you better hold on." My voice comes out raspy.

I hold on to the bed frame for support, pressing into her pussy. Diving deeper when she begins to shatter underneath me. She screams when the last orgasm comes in, milking me dry. Rolling off her, I kiss her hungrily.

"Damn, baby, I can get used to Horny Mila."

"Stop it, I don't think you can handle me," she hisses and flushes with a grin.

"Watch me, baby, I'm ready for an all-nighter," I say, leaning I kiss her pregnant stomach.

"Hi, baby, I'm your daddy. You have a big brother who's going to be excited to meet you." I pepper kisses all over her belly.

She runs her hands through my messy hair. "Dante's going to be ecstatic." She beams with a smile.

I kiss her belly to her breasts, making my way to her mouth. Lifting her chin to meet those big alluring glass-green eyes staring back at mine.

"Angel, you make me so happy. You have given me two precious gifts. In the last couple of months, I found out I had a son. It meant the world to me, having a child with the only woman I've ever loved. This baby we're having is coming in perfect timing," I murmur rubbing her belly.

A tear rolls down her cheek. I catch each one with my lips, kissing them all away.

"With all the shit happing. This is the best gift, baby. No one will ever come between us, Angel. I'll protect you, *our family*, with my life."

Her glossy, beautiful eyes spill more tears, catching each salty tear with my mouth. It's true, I'll never let anyone hurt her. She's been through so much. Day-by-day, the pain in my chest has lessened. Mila and Dante have shown me what family and love mean. I had not realized until now my mother was manipulative and toxic. My new purpose in life is to become the best father and man for Mila. I'll never stop fighting for *us*.

MILA

Mila

A month later

A SHAFT of sunlight splits down the middle of the bedroom. Stretching, I yawn, rubbing my pregnant belly. Two months pregnant, nausea has finally subsided. Thank God. Picking up my phone from the nightstand, I gasp. Oh shit, it's noon. I slept all morning. I grab a pair of leggings and a long sleeve shirt and make my way to the shower. Walking into the kitchen, it's empty—no sign of my guys. I notice a note on the table.

Good morning, baby, I didn't want to wake you up. Dante and I went to run some errands. Get dressed. When you're done, let's play a little game. Do you remember the place I first kissed you on the lips when you moved back? Make your way to the spot.

I grin stupidly.

This is spontaneous. Slipping on some sandals, I think back to the day. Hmm, it has to be the studio when he found out about Dante, and he smacked his hot lips on mine. Making a beeline to my Ranger, I drive to the studio.

Sophie stands with a big grin. "Hello, their sleepy head."

I groan. "God, I'm sorry I woke up so late. Good thing I don't have clients until three today."

She walks to her desk, pulling an envelope from her drawer. "I rescheduled your appointment for today. So, here you go, babe." She hands me an envelope.

I pry it open with eagerness.

You made it, Angel; you did well. Now next stop, Angel, where I sat you on my lap and kissed the hell out of you and where you decided to give us a chance.

I chew on my bottom lip. Well, this is easy, it's his restaurant Delgado's.

"Thank you for rescheduling for me."

She rubs my tummy. That seems to happen a lot. Even Santiago and Mark were over the moon, rubbing my tummy every time they see me, and my baby, Dante. He was so excited he kept telling me, thank you for my brother. He's determined it's a boy.

"Your man had me reschedule. He wanted to play scavenger hunt." She shrugs as she picks up her cell, texting someone. "What's your next stop?"

"Umm, the restaurant," I reply.

"All right, see you later." She shoos me off.

Opening the big double doors to the restaurant, I spot Mario standing waiting for me, looking handsome with his long sleeve button shirt and khaki pants.

"Mila, how are you doing?" He smiles boyishly.

"Good, Mario. How about you?"

He rests his hand on my back, guiding me to the private back room reserved for parties. The room is quiet and empty. Then, I spot an envelope and a bacon cheeseburger and fries with a strawberry shake.

"Doing good, just busy with the kids. You know how it goes?"

I nod in agreement. "Yes, I do."

He pulls out a chair so I can sit. "Dominic ordered your favorite. He figured pregnancy would have you craving a shake with it."

"He's sweet. It all looks delicious. Thank you, Mario."

"You're welcome. I've never seen him this happy. I met Dominic in culinary school. He was always grumpy, unhappy with his life, then you walk back and light him up," he admits. "I'm just happy I don't have to deal with his grumpiness, and when I do, I'll call you to set him straight."

We both laugh as he walks out. I open the envelope as I squirt ketchup on my fries.

Angel, enjoy your lunch. I figured you'd be hungry. Can't let my girl go hungry and the baby. Next stop, Angel, the place where it started, the place where I fell in love with you, the moment I first saw you.

Tears spill down my cheek. Pregnancy hormones make you crazy. This has to be my dad's restaurant. I haven't been there in years. When my dad passed away, it was taken into the bank's possession. My dad had lost a lot of money, and now we know Rachel had been stealing money from him. Last, I remember someone purchased it from the bank, and converted it into a deli. I'm not sure if it's still occupied.

Pulling into the parking lot, I spot the restaurant. My hands shake. It's for sale. Well, it *was* for sale; it says sold. Then the memories of my dad hit me. After school, I would help him when he needed it or simply eat dinner with him. The memories of Dominic and me. The night he walked in the door, I knew he was it for me.

Santiago stands in the parking lot, waiting for me. I step out of my car, Santiago wipes away my tears, handing me an envelope. "I know this is hard for you, Mila, and I'm sorry. Things will get better. Good memories, right?"

I nod. "Yes, very beautiful memories. Thank you. I see you're the messenger at this spot."

He grins, showing his white, bright teeth. "My brother, the romantic." He shakes his head laughing.

"Hey, when you find love, you'll be Mr. Romanic, all gooey on the inside."

He scoffs with a smile. "I don't see that happening."

"Oh, it will." I wink.

He pats my back. "Take care and of my little nephew or niece."

"Laters."

Santiago jumps into his pickup. Opening the envelope, I read.

Angel, this place has so many significant memories of us and, most of all, your dad. So, in honor of him, I bought this place. We're the new owners of our second restaurant, baby. How about we call it Mila's Diner? Let me know what you think, or you can name it anything you want, baby.

I gasp with shock. I break down with an ugly cry. God, Dominic is so amazing. He bought this place for us... for my dad.

Last stop, baby. This next stop is our favorite spot. The night you became mine seven years ago.

The beach is our spot behind the rock. Smiling goofily, I melt with all these memories. We were wild and free teenagers, having sex anywhere we could. Our prime spot was the beach, a giant rock blocking anyone from seeing us. Taking off my sandals, I walk along the coast. I feel the fresh, moist sand on my bare feet. My two guys stand waiting for me. Dominic looks hot in his jeans that fit him perfectly, along with a black t-shirt which hugs his biceps, muscles popping out of them. Dante is dressed similarly to his father. They look so cute. A smile breezes over me when my eyes catch the heart traced on the sand with Dominic and Mila. I'm crying all over again, damn you... hormones. Dominic jogs to me. His handsome face is washed with concern.

"Baby, are you okay... what happened?" he asks as I throw my arms around him, sobbing. "Baby, you're scaring me. Did someone hurt you?" He pulls me away from his hard body, his eyes roaming up and down my body with concern.

"No, no, I'm fine."

"Thank the fuck, you scared me, but why are you crying?"

"The restaurant; you bought it?" I ask.

He frowns worriedly, his hands still wrapped around me.

"Shit, I'm sorry. I wanted to surprise you. I should have asked you first."

I cup my hands on his cheek. My eyes pinned on his. "I-I love you. You're right. We have so many good m-memories, it's perfect. I'm just o-overwhelmed with emotions. I- love you, Dominic. You're the most amazing man. My d-dad would be p-proud of you." My sobs make it hard to talk.

A bulge in his throat wrenches up and down.

Dante runs to us. "Hi, Mommy, I got some crap in my bucket."

"Crap? You have crap in your bucket?" I ask worriedly.

He nods. "Yes."

Dominic barks a laugh, head tilting back, laughing. "He means crabs."

"Oh." I laugh too.

Dominic hands me a red rose, holding my hand as we walk behind the rock. I'm lost in the fresh breeze of the ocean, blue waves hitting the rock, seagulls squawking. I am overcome by a sense of calm. I turn to look for Dominic, he's kneeling and looking right at me. My heart beats wildly, gasping when I see the box in his hand. My hand slaps over my mouth. His eyes are glossy, those whiskey eyes, gaze at me with so much love.

"Angel, I love you more than words can say. Loving you is the happiest I've ever been. You're my soulmate, my other half. Without you, Mila, I'm empty. I hate the feeling of emptiness. I never want to feel it again. Until we are gray and old, I want to be with you. Even in another life, I'll find you. I know I don't deserve you, baby. You're too good for me, but I promise I'll spend the rest of my life trying to deserve you. God, Angel, I'm so in love with you. You're my queen, my everything. Mila Amaro, will you marry me, baby? Spend the rest of your life with me."

I'm a sobbing mess. I throw myself on him, knocking us both to the ground. "Yes!" I scream. "I'll marry you."

I hear clapping all around us. Dominic slides the beautiful

ring on my finger. He slams his lips on mine. Pulling away, he smiles with satisfaction, leaning my forehead onto his.

"I love you so much."

I still haven't glanced to see who's around us, reveling in the special moment.

"This was a perfect proposal, baby, everything a girl can dream of."

He whispers, "You deserve every bit, baby, and more. I'm relieved you think it's perfect."

When I spin to see the people behind us, I see Santiago, Mark, Sophie, Daliah, and Liam all clapping and yelling congratulations. Dante comes running, throwing himself on us. We're still on the ground.

"You're getting married," he shouts excitedly.

We hugged him. "Yup, little man, Mom said yes."

This has been the most amazing day, overflowing with so many emotions, all happy tears, tears of love. We walk hand-in-hand, the three of us making our way back to Dominic's truck. Handing Mark my car keys, I ask him to take my car back home. Staring at the man I love with my whole being, we've been through so much in the last couple of months and years.

Love isn't always perfect, and it doesn't always come easy. Love is overcoming obstacles and facing the challenges that life throws at us. I found my soulmate, my true love, the man I want to spend the rest of my life with.

Forty

MILA

Mila

Two months later

OUR NEW RESTAURANT has kept us quite busy, plus planning our wedding. We decided on a small wedding. This weekend is the big day. I watch as men put up the neon sign for our new restaurant. *Leo's Diner.* I felt it was fitting to keep my father's name to honor his memory. He died a tragic death. I wish to keep my dad's and my mother's dreams alive.

Dominic stands behind me, wrapping his powerful arms around my waist as we watch the men switch on the lights of the sign. As I watch, tears begin to flow. Dominic's thoughtfulness leaves me speechless and full of gratitude. It means so much to me. I tilt my head back to look at him.

"I love you so much, thank you for this."

He wipes my tears. "Baby don't thank me. I'd move mountains for you, Angel."

Right then, my little peanut kicks.

Dominic gasps with amusement. "Wow, it felt amazing, baby. My heart just wants to burst."

I want to melt just looking at him in awe.

"Hey, little guy, a couple more months and we get to meet you." We found out just the other day it's a boy. Little baby Luca kicks again.

"Two boys, I think we will have to keep trying until we get the girl," I tell Dominic.

He keeps rubbing my belly as he kisses me along my collarbone. He grins, one corner of his mouth showing his dimples. "Even after we have our girl, we should have about six kids."

I turn to face him. I'm about to say he's crazy. I can't say it now he's hot as hell and wearing his hat backwards, which sends lightning strikes down my spine. My arousal is at an all-time high. I'm not sure he knows what he does to me when he wears his hat backwards, or maybe he does because he's smirking like an idiot.

"Stop it," I sneer at him, annoyed.

"Ahh, let's get you home before you rip my clothes off."

I swat him away as he reaches for me, but he lifts me up bridal style, carrying me to the car, kissing me deeply. "Let's get home quick," I murmur in between kisses.

"QUE HERMOSA, *HOW BEAUTIFUL*." Nana sneaks up behind me.

Sophie styled my hair and makeup beautifully. My eyes roam my reflection in the mirror. My dress fits flawlessly with my round belly. I feel like a queen. I went with a mermaid chapel train, off-the-shoulder, tulle, sleeveless, white dress with lace all around. It shows a lot of cleavage, more than I wanted to show. Pregnancy has my breasts popping out.

"Thank you, Nana."

"Whoa, you look so beautiful." Uncle Roger snaps his camera, taking pictures from all angles.

"Your father and mother would be so proud of you. You've

become a beautiful, strong woman. I'm so proud of you, Mila."
Nana strokes my cheek lovingly.

"Thank you, Nana, for being a mother to me, for showing me
how to love, to be strong. You helped me become a better person,
the best version of myself that I could be, a strong woman and a
loving mother. I am who I am because of you. Thank you, Nana,
for being my strength."

She Wipes our tears.

"Hey, you two, no more crying now. I need to fix your make-
up." Sophie scowls at us.

Nana, Daliah, Rosaline (Liam's cousin), and Liam's mother
all load into the limo. Sophie, my bridesmaid, and I round out the
group. A May beach wedding is our plan since it was where our
love started to develop. Sophie did an amazing job decorating the
gazebo with twinkling fairy lights and white roses.

"Are the guys ready?" I ask, nervously, chewing on my lip as I
glance at Sophie's beautiful blue eyes in her blue maid-of-honor
strapless dress that makes her eyes stand out gorgeously. I'm
excited to start a new chapter in our life.

"Well, I sure hope so, unless he ran for his life," she teases.

I hiss, side-eyeing her.

"Kidding, kidding they're here. Liam, Santiago, Mark, little
man, and all the guests have arrived. I think this is it, Mila; you'll
be married in less than thirty minutes. God, you're the most beautiful bride I have ever seen. I'm so proud to be your best friend,
Mila. You're the strongest woman I know. You've been through so
much, and here you are with a huge smile, a man that would kill
for you, and a beautiful family.

"I don't know why this feels like a goodbye, even though we
work together and will see each other daily. It's a milestone in
your life, a new chapter. I love you, Mila, I wish you the best. You
deserve all the happiness in the world, my best friend, my sister."

I swallow the big lump holding the unshed tears, wrapping
her in a hug. "I love you. Thank you for always being my rock.
You've seen me at my worst before you saw me at my best; you're a

true friend, a friend few people find, and thank God you rubbed my belly that day."

We both chuckle, trying to keep the tears in.

Uncle Roger walks up to us. "It's time."

THE MUSIC BEGINS TO PLAY. Uncle Roger walks me down the aisle, holding a bouquet of white roses. My eyes roam to my handsome man in a tux—broad shoulder, chiseled jaw, whiskey brown eyes drowning me in deep. His mouth gapes open as his eyes trail up and down my body, dancing with lust, adoration, and love. He swipes a tear off when Uncle Roger hands me to him. He leans in to kiss my forehead.

"You're so beautiful, the most gorgeous woman, Angel." He chokes with emotion.

"You look insanely handsome," I whisper in his ear.

My little man looks adorable in his little tuxedo. The priest begins the ceremony. Dominic and I get lost in each other as our eyes devour one another. It's like we can telepath with one another. My body heats at the way he bites his bottom lip. As we say our vows, Dominic says,

"I do."

Right when the priest pronounces us man and wife; you may kiss the bride, Dominic sweeps me into a deep kiss. I almost forgot we had an audience. Tears spill from my eyes, tears of joy and love.

"My beautiful wife," he says between each kiss.

His hand traces each curve and when his hands meet my ass, he squeezes. He seems to do that a lot.

"Been wanting to do that since the minute my eyes landed on you baby."

Our family and friends gather around us, enveloping us with hugs. My little man runs up to us.

"Are you married now?" he questions with a confused look in his brown honey eyes.

I try to get on his level, but I can't because my dress is too tight around my tummy and ass. It's not happening. Dominic lifts him up, chuckling when his lips twitch into a grin.

"We are married, buddy. She's, my wife."

Dante's nose scrunches up. "Ok, can we go now? This is so itchy." Not affected, more than likely doesn't know what's going on.

"Sure, when we get to the restaurant." Dominic holds my hand as he holds Dante in his arms. We make our way to the limo that's waiting for us.

"Let's welcome the newlyweds, Mr. and Mrs. Delgado," the D.J. announces as we enter Delgado's Steakhouse.

We managed to shut down and move all the tables and chairs to make a dance floor for the reception. The place is filled with elegant white linens and delicate glassware, and further adorned with a multitude of colorful floral arrangements. Every corner is decorated in fresh white roses, baby's breath, and ivy garlands intertwined with fairy lights, creating a whimsical paradise. Dominic hired a wedding decorator, and they outdid themselves.

Looping my arms around Dominic, we make our way to the dance floor for the bride and groom's first dance. When the song plays... my knees wobble. The song Dominic chose is perfect. I wrap my arms around his neck, his hand below my waist. *Dressed up in White* by Cal plays.

He croons the lyrics for me, only for me to hear. I'm melting into a puddle of mush. Good thing I'm holding onto him, or my legs would go out.

"I've dreamt of this moment for so long. To be able to call you my wife, baby, and for you to be the mother of my kids. My dream was *always you*. How about we get out of here?" A slit smile unfolds.

I gaze at our guests. "We just got here; we can't ditch our own wedding."

"Sure, we can. Look, everyone will be drunk in no time. Besides, I have a surprise for you, and Sophie, and Nana agreed to watch Dante, so my love, we are covered," he assures me with a dimpled smirk on his handsome face.

"A surprise, you say?"

As we're still swaying to the next song, our guests join the dance floor. My gaze sweeps over the dance floor and I see Liam and Sophie dancing; I also see Mark and his girlfriend dancing. I spot Santiago dancing with Liam's cousin. She's Mark's age. Dominic lifts my chin and kisses my mouth. Sneaking out sounds good now.

As Dominic drives, his hand entwines with mine. He kisses the base of my knuckles every couple of minutes until we make it to a beautiful, stunning house with a beach view. My mouth gapes open like a fish.

"Did you rent this place for the night?" I ask.

"You like it?"

"It's beautiful. Whoever this house belongs to, they're lucky fuckers."

He chuckles as he makes his way to open the door for me. Stepping into the immaculate home, I gasp. It's just as stunning on the inside, a huge marble kitchen with copper sinks and a colossal island. Holy shitballs, the living room is enormous with a gorgeous fireplace.

"Wow, this is so beautiful. How many bedrooms?" My mouth is still open. When I glance at Dominic, he's smiling at me, a smile so big it has my heart fluttering.

"Come here, baby."

I take little steps toward him, afraid of tripping on my dress. His lips slam into mine thirstily, consuming me fiercely. God, it feels good.

"Before I lose control, Angel, because God, it's easy to get lost in you. First, it's a four-bedroom house, huge backyard, with a firepit, beachfront view, three baths and a lot of other shit." He pecks my lips with a smile. "And, my Angel, it's our new home, baby. We are the lucky fuckers."

My mouth is now on the floor. *What the hell?* Eyes wide on him in shock. *Our new home,* I repeat to myself.

"Really?" I choke out, unable to speak.

"Uh-huh, baby, it's our new home. We needed something bigger for our growing family. I've saved money throughout the years. You deserve it."

All right, that's it. I sob. He's so perfect; he surprises me every day. Dominic is beyond everything I've ever wanted in a man.

Dominic carries me bridal style, I assume, to our room where a king-size bed awaits. I spot a duffel bag with our clothes. As he unzips my dress, it falls to the ground. His eyes caress my body, pinning me with a feral look, the way his eyes dissolve into the slopes of my breasts. My breathing picks up. How can he look at me as if it is the first time? He sees me with so much love, longing, and lust.

It's because we were destined to meet no matter the distance.

When I look into his brown whiskey eyes, I see a reflection of my soul, our hearts beating in harmony. My hands shake as I unbutton his dress shirt. His eyes never leave mine, holding him by the shoulder as my green eyes bore into his soul. No words are needed: our eyes, our mouths, our bodies do the talking. As he lifts me, placing me gently on the bed, our bodies connect, we're so in tune with one another. His kisses are gentle, sweet, and perfect.

We've overcome so many obstacles in our life. Our love for one another is so vital that if the world crashed, we would be the only ones left standing. Our love story is raw, unique. In the end, it's *ours*.

Epilogue
DOMINIC

Five years later

I GRIND my erection on Mila, spooning her in bed. She's such a heavy sleeper that I could have my way with her, and she would be limp as a noodle. The last five years have been a hell of a ride. Life with Mila only gets better every day. I fall in love with her all over again.

Sliding the covers down, I get a peek at her breasts poking out of her tank top. Sucking on each one, I try to wake her up, and fuck, she's still asleep. Goddamn, this woman. I sucked a little harder, biting them.

She stirs in her sleep. A soft moan escapes from her plump lips. She's so beautiful, trailing soft kisses on her lips, and nope. My wife is wholly given over to sleep. I don't blame her; the kids wear her out. My erection is only getting harder, begging for her attention. So, I do what I'm positive will wake her the fuck up.

Rolling her red-laced underwear off, I place myself in between her legs. My tongue lashes inside her, working her open, driving her wild. I chuckle in between her legs. She moans as she rocks back and forth. I groan and growl as I lavish my wife.

"Don't stop, that feels good," she purrs with pleasure.

"Don't plan on it, Angel," I mutter as I suck.

"Mom, Mikaela peed on the bed," Dante shouts from the other side of the door.

I don't stop, fuck, I can't. Damn, kids can wait. I keep devouring her while Mila tries to get up, pulling her legs down.

"We'll be right there," I shout to them.

"Dominic, I need to change her."

"Baby, I've been trying to wake your ass up for the last thirty minutes before the kids got up. Now let us finish."

Thirty minutes later, I pour Mila and me a cup of coffee as she makes pancakes. Dante is ten now, building a model car while Luca, who's five, watches closely, and my princess Mikaela, who looks just like her mom with the same piercing green eyes, sits eating her pancakes with her frozen dress on. Mikaela is three years old.

She groans, "'Tis good."

"Dante and Luca, come get your plates, boys. Take them outside so we can eat," Mila shouts for the boys.

We all like to sit on our backyard patio and have breakfast, watching the waves hit and enjoying the fresh smell of the salty ocean.

"Dad, what are we doing today?" Luca asks, with a mouthful of pancakes.

"Dude, don't talk with your mouthful; it's gross," Dante grumbles.

"Leave me alone; I can do what I want."

"All right, boys, that's enough." It's too early for this shit, they bicker like Santiago, and I used to. Mark was always pulling pranks on me.

"Dante has his baseball game, after we can do whatever you guys want. Then your mom and I are going out. Your Aunt Sophie is babysitting."

I've been coaching Dante's team for some time now. With running two restaurants, Mila's studio, and three kids, life has been hectic, but we make it work. Every other weekend I have my brothers, or Sophie, and Liam babysit so I can take my wife out on a date. Tonight, will be a special night. I have something planned. I love surprising her.

"GO, DANTE, RUN!" I shout as he makes a home run.

"Good job, baby," Mila yells from the stands.

I snort as I watch Dante blush and groan when she calls him baby. Being a dad is the best feeling in the world.

As for Rachel, she sends my brothers letters, but they toss them out. We haven't seen her since that day in court. She's a memory I don't want to remember. She made her bed now she must lie in it.

"Good job, boys, you played a good game." We're on a winning streak.

"All right, kids, line up for snacks and drinks. Good game," Mila praises the kids with a beautiful, beaming smile.

She took on the role of team mom, and she loves it. *God, I can't wait to have her to myself tonight.*

Smacking a kiss on her cheek, I whisper to her softly, only she could hear, "Can't wait to finish what we started this morning, baby."

Her eyes crinkle with a smile. As her sparkly, enchanted green eyes take in my profile, the heat in her eyes has me wanting to erupt like a damn volcano. The way Mila chews on her bottom lip always captures my attention. Mila is the most stunning woman I've ever come across. She just turned my hat backward, and fuck, it turns her on. Those predator's eyes tell me all I need to know. So, I fuck with her, teasing her, and at the end of the night, all that sexual tension will make for one hell of a night.

Placing another kiss on her cheek, I take Mikaela from her arms. Her eyebrows jog up to her forehead. Her breathing picks up like it always does. As I walk away, I shoot her a wink in a way that makes her flush—making my way to the kids, feeling her gorgeous eyes on me burning right through me.

AFTER THE GAME, we took the kids out for ice cream. Tommy's Frozen Custards is a new ice cream shop that just opened. Unbuckling Mikaela from her car seat, her beautiful green eyes sparkle like the stars.

"Look, Dada." She points to the ice cream shop.

"Yeah, princess, you want ice cream?"

She nods, her doe eyes blinking with happiness. My baby girl wraps her hands around my neck. I reach for my other girl's hand.

"I want a strawberry sundae," Luca says with a mischievous grin as he runs to Dante, pulling his underwear and giving him a wedgie.

Dante yelps as he glares at his brother with a sneer. For fuck's sake, pinching the bridge of my nose. I don't know if I should laugh or yell at them both. They are constantly fucking with each other; Luca enjoys aggravating his older brother.

"Luca, behave yourself." Mila narrows her eyes at them.

They shrink in size when Mila gives them, *I'll fuck you up if you don't behave* look. Shit, that look has me shrinking in size, and I didn't do a damn thing. I squeeze her ass, getting her to relax and continue the teasing. My hands always seem to land there. She smiles as she leans into me.

WALKING INTO OUR BEDROOM, my incredibly beautiful, teasing wife parades in her little lace underwear and bra as her breasts spill out evenly.

My erection grows ten times its size. Shuffling to her, I groan, observing every beautiful, lush curve perfectly made just for me. Heat spreads throughout my body.

"Can I help you?" She tilts her head with an amused expression.

"Yeah, baby, you can help me with this." I point to the bulge in my pants.

She tippy toes to kiss me, I open my mouth to give her all the access she needs, but no, all she does is peck my fucking lips and squeezes my dick over the material of my jeans. And sways to the bathroom, unclipping her bra as I watch her breasts spill out and bounce as they do.

"Fuck, that's cruel, baby," I shout.

She giggles like it's the fucking funniest thing on the planet to tease her husband on the verge of his dick exploding.

"Mila!" I shout again, coolly and a little desperate.

She spins around, a satisfied smirk plays on her sexy lips. Her long, thick eyelashes flutter as her gorgeous eyes dance all over mine. Hot damn, my body is turning into a sauna, heating as she rolls her lace underwear down and tosses them to me.

Catching them, I stuff them in the back pocket of my jeans.

Fuck, are they soaked.

"We need to get ready, Dominic. I'm showering."

She stands naked exquisitely, as Michelangelo sculpted her himself, sexy as sin. My mouth is still drooling over my hot, sexy wife.

I strip my clothes off—more like ripping them off. I'm starving for my wife. My teasing was a complete failure. I'm the one paying for it, hauling ass to jumping in the shower ogling the wife. This time I'm the predator catching its prey and fuck am I starving. She moans as she washes her hair. Trickles of water beam from her milky soft skin. Ahh, she knows perfectly well what she does to me.

"Angel, cut the shit already. You won all right; you always do. You're mine tonight. The kids are at Sophie's, let's skip the date and let me have my way with you all night."

She squirts lavender body wash into her red cleansing pouf, massaging her body, droplet of water drip from the tip of her nipples. Never been so jealous of a droplet of water. My mouth waters at the thought of licking them off. She finally acknowledges me, looking up at me with a sense of eagerness.

"Oh, Dom, you wanted to play a dangerous game. Hmmm, you never win, maybe this time. I'll hold out a couple of days to really teach you a lesson." Her voice is raspy with a mixture of seductive tone to it.

"Fuck no, baby, I'm sorry, never again." I make my way to her, our shower is enormous, big enough for five people, I pin her to the wall.

"I think we should get out and get ready to go," she says as she tries to escape my hold.

Oh, baby, we're not going out tonight, I say inwardly.

She's playing hard to get. I brush my lips onto her forehead, stroking my fingers between her legs, and Mila's head tips back against the tile, giving me better access to her neck. Assaulting her with kisses while I keep working my finger in her stroking, she moans. I grin and laugh on the inside, my baby thinks she always wins, but I do. I always do. I let her think she won. She's so wrapped around my finger. I give her anything she wants. I'm at her mercy.

Our love is full of magically beautiful sparks. My love for her is deep, it is strong. I could literally start fires with what I feel for her: *that strong, that passionate, that magical.* My love for her shall burn for eternity. I kiss her forehead, sealing it with a promise to love her forever, to protect her from the world.

It was *always you,* Mila.

THE END

Acknowledgments

Thank you for taking the time to read *Always You*. It means so much to me. I want to thank my husband Raymond, sons, Nathan and Julian, and my daughter Maia for their support and encouragement. You've been supportive while I locked myself up and wrote for the last year and now, I finally get to share it.

I want to thank my betas who helped in more ways than you think. I appreciate the encouragement you gave me to keep going. Especially to Emillie Magda, you gave me the push to write the series so that they each have their own book.

Thank you to my editors, you really helped me in so many ways. I appreciate your patience.

Connect

Thank you for taking the time in your busy life to read Mila and Dominic's story.

If you'd like to follow me:
Instagram: @aurtorj. Morales

Facebook: @authorJ.Morales
TikTok: @authorj. Morales

No pressure but my heart would explode reading your kind reviews. Leave your reviews on Amazon and Goodreads.

Printed in Great Britain
by Amazon

28352677R00202